TOMMY LELLAN

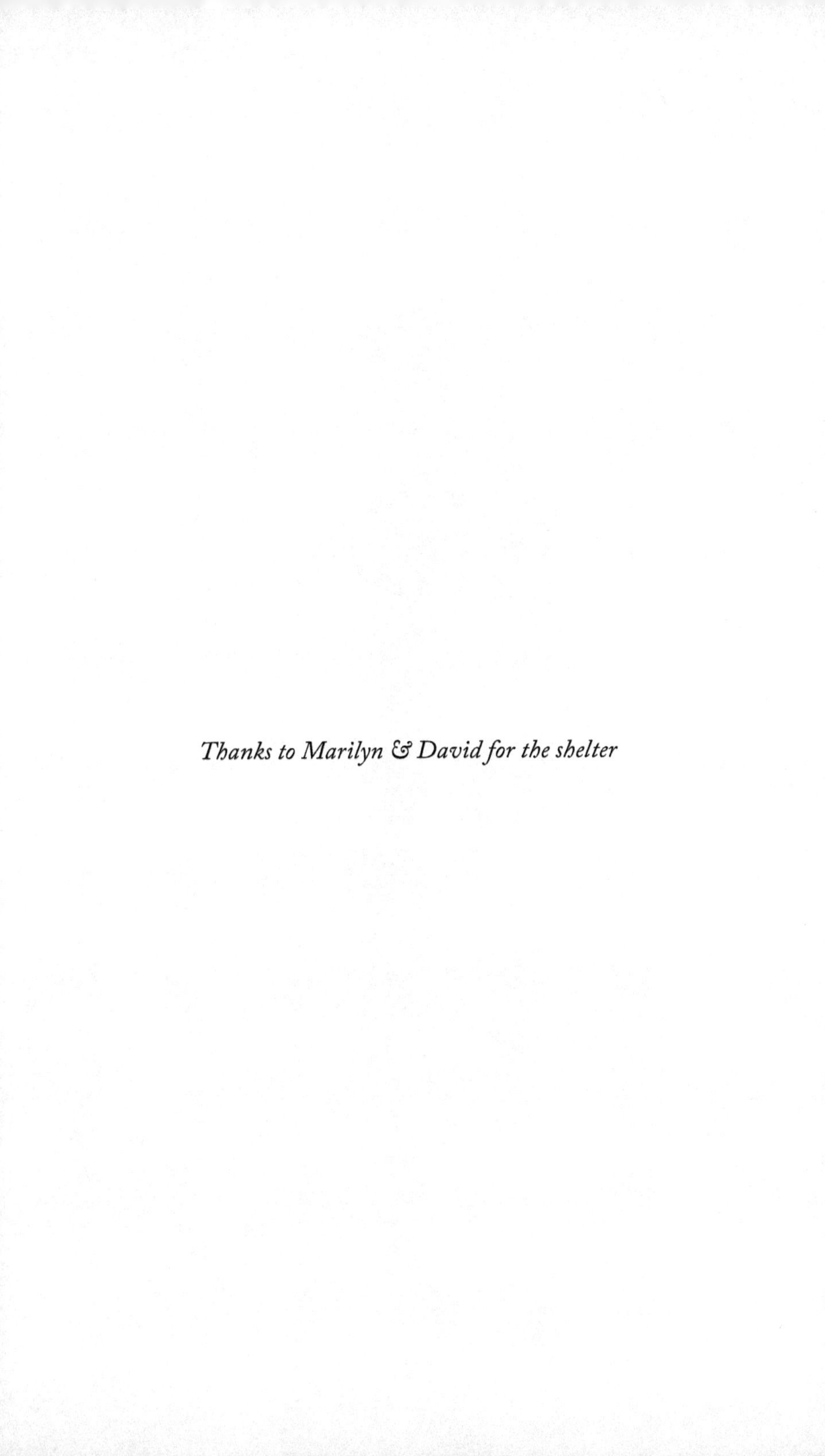

Thanks to Marilyn & David for the shelter

"Let me just say, this is my all time favourite fantasy series. The plot kept building upon itself drastically with every page."
- Ceara, Goodreads

*"The f***ing bee's knees."*
- Tamara Presley, Goodreads

"One of the most mind-bending fantasy stories I've ever read!"
- Marina Levy, Goodreads

"Got to be the most original series out there. The twists are insane. I found myself laughing because I was loving where it was going."
-James McDonald, Goodreads

"I see huge things for this series, and I can't wait for the next one."
- Jesse Elliot, Amazon.com

"I completely connected with the main character. Perfect for young adult fans who love humour and horror."
-Rory, Goodreads

"This was the strangest book. I just couldn't put it down!"
- Merry Chapman, Amazon.com

"A stand-up comedy. And then there are the amazing odd twists!"
- Gloria, Amazon.com

"This book was magic! It keeps you hooked until the very end."
- Alex Murakami, Alextheshadowgirl Blog

"Try reading this on a train and looking like a normal human being."
- Charlotte Geller, Goodreads

"Horn-Horn is a breath of fresh air in a time when many books seem to follow cookie cutter plot-lines."
- Brian Gates, Amazon.com

"Too friggin' funny. It reads like a classic novel. The narrator has such a witty elegance to her voice of reason in this whacky setting. You can't help relate to every woe she suffers."
- Lucianne Neptuna, Goodreads

"It's giving me Beetlejuice vibes! I engulfed this in two days, then went back and re-read it all again. There are heaps of clues in this novel that blew my mind the second time. It's hilarious, scary and thrilling."
- Jackie Perotta, Goodreads

"I've long been an avid avoider of the comical in novels. Horn-Horn changes that, as the genre is firmly set in the absurd. I'd recommend for people who love the rebellious in nature, and who love their modern stories doused in an array of intense, sometimes scary, magic."
- Malwina Ricohard, Goodreads

"Very addictive! I need to know what happens in the next one."
- Emma Moore, Amazon.com

"Wonderful premise for a story!"
- Melonie Purcell, Amazon.com

"Even the characters from another world seem to be in on the gag. Nobody is particularly normal and that, ironically, seems to be the norm within the Horn-Horn universe."
- Alyssa Whicker, Goodreads

"These are the funniest fantasy books I've ever read!"
- Callan Murphy, Goodreads

"Major potential for successor to The Hunger Games — a must-read."
- Renae Ciuffetelli, Goodreads

PROLOGUE
THE AMBER NECKLACE

Ursula only bit her nails on the oddest of occasions. The soon-to-be orphaned princess sat in her pristine bedroom, legs crossed at her vanity mirror, wearing a fine silk dressing-gown. While she chomped and tore away at her nail plate, her eyes skimmed intensely across an article that had been written about her. One that featured an especially troublesome quote:

"Upon this magical Planet of Danube, we continue to observe the Planet of Earth from a distance, through the art of gravitational lensing. Its inhabitants, particularly the magically stunted human race, continue to draw parallels to our own society. Shall we ever accept them as our descendants, or will we continue to let them ruin their resources, as yet another war breaks out? I for one think we should lend a helping hand. Let them know we are here! Bring them up to speed. Or perhaps my fellow Danubians have a superiority complex - belief in our own grandeur being such a dominant component that we cannot bear to entertain the idea that a 'subclass' of souls on a planet within our reach... may contain our own?"
- Ursula the Viking Princess, Author of 'Can You Travel Light Years? I Can'

The servant named Pier burst through the heavy wooden doors of her bedroom, out of breath. He had the same article in his hands. As soon as he saw her face, his dropped.

"Oh, no. You've read it."

Ursula glared at him through her mirror, not saying a word. She examined his caramel coloured hair, his bow-tie, blue pants and black shoes. He was a descendant of goats and humans. A terrible mix. The only thing shared with his bleating ancestors was his style of facial hair. Also, he could scratch his head with his feet.

"Damn him!" she cried. "Damn that Rudnick van Pan. I've now read his blasted piece so many times that every word makes me want to laugh. Angrily, though."

Rudnick van Pan was a hideous creation, a man so nasty it often made the hairs stand up on the back of Ursula's neck. She'd been burdened with his company since childhood, with the unfortunate coincidence of sharing every single class at school with him until graduating in her early twenties. Now in their early forties, he was a politician and journalist very close to her father's private staff and the inner circle of the current ruling monarchy. He had his own manor, a stone's throw from the Palace, where he was afforded greater luxuries than most of his stature. One such luxury that made Ursula green with envy was the fact that he had not one, not two, but *three* personal assistants who served him day and night and managed his affairs. While van Pan insisted he kept all three simply because they were brothers and couldn't bear to be apart, Ursula highly suspected he used this as a convenient excuse to lessen his own workload. On top of that, they sometimes stood in at meetings, and travelled in his place whenever he wanted time alone. All very unfair, Ursula couldn't help but think, for she, the princess of this land, rarely had a room to herself.

Sighing in misery, she opened a pine jewellery box the guards had brought over earlier, and admired the orange necklace inside. It featured a large burgundy stone in the middle.

"Pier, old friend, I've never been so humiliated in all my life. Those were private thoughts I'd written, from when I was a teenager, stashed away in my father's office for *years*. He specifically instructed me never to reveal my controversial thoughts on Earth to anyone. Now they're out there for all of Danube to read! I'll be a pariah in no time. Much worse than that Jezebel piranha pariah named Mariah

Miranda from Summers City. I just don't understand why van Pan would print that in his pretentiously artsy, misogynistic newspaper column? It has nothing to do with anything!"

"Woebegone. He has quoted you, and acknowledged them as your words," Pier scratched the back of his ear with a hind leg, splitting his pants. "Oh dear…"

"Let's hope we can handle this as we did those accidental murders, and easily sweep them under the rug. Stop sewing your pants and go back to the headquarters," said Ursula suddenly, and she collapsed on her bed again. "This needs serious attention. Call the literary agencies. Call the Heads of the Universe. Call the lawyers! Most importantly, tell the guards I won't be wearing that abysmal excuse for a green dress my father picked out for me tonight."

"But…"

"No, it's my night. If they have a problem they can come and find me," she replied. "I'll be in the *other* home until the celebrations begin. Is that alright?"

Knowing when to let things be, Pier backed out of the bedroom. He shut the giant doors behind him, and Ursula was left alone again. She took the time to stare about her room, admiring the many gifts and treasures she had inherited. Vases from the Fa-Fa Belt, magical beads from many stardust societies in the Crux constellation. Yes, she was rich and of royalty, but still she felt… unnecessary. Sometimes she wanted to cry, but she would always feel silly for it. Her troubles were so trivial.

The pressures of being a princess weighed heavy on her chest with such force that for a moment she thought the giant stone on her new necklace weighed a million tons. She breathed in and out to calm her nerves.

"Oh, I just want to curl up into a hole and pretend I'm a sand lizard!"

With that, she curled into a ball on her sand lizard-skinned bed-spread and wept. She would have stayed like that for much longer if not for the stomping footsteps rushing down the hallway. She jumped up, grabbed the first dress she could find, and her long wooden staff. With one click of her fingers, she and her abysmal green dress vanished into thin air. The half-zebra guards entered through the large doors and inspected the empty bedroom.

"I guess the princess decided she would wear the dress her father picked out for her after all," said one to the other. "Look, it's gone from her hanger on the closet door."

"Shame. It's a stupid green dress if you ask me."

"Crisis averted, then."

"Yes. Cup of tea since we're near the kitchen?"

—— · · · ——

Miles away, Ursula appeared several metres above the snowy ground. Suspended in the darkness, she was momentarily bewildered, and she clawed at the air in panic. But at last, gravity found her and pulled her down. She climbed up off her hands and knees from the snow and looked around her. The two demented moons were nearly passing overhead, and their gentle mingling light gave her enough source to discover that she was about sixty feet from the tiny cabin she had intended to arrive inside.

"Stupid magic," she muttered, wiping herself down.

Inside that cabin, the young boy with jet black hair threw a log into the tiny stone fireplace. It did little to warm him, as the spell put on it earlier was starting to wear off. Ursula burst through the door ferociously, and he leapt in fright. For a moment he transformed into a bear, a powerful magical ability he possessed but did not often reveal. He returned to his normal form almost at once.

"It's only me!"

The young boy remained shaking.

"Timothy, the Dreamcatcher out on the veranda has an eagle caught in it," she told him, taking off her gloves. "Make sure it devours the whole body before disposing of the skeleton."

Timothy nodded and sat down at the wooden table.

"Oh my, I am in such a state. I just had to come and see you, my dearest husband-to-be." She leant forward and stroked his chiselled, youthful face.

"What happened?"

Ursula closed her eyes and grimaced. "Rudnick van Pan, that ham of a man. He… Oh, it's ridiculous. You'll find out yourself when you read his next book."

"I'll never read his book, for I cannot read," he reminded her. "Figuratively of course, due to the fact the King prohibits me."

"Perhaps I shall have a word to him about that when I go see him," Ursula smiled. "Maybe you could dash that rule upon hitting puberty… Which I'm hoping will come along any day now."

Ursula knew that in her world, the average individual remained childishly youthful until one unpredictable day, when their body would mature, in which case they would mysteriously erupt and grow in the space of ten seconds. Hair would sprout, vocal cords would change, fingernails would turn jagged, breast tissue would expand, and in some frightful but not completely uncommon cases their eyeballs would shrivel and a lifetime of blindness would ensue. They called it 'Suffrolens'.

"I'd like puberty too, but… not for the same reasons as you," said Timothy, and he stood up to get a drink from the tap.

A smile suddenly spread across Ursula's face. Timothy knew what this meant. An idea. Usually, her ideas were terrible. In all the time he'd known her, not one idea of hers had gone down well with her father. In fact, even her popular inauguration had failed to impress His Royal Highness. Probably because he was still alive.

Ursula stroked the staff she'd brought with her. It was crafted from five very strong roots ripped from the greenest of trees, each one wrapped around another like plaits, with the five ends curled like a hand around a large crystal ball on top. That very moment, inside the ball, an electrical storm seemed to be brewing of purple smoke and lightning. Although silent, it spat about inside, furious to be contained. Timothy watched it in dazzlement.

"You know, my father… He has a *place*. It's been rumoured to prevent *Suffrolens*. You don't lose your eyesight. There's no chance. Of course, these are just rumours. But say the word and I can take you there. After all, you fit all the standards of a typical patient. Young, undernourished, orphaned. Or perhaps I could… make you a man right *now*. Then my father wouldn't be so hell-bent on keeping you trapped in this cabin!"

Terrified, Timothy left the tap and backed up against the nearest wooden wall. He knew of her staff's power. Every soul on the planet had their own special gift. van Pan's was to transform into any object, albeit with an amber tinge. The King's was the power to numb another's limbs. The Duke's was to control static electricity around him in order to communicate with others far away. All these unique powers came to one in the womb, while their usual run-of-the-mill powers such as willing electricity and defying gravity came along with puberty. Ursula's birth-gift lay in her crystal ball, which she'd given birth to directly after being born herself. Her gift was that of bringing youth, or stealing youth. She'd killed five people with it, all accidental of course. And being the daughter of a King, she'd been acquitted on all four trips to court.

"I don't want you to," said Timothy. She wanted to age him with her crystal ball.

"Oh, come now," said Ursula, who was standing and aiming the staff at her youthful fiancé. "Don't you want to be six feet tall, with stubble and a deep voice? Don't you want to be accepted into the Kingdom by my side instead of being shunned to this heathen spot until you finally grow them on your own?"

"But what if I hit puberty tomorrow?"

"Wonderful. Wouldn't make a difference," said Ursula. "But this way, if I grant you puberty with my staff, you won't have to worry about the threat of shrivelling eyes."

"I don't know…" said Timothy, turning his head to the side.

"If it helps, I shall try and scrape a few lines off my own face," she coaxed. Upon reaching him she ran her fingers through his hair. She leaned in and spoke softly into his ear. "Please? *I want a man.*"

Timothy burst into tears and collapsed on the floor.

"I'm only eight!"

Ursula watched as he shifted before her very eyes into his favourite form: a black cat. Failing to impress, she rolled her eyes and headed for the door.

"You know, here on Danube, that's usually *far* too old to still have your giblets lurking in the rafters. Send the Palace a telegram when you find your first chest hair."

She opened the door and battled against the raging winds.

"Oh, and happy bloody birthday to me."

Ursula punched the struggling eagle in the dreamcatcher, knocking it cold, and disappeared into the darkness.

———— • • • ————

The trumpets blared. The guests had arrived from all corners of the universe, and were now waiting patiently in the castle's many smoking rooms. The dust particle family from Dust Particle Alumni, the flamingo prostitutes from Whore Alley, the small gnome guardians of the Crux, the Giravers Clan (a terrible mixed race of giraffes and beavers – they were infamous for forming gangs), and even two Earthling humans: one being a President, and the other being his long-term mistress. A thousand more stood amongst them in the crowd, waiting for the princess to arrive for her birthday celebrations.

The great Palace of Danube lay beneath a titanic dome of protective crystals and ice. A kingdom so grand that it defied the imaginations of great intellects. Made entirely of crystals and ice itself, it would likely rest forever in between the two large mountains that it sat against, which had formed millions of years ago over the bodies of two dead ogres. The inhabitants lived in harmony. There were hardly any murders. In fact, in the entire history of the Palace of Danube — which, confusingly, was named after the large Kingdom they lived in, which in turn was named after the small planet they resided on — there had only been five murders. And this society partly lived in such peace due to the invincibility of the dome. Somehow, some way, the crystals and ice were beyond that of the normal kind. They simply could not be destroyed, not by heat, not by force... A theory proven at one point when a rogue dwarf planet catapulted into Danube. Rather than the Palace being crushed (or even the outer kingdom for that matter), the dwarf planet simply exploded into millions of tiny fragments. The repercussions of this event for the souls of Danube had been relatively minimal. Temporary blindness, fatigue, deafness and the releasing of one's bowels due to the seismic rumblings such an explosion tends to create. All the injuries were forgotten within a week, but the event never ceased to rouse the tongue.

"The princess's birthday is almost as big an event as when that rogue planet Madonna crashed into us," one guest whispered to another. "Thankfully, it reformed in space and adopted some other planet's moon."

"A lot of people weren't happy about that," said another.

As the guards thundered into the main hall, a great voice echoed from above, from an invisible system. "*Dear guests, welcome to Danube. Chai ju, thunter ou Danube. Dor gasts, vilkum tue Danube. Please find your allocated seats. Heill guize sa bullable tunmars. Seine allovere seats tan muilles.*"

The legions of guests, cluttered together socially, heard the request and were slowly escorted to their seats. The giant hall they were led into was so large that the back had a magnified mirror-wall so people with impaired vision could simply turn around to see the front better.

Discussions and whispers licked across the way as everybody found their tables, some appreciating the company, others biting their tongues. The trumpets bellowed once again from nowhere distinguishable. They stopped when the back entrance opened up to reveal fifteen guards. They stomped in, their grey leather shoes creating gigantic tremors. They were carrying a King sized bed above their heads, which carried in it the King, who was currently so ill of health that he was certainly not fit for a King sized bed, or the size of what one would expect for a King. The guests remained in their seats, spell-bound and staring in disbelief. There had been rumours for many months that the King of Danube had been sick, but until now it had all been hearsay. Everybody was so shocked that they didn't even notice as Ursula followed behind the guards, wearing a greatly revealing dark green silk dress, and the orange necklace given to her. The gigantic burgundy stone attached to the necklace was resting firmly in the middle of her bare chest, holding the middle of the dress together. Her cleavage was so immense that if anybody had actually been paying attention to her at that time they would have declared 'Oh my word!' purely out of reflex.

The King's bed was carried all the way to the front of the hall, where it was finally hoisted up onto an empty stage, which was often filled with jokers and hatters who would keep the royals entertained on dull weeknights. The guards then departed as noisily as they had come.

Ursula looked out upon the seated crowd as she stood by her father's bedside. Behind her was a large velvet red curtain. She glanced at it in wonder, and then smiled sweetly at her father, hoping for at least some hint of attention. Nothing came, for he was fast asleep. Her smile faltered slightly, and then she coughed. The sound of heads turning in unison stunned her.

"Oh my word!" they collectively cried.

"Thank-you all for coming to my birthday celebration," Ursula spoke, and she shook her blonde hair loose from the bee-hive style she'd had set, letting it drape across her shoulders and down past her bosoms. "I am so glad you could all come. And for many, from so far."

They clapped appropriately. Ursula smiled appropriately. It was a very appropriate occasion.

"My father told me that so many of you were very eager to make it here tonight. It really warms my heart. And thank-you for your donations to the *Make a Fish!* Foundation. All the baby fish you helped create can be seen later tonight, separated by species placed around the ballroom in between the punch bowls. Please read the signs as we don't want anyone to mistake one bowl of chunky floating stuff for another." She laughed to herself. Then she paused to glance across the room. She couldn't spot that dastardly vermin Rudnick van Pan anywhere, with his horrid slicked-back hair and billowing red silk vest. He hadn't turned up. She was surprised, but relieved nonetheless.

"As many of you may have heard, my father is ill. His medical team have informed me that he won't last a week."

A few guests gasped in surprise. Vastly appropriate.

"Although, doctors have recently been proven wrong on all accounts by leading experts, so it has been extended to six months."

A few guests sighed quietly. Vaguely appropriate.

"Yet, I'd prefer not to dwell on things that haven't happened yet," she said. "I do believe it's time to open my presents!"

She clapped her hands demandingly. The large red curtain behind the King and Ursula began to rise, to reveal a large brick wall behind it which then vanished into thin air (technology that had been around for hundreds of years on this planet). A mountain of wrapped gifts tumbled magically out of the hollow space behind the vanished wall. The pile fell so close that one gift landed gently on the King's sleeping stomach. Ursula picked it up and shook it. It made no sound. She then shook it with much more force and a sudden rattling arose. "Oh no, it's broken," she sighed, feigning sadness. It was from Rudnick van Pan.

It was then as Ursula scoured the gifts lying around the bed that she noticed her father's eyes were open. She paused where she was, one of her hands on a pink gift. He looked right up at her.

"King Frederick is awake!" somebody in the crowd cried out.

Ursula smiled at her father, tears welling in her own eyes. She stroked his forehead.

He was completely bald, with dentures, and was one of the oldest men on the entire planet. Rounding one-hundred, he was much like a prune that had once been a lush apricot. His abnormally small eyes had sunk into his skull. His nose had spread so far across his face that it was almost flat and hollow. His jowls lay like fallen curtains on his neck. His lips thinned and chapped.

"My dear Ursula," he said quaintly. "How I recognise your scent. If I could only see you with my own eyes, I would tell you how beautiful you are."

Ursula spoke: "Father, you cannot. You lost your eyesight at puberty, remember?"

"Yes. I remember," he said, slowly. "If only your step-mother was still with us. She was equally beautiful." He raised a thin hand to stroke her face, his mechanism for detailing how one looked. "I do miss her old ways."

"So do I."

"Now, it's time to open my present, dear." Her father was quick to change the subject, for he didn't like to dwell on his fallen wives, particularly his second. He motioned his hand out to the pile of gifts he had smelt upon opening his eyes. "It's the medium sized one wrapped in orange."

Ursula stared out upon the pile of multi-coloured presents, many of which were orange.

"More like salmon," he added.

Ursula found it and picked it up, and opened it. Throwing away the shredded wrapping without care, she stared hungrily into the box beneath. "What's this?" she said, her smile dropping. "All that's here is some sort of a… A head made of clay."

"Exactly," said King Frederick. "Open it and look inside."

Ursula braced herself. The clay head, which was orange and about the same size as a child's head, appeared to be completely hollow from what she could see. It had two gaping holes for eyes, and one for a nose, and a giant one for the mouth which was shaped in a grin. On top of the head was a separate piece of clay which had been sculpted to look like a beret. It sat quaintly on top as a lid. She took the beret off and looked inside. Astounded by the sudden bright yellow light she saw, she put the top back on and looked to her father.

"You're giving me this?" she said, blinking away the spots.

"Oh, I think it's about time," he replied with a kind smile.

Ursula beamed. This clay head had sat in her father's office for years. It was given to him by a merchant from the black markets on his last trip to the touring Fa-Fa Belt between here and the end of the Crux constellation. Inside was a boy who had been born and orphaned on the same day in the slums of Summers City, which lay on the polar opposite side of the planet of Danube. He'd been born with the ability to grant wishes, but a good soul had bound his magic only to those who agreed to house him. King Frederick had kept him safe, but never taken advantage. Ursula had only met him once before, when he was an infant. "Where is he, then?"

"He's anywhere you want him to be. Zag, my boy, come here."

A sliver of light shimmered into view by Ursula's side. All of a sudden the body of a young boy appeared there. He was wearing blue pyjamas, and a nightcap over his red hair. Buck teeth protruding slightly from his lips, he scratched his left ear with both hands, which were bound by shackles attached to the clay head from the base.

"Fred, what gives?" said Zag, bewildered.

Ursula could only gape at the boy beside her. His similarities to Timothy disturbed her. If not for the red hair and buck teeth, he could be a carbon copy. Right from head to toe.

"You've grown," she said quietly to him. He looked up at her shyly, and didn't respond. She looked back to her father. "Does this mean I can wish for anything I desire?"

"Yes, but you must remember what you were taught in school about the dangers of orphaned children born to the wishing curse," said Frederick.

"*Be careful, always think before you wish, no more than ten a year to be on the safe side,*" she recited the words that had been on the board as a teenager. "*Children of the Crux must always be bound to something by metal to prevent the wishes from electrically turning negative.* I mean, father, I could recite the entire chapter if you wish." With the magic word uttered, the chains around Zag's wrists glowed a bright blue, then faded out when no more was said.

"Be *careful,*" said King Frederick after hearing the familiar moans that emitted from the shackles.

She stared at the chains around Zag's wrists, and how they seemed to vibrate ever so slightly. What was she to do with him? Where would she put him? She already had one child to take care of, feed him every day and check the bowl of water for him at least twice a week. Caring for another boy was not in her future plans, but if she wanted the wishes she simply *had* to care for him.

"I can think of a *hundred* better presents you could've given me."

"Sweetheart, you're forty-three, you've got many birthdays ahead of you. This boy needs a good home. You'll learn to appreciate him. Stop taking and try giving for once."

Ursula paused in disgust. "On my *birthday?*"

"No, no, throughout your entire life. Balance the two. When I was your age, in fact when everybody alive was your age, we had our looks, our complete and utter youth. Ursula my dear, I've heard from certain guards that you are not looking youthful for your age."

Ursula touched her crow's feet. "You think I'm ugly? It's my nose, isn't it. It's a fugly nose! Sculpted by the Gods, my ass. Sculpted by the God's ugly step-niece who hated sculpting, more like."

"Your nose is fine. Take this as a warning, my dearest daughter. You are not looking the way you should for your forty-third birthday. It's all a sign from above. You should take it as a warning. Self-centredness makes you bitter on the inside, and it shows on the outside. You have wrinkles and your bosom is beginning to sag, and you're dev…"

"Who told you all this? You cannot see for yourself!"

"It doesn't matter. The whole point of keeping you-know-who locked away in the cabin was so that when he finally develops, you won't look so strange together. You were supposed to appear the same age. There's no use keeping him hidden if when he develops, you still look like you could be his mother."

"Why, I ought to cut your cords!"

"All you do is take, take, take… Frankly, I blame that wretched crystal ball you were born birthing. It's getting to your head."

"I know you don't like my power, father."

"I see no use for it. It's a burden, particularly on you, for if you are looking as old as some claim, then it can only be as a result of your age-bending crystal ball. That thing has a mind of its own."

There was silence between the two, and Ursula sensed an end to their argument.

"In the meantime…?" she offered.

Her father's shrivelled eyeballs were burrowed beneath a frown. "In the meantime, enjoy your gift and happy birthday."

"Oh, father!"

Ursula collapsed on top of him and hugged him with great emotion. As they embraced, the many guests in front of them clapped and cheered. She jumped slightly, for she'd forgotten they were there.

Zag, unmistakably troubled by the audience watching them, began to tug at Ursula's dress. "I'm tired. May I have the clay head?"

Ursula remained over her father. "I suppose so, soon. Tell me, do you live *inside* it?"

"Yes, but it's bigger inside. I want to go now."

Ursula was becoming agitated by his tugging on her dress. She batted him away with a spare hand, and when that didn't work, she tried with her leg. Finally, she jumped off the bed and picked the tiny boy up by the collar of his pyjama top and pointed her staff at him. "Not yet! It's *my* birthday and I will sire you if I want to. I want you to go and clean the bathrooms before the guests leave for intermission. After that, you can go back inside your precious clay head."

"Is that a wish?" asked Zag, noticing the chains around his wrists begin to glow again.

"No, that's an order," said Ursula. The electrical storm started again in her crystal ball, and with not even the blink of an eye the boy and his clay head vanished into thin air.

Ursula smiled happily at the clean and proper dismissal of her servant, and turned back to her father. She immediately felt something was wrong. Firstly, her amber necklace had fallen off, and she noticed her dress was in a heap on the floor. She stood there naked in front of many, all of whom stared with open mouths. She laughed in embarrassment, swept up her dress to cover herself, and went over to pick up the necklace. It lay with the orange stone firmly planted on the King's neck, indented furiously. As soon as she peeled it off, she reeled at the damage.

It had suffocated him. He was dead.

Her dress dropped again, and the crowd cried: "Oh my *word!*"

———— . . . ————

Five elaborate halls away, Zag rolled up his pyjama sleeves to start on his tedious work scrubbing away the filth and grime that came with used bathrooms. He opened the first stall, expecting a mess. What he found instead was a toilet roughly ten feet tall, clearly made for giant guests.

"Mother!" he cursed, and started to climb.

An explosion rocked the cubicle as he reached the top. He slipped and fell into the bowl. When he swam to the surface, he looked around in bewilderment. A shrill scream echoed around him.

"ZAGREUS!"

Ursula was in a rage. Zag was too afraid to ignore her. "Yes?" he called. His voice reverberated in the small confinement. A tiny turd floated past.

"You killed him!"

Oh no, thought Zag. Wondering what she would do to him, he looked above just as a dark shadow cast over him. He saw his new owner's face, furious and wrinkled. She reached in with one of her menacing hands and pulled him out. She plopped him on the floor with no care in the world. He dropped his clay head, but it dangled from his chains mid-air.

"The King is dead?" he asked.

Ursula had her staff pointed at him, determined to do some damage with it. A bolt of green electricity shot out of the crystal ball and impacted a small potted plant by the exit near Zag. He watched as it shrivelled into itself, ageing and decaying within seconds.

"My father shouldn't have kept you. People have always told me that Crux children were cursed. Now I know they were right."

Zap!

Another bolt singed the ground near him.

"You must leave," she said, her voice low and hushed. "I want you to go far, far away where you can ruin somebody else's life."

"But... I don't know anyone else."

The crystal ball atop her staff vibrated with the power and fury that ran through her veins, and she picked a place in her mind. She wasn't even sure if it was a real location, or if she'd made it up in a dream. "Take your clay head — which you so desperately cling to — and leave my Palace. Now, Zagreus. *I wish for it.*"

Zag stared frightfully at her crystal ball, which was now glowing the darkest red possible. Before he knew it, the colour had taken over everything. He couldn't look away. The chains attaching him to his clay head hummed, and the ground left his feet. The chill of the bathroom vanished. All he could feel now was the sensation of flying so fast that it should have hurt, but it didn't. Then the red light began to fade.

Soon, he was gone.

PART
ONE

WELCOME TO
HORN-HORN!

1
FIVE BIRDS
A BOILING

If Mr. Banting hadn't started mowing his lawn at two o'clock in the morning, none of this would have happened.

I was certain the poor ageing man, diagnosed with chronic insomnia three months earlier, had lost his mind. Otherwise he surely wouldn't have decided to mow his lawn every weekday at such an ungodly hour, waking the neighbourhood as a result.

We were too polite, or perhaps sympathetic, to say anything about it at first. The clincher came (so to speak) when my eleven-year-old brother woke up one night and looked out the window to find him striding naked across his lawn pushing a mower with one hand and having a good time with the other.

Mom and Dad had been looking at selling for years, ever since my father's first heart attack at the age of thirty-nine. We held no grudges against Salem; it was a beautiful shindig and rich with history, but my parents wanted a lesser-known coastal town to live out their days in. I couldn't blame them, either. Halloween was torture.

Tourists clogged our roads, which meant we often had to leave home for school and work half an hour earlier. With Mr. Banting keeping us up, that extra half hour of sleep was non-negotiable.

So here I was, months later, the early days of September. I'd been sixteen for one month and thirty days. I was counting. My sweet sixteenth had been on a Monday, and I'd suffered a run of bad luck ever since. Now I stood in a line in a fast-food outlet in the middle of nowhere, with three other girls, waiting to order some disgusting grease-covered piece of garbage claiming to be a 'meal'.

"*Cassandra Lillian Gellar*, are you even listening to me?"

I stopped staring at a bug stuck on its back on the floor, and met my sister's gaze. "Yes, Annie. You said that the sun sets around nine thirty-five for the next few weeks, and then it will start getting darker."

"Well, alright..." said my sister suspiciously. She pushed her giant glasses up and continued talking.

We finally got our orders, consisting of far more than either of us could eat, and managed to dump it all on the nearest table to check before leaving.

"Is it customary to leave a tip?" Annie asked me.

"No," I sighed, and then yawned so much that it felt like one of my eyeballs dislodged itself from the socket.

"Dad likes sugar, right?" she said, pouring a packet into one of the coffees. "Or was that Mom?"

"It was Mom. Dad can't have sugar because of his worms."

"Oops, well, let's not tell him."

I watched as she poured another packet into the second one.

"You could have just left one of them without sugar and given it to Dad instead."

Annie paused to understand, tilting her head again. Somehow, this brain-freezing grinky was a certified genius. And by genius, I don't mean 'quite a smart one', but literally. *A genius.* She took a test at school last year. Boasting was her middle name now, along with May. If someone debated her, she would raise the old "I surrender... but... I *am* a certified genius" flag. And let's get one thing clear. *I'm* not a certified genius. Nobody in our family is besides from her. It really makes you feel even less intelligent when you have a sister who's smarter than your teachers. It raises the question deep within your soul: *Why didn't my brain get that thing?*

Mom, Dad and my brother had decided to stay in the parking lot. Embarrassingly, we were driving around in a borrowed school bus from the seventies. It was painted white, with purple and green graffiti obscenities all over it. Five people in our family. The equivalent of six bodies. Just that one too many for our own car. Plus the dog. Then the cat. Thankfully there wasn't a partridge in a pear tree, although we were a family riding around on a bus.

I kicked the rusty door open with my left foot, and climbed the steep steps. I chucked the food I'd carried onto the front seat next to Mom, and raced for my seat at the back. Dad, who was in the driver's seat (and was sort of stuck there) reached behind him for his bag of food and coffee, but couldn't reach. Mom handed it to him kindly.

Upon sitting down in the back row, very middle, I placed my music earbuds in and pretended I was listening.

"Where's the toy!?"

My little brother sifted through the colourful take-away box that contained his kids' meal. Apparently he needed a plastic figurine to continue living.

I took my earphones out and spoke to him. "Sorry, I forgot that you're still a six-year-old."

Brendan stared daggers from next to Mom, but he corrected me in a pompous tone: "I *happen* to be *eleven!*"

With that, he stuck out his tongue at me.

Once we'd finished eating our dinners, we were back out on the open road. Conversations generally petered out; it seemed mutually understood that it was too hot and stuffy in this old bus to do anything but think, or listen to music. Then, as we glided along a dark patch through a pine forest, Dad said something alarming:

"Did somebody put sugar in my coffee?"

Terrified silence.

"Ichabod, honey, you gotta scratch?" asked Mom.

Dad laughed, but it was one with very little humour. "Oh boy, Lesley, I've gotta do more than that. I'd better pull over."

Annie and I moaned so loudly that we ended up in harmony. This was the fourth time today we'd had to stop for him. To pee, to poo, to vomit, and now to scratch his butt because of worms he had gotten in the first place from letting the dog lick his face too much. The thing with Dad was… well… He was too big for britches. Some might say *obese*. He'd been that way since he was little. Claimed it was a disease. Which wasn't completely impossible, but Grandma told me once that the disease was his desire to eat everything in sight. She told me when he was a teenager he'd even taken a bite out of a very off piece of Brie and was rushed to hospital. Therefore because of his weight, he kept getting wedged between the seat and the cup holder in the driver's seat of our bus. It was the same with him for every vehicle, which is why he didn't normally drive. It's one giant leap for mankind when he gets out of a Four-Wheeler. Getting in is another story.

"Don't go too far!" Mom shouted from the door as he ran off into the woods. "There could be deer and bears and moose out there."

He swiftly ran back into view, frightened of such prospects. He decided to do his scratching behind the bus instead. I prayed nobody would drive past while he was doing it, to no avail. The honking and flashing of lights added to the humiliation.

"Thank God we're moving to a new town," I said loudly, mortified, as the bus shook from side-to-side. "I think I'll get the *school* bus from now on. I don't want any new friends seeing something like this."

"If you *make* new friends," said Annie.

"Oh, please. I had more friends than you ever did."

I'd had one friend, Nicole.

Ten minutes later, Dad had finished damaging the exhaust pipe, and we continued on our way. Again. Just to let you get an idea of how long we'd spent on the bus that day: We'd left our old town of Salem at precisely six in the morning, after having loaded the bus for an hour before that. So 'early start' was an understatement. We said goodbye to our empty and sold house, and travelled practically right across the country in the process. It took *forever*. Much longer than it should have. We should have arrived in the new town by at least five-thirty that afternoon. It was now nine-thirty at night.

Brendan had seen a sign for a superhero convention one quarter in, so we'd had to stop in Shrove. Annie spotted a fellow dork hitchhiking, so we gave him a lift to Camberwell. Then selfishly, I faked needing to relieve myself of women issues so that I could go to a mall to get an album I wanted. Which I got. It amazed me how different the accents were with every place we stopped. I had misheard the salesperson saying: "That's seventeen dollars, thanks," for "That's never been more hollowed, skank." I looked at her weird and she looked at me weird, and it was just an incredibly awkward moment. After that pit-stop, we parked for lunch at about 1pm at a fast-food outlet, which we didn't expect to do again for dinner, but we were desperate.

"Which-one-of-these-guys-will-I-have-sex-with-at-the-reunion?"

said Brendan, playing with his paper fortune-teller.

"Honey, don't say that out loud," muttered Mom.

"Sorry, Rhoda."

It was nearing twilight. We were still on the highway and Dad had just turned on the lights. I shuffled across to the left-hand side of the bus and rested my head against the window. I gazed out, appreciating the weird massage I got from the vibrations.

Suddenly, through a break in the trees, I caught a quick glimpse of what looked like the ocean.

"Horn-Horn's near the beach, right?"

I already knew the answer, but Annie was quick to confirm.

"Then… I think we're here."

Brendan and Annie rushed to the left side of the bus and pressed their faces against the windows. Giant oak trees kept blocking what I'd seen. Finally, a hint of…

"Oh, I see a kite!" said Annie excitedly.

"I see a dolphin!" said Brendan.

"Don't be stupid."

"Well, don't be a dolphin."

A moment later the words: 'HORN-HORN – NEXT EXIT' appeared on a giant reflective green sign up ahead, and we all cheered.

Dad wriggled as he did so.

2

BY MOONLIGHT AND FIRELIGHT

I feel I need to point out that by way of family inheritance and clever banking, the Gellar family was pretty darn set. Our great uncle was a well-to-do businessman of sorts (possibly a criminal) and that's all you need to know. Regardless of our financial issues, however, my parents preferred to work hard to maintain stability in our lives. As if they were good parents or something. We were raised on pocket-money and chores like normal children were. And we'd always lived in average sized houses. Not one for flaunting their wealth, Mom and Dad had temporarily lived below the line before we came along (to prove a point to my grandparents, disagreements and so forth, which had resolved somewhat due to the arrival of baby Annie). This stigma against their own parents' money had somehow evolved into us always living in cute little wooden houses. Until, earlier this year, they'd announced plans to move, and in doing so, upgrade. The new house was indeed fairly large. Actually, I'm being fairly modest. It was fairly gigantic to be fairly honest. A double storey, 1932 commissioned French Normandy styled house that was shipped over from Champagne in 1962, made of beige stucco, with a steep roof, complete with original green shutters on the windows and one of those dumbwaiters in the walls that go up and down each level by rope. All this information we gathered from the net, of course, for we hadn't officially seen it in person yet. Basically the land we now owned was about three times as big as our previous one. It was technically on a residential street, that being Philips Street, but the properties on this stretch were bigger, wider, affluential. Only Mom and Dad had seen pictures of the house before arriving, and even they gaped in awe as we pulled into the driveway. Whatever photographs they'd seen or three dimensional tours they'd taken online obviously didn't compare to the wonders of reality. It was a mansion.

"This place is borderline mansion!" shrieked Brendan.

The vast property was littered with oak trees, making an impressive hiding place for the house in the dead centre. The fences were smothered by large vines on the left, right and back, but there was no front fence or gate. The driveway spiralled kindly around the oaks, which towered far above.

One step in the front door and it felt like we'd walked onto the set of *Gone with the Wind*. The foyer was unimaginably large, round in shape, with polished white marble floors. In the dead centre was a very large maroon-carpeted staircase that led up into the second storey landing, most of which could be seen from where we stood at the entrance. It was a treat to the stunned eyes, yes, but unfortunately not to the nose. There was an un-lived-in odour that sat heavily in my nostrils, one which suggested nobody had lived here for a while. It seemed absurd, given what a wonderful steal the property was. Maybe it was a murder house.

We ended up congregating in the foyer for about two hours, yes, two hours, since the removalists had obviously gotten lost along the way (they'd been following us). First we sat and talked. Then some of us argued. Then we told ghost stories. Then Annie read to us from the town guide she'd printed off weeks earlier. Then we started to get snoozy, so Mom pulled a few bed-sheets from the bus and we all snuggled around one another like we were on a camp and staring at an invisible camp fire. I pretended to get burnt by it, but nobody got it, and I felt stupid.

"Are these people ever coming with our furniture?" said Brendan. He was resting against our dog, Pigsworth.

"Hopefully soon," said Mom, lifting her head from her slumber. She stretched and then hopped up to go to the windows by the door. There were dusty net curtains covering them, left from the previous owners, and she lifted one up to look out at the front lawn. "Ichabod, maybe we should call them again?"

"Don't worry about it. They'll still be out of range. They've probably driven past the house ten times without realising this was it. This street needs clear numbering."

"Park the bus on the street," suggested Brendan.

I raised my voice. "No, don't even, ever. Thank you very much."

Midnight rolled around. We were all feeling the strain. Dad suggested letting our cat Tigger out of his cage to get used to the new surroundings. I wouldn't be around for that. I had an illogical fear that the worst would happen to him – he'd jump at the window and smash it, cutting off his back legs. He'd then drag himself off into the darkness, get lost in unfamiliar surroundings and eventually fall victim to a hungry owl. I decided to ignore my crazed imagination, and instead headed upstairs to pick a room.

I flicked on the upstairs hall light and got a better look. The hallway was painted white, and there was a fake fern plant at the very end, near a giant closed white door which seemed to have a crack straight down the middle of it. I felt immediately drawn to it, so I crept up and rubbed my fingers gently along the crack. I wondered how it came about. Maybe there had been a really bad earthquake and it only affected this one door. Or maybe Jack Nicholson had come looking for someone but his axe was blunt. In the dull light of this unfamiliar hall, such a thought gave me the willies. I turned the doorknob and went in.

Click!

This was it. This was my room. The moment I turned the light on, I knew it was mine. I stood at the doorway, my hand frozen on the light-switch, speechless.

"Ooh," said Annie, leering behind me. "Nice room. I call it."

"No you don't, I was here first."

Annie shrugged. "But I called it."

"I already called it, in my head!" I said, and I started to yell to try and scare her off. "Why don't you stop stalking people and go find your own room! I was here first, go away!"

I gave her a few sharp pushes and she tripped over the hall rug.

"*Jeeee-*sus!" she screeched, running off.

I could see it now. Bed against the window, computer desk against the back wall, chest of drawers next to that... Oh, wait. Hmm, maybe the bed could go against the back wall, and... No, that wouldn't work... Well, I'd sort it out eventually. The built-in wardrobe, on the same wall as the door, was large and painted white like everything else. It was almost inconveniently large, but given the amount of jackets and tops I owned, I couldn't complain.

Downstairs, my mother was lying on the tiled foyer floor alone. She stretched her arms and legs wide, making a starfish.

"What are you doing?" I asked.

"Yoga," she said.

"I don't think that's yoga."

"I've lost my DVD, so I'm improvising."

"Have you seen Dad?"

"He's running around looking for Tigger."

"What? Where's Tigger gone?"

Mom sighed in annoyance and sat up on her elbows. "I don't know, sweetie. Why don't you go see your father, and find out?"

Worried, I ran away into the downstairs hall, through dark rooms and finally, into the kitchen. Lost, I turned back to go the way I came, but realised it wasn't the way I came. I sat down on the cold floor and muttered: "Where is everybody?"

Annie came out of the pantry, startling me. She looked equally lost. Turning back to examine where she'd come from, she said: "Okay... The pantry is also a short-cut to the bathroom."

"Where's Dad?"

"He was out in the front yard with Brendan."

"That means Tigger is *outside*?" I cried, running away. My worst fear was coming true.

Through the pantry I went, into darkness, then I found myself in the bathroom somehow. I opened the door, ran out into the hall, through to the foyer, down the stairs, past Yoga Mom, and to the front door, which I swung open. I couldn't see Dad anywhere. So I ran out into the front yard, sprinted past oak tree after gigantic oak tree. I knew which direction I was headed, but it was terribly confusing being out in the dark all by myself. I was helped by a sudden dull source of light that seemed to be coming from my right. I pressed against one of the trunks and spotted a lit-up window in the house next door, upstairs. There was nobody in there, though. A second later, the light turned off. After a moment of staring blankly at it, a girl's face appeared in the darkness, helped out by what was probably the hall light outside their room. She seemed to be staring in my direction. I wondered if she could see me out here, so just in case, I continued searching again. I ran until I finally reached the end of the driveway. I tripped and banged my head on the white letter-box.

"Ow," I muttered, rubbing my eyes. As I stood up, I allowed my vision to adjust to the darkness. I immediately saw Dad standing nearby, looking out at yonder. At least I assumed it was him. He had a cage in his hands. Perhaps, I thought, it was a different man who just happened to have a cage, and planned to chop me up and fit all my pieces in there. Or break my back so I would fit in. Or maybe this man had already killed my Dad and had ripped off his flesh, and put it on like a costume and was trying to trick me into thinking it was my father when actually it was not.

"Who's that?" I asked shakily.

Dad shrugged. "Who do you think?"

"Where's Tigger?"

He placed the cage down and put his hands on his gigantic hips. "We really are Jewish, aren't we? Answering each other's questions with questions?"

"Are you going to answer my question?"

"Maybe I'm afraid to?"

I frowned, my heart still beating. "Dad. He's only a year old." I turned to look down the road, which seemed to lack any light source from the street-lights.

I flinched at the sight of a midget figure by my side.

"I say we go downtown and look for him," said Brendan.

"Why would he go down there? He doesn't know where downtown *is*. Just like we don't. We don't even know this place. We'd get lost in the day-time, let alone at night."

"Listen to your brother for once. Brendan, take the lead."

Brendan turned on his heels, excited. "Downtown-a-ho!"

———— • • • ————

Downtown-a-ho was… well, it was hard to tell exactly where it was. Being a very balmy night, a gentle sea breeze welcomed us as we *assumed* our descent to the lower parts of Horn-Horn.

"Street lamp… turn… *on!*" said Brendan, pointing his finger at the nearest one available. It didn't turn on.

I snorted.

"I can't believe you actually thought that was going to work."

A car drove by quickly, lighting up our surroundings. I took great pleasure in noticing a very big sign in that moment, which I looked fondly upon for two reasons. One, I had been seconds away from walking into it. Two, it said simply: *Beach*.

"I'm going to the beach," I called to Dad excitedly, and I began to run towards the sound of the waves. I'd hardly seen the beach in my short life.

"I'm going with her," said Brendan, chasing after me.

"Don't leave me!" cried Dad.

The moon was but a crescent in the clear sky tonight, and it hovered above the sea. Its quivering reflection sat not far below, in the calm ocean. I could see fairly clearly now. Thanks to a weird carrot faze a year ago, my eye-sight was superb at night. Unlike my mother's. She was super paranoid when driving any time past twilight. If she saw a tree stump on the side of the road she'd practically flip the car to avoid it, thinking it was a psychotic elephant on the loose.

My feet landed on the soft sand and sunk in gently. I gained my balance and slowed down, then took off my shoes. There was a sparse stretch of sharp grass, but as I walked closer to the shore it disappeared. The sand was warm, the heat of the day still remained under my toes.

Brendan finally caught up to me, and I turned to see him just as he reached the sand. He lost his balance and fell over. I gave him my hand and helped him up.

"So... If I were a cat, would a beach be the first place I'd go?" he asked himself. "Hmmm, let me think for a mi – *No*." I could see his livid eyes in the moonlight.

"Brendan, if you were a cat on the loose, I don't think you'd really *know* where you'd end up. You'd probably climb a tree at some point and lick your testicles."

"You know me so well."

Nearby was a pier that stretched out into the sea. Its silhouette intrigued me, and I decided that one day when I was older I would come out here during a full moon and paint what I saw. I wasn't really an artist, that was more Dad's territory, but the view was beautiful and peaceful.

"There he is," said Brendan.

I snapped my head back to see him, pointing towards the pier. I immediately felt sick, fearing our Tigger was about to commit suicide by jumping off the very end, but as my eyes scoped the entire platform I suddenly noticed a tiny spec of orange light poking out underneath the pier. Concerned, I stayed in place while Brendan rushed forward.

"I saw him run underneath!"

"Brendan, wait," I called in a hush, but he didn't hear me. My mind congested with horrible notions again. What if the orange light was from a fire? With homeless people gathered around it. Or worse, perhaps not homeless people but *teenagers*. "Brendan!" I called loudly, running after him.

He was completely hidden by the darkness now. The pier grew larger and larger as I ran towards it. The sand was damp and solid the closer I got. I could see the orange light more clearly now, coming in and out of view as the large supporting wooden pillars passed by me. I ran around them and squinted. It wasn't a very big fire, and as I slowed down, completely underneath the shallow end of the pier now, I noticed that people were indeed gathered around it. One of them was Brendan, standing behind a man. A tall man with black hair, wearing board-shorts, flip-flops and a wife-beater. Two other people were around the fire. One of them was a slightly shorter man, black, wearing a beanie, a white T-shirt, shorts and no shoes; and resting on his lap was a female (which made me slightly relieved). She had long blonde hair and was sporting very little. In fact, just a fluorescent green bikini-top with a towel wrapped around her bottom half. The three of them were sitting on two plastic orange milk crates.

I half hid behind the nearest pillar and watched with wonder. Was it safe to fetch my brother from these strangers, or was he standing behind them because they weren't letting him leave? I couldn't imagine much had been said between them in the short period of time I'd been separated from him.

"Look, no, I'm serious. There she is right now."

My brother pointed at me, and my stomach twisted as they all turned to look in my direction. I decided there was no use hiding anymore, so I came out of the shadows and revealed myself in the fire-light. They all gasped. I immediately felt very self-conscious.

Brendan giggled. "Gotchy'all."

"What the hell, Brendan? Don't go chatting to strangers."

The girl stood up and walked towards me. She seemed incredibly amused, possibly high. "You're not a ghost?"

"No… Why do you ask?"

"This kid told us to save him from the ghost girl that was following him," she said, chewing incessantly on a stick of gum. "I just figured it was easier to ask than to run off without checking."

"Oh. Well… I'm all real."

"I can see that."

I folded my arms across my chest and addressed my brother. "Okay. Let's go."

"But they found Tigger," he said.

I paused where I was, and blinked once. "Where is he?" I moved around the fire to get closer. As I did, I noticed he was scratching our sand-bound feline with his left foot. Tigger looked content enough. But this wasn't good enough for me, so I scooped him up in my arms and coddled him. "Oh, my poor baby! I missed you so much, I was so *worried!*" I hugged and squeezed him tight, declaring these ridiculous words with such overdramatic cutesy emphasis that I couldn't believe they'd left my mouth. I looked up, and went red. Thankfully, the orange light hid it.

"We found him strolling along, looking unsure of himself," said the girl. "The cat, not the kid. And then this little guy came along… The kid, not the cat."

"Then you came along and we thought you were a ghost," said the guy with the beanie. He scratched underneath it and grinned like he found something vastly amusing.

Oh yeah, gotta be stoned, I thought.

"Thanks for keeping him okay until we found him," I said, looking at all of them except for the quiet guy with the wife-beater. "Both the cat and the boy."

"It sure is weird, though," said the girl, and she drew a circle in the sand with her right foot. "I mean, if *I* were a cat, I wouldn't go anywhere near the ocean, because, you know… cats hate water."

"That's what I said!" laughed Brendan.

"No, that's what you *alluded* to," I corrected him. "Well, um… thanks for everything."

I handed him our cat, then swung my arms nerdily.

"You already said that," the beanie guy muttered serenely. I felt like maybe he took pleasure in other people's discomfort.

We stood there for a while, ho-humming, and I kept my gaze on my feet. I couldn't think of a single other word to say. Finally, our father's desperate calls broke the silence. They were far off.

"Coming!" I yelled.

Brendan ran away immediately, in hopes of winning Dad's favour by arriving first. I lingered by the pillar I'd hidden behind. Perhaps these guys were my age. They didn't look like they were over twenty or anything.

"Do you guys go to Horn-Horn High?"

The girl snorted. "High-High."

"Beg your pardon?"

"Yeah, we go there. Do you?"

"Yep. Well, I mean… I will do… *start*. This week. I'm new to town. We just moved in."

"So you're a Parker virgin," said the beanie guy.

I smiled politely, but had no idea what this meant.

"Yeah," I laughed.

He looked to the other guy and shared a sort of secret amusement with him. I guess whatever I'd responded with was the wrong kind of answer. Once again, I went red.

"I'm Cassie," I told them.

They didn't react.

"Gellar…"

I peered at them with no courage at all. As soon as my Dad called my name again, I turned without saying goodbye and ran off.

I wasn't good with people.

3
ELEANORE PARKER

The removalists never came. I personally gave up and collapsed on the floor of my new room. Like all non-poverty-stricken individuals, I was not accustomed to sleeping in such harsh conditions. I sorely pined for my beautiful queen-sized bed, which I had shared many a dreams in since my fourteenth birthday. I called it *LOL*, which was short for '*Legs of Luxury*'. Also, after a hard day of being on my feet, I would jump under the covers and find myself so ecstatically comfortable that I'd often wriggle about in the confines and laugh out loud.

I woke up the next morning with a stiff neck, feeling like I had betrayed *LOL* since I rose surprisingly well-rested. I stood up, yawned, and looked around. I grabbed the suitcase of clothes I'd left by the door, and quickly changed all but my underwear. I liked the idea of looking good if I was to head into town today, so I put on the Porky Pig T-Shirt I'd adopted from my dad (which was too big for me, of course) and some white shorts.

Downstairs looked exactly as it had the night before. There was no furniture, and the sun was shining fiercely through the foyer windows. I expected to see my parents asleep on the floor where I'd left them last night, but they were gone. So was Annie. Instead, Brendan lay naked under a white bed-sheet. I tip-toed down and gently poked him. He immediately woke with fright and whacked me across the face. By the time I looked back, he was gone.

I headed into a large room that was closest to the kitchen. It had to be the lounge-room. There was a place by the window where the TV could sit, a fireplace in the corner… The only problem was that it was a room attached to the kitchen. There was no wall separating the rooms — simply a few small carpeted steps that led down to where we would eventually put one of the couches. I wondered if Mom would like the idea of a kitchroom.

There was a knock on the front door. I jumped about a foot in the air. Nobody knew we were here yet, except for the delivery men, and maybe the real estate agent, Penny. She always had lip-stick stains on her teeth. So I snuck my head around the corner to see who was outside. Through the narrow window, all I could see was an elbow. I wondered if my parents had gone for a walk and locked themselves out. Or perhaps it was those strange people I'd met last night under the boardwalk.

But no, it was a family. Five people: a middle-aged man and woman, as well as three children: one being a dark-haired teenage girl and the other two being blonde, a little boy and a girl who looked very similar.

"Hi," I said, peeping my head through the open door.

The middle-aged man was bald on top and roughly six foot. He was dressed in a lavender buttoned-up shirt, khakis, sandals. He held out his hand and I shook it and he said: "Hello. We're your neighbours, next door." He pointed to my right. "I'm Eric Parker, this is my wife Ella-May, and my three kids: Eleanore, Elliot and Eliza."

The two blonde kids smiled up at me. "We're twins."

The mother was a brunette and she looked like a scarecrow, dressed in overalls, a patterned purple shirt, and a straw sunhat sitting on top of her head. She smiled at me in a way which suggested, oddly, that she was not a very strong person emotionally. "We heard you all last night when you arrived late. We thought you'd gotten lost. We knew you were coming, of course, because of Penny the realtor." She poked her head through the gap. "It's still as big as I remember it."

I smiled, but I didn't think to let them in... or respond, it seemed. Eric noticed this and pulled out a large champagne bottle he'd been hiding behind his back. "We obtained this. For your parents. Daughtrey's best. 1938. *Quite* the find. Are they here?"

This seemed to bring forth a few more words, and I took the bottle off him. "Yeah, they're upstairs, I think. Asleep."

"Oh. Well..." started Eric, but his wife suddenly barged past me and delighted in examining the empty foyer properly.

"Eric, it's *beautiful* without all that bizarre clutter they had before! I've always loved this place," she said to me. "The last tenants weren't the most normal folk I've ever come across, so I've only had the honour of seeing inside a handful of times. I used to be a real-estate agent, before the kids came along — that's how I know Penny. We've lived next door since before our eldest was born." She regarded the tall teenage girl, who I now recognised as the one watching me from the darkened room last night. "What's your name?"

I snapped out of it and searched for the words. "My name's Cassie Gellar. My parents are Ichabod and Lesley. And you're Eric, Ella-May... Eleanore, Elliot and..."

I eyed the little girl, who immediately scowled.

"It's Eliza," said the teenage girl, Eleanore, and she came to me and grabbed my elbow and pulled me away. "Don't worry, their names aren't worth remembering. Mom, Dad... hang tight." Before I was dragged out of the foyer, I screeched my parents names, hoping it would wake them up from wherever they were and get them down here so they could tend to the strangers left behind.

I was thrust violently into the kitchen, almost dropping the champagne, and Eleanore let go of me. She started going through all of the cabinets. I watched in amazement. Was this okay behaviour? Now that this was my house, could I tell her to stop?

"Oh, all of your glasses are missing," she sighed, and she stopped looking and put a hand to her hip in confusion.

I eyed her quizzically. "We just moved in."

"Where's all of your furniture?"

"We *just* moved in."

She smiled dramatically, revealing her porcelain-perfect teeth. She was extraordinarily pretty and was so dark-skinned I wondered if it was just an incredibly deep tan or if she'd been adopted by her very white parents.

"I know that, silly!" she laughed, and she punched my shoulder jokingly. Then she stared at me for a moment, perhaps waiting for me to punch her back, but when I didn't she turned away. "I love your house. We always have. I hope we can become the best of friends so I can come over here more often. Hey, are you going to the private school or the public one?"

I went to the pantry and pulled out a small coke bottle for her. "The public one. My parents wanted me to go to the private one but I didn't want the extra pressure. I just want to get through school. That's my main initiative. And now it's theirs, too." I laughed innocently at my mother and father's concern over my apparently bleak future.

"Hmmm..." said Eleanore, and she declined my drink offer. "Let's see. So, you're sixteen, which means you'll be in the tenth grade, and judging by your acceptance letters you should be in Ms. Weiss's form, and start on Monday."

I stared blankly. "How could you possibly know that?"

She bared her teeth again with a vicious smile. "Silly! *I* go to the public school, too. And I'm in Ms. Weiss's form. Plus, my daddy is the Principal of that god-forsaken place, so I pulled a few strings when I heard that a new girl was going to be joining our year, and he put you in with Weiss."

"Wow. Thanks, I guess." I said. I was kind of flattered that somebody had paid attention to my wellbeing before even meeting me. I smiled to be polite, sniffing out what *hopefully* could *possibly* be a new friend *maybe?* My mind's fingers were crossed.

"Come to think of it, the name Weiss does sound familiar," I told her. I'd glanced at the school letters about twice, given school brought me such little interest.

"That's good, that's very good," Eleanore turned the tap on and poured herself a drink in her hands. She slurped it quickly, and went for seconds. "Ms. Weiss is such a nice teacher. She's always very considerate and warm. We've been lucky enough to have her for almost every class since the seventh grade. I know that's not the norm outside elementary, but it's simply a case of serendipity. You really couldn't ask for a better teacher to introduce you to the *horrors* of a new high school. She was made redundant last year due to a bitter temp vice-principal, but every student she's ever had practically backflipped in protest. So she's a keeper, trust me. Just don't ask her about her gnome collection."

I shrugged. "I wouldn't have thought to..."

"She will go on and on forever about them. She has over two

hundred, you know. Here and there. They lurk in her garden, mainly. I went to her house once with my father and I was literally *scared* for my *life*." She put a hand to her collar. "I was so traumatised that I nearly reverted back into the nasty old habit of sucking my thumb." I noticed her thumb twitch. "That was actually three weeks ago."

"Duly noted," I muttered. My mind was buzzing. So much school information in such little time. It was horrible. Summer was still technically on the clock, and I felt betrayed.

"HEY!" my new neighbour screamed, causing me to jump. "Do you want to come with me in an hour to the mall? I need some serious clothes shopping before the semester begins."

I nodded.

"Ten thirty isn't too early for you, is it?" she asked, and smiled when I shook my head. "Great. Oh, this will be fun. We can treat each other if you're into that. Oh, and I can't wait for you to meet my friends Wednesday and Friday. You'll just love them!"

She turned to leave, excited, but I grabbed her arm to check on something. "We're still going out *today*, right? Not just Wednesday and Friday?"

Her smile faded, and then she nodded and left. Phew. Perhaps it had been a stupid question to ask, but at least now I was sure. Plus, I had three dates. One today, for shopping. Another on Wednesday to meet some of her friends, and another on Friday. The question of why I couldn't meet them all at once instead of two days apart did cross my mind briefly, but as I cleaned my face upstairs I figured it was because she had so many friends, it was impossible to meet them all in one day. I mean, I'd never been popular, so I wasn't sure what it was like.

• • •

I was ready fifty minutes later. By then, the reality of the situation had hit me like a stack of bricks being thrown by a pack of Care Bears: It was a real rush, but it made me feel delighted. My terrified fake smile in the mirror soon turned into a real one, and I started to laugh. I think my parents thought it was weird, especially as it came after the Parkers had left and mere *seconds* after they yelled at me for screaming out their names earlier.

I kept what I had on. Porky Pig had always been in, especially when I was younger, and although the white shorts were completely hidden by the extra large tee, I thought I looked quite good.

Turns out, I was wrong. Way wrong.

Eleanore confronted me about it as I turned on the outside sprinkler in the front yard. If heat fell under any form of constitution, it would have been considered illegally hot. So I was just that little bit less surprised when I saw her strutting across our lawns in a fetching piece of… seat-belt, apparently. Two strange items of white fabric were crossed over her brown chest and somehow made a top. A mini-skirt covered her bottom half. Other than that and some glittered high-heeled flip-flops, she was all but nude. First thing she said to me was: "You look like a frump-gump."

I crossed my arms self-consciously.

Eleanore rolled her eyes as she stopped by my side. "Not literally. In our little world, there are certain types of people. The hot guys, which we call pugs, are an example. Then there are the frump-gumps. Girls that are… undesirable to the eye." I nodded in understanding. Still, the explanation served as pointless given I was equally offended. "Tanya got us onto them. Slang doing their rounds in Hollywood at the moment. Oh, she's another friend, by the way, Tanya. She's the queen of useful phrases when you want to express yourself incognito-style in public."

Moments later we were half-way down Philips Street. It was abandoned. Most people were still asleep, since it was a Sunday morning. It was quite a steep road, too. As we lived in the more affluential neighbourhoods, our houses were built higher than the rest of the town's. The Horn-Horn Hills, as I found out soon enough. So it took a lot of hiking to get to where we lived, and back, without a vehicle. My feet were already killing me.

"Tell me a little about yourself," Eleanore said. She was so tall with her high-heels on; I assumed she might only be my height or a little bigger if she took them off.

"Like what?" I asked, unsure of what to say.

"Well, stuff like…" She thought about it. "I'm not exactly sure what, but Daddy asked me to ask you that, so I thought I would. Okay, let me tell you a little about *myself* first. You know, to get the ball rolling."

"Good plan," I said.

Eleanore seemed delighted to be discussing her favourite subject. "My name is Eleanore Crapchel Parker. I was born here, and in doing so, I have lived my entire *life* here. My father was born here too, and my uncles all live here, and my aunts and cousins. My grandparents, not so much, but my *great*-grandparents..."

"Wait, hold the phone. What's your middle name?"

She'd been expecting this, and sighed angrily. "My middle name is Crapchel, alright? Crapchel. *Crap*chel! It was meant to be Rachel, but my father was eating Alphabet Soup when he signed my birth certificate. We don't like to talk about it.

"So as I said, I was *born* here, which means that I know everything about this town, and everyone's business. Not in a trashy housewives kind of way, though. I'm also the most popular girl in my year level and I even got an award for it one time!" She stopped and turned to me, beaming. "Your turn now."

I was on the spot after that weird rambling of hers, so I stumbled for a second. "My full name is Cassandra Lillian Gellar. My middle name is actually Lillian, in case you were wondering, and my mother chose this name for me because when she was ten she had a pet frog and she named it Lillian, and a few weeks after getting it, it went missing, and she found nothing but its skin when she opened her bedroom window a year later." I giggled. I loved that story. The poor frog had been crushed when Mom shut her window one time.

"*Oh!*" Eleanore seemed repulsed; not in the least bit amused. "That's terrible. Is your mother okay? I mean... *Oh!*" She gulped and looked like she was about to keel over.

"Yeah, she's fine..." I checked her face to see if she was serious. "She's moved on..."

After that I didn't want to talk about anything to her, in case I offended her again. I knew I'd have to pray for us all if I let something vile slip out and she turned her nose up at it.

At the corner of Philips Street, we passed by a very big, old property. Trapped inside a peeling white picket fence, a dilapidated double storey stood amongst a forest of sugar pines. Somewhere on the front porch, out of sight, apparently sat an elderly woman with crazy white hair. A hefty repetitive creaking gave away the rocking of her chair. We could hear her cackling away like she was in some kind of Warner Brothers cartoon. I soon learned that this was the local Emmett residence and they had taken charge of being the town kooks in 1978, which was quite a big honour in such a strange town. Eleanore also pointed out the red fire-hydrant across the road. Its colour was faded, and that was because the same dog for the past five years walked by every single afternoon at four and urinated on it. Other worth-knowing goings-on my tour guide thought I should know about consisted of, deeply truncated for your own sake: The house that kept burning down mysteriously, the flame-thrower who lived next door, the Alice in Wonderland fanatic, the family that owned a flamingo because their daughter wanted it, and the bachelor who was now a paraplegic because he fell through the ground in his back-garden into an underground cave. I wished I could turn Eleanore's voice off and just smile and nod every once in a while, but I couldn't. It wasn't until she finally asked me about my T-shirt that I looked up and realised I had no idea where we were anymore.

"Does it pertain to your designated religion?"

This day was getting weird. I looked down at Porky. "Are you asking me if I'm part hog?"

"I'm asking if it's in any way related to your ancestor-hood... ness." She looked around. "I'm asking if you're Jewish."

The connection between pork and the religion of which she was referring wasn't entirely hard to grasp. "Oh. Sort of," I muttered. "My father's father is. So... it's hard to explain. We don't stick to that religion. Just another typical Christian, I guess." I thought for a moment. Perhaps we were Catholic? We never really discussed it at home, unlike the touchy sex subject.

"Well, you can tell you're *part* Jew," said Eleanore as we turned down a long gravel road lined with eucalyptus trees. "FYI, you might want to trim those eyebrows a little...

"I'm not, like, a Nazi or anything," she continued, sensing the tension. "I'm sorry, you'll learn to love my quirks. I tend to say what's on my mind. I'm not racist at all. One of my top two best friends of all time is black. In a town like this, that's saying something. I don't know why, but minorities seem to skip Horn-Horn. It's just us whites and... and Jews."

There was a long pause. I sensed more to her thoughts on this. In case she was hinting at anything suss, I said: "I'm not racist, either."

"Of course you're not. You're *one* of them, silly!"

"Right," I laughed awkwardly. "But my grandparents *are* racist. On my mother's side. You see, my mother's parents hate us, and my dad. Because of our Jewish heritage."

"They sound like real Nazis," Eleanore seemed intrigued.

"Well, they were," I said. "Back in the day, anyway. During World War II. They're German, so they had to be, really."

Eleanore's mouth was wide open. "Get out!" she yelled, and she pushed me quite harshly. I found myself lying in a shrub, but she helped me up and apologised. "That's a little bit like my great grandmother Helga Emmett. I've never officially met her because she is sure I was adopted from Jamaica. But I wasn't! I can't help it if my skin is naturally olive. So I hear her every day, sitting on that porch cackling away, and I wonder: What traits do we share, old woman?"

I smiled thinly, but kept quiet to veil my concern. It didn't matter though, because out of the blue Eleanore veered off the road and over the ditch. I followed promptly, scratching my hand on the decrepit barbed-wired fence containing the land outstretched in front of us. Soon she had me trenching through some nearby woods, probably part of a private property. Thick with eucalyptus trees and wattle, we walked through tall, dead grass. Up steep banks, past giant rocks. It was darker here and I was getting anxious. I looked up as the wattles thinned and we became swamped by gigantic pine trees, probably hundreds of years old. They were so tall. Like sky-scrapers. I became dizzy looking up so I focused on my shoes, and realised that my friend was a hundred feet up ahead. I jogged to catch up with her.

"Where are we going?" I asked her.

"The mall, remember?" she replied, walking briskly.

"Shouldn't we stick to the…" I stopped talking. A thought had crossed my mind. This could be some sort of hazing ritual. The new girl was led away from the safety of her home by the really popular girl, taken to the middle of nowhere, tied up to a tree stump and left overnight. Perhaps throwing egg-yolks over the victim to provoke night animals.

"Hey, wait a minute!" I said firmly.

Eleanore turned around to see me standing absolutely still in the middle of a thick field of dead grass. She didn't look very happy. In fact, as I examined her closely, she looked rather distracted. My fears started to pour out in sweat.

"What?" she said, looking from left to right.

"Please don't haze me," I said.

"Come again?"

"If you're leading me to my doom, I think I should warn you. I bite deep."

"Speak English!"

"Where are you taking me?"

"To the mall, alright?" She came over and grabbed my hand

and we continued at a quick pace. "If you're concerned because I'm walking so fast, it's because quite frankly I hate these effing woods. Oh sure, it's a tremendous short-cut to town centre from our street, but there's just something creepy about them."

I looked around, feeling relieved. "But it seems nice here."

"You don't know what I know."

"Then tell me, and I'll know."

"I'm not going to tell you, it will scar you for life."

"Oh..."

Eleanore let go of my hand, but we kept walking. "Well, since you've twisted my arm, I'll tell you. When my daddy was a little boy, this was before his mother didn't off herself properly, she led him through these woods every day to try and lose him or drown him. It's a long family story that I won't get into. Anyway, one day she left him here alone and he was on his usual trip back when he says he saw a giant ball of light in the sky and the next thing he knew it was night time, and he walked all the way home in the dark and when he got home he realised that his family didn't live there any more. So he went to the local police station and they ran his face through the system and found out who he was, but they told him that he'd gone missing eight years before, except he hadn't aged a day. And when he went home, his parents had aged, like a lot. And so these scientists and all that came and took him away and did experiments on him. And I forget the rest, I think I started blow-drying my hair when he got up to the boring NASA stuff..."

I toyed with this story for a moment. "Eleanore, that's the plot to *Flight of the Navigator*."

Eleanore cleared her throat of phlegm and dug some wax out of her ear. "What's that? Oh, anyway, aside from that creepy story, I saw something once when I was crossing a stream nearby with my friend Tanya."

We trekked over a small hill and were met with even more woods, thick and dark. In front of us, at the bottom of the hill, was a stream. Eleanore stopped and crossed her arms indignantly.

"It wouldn't happen to be *this* stream, would it?" I asked.

She frowned, and pointed to a tree which stood on the other side of the stream. A very strangely shaped hollow tree. It wasn't a pretty sight to look at, either. It was dead. Very dead. Pitch black.

Burnt.

"She was halfway across the stream when it burst into flames."

I looked up at her in disbelief. "Nuh-uh... The tree?"

Eleanore nodded, looking rather wary. "Out of nowhere. Like *that*." She clicked her fingers. "I got so freaked that I ran away as quickly as I could. I left Tanya behind."

I dreaded the ending to this story, which didn't sound like it had come from any sci-fi eighties movie. "Did Tanya disappear...?"

Eleanore snapped out of her daze and looked at me in wonder. "No... Of course not. She came back about an hour later. She's in our *class*, Cassie. Not that she'll be there tomorrow. She's still 'holidaying' in Italy."

"Was she alright?"

"What? Oh, I don't know..." said Eleanore as we hopped over the stream. "I guess so. I didn't ask, really." She glanced back at the tree, which seemed to gape right back at us. "But how that tree caught on fire... I'll never know. Tell the truth, I don't *want* to know. Come on, let's get going."

4
WEDNESDAY & FRIDAY

It wasn't long until we reached the end of the woods. Although it had been quite a strenuous journey in this heat, I trusted Eleanore when she said it was a short-cut. The town was such a big place; I couldn't imagine how long it would have taken normally.

The sun shone directly down upon us in the morning light and I shielded my eyes for a few moments. When I could see clearly at last, it appeared we were standing on the edge of a great field, high on a hill. It looked down upon the rest of Horn-Horn.

At least, a busy version.

"This town is separated into two parts," said Eleanore, continuing on through the empty field. "The part we live in is the quiet side of Horn-Horn. Or the residential area, at least. This side is the real Horn-Horn. Where the bustling businesses, schools, and beach are. All that. Those woods are there as boundaries between the quiet and the busy sides. They also block out a lot of the noise from the busy side so we can't hear it where we live. Cool, huh?" She smiled. "Careful. Snake."

I checked my feet, saw nothing, then examined the town from where we were. We weren't that much higher, but we were high enough to see everything that lay out in front of us. Beyond the field lay a steep slope that led down to a busy section of road. Directly across from that was a parking lot, and the mall. So it was actually much closer than I thought it would be. Beyond the mall, from what I could see, were streets and streets of businesses, apartments, shopping alleys, tourism venues, restaurants, and somewhere near the end, the beach. I could see the ocean spread out on the horizon and in the morning light, it looked very inviting.

"Maybe we can beach it later," I suggested as we reached the end of the field. We started down the slope for the pedestrian crossing.

"Not after my tanning sesh," laughed Eleanore.

Well, that was that then.

Soon enough we were walking through the empty mall parking lot. Besides from about ten cars and a few upturned shopping trolleys, the only signs of life were two crows battling it out with a used burger wrapper. It was at this point, as one of them flew away in victory, that I noticed the sign above the mall in large black block-writing.

"Horn-Horn Mall II… Why's it got two at the end of it?"

"This is the second mall in Horn-Horn," my friend told me casually. "Even though this one was built after the other one, this is still the best mall of the two. The other one is gross and going out of business, and everything in it is cheap."

"I like cheap."

"Of *course* you do, Jew."

I stared at her, dumbfounded.

"That was a joke. And no we *don't*," she reminded me in a sing-song voice. "It's the mall where all the bogans and losers go. We call it 'The Mall of Shame'. Because of the lower levels of society who go there, but also because a few years ago an escaped panther mauled a guy in one of the bathrooms until he was naked, and for a while nobody went back there."

All of this I found only mildly interesting, until I spotted another weird building not too far off. A large, slightly leaning building, much like an enlarged mausoleum, sat on a hill. It looked like it had sunk greatly into the ground on one side, but I think it must have been one of those new-age 'odd for the sake of being odd' architectural designs.

"And that eyesore?"

"Well firstly, we're not going in so don't even ask. That's the Horn-Horn National Gallery and Cemetery."

I paused, then laughed.

"No, really," Eleanore said. "Inside it's just like any other Gallery, like the Louvre. Except it's got cheap home-made paintings hanging up on the walls, like Mr. Gan Vogh's *'Vinnie's Bedroom in Flames'*, Borlan Bennet's *'The Outsider Inside Her'*, and my personal favourite: *'Britney & Justin: A Portrait'*."

"And the cemetery part?"

Eleanore huffed. We'd stopped and were standing at an enticing distance from the mall entrance. "Daddy says it is an insult to the town. It's pretty much what the title suggests. All the paintings on the walls are surrounded by graves."

"No."

"Fifty years ago, the Mayor of Horn-Horn ran out of money for a gallery, and the old cemetery downtown was and still is completely full. Instead of building a new one, they just mixed the two together. So this way, when people visit their dead relatives, they can be soothed by the art on the walls."

"Are the graves buried underneath the floorboards?"

"No, it's an open roof. All of the paintings are in glass protectives. Daddy only puts up with it because Ellana Fork-Flame's dead husband is buried there. She's the mayor."

I remained where I was, staring at the building in awe, until I sensed I was alone. I turned and saw that Eleanore had wandered off towards the mall again, and I ran to catch up. But I didn't need to run. She stopped right in front of the automatic glass doors that led inside. She was looking up at the sky angrily, arms crossed again, tisking, and tapping one of her feet.

"What's wrong?" I asked. I walked past her, and the doors opened. She shot past me to get inside.

"One of the stupid workers here. Every time I come, he or she keeps turning off the automatic doors so I can't get in."

"Maybe you have no soul."

Eleanore laughed, thinking I was joking. Inside, we were hit straight away by a burst of fresh cold air. It was a tremendous relief. I closed my eyes for a moment, still walking, and relished it. But when I opened my eyes again, I turned to see that Eleanore was on the other side of the walkway, peering into a window at a flashy number in one of the stores. I checked to see if anybody had noticed me. Of course, nobody had. The town seemed to be deserted today, entirely. If it weren't for the security cameras I could strip off and play jacks with my nether-regions and nobody would know.

"Are you going to buy that?" I asked Eleanore, joining her side.

She shook her head, and walked off silently. I quickened my pace as she strode from one store to the next, glancing sometimes briefly into one, then thoroughly inspecting items in another. Eventually, I started: "So are we going to…"

But she interrupted me with a: "Ssshhh," and continued studying the price-tags.

"Okay," I turned, annoyed. "I'm going to look around on my own."

"Stay where I can see you," I heard her say.

My cheeks flushed in outrage. Who did she think she was, my mother? She was about a dozen lbs and a kind soul short of that. I looked around, panicking. Perhaps it was an anxiety attack. I couldn't remember how to get home from here. I strode towards the other end of the mall, to get to the closest exit which was beyond the food court. I'd made a bad mistake. An awful one. I decided at the last second to walk into a tiny Mexican restaurant on my right. I needed something to eat, and some water. Inside the empty establishment, the tables were dirty and the fluorescent lights made the whole place seem seedy. I went straight to the counter and ordered some nachos with melted cheese, and was told to take a seat and wait.

I wanted to cry. Was I perhaps being a little overboard about this? It was definitely an anxiety attack. I poured myself a cup of complimentary water from the water-cooler and plopped myself down at a table, my seat scraping noisily on the ground. I focussed my attention on the wall opposite me, and tried to relax. My heart was beating fast. I could hear it in my ears. Then I became distracted by a movement to my left. I turned to see three people, two tables down. The three people from underneath the pier. My heart stopped. How had I not seen them sitting there? I'd walked right past them as I ordered.

"What's up?" said the blonde girl.

I shrugged and tried to swallow as quietly as possible. It didn't go to plan. "Nummusch…" I muttered.

She was sipping a coke, resting into her beanie boyfriend's body casually. Eating the same thing that I'd ordered, and he watched me like a hawk. He winked. The other guy was sitting opposite them, so he had his back to me. All I could see was his shaggy, wavy black hair. But he turned his head and our eyes connected. I couldn't keep it up for more than two seconds, and I had to look down. My cup of water was that interesting.

My nachos were ready. I got up and collected them from the front counter, and turned around. I stood there, staring at the three of them, who in turn stared at me. Suddenly I noticed the heat of the nachos and melted cheese; I hissed and released its scolding bowl from my grip. It landed noisily in front of them. Stupid reflexes.

"Spare seat," said the girl.

"Huh?"

She lifted her eyebrows. "Spare seat. Take the spare seat."

At a table with four seats, I could think of nothing else.

"Okay," I said. With a wobbled movement I picked up the spare seat and began to walk away with it.

"No," the girl spoke slowly. "I mean, sit down in that seat. *Here.*"

I shook my head and laughed at myself, and I took the seat back to their table to join them. Once I sat down, I started to eat as an excuse not to speak first.

"How's your pussy?" said the beanie boy.

"Fine." I picked at a submerged nacho. I knew what he meant.

"We keep running into you," said the girl.

I smiled politely. "I know."

"And you just moved here."

"Yeah. Weird, huh?"

"People move here all the time," said the beanie boy.

I looked up at him. He challenged me.

"What's your name again?" asked the girl.

I was about to answer when all three of them moaned and groaned and rolled their eyes. I wondered why.

"*Cassandra Lillian Gellar!*" a voice shrieked into my right ear.

I leapt a foot in the air, striking my knees on the underside of the table. Eleanore stood next to me, her arms crossed, gazing down.

"Yes, Eleanore?" I said, my eyes wide.

"May I borrow you?"

I stood up with my nacho bowl. "Okay."

"Wassup, Parker?" said the beanie boy.

Eleanore didn't look at him. "Come along, Cassie." She grabbed me by the arm and I found myself yanked out of the restaurant. We walked a good mile before I decided to confront her.

"What was *that*?" I said quietly.

Eleanore stopped at the sight of some jackets on half price. "Hmm? Oh. That! No, we don't talk to them." She tsked at a purple hoodie and threw it back into the basket. "They are what we call *back-seaters*. Neither pugs nor frump-gumps, but not shy of a flamingo."

"Your terms are like mathematics to me."

"Look, they are just poor losers who will end up living on the streets. Or if they're lucky, in cheap apartments infested with rats."

"They seem cool."

"Cool, yes..." Eleanore looked at me. "If you think wearing your pants down to your knees or... or sleeping in class is fun, then yes, it would seem cool. But we are not like that, Cassie. We like to cover our behinds with trousers, because we are not seeking anal sex. We go to school to learn, don't we? Then learn we do. Once Wednesday and Friday get here, you'll learn a thing or two, trust me. In the meantime, keep away from those... people. They're like poison ivy, only without the urushiol-induced contact dermatitis."

Two screams made me yet again leap a foot in the air. My bowl of nachos smacked to the ground by Eleanore's feet. She looked at me with a sharp eyebrow. Two girls were running towards us, both utterly gigantic and possibly seeking snu-snu. I felt the urge to flee, but they called Eleanore's name. Upon seeing them, she screamed too.

"*Wednesday!*" Eleanore cried to the black girl, hugging her gently.

"*Friday!*" She hugged the red-haired girl.

Their gazes fell upon me.

"Ohhh."

It finally dawned on me that when Eleanore had said Wednesday and Friday, she was actually referring to the names of her friends. The days of the week would never be the same again.

"This is my new neighbour, Cassie G —"

"Eleanore, please, we know!" said Friday loudly. "Cassandra Lillian Gellar. Born July 2nd 1985 in New York, lost her first tooth at age six, has a dog and a cat and is allergic to..."

"Eucalyptus oil, black currants and incontinent pads," Wednesday finished. "We've heard so much about you from Eleanore! Well, from Eleanore and the school records."

"And I've heard absolutely nothing about you two. Other than your preferred weekdays."

"I'm Friday Sheppard," said Friday, pronouncing it as '*Shepp-paahd*' quite pompously. "And this is Wednesday Shalom."

"Hi."

"Shalom," said Wednesday. I was shocked to notice that she had fierce blue eyes.

"My *God*," cried Friday fiercely, pinching the cloth on my upper-arm. "Did you pick these clothes up at a two-for-one sale back in the early David Bowie days of yore? Because they are totally Dumpsville, like, *off!*"

"No. This was my dad's, and the rest were my sister's until she grew out of them."

Friday looked above in disbelief. "Recycling items of clothing is *so* juvenile, bar diapers according to my mother. But this... on you... Well, it's just unnecessarily awkward."

Eleanore rested her heavy arm on my shoulder. "We have much to teach you before tomorrow. Let's begin!"

Before I knew it we had all linked hands, and I tripped along with them as they embarked merrily down the yellow brick road. We soon entered a gigantic women's clothing store. Friday was the first to break away. She turned to the other two and flashed them a weird baseball signal with her hands.

"Spread out!" Eleanore declared. They set off through the fields of clothes, like raptors in tall grass.

"Got one!"

"Got one!"

They returned with a couple of items each.

"Friday..." Eleanore tsked, looking down at her choices. "Fluff just isn't good for summer." She looked at Wednesday's choice. "Other than the skirt, it looks fine. Good work."

Wednesday and Friday smiled; Friday half-heartedly.

To my *supreme* exhaustion, we spent the next *two hours* picking out clothes. For me, and only me. I didn't even like the choices. The one item I picked myself, a black pair of sweatpants, was snatched off me by a worker who happened to be passing by ("How did they get there?" she muttered).

"*CASSIE!*"

Friday swung open the curtain to my changing cubicle. I was in my underwear and I squirmed into a ball. She showed me the clothes I'd worn here, holding them like they were toxic. "Where do you want me to put these?"

I paused, thinking. "Spare bag?"

Wednesday barged into the cubicle without hesitance. "Are you sure you wouldn't like us to burn them? They are *hideous!* I could just give them to that worker with the sweatpants."

"I like them."

Eleanore clambered in, looking like she was busy at work. "No you don't. You just don't know any better, sharing a house with a grotty little boy and a pod-person for a sister."

"Brendan *seems* grotty, but he's just putting it on because he's trying to go against gay stereotypes."

"What? He's *gay?* But he's only eleven!"

I could see they were doubtful. "You've got to know him to get it." I paused, looking down, but suddenly something struck me. "Wait, you've met my brother and sister?"

"Oh my, no," Eleanore said. "I saw them last night when I was watching your house. I know you saw me. I can see into your upstairs from my brother's bedroom. Before your sister closed her curtains I could see right into the hall and into your room, and your brother's. He's such a cutie-pie, but he needs to clean his ears. And have them surgically taped back. They look like squishy dried apricots. And your sister... I don't know quite what to say. She is a *bit* of a nerd." She said it comically, as if she knew it was a wicked thing to say.

All three of them laughed meanly.

"She's my sister."

"And we don't hold that against you, Quinn. Now, these jeans need out. Wednesday, what were you thinking? Did you see the smiley-face flower patterns on the back?" Her best black friend of all time shook her head. "Wednesday dear, if you don't examine, you'll never learn. Put them back where you found them and write an apology note to the store for creasing them!"

Wednesday left with the devil's jeans, but didn't close the curtain. This cubicle seemed more like public domain.

———— • • • ————

I wore a tight grey top and long red skirt out of there. Eleanore had squished my boobs up to make way for some mega cleavage I didn't even know I had. She also slapped some bright red lipstick on for me. I felt like a thirty year old Special K model.

"Oh look," said Friday, as we passed by the Mexican restaurant. "There's Moe, Larry and Curly."

Sure enough, the 'back-seaters' were where we'd left them.

"Don't they ever get tired of staying in the same place?"

I stifled back my disbelief.

They looked up just as we passed by. The boy with black hair was the first to catch my attention as he turned in his seat again. Even from across the walkway, I could see how piercing his blue eyes were. They absolutely made me nervous to the point where I thought my brains would melt and dribble out of my ears. The others... the girl, and the boy in the beanie, stood up at the table and pointed at me. The boy cat whistled and the girl snorted with laughter. I guess they didn't like my new clothes.

"Oh, Cassandra! How very *selective* you look!"

I blushed. Wednesday and Friday glared at them like tigers, encouraging me onwards with their hands on the small of my back.

"Ignore them. They aren't worth the trouble."

"I bet she don't even knows that her sentence made none sense."

The three girls stuck their noses up into the air and walked faster, like a pack of pompous springer spaniels. I, of course, made quick work of catching up to them, but I chanced a look back to see the boy I liked still staring blankly.

Is he even aware he's doing it? I wondered.

When we emerged from the mall into the great outdoors, we discovered with great regret that the sun had picked up its strength and was causing death and destruction to everything within its reach.

"Who *were* they?" I asked as we crossed the parking lot.

"That was Hayley Gauche, JT Walker and Greg Cooper. The losers of our class," Eleanore told me. She snorted, holding back a laugh. "They *so* want to hang out with us."

"Which one is the boy *without* the beanie?"

"Oh, Greg?" Wednesday said, smiling slightly. "He's not all bad..." Eleanore shot her a grim look, so she continued, "... in an abominable and distasteful way, though. Kinda like sour worms. Hey, let's take the short-cut through the woods again."

"We went that way to begin with," said Eleanore.

"So did we," said Friday.

"Get *out!*" laughed Eleanore.

She pushed her friend over.

"Sorry. I've got to stop doing that."

——— · · · ———

My mind eventually took control and blocked out their voices. I focused on the ground beneath my feet for the rest of the walk home, except during the time spent in the woods. Now that Eleanore had mentioned it, there was an eerie vibe to it.

The walk up Philips Street was painful. I was not dressed at all for walking uphill. But I wasn't the only one suffering — the others had gone relatively quiet during the last quarter of the hike. Still, there was a bit of breath left for light conversation.

"I got an email from Tanya last night," Friday broke the silence.

"How is she?" asked Wednesday.

"Good! She'll be home soon, depending on her sister."

"How is she?"

"I just said... She's good."

"No, I mean her sister."

"Oh. I didn't ask."

"What's wrong with her sister?" I piped in.

"Her sister Cindy had a rock climbing accident in Rome," said Eleanore. "One of those indoor walls was driven into by an old man. Poor Mustang. Dozens were injured, blah-blah. She's in one of their hospitals, and depending on when the doctors give her the all clear, Tanya and her family will bring her back home with them. Shouldn't be more than a few days."

"Great excuse to miss school, though," said Friday.

We spent the rest of the day hanging out in Eleanore's bedroom. It was a session of clothes this, clothes that, ringing up boys and hanging up, and as the sun set even a mild pillow fight which I decided to sit and watch rather than partake in. I was considering quietly slipping off to the bathroom and punching the mirror in anxiety, when Mom called. She informed Eleanore that it was dinner time, and I had to go home.

I was so relieved, I actually jumped up and started to scream: *'Hallelujah!'*, but caught myself after *'Ha'* and yawned out in a southern drawl: "*Haaa*... wonder what we're having for dinner, *tharrr..?*"

Eleanore didn't seem too disheartened by my departure. As she ushered me down the stairs to the front door, she told me to come back as soon as I'd finished eating. I crossed her lawn and into mine. My shoulders were sore from sunburn, and all of those heavy bags of clothing that pulled my arms down were not helping. If I held them until I was twenty, I'm sure my fingers would reach my toes naturally.

I opened my front door. Dazed, it took me a few moments to

realise that there were familiar items of furniture in the foyer. I dropped the bags and rushed to one of them, hugging it firmly.

"Oh, cellarette!"

Mom came to greet me in the foyer, a dish-towel in her hands.

"Dinner is in the dining room," she said.

I stood up, sniffing. "And where would that be?"

She pointed to a mysterious hallway I'd failed to notice.

"You go two doors down, turn left, then open the french doors at the end of the hall."

I did just that, and was met with the rest of my family sitting at our familiar mahogany dining table. It was weird seeing stuff from our old house in new rooms. Dinner was not as extravagant as our furniture, though. It seemed to be a bunch of paper plates with pizza slices on them.

"Compliments to the delivery boy!"

I sat down next to my father. Mom followed me in with a bottle of coke and five glasses stacked on top of each other.

"So," she said, sitting down. "How was everyone's day?"

"Horrifying," I decried immediately.

"Mine was engaging," Annie said in her typically snobby way. "Once those plebs from the removals company found us, I got out all of my books and put them on the shelves in my room. *In* alphabetical order, mind you. It was quite a task, but really very rewarding in the end. You know, I even found books I forgot I had."

"Yeah, well, while your day was wonderful, *loner*… I had to deal with our neighbour, Eleanore Parker. She's the Principal's daughter. Yeah, Annie. Prepare for her at school." I dabbed the corners of my mouth with my napkin. "Her friends call her 'Marcia, Marcia, Marcia' as a joke, they named themselves the *'Saviours of Tomorrow'*, and she considers the desire to read to be contagious."

"Ewww. Ein Fluch auf die Erde!"

Brendan giggled between hefty mouthfuls. "Only nerds read books, and I poo on nerds."

It took Annie a moment to catch on, then she choked down her bite to speak. "Oh, it was once, and you were a baby!"

At that point, Mom reminded me that I was expected back over at the Parker household as soon as dinner was over. After a moment of stressing about it, I decided sneakily that dinner would simply never end. My plan of slowly eating tiny amounts was going perfectly, until Mom guided the pizza slicer in my hand as a hint that she knew what

I was up to. I pleaded with her to phone Eleanore and lie for me.

"Tell her I've suffered mild heatstroke and need to go to sleep!"

My mother begrudgingly agreed, and I happily spent the rest of the night unpacking my things.

5

HORN-HORN HIGH-HIGH

I was fast asleep in my cosy *LOL* when Mom came in to wake me up the next morn'. She pinched my nose, through which I was breathing, and waited. I sat up, gasping.

"Why?" I choked.

"School."

"Another year added to my sentence for, what this time, manslaughter? Oh, no. Just being a kid. How awful of me."

As she left to wake the others, I started thinking over what to do with Eleanore. I could always just come out and say that I didn't want to be her best friend, only a next-door-neighbour-type friend. Hanging out with her and her company for just one day had been more than enough for me.

Just then, a rock hit my window. I went over, opened my blinds and looked down. There they were, the Saviours of Tomorrow, standing merrily-dressed in the garden bed below. They waved to me like stranded passengers on a deserted island. I shot them a curt wiggle of the fingers, and snuck down the hall in fear.

I dressed in one of the outfits from yesterday just in case, with a great big magenta belt holding everything in place. I was out the door half an hour later, paranoid of course, but long after Mom had gone outside to tell them she would be driving me. Another lie. Annie actually did want a ride to school, but I was walking. I was determined to start the school year independently. Now, if the town map was not outdated, then it was safe to say that the woods I'd walked through yesterday would still be a sufficient shortcut. Even though this time I'd have to cut it even shorter since the school was on the east side, while the mall was on the north side. Confusing? Thankfully I had GPS on my phone in case I got lost.

My slightly altered trip through the woods was completely uneventful. So much so, that I was a little bit disappointed as I left the eerie darkness. The school was now directly in front of me, at the bottom of the hill I was on. I walked down the slope towards it. The school sign came into view. It read:

<u>Ellana Fork-Flame High School</u>
For children and stunted adults

The school was very tech-savvy from what I'd heard. It wasn't a private school, but Eric Parker apparently invested quite an amount of his fortune into the place. The buildings weren't dilapidated, and most of them were oddly metallic purple structures. The main building was directly in line with the front gate, which I walked through and stopped under the cover of a eucalyptus microtheca to check my backpack. Through the mail, I'd been given information on my first day. No curriculum or anything, just tidbits about what to expect, where to go, with a map of the school.

My class home room was in B block. I looked up at the main building. Underneath a sign saying: '*Reception*', was a tinier sign saying: '*A block —>*'.

I followed the arrow around the side of the building, ignoring teenagers in groups as they sat gawking, until I found A block. Then there was a sign pointing to B block. I followed, past the library, until I found the corridor for B block. My new home. It was a dark corridor, with lights on the aqua coloured walls above the orange lockers. Quite busy with it being quarter to nine, I found my supposed assigned room and entered, shutting the door behind me. I thought it was empty until I heard a squeaking of chalk. I spun around to see an old woman writing on the board. She had short white hair, and was dressed in a dark pink blouse and skirt, with light pink pearls around her neck. When she turned, the first thing I noticed was how kind her face looked. With pink lips and blush that spackled her wrinkled cheeks, she took me in with the largest blue eyes I'd ever seen.

"Hi," I said quietly.

"Hello," she replied in a husky voice. "Not lost, are we?"

I thought for a moment. "Are you Ms. Weiss?"

She put the chalk down. "You must be Carrie Glandular."

"Cassie Gellar."

"Welcome to Horn-Horn High-High, dear," she said, and she walked all the way over to me just to put her hand on my shoulder. She promptly walked back to the chalkboard and started writing again. "That's what everybody calls it. *Horn-Horn High-High*. Don't worry, it's a running joke in town. Now, be a sweetheart. Sit down and wait for class to start."

I gazed across the empty room, and chose a desk near the back. Not at the very back, that was scary. The second last row, smack dab in the middle. Ms. Weiss had written *'Welcome bak!'* in big, shaky handwriting. I wondered if I should alert her of the mistake, but I didn't want to tell her how to do her job. Last time I did that, I got a nice shade of purple around my neck and a new Girl Scout leader.

"Now, Cassie, is there anyone in this class you already know?" Ms. Weiss asked me. It was a welcome relief from the awkward silence between us. "The reason I ask is because we have a buddy system for new students. While we like to promote new friendships, it can be beneficial when one already knows someone and therefore has a good excuse to sit with them. They can be your tour guide for the first week of school. Just to help you get used to things around here." She put the chalk down again and went to her desk, emptying some folders of paper out in front of her to make it look like she'd been there a while.

"Let's see, I know..." I began, but fate sent a bubble of genius into my throat to stop it. "I know Hayley Gauche."

Ms. Weiss's face dropped like an anchor had been tied to it. "Oh, Hayley, that..." She said it with incredible spite in her voice, but then she caught herself and beamed at me. "That unique go-getter!"

When the bell rang five minutes later and the class filled up fifteen minutes later, people seemed to sit away from me. Despite Eleanore's comments to the contrary, there were many different varieties of students, too. I felt like I was watching cable. I know they called this county the multicultural cesspit of the continent, but I wasn't expecting *Hands Across the World*. There were goths, cheerleaders, jocks, nerds, loners, bogans, big-breasted sexed-up librarian types, large acne-faced scaredy-cats, hippie-wannabes... My eyes lost control as I examined them all trundling in. Last but not least, as if the universe had planned it: Eleanore and Hayley waltzed in, their cronies chasing their tails. I straightened up, preparing myself. The Saviours of Tomorrow gathered around me.

"How's your neck?" Wednesday asked, sitting down by my side.

"Huh? Oh, fine. I just needed a good night's sleep."

Eleanore faced me head on, and for a moment I thought she knew what I was planning. "Ms. Weiss is going to ask if you know anyone. Don't forget to mention me!"

"Okay," I lied through gritted teeth.

A dozen angels must have been passing overhead, for all at once the room stopped its chatter and faced the front. Precognitive it would seem, as Ms. Weiss stopped writing assessment details on the board and strutted in front of her desk to plop her butt against it.

"Welcome back, class!" she addressed us quite gleefully, pointing to the board. She finally noticed her mistake, and blushed. "How did everybody enjoy summer?"

Mild mumbles spread across the room.

"I thought you'd all appreciate the sunlight. Except for you, Jared. I'm sorry. I keep forgetting. Now, while most of the morning will revolve around sharing your summer adventures, we'll have to touch lightly on our assessments and requirements for the first term, including an outline for what to expect from the rest of the year. With a new age and a new grade level, one must expect fresh and tougher responsibilities..." She started off on a speech that sounded vaguely stolen, and I soon drifted off into my own world of thoughts. Great start to the academic year.

"Next she'll make you stand up in front of everyone," Hayley whispered on my neck from the back row, her hot breath filled with mint. I turned to face her. She was smirking horribly at me. "Then everyone will be looking at you and she'll lay the hard stuff on you. After that, she'll make you hang out with Eleanore and you'll talk about dresses and boring stuff and..."

"Excuse me," Eleanore turned around and whispered harshly. "Please be quiet. Class has started." She faced the front, then turned back again. "And not boring stuff. Cardigans and new suede boots and gloves made out of Yearling skin, too."

"*Yearling skin?* Are you serious? You are a Disney *villain!*" Hayley hissed quietly at her. Finishing that, she turned her attention on me again. "Do you know what you've gotten yourself into, *Cassandra?* Schools and their tags, they stick with you for life for some reason. Once a Saviour, always a —"

"Miss. Gauche!" our teacher called loudly. "Spit out that gum."

Looking around to find no bin, Hayley gave her a disrespectful stare. "Where shall I put it, oh wise one?"

"Open Sesame and find out," Ms. Weiss played cooly, pointing to a closed cupboard behind us. Then, she used that same hand to point at me. "Also being a new year… We must welcome new people to our class. I'd like you all to say: Hello, Cassie Gellar."

Several people muttered my name unenthusiastically, while Eleanore and her friends said it with fierce enthusiasm: "*Hello, Cassandra Lillian Gellar!*"

I sank down in my seat, just as Ms. Weiss lifted her arms into the air to catch my attention. "Cassie, why don't you come up to the front and grace us with your presence?"

"Do I have to?"

"Yes."

Slowly and nervously, I stood up and walked to the front with my head down. I heard the tiny whispers and giggles as everybody judged me, wondering if I was cool or if I was lame. At the front, I focused on the back cupboard. Hayley hadn't bothered closing it, and her moist green gum sat on the edge of the exposed bin.

"Hi. I'm Cassie Gellar. Sixteen. I come from Salem." They were all listening without any ridicule. I continued, feeling braver. "You know, the ghost town. Can't step out of the front door without tripping over a black cat and falling into a grave." That was my attempt at being funny, yet they looked on in silence.

"Hmmm…" Ms. Weiss gazed at the floor for a moment, then she made the gesture for me to sit down again. "Thank you, Carrie. Now, the little matter of who will take care of our new classmate for the first week must be dealt with. After much careful thinking, I have decided to pair her with Hayley Gauche."

"Present," said Hayley. She'd been gazing out the window.

"No, Hayley. You'll be taking care of Cassie for the first week."

Hayley's head made a whooshing sound as she turned to face the front. She gave Ms. Weiss an almighty evil stare.

"*What?*"

Eleanore stood up, laughing in disbelief.

"If you don't mind Ms. Weiss, I would like to take care of Cassie. After all, we are neighbours, and…"

"No thank you, Eleanore," said Ms. Weiss. "Although I am grateful for your enthusiasm to show the new student around, again… Your help will not be needed *this* time around… again."

She smiled forcefully at Eleanore, who reluctantly gave up.

"Cassie, why don't you go and sit in that spare seat alongside Hayley in the next row down?"

The back row! What world was this I'd fallen into? I got up and did as I was told. The class ooh'ed as if I were in trouble. Hayley's almighty evil stare was now set upon me. She looked like she would rather eat twenty pregnant slugs, spew them up and eat them again as the babies wriggled down her throat. Still, I smiled at her. She'd been nice to me until yesterday. Maybe she would change her mind.

"*Saviour…*" she mouthed slowly and malevolently.

Or not.

6

HOW TO WIN FRIENDS AND ALIENATE PEOPLE

I t felt like a lifetime until the recess bell rang, and everyone hurried out of the room as fast as lightning. I took my time. I didn't want to leave so soon. This classroom was like a safe haven.

Hayley waited until Ms. Weiss was facing the board, then took her chance and bolted from the room. But Weiss turned just in time, ran to the door and ordered her back. Fuming, Hayley returned, grabbed my arm, and forced me to follow her down the hall. I was dragged all the way to the very back of the school, to an abandoned area of flat land littered with red dust. Resting against the cyclone fence was a hefty sheath of vines.

Hayley let go of my arm. I was about to say something, but found myself being pushed forward. I fell dramatically through the twines and landed on something hard. I opened my eyes. I was resting on Greg, who looked embarrassed enough for the both of us.

"Chick magnet," JT smiled next to him. "Greg, you dog."

I quickly jumped off him and apologised. Trying to act casual and make it out as no big deal, I flopped down beside him.

"Did you ask to be put with me?" Hayley said, looming over me with her hands on her hips.

"Of course not."

"You're such a liar," she picked me up by the hair, and my eyes began to water. "You're a loser. You hang out with the Saviours and live up in the Hills. We don't talk to snobs like they're humans, because they're not. You're not. You're a — "

Without even meaning to, the palm of my hand came into blunt contact with her forehead. I guess the many times Brendan had done it to me triggered some kind of kin-connection or something. But I wasn't thinking about that as my hand quickly snapped back into line against my thigh.

I was thinking: '*Omygod-omygod-omygod!*'

Hayley blinked a couple of times, and moved her eyes around to make sure she was alright. The silence between us was unbearable. My lips quivered as I tried to keep them closed, but alas, words spilled out.

"You know, maybe you should get your facts straight before you grab someone by the hair."

"Fine," she sounded like a surly child.

"Eleanore lives next door to me now, and she ambushed me yesterday morning. I'm not... We don't..."

I struggled with the belt buckle cutting off my circulation.

"It's just... not... *me*. And, I mean, it's my first day, and I'm trying *really* hard to like it here. But if everybody is as crazy as you and her, then I don't know why we bothered moving here."

I felt I was on the verge of slicing some crap.

Hayley did something I never expected in a million years. She smirked. She then promptly thrust her weight atop one of my shoulders, pushing me to the ground again. She lowered herself to sit next to me, taking some of her recess food out of her gigantic flannel shirt pockets.

"This is my boyfriend, JT," she pointed to the one and only, who pulled a juice bottle out from under his beanie. "Jonathan Thomas is his full name but call him that and die. Only I get to call him by his real name. Oh, and this other neanderthal is Greg."

The boy with shaggy black hair scowled at her.

"Hey! My brow is naturally furrowed, thank you very much."

I smiled gladly at him and waved hello. I was so relieved; up until that point, I'd thought he might be a mute.

"This is where we sit and waste our lives away," said Hayley, pointing at the vines shielding us from the outside world. "I guess you can hang here if you want. People call it a vine-plant, because I guess that's what it is. That sounds so informal though, so we call it the Vineyard, just because. Also, it's magic."

"It is not," said JT.

"Yes it is, you idiot!" she shouted. "Don't ask me why, but it's magic. It just is, and I know it. If you debate me on it, I'll pound your face in."

Hayley was a bit like Nicole, my friend back in Salem. In a way. She wasn't a Goth, and the way she acted with JT certainly didn't make me question her sexuality... But there was a fight-against-the-authority vibe that came naturally to her, as if it were implanted in her genes.

Danger sounded by way of clip-clopping heels nearby. Hayley poked her head through the 'Vineyard' leaves to examine the school yard, and grumbled.

"Don't you even *think* of inviting them over here," she snapped at me, hiding. "Whether you're trying to be polite or not, if they find out where we hang out, she'll get her father — Principal Pauper — to have this place knocked down."

"Why would she do that?"

"Why not?" JT sat up, grinning.

"She doesn't like us, that's why," Hayley said, sitting on her knees. "It'll just add to the kick she gets from being the Principal's *innocent little baby*. Plus she's not very environmentally friendly. I saw her once in her backyard when I was little, slashing one of those giant oak trees with a hatchet. Says she was just playing, but I saw the fury in her eyes."

I noticed an eye peering at me through a gap in the vines. Eleanore moved forward, revealing herself like the raptor right before it killed Muldoon. *Clever girl.*

"Ring-around-the-rosy, a pocket full of *vines*," she said.

She turned for support from her two crones, but they weren't there. In fact, they were already sitting beside Greg and JT, looking about in wonder.

"This place is so cool," said Friday.

"*Girls!*"

Hayley made the movement of a hatchet against wood.

"Come along, Cassie," Eleanore addressed me. "Let us leave these gingerbread men to wait for the fox that is their lives."

Hayley cracked her knuckles and neck, and stood up. Eleanore balanced on her tippy-toes as the two rivalled off with their glares, their stares, their hypnotic eye-power or whatever struggle they were going for. It was like watching two spiders having sex.

"She doesn't want to be your friend," they declared in unison.

Eleanore took the words in and faced me. "What on Earth is this little cabaña on a swizzle stick blabbering about?"

I was stuck on the spot, panic ruining any chance of wooing smoothly. "I'm sorry, Eleanore. I mean, you're nice, but... I'm new and... I just want to... I think I want to hang out with these guys for a while. You know?"

It was as if a rock had fallen from a nearby cliff and landed on a see-saw and then flung a kid into a bike stack and the last bike to fall had landed on a dog's tail and the dog had been tied to a gazebo and as the dog ran off the gazebo's support was broken off and the gazebo had fallen down and revealed a man and woman having intimate relations inside. The Saviours of Tomorrow let their mouths hang open in utter disbelief.

"You... You want to spend time with... You want to spend time with these... these sad, pubescent, rebellious, wretched, cheerless homo-sapiens?" Eleanore laughed angrily, hands on hips. *"Why?"*

"Well, I don't like to shop —"

Friday moaned.

"Or gossip —"

Wednesday moaned even louder.

"Or prank call boys, for Pete's sake —"

Wednesday and Friday moaned together quite loudly, but Hayley cut in: "Oh, stop it! Go home and sit on your washing-machines."

"Can't we all be friends?" I reasoned.

Eleanore's gaze sent a sudden chill down my spine. She licked her lips and snorted menacingly. "I should have assumed when we first met. What with those *dreaded* clothes I caught you in. I tried to be a Cher and make you a Betty, but it seems like you are not the next in line to be a member of the Saviours of Tomorrow Club."

Hayley snorted back. "Rack off, Jurassic Parker."

"You, Cassie Gellar," Eleanore pointed a finger at me as she headed to leave. "You may be my next door neighbour, but that doesn't mean you're *rich*." She glared at me like a cat.

I thought this over for a minute. "Yes it does."

"Okay, maybe it does," Eleanore said, thinking quickly. "But it doesn't mean you're rich in the sense that *I* mean... yes... You may have a lot of money to your name, but you, *just you*, will never be worth *anything*. Because you are one of *them*. You are officially a loser, and you have just gained your first major problem in Horn-Horn." With a quick stride, she was out of sight, and her friends gave me one last look of horror before they ran to catch up with her.

Deeply in awe, I sat down next to Hayley. What happened? Was I hit by a plank of wood? Was I really lying on the ground, slipping into a coma, merely dreaming I was by Hayley's side?

"You have the worst luck," JT said to me as we walked towards B Block. "You only just started and you've already made enemies with the daughter of the Principal. You're totally screwed."

"Thanks for reminding me," I muttered.

"Good thing you don't have anything to do with the Loony Bin downtown, or else I'd think you were cursed," said Greg casually.

"Why would that be so bad?" I tried to sound nonchalant as I asked, but I was sweating. My mother would be starting part-time work there in a few weeks.

"Oh, it's nothing," Hayley brushed it off. "Mrs. Parker works there, that's all. I think she's the secretary or something. She can't type for peanuts, though. I remember she printed out the invitations for Eleanore's thirteenth birthday party a few years ago. I was invited back then, and she misspelled her own daughter's name. *Eleanore Crapchel Parker*, she wrote. What a doofus."

I grunted quietly. So my mother would be working with my enemy's mother. My life was gradually revealing itself to be a soap opera.

For the rest of the mid-morning, as we listened to Ms. Weiss talk about the planet Mars and her *fascinating* theories about its canyons once providing water for thirsty space-antelope, Eleanore and her friends gave me the cold shoulder. Hayley said not to worry about it, that it would soon go away and be replaced with nasty rumours and mean tricks. Which, apparently, was much better. Despite this, I was feeling much less unwanted than I had been before recess. I hoped, I prayed, I begged...

Somehow, I'd made friends.

7
SHACKLED

As the day went on, I was met with the typical strains of first-day-itis: Too many things for one brain to remember, slip-ups and what-not, the constant movement from classroom to classroom, and then... physical education. A shy, mopey woman with ridiculously large glasses introduced herself as our gym teacher. Her name was Ms. Berry. Dowdy, with a brown bob-cut, she was probably in her mid-forties and dressed in grey sweats. She had huge sagging lines on each side of her mouth that suggested years of misery. According to decent sources, she'd once married a man with the surname of Hamilton. They were since divorced but she had refused to take her maiden name back, convinced that the divorce was just a phase her husband was going through. Everyone called her Ms. Berry though, and most of the time she would let it pass. But then, on the very odd occasion, like a shooting star in the sky she would snap and go ballistic. That's what people were saying, anyway.

The gym class that day consisted of rope climbing, and for some reason I just couldn't climb that rope. I'd never been good at climbing them, but it was the fact that everybody else in the class could do it that got to me. I felt like an outcast again. At least this time I had some people to hang around with so that if any insults were thrown my way, they could easily be deflected by Hayley's sharp tongue.

"Just try it one more time and wrap your legs around the rope," Berry urged me.

I clutched at the rope and heaved in my efforts. Easier said than done for someone with bendable shins. Then, as if a miracle had befallen me, I began to climb. I looked down at my peers, most of whom weren't even watching, and grinned in triumph. *So this is how you do it,* I thought. Hayley reached and tapped me on the head in congratulations. I would have climbed up to the very top, but a loud plane flew overhead, shaking the entire gymnasium. I became startled, and jumped down. Heights weren't my friend anyway.

"What happened? You were going so well," said our teacher.

"It was that plane. I got scared. I'm sorry, Ms. Berry."

An immediate silence followed and the class turned to her.

She smiled and shrugged. "We'll work on it."

I was free.

• • •

When school finished that afternoon, I said goodbye to Hayley, JT and Greg, and went to find my sister. I found her in Z Block. She was at her new locker, retrieving her backpack which had been wedged inside. I stared at her locker in jealousy. My back was killing me. Unlike her, I hadn't been given a locker yet, so I'd been forced to cart my own backpack full of books around all day. I must have looked like the Hunchback of Notre Dame.

"How was your first day?" I asked. We headed out the back gate.

Annie ho-hummed for a minute. "The student average expectancy for my year is pretty... well, *average*... and my main teacher is bit of a worry. I think he eats salami for breakfast, and when he talks to you he leans in close. Grandma Helen always told me if someone is close enough to you that your tongue could touch them, you should stick out your tongue."

"Random... And the work load?"

"Quite satisfactory. Yours?"

"It's so easy, you could say it's *peasy*."

"Really?"

"No!" I held my hands up and scrunched my nose. "I *wish* it was just the work load I had to worry about. There's too much to remember, for one thing. Another thing, there's all these... what do you call them?... cliques? Too many of them. Then there are the teachers. A few of them have control issues. Some of them also have daughters who now hate me. And to add to the mental exhaustion of it all, there's also the physical education making me *literally* exhausted. We had gym right before lunch. *Gym.* On a day like this. Come lunchtime I could barely lift my sandwich to my mouth. And then a seagull swiped it."

"Made any friends?"

I nodded, distracted. We were heading across a busy street towards the steep hill that led to those strange, dark woods. I collected myself. "Yes. I mean, I sort of made friends with them yesterday, oh the day before actually, but... Well, it's a long story. On the plus side I don't have to worry about Eleanore any more."

"Oh good," said Annie, and she looked about. "Hey, where are we going?"

As someone who wasn't as familiar with the town landscape as I was, I took the knowledge smugly out of my back pocket and flaunted it in front of her. "Don't worry. It's a short-cut."

To anyone watching from a distance, it would have appeared at that moment as if we were being engulfed by a giant shadow monster. We crossed the barrier, the outskirts of the woods, and soon were so far in the thick of it that nothing but my phone's GPS could tell us which direction to head in. The notion of 'just going straight' wasn't lost on me, but according to Annie that was naïve and simplistic. Just like her face.

As we swept through large thickets and stunted bushes, I tilted my head to look up at the sky above, or whatever amount of sky the trees allowed into view. It was fascinating, like a moving painting. Far, far above I could see the top of the pine trees around me, and above that was the clear blue sky. Not a single cloud up there. I stopped to stare in awe, to take a mental picture. I probably would have stayed that way for longer, but a pine cone began falling from one of the highest branches and was hurtling towards me in what appeared to be slow-motion. I moved forward but bumped into Annie, who had turned to face me. She wheezed for a moment in shock and inhaled from her asthma pump. "We aren't lost, are we?"

"No," I jumped back on my phone and searched. "According to this we are... not that far from the other side of the woods. If we're going in the direction I think we're going."

"And if we're not, where will we end up?"

"The old abandoned train station."

The pine-cone crashed into the ground between us. Annie took an extra serving from her inhaler, and continued walking. I followed promptly, keeping a nervous eye on the map lit up on my screen.

Twenty minutes later and we were no further along. The map was lying to me, I knew it. I was all clammy and my clothes were sticking to me. My neck was sore from the sweat drenched into my collar, and my back was itchy. I really hated the heat. Coming across a fallen pine tree, I plopped my butt down and searched my bag for a drink. Drat. I'd guzzled my water down to the last few drops straight after gym class.

"Don't sit down," said Annie, her hair matted with sweat.

I batted her prying hands away. "No, I need a break. Just a short one. I'm seeing a huge blob, and it isn't Dad for once."

"Cassie, I've got a heavy bag on my back and my body's starting to chafe. If we're not home in twenty minutes, I'm stripping." She pulled me up, but her nudity was motive enough.

Ten minutes later, when our hike reached the next fallen tree, I finally remarked on something interesting: "Have you noticed there are a lot of trees down around here?"

Annie wiped her forehead dry and straightened her glasses. She didn't say anything, but the look on her face told me I was right to question it. I watched her disappear into the woods in front of me. I reached back to grab my bag off the ground. Then I saw something strange. Something blue on the bark of the fallen tree I'd been against. As I leaned closer, I noticed it was some sort of goo. Maybe blue moss? If there was such a thing. I touched it and it burned slightly. I hadn't felt anything like that before. Moss didn't burn.

Annie called out my name. I hopped up and ran after her. It took me a few moments to find her. She was standing on the edge of an enormous clearing, about the size of a football field. Why it was cleared of trees wasn't obvious to me until I joined her side. My jaw dropped. There were at least four dozen pine trees, all laid down perfectly on their sides in a circular pattern which filled up the entire clearing. It couldn't have been a freak of nature. The wind hadn't knocked them down like that. They were almost logs, stripped of their roots, and their branches whisked to bristles. It was like a crop circle.

I tugged at my sister's arm to leave.

"Let's stay," she whispered, and she moved forward to climb over the nearest tree. Once she had done so, she stood on the top and looked around. She covered her mouth and jumped in delight. "It's like a maze! It leads to the middle. This is amazing. It could be *aliens!* I need to take photos. Alright, I'm going to check what's in the centre of it." With that she jumped down to the other side, out of sight.

A sense of dread washed over me and I hesitantly edged to the tree my sister had climbed, touching it with sensitivity. I climbed quickly, and saw my sister's head disappear over the one in front. The logs were pretty hard to climb, too, but thankfully their patchy, thick bark was good for foot holds.

"Wait!" I grabbed onto the next fallen tree to chase after her.

Something mumbled to my right. I paused and looked around. Nothing was there, but I had definitely heard it. I struggled for a moment to listen, the wind in the standing trees and the birds near-by drowning out whatever subtle noise it'd been. I jumped on top of the tree in front of me and scoped the landscape. Annie was about five trees ahead of me, making her way furiously forward. In the middle of the circle, which was very far away, I spotted something white. I hadn't noticed it before from the ground, but now it was quite evident. Only the top of it was showing, as the pine tree near-est to it blocked the rest of it from view. I couldn't make out what it was, either. After a moment of squinting and deciphering, I jumped back in fright and fell to the ground.

It moved.

The same mumble arose. It was muffled. An animal, perhaps? Or a human. Maybe hurt. But now I knew where it was coming from. Right in front of me. It was coming from inside the fallen tree. I jogged to where the roots had once been. There was the tini-est gap between this one and the one lying down next to it, where the assaulted branches that once made up the pointy top lay butchered in death. I faced back to the tree I'd climbed, the tree I had heard the moan from. As suspected, where the roots had been was now a large gaping hole that led inside its perfectly hollowed centre. I stared into the darkness within, looking for any signs of life.

I heard the mumble again, clearer now, and it echoed. It sound-ed like a half-conscious puppy. The thought of a trapped dog braved my senses, and I turned on my phone's light, placed it in my mouth, and crawled in on my hands and knees.

It was damp. That was the first thing I noticed. Pointing the light on my phone ahead with my tongue, I could see tiny droplets of water dripping from above me. Or so I thought. As I got closer to a few of them, I noticed they were the same blue droplets I'd mistaken for moss. My heart was beating a mile a minute, but I couldn't stop moving. This was too curious. Besides, it would be a really exciting story to tell my new friends at school. How heroic I'd been, possibly saving a puppy from its wooden grave. I would name it Pretzels if it was a boy dog, or Luna if it was a girl dog. I could even bring Hayley, JT and Greg here after school and it could be a new place for us to hang out in. Then they couldn't ditch me when they realised how uncool I was.

"Hello?" I said gingerly. "Pretzels?"

The low mumble rose again. This time it was a voice. A human voice. I backed off. My heart was in my throat. I couldn't see anything ahead, as if the centre of the tree forbid the light. Slowly, very slowly, I crawled backwards. I needed to get out.

I was just starting to see light from outside when my hand came into contact with something sharp. I pointed my head down to see better. I'd whacked into what looked like an orange sculpture, made of clay. In the shape of a head, roughly twice the size of my own fist. It wasn't very well shaped, mind you. It was acutely dimensional. Hollow, as well. I could see the shadows dancing around the inside through the holes of its eyes, nose, mouth. It also had the remainders of some bolts attached to the sides of it, as if a pair of shackles had been ripped off long ago. I picked the head up in my free hand to take it away with me.

At that exact moment, the world lit up. The tree, I thought for a moment, had caught fire. I soon realised it must have been so bright outside that amazingly some of the light shone through the tree's wood, like when you shine a torch against your fingers. Within an instant I saw the boy not three feet in front of me. No older than seven, and fast asleep. With the light came a deafening trombone-like cry, a never-ending alarm. It soon morphed into the same roaring noise I'd heard in gym class. *A plane is crashing down on me*, I thought.

The boy woke up. He checked his surroundings, then saw me. Saw what I held in my hands. And, chased after me. I screamed and backed away as fast as I could. He had the other end of those shackles around his wrists. He was wearing blue pyjamas, too, and was barefoot. I backed right out of that tree trunk and ran away as fast as I could. Out in the fresh air, I was blinded by the light, and then before I knew it I was shrouded in darkness. I pressed against one of the trees and breathed heavily. The noise had stopped, and my eyesight slowly returned to normal. I could see again.

Within a second, the boy from inside the trunk had tackled me to the ground. I dropped my phone and spun around to find him on top of me, putting his hands over my mouth. He was unnaturally strong for someone his age. I tried to scream out, a cold chill running down my spine, and I punched at him with all my might. I clocked him in the temple with the clay head and he fell into a heap by my side. I scrambled to my feet and ran away, climbing over those pine trees, desperate to find a way out. I had to find my sister. I had to call the police. I checked my pockets for my phone, and realised with dismay that I had dropped it during the struggle. I slowed myself as I climbed another tree, and then stopped entirely. I looked back and bit my lip. My ears were still ringing and somehow their hindrance to hear the natural world made things worse.

I could see a shadow as I returned. I peeked around the corner near one of the stumps, and saw him, either muttering or sobbing quietly. Barefoot, red hair messy. Pointy ears. *Pointy ears.* Small. He was wiping himself down, talking to himself, and inspecting my phone in his tiny hands.

His head jerked sideways and he spotted me. I ducked out of view. *Pointy ears. A boy with pointy ears and shackles around his wrists.* I waited there, pressed against the tree and hiding from view, praying he wouldn't come after me. I leaned forward again to see if he'd disappeared. In fact, he was closer, and standing there waiting for me to rear my head. I couldn't move. I just stared at him. Not directly into his eyes, but at his dirt-covered face. I examined him. All three-and-a-half feet of him.

"Whoa."

"You have something that belongs to me, and I want it back," he said firmly.

I looked down at what I was carrying. The clay head. I noticed now in the daylight that it was made of orange clay, and had a lid on top that resembled some sort of a beret.

I eyed my phone in his hands. "Let's trade."

He threw it at me with little warning, and I dropped the clay head to catch it. He dove for his object and caught it in his tiny hands, crashing into my shins as he did. I wriggled and writhed in horror and jumped over him and ran away. I absentmindedly cried out for help, and dialled home.

Around the corner I bounded, and I barely punched in two numbers before I catapulted into the firm behind of a gigantic white moose. It was such a violent collision that I landed on my back. I looked up at it in horror. It turned to face me, its eyes glowing a violently rich, dark orange. It had giant stained fangs, and its mouth was open loosely. A deep, rolling rumble rose from its throat and into a fierce roar. Frozen, I felt something grab my hand. I was jerked to my feet as a stream of strange glowing orange energy shot out of the moose's eyes and burned thoroughly through where I had been lying. The ground erupted into the air and showered me with dirt and stones before I disappeared around the nearest corner.

I was too shocked to care that the boy held my hand, that the boy was saving my life, and he pushed me into the darkness of another hollow tree. There I collapsed in exhaustion and disbelief.

"Crawl!" he yelled.

I got on all fours and crawled into nothingness, into the unforgiving darkness as fast as I could. My hands scratched against too many objects to keep count, my head bumped into different things, but I couldn't see what they were. The further in we went, the darker it got. I couldn't even remember when we left the safety of the inside of the tree, or obviously trees, as we wound up on the other side of the clearing. I thought distantly in our rush how the trees placed like that were simply a mechanism for manoeuvring from one side of the clearing to the other, whilst staying protected inside.

In the daylight again, I left the boy's side and bolted for the woods, my mind set on escape. It wasn't until I found myself gallivanting over a muddy slope that I fell onto my hands and knees, rolled onto my back, and glided to an abrupt stop in the middle of an orange burr bush. Silence overwhelmed me, but it wasn't the after-effects of that deafening noise. My ears had popped somewhere along my travels. Now I lay there, staring up at the treetops. This silence was real; the birds and the breeze having ceased long ago. Time stood still, and I couldn't think. I couldn't move. The beautiful view of the trees above — this time, I couldn't take it in.

8

WHITE MOOSE

It felt like a dream, soft on the edges, complicated with heavy weeds and roots in the middle. Suffocating my senses and numbing me at the same time. Then with a rush I found my concentration to be very sharp, as if my ears had popped again. I knew where I was now, I knew what had happened. I was being dragged along by Annie, who was sweating and grunting under my weight. We weren't in the woods any more, we were on the steep ascent of that familiar dirt road lined with eucalyptus trees. She took a few breaths and stopped, but didn't let me go. She was muttering to herself things like: "I thought I'd gone blind…" and "… ears are still ringing…"

"I can walk," I told her.

My feet steadied on the ground and I leaned my right hand against her shoulder for a moment. She looked unharmed. I could tell the same didn't apply for me. I could feel the dirt on my skin, under my nails, while my hair was disheveled, and my top lip was pulsing with a fresh cut. Reality crept up on me like a ghoul in the night, and I shuddered.

"What *happened* to you?" she asked slowly. She flattened down my hair, then got a wet-one from her bag and started to clean my face.

I fiddled with my cut fingers. "Monster."

"Was it the moose? I saw it."

I nodded, though I wanted to say more. It wasn't just a moose.

I heard the familiar sound of a vehicle coming towards us. It was our black four wheeler, the one the car company had delivered the day before, and it skidded dramatically to a halt on the side of the road. Ashen faced, Mom jumped out and ran to me, and she cupped my head in her hands.

"Thank God you called," she said to Annie. Then she pointed to the car and ordered her to get in. My sister was quick to comply. "Honey, what happened?"

I suddenly felt very embarrassed. I shook my head and looked down, feeling tears drying on my filthy cheeks. Whatever truth I told her would not help the situation. I couldn't explain it, it wasn't real.

"It was a moose," my sister called. "A white one."

Mom stared carefully. "What? Out *there*? Did it attack you?"

"I don't remember…" I muttered.

With that, I started to cry. I nestled into her bosom.

Brendan was quiet in the car-ride home, for the first time in his short life. The only person to talk was Mom, who went on an angry rant about how the woods should be off limits. Since this town was still a stranger to me, I could only stare up at the clouds. I needed something familiar to look at, and the sky was the only thing.

———— · · · ————

The local doctor came to our house that night to check up on me. Once he was gone, I sat in bed and watched television. Or rather, I watched the television screen. The lights and sound washed over me. My favourite show was on, but I couldn't focus. All I could think about was what I remembered in the woods.

The next morning I woke up with the sun shining in through the window. I'd forgotten to close the blinds, having fallen asleep upright while attempting to read a magazine. I must have been asleep for a full twelve hours.

My neck was aching like a mother. I hopped out of bed and

went into the bathroom. It was the first time I'd looked at myself and I was a mess. My neck was bruised, and I had dozens of tiny little cuts and scratches on my face, my hands, my arms and legs... From what? The ground exploding. The rough interior of those trees as I scrambled through them to safety. I tried not to think about it, and showered.

It wasn't long after I hopped out that I noticed how silent the house was. I wrapped myself in a towel and snuck downstairs. The place was empty. There was more furniture though. Or maybe it had just been rearranged. It was starting to look more homely, and familiar.

The time was 9:50am, so I guess I'd slept longer than planned. It's not like I had anywhere to go. Mom was heading to the Mayor's office that afternoon to lodge a complaint about the 'white moose'. I could see the newspaper headlines already: '*White Moose Attacks White Goose While On The Loose*'.

What was I to do? Sit in bed and watch television, or stare at the wall and break off strands of hair while my mind wandered? For a while, I tried both. I went for a walk at midday. I took our dog Pigsworth with me, but he didn't really feel up to it and maybe he was sensing how unmotivated I was. He stopped halfway down the street and looked up at me with understanding eyes, so we went home.

By one in the afternoon I painfully wished I'd gotten up and gone to school. I would definitely be going tomorrow. I guess I was traumatised, maybe that was it. Maybe it hadn't hit me yet. It didn't matter. I could still function. I wanted to know what my new friends were up to. I wanted to be involved in everything.

The rest of the afternoon was filled with tiny little chores around the house, and time spent putting packed stuff out on display. We still had eighteen boxes to unpack, so I got a start on it while playing happy music. I'd found my old music dock in one of the boxes next to a wind-up mouse toy we'd gotten a while back for Tigger. I wound it up, called for him, and waited. Of course, hearing my voice, both my cat *and* dog came bounding into the foyer. I let the mouse go and it spun away, heading for the staircase. Tigger gave chase. Then Pigsworth did too. Soon enough the two of them were engrossed in a war of hissing and growling until Pigsworth bettered Tigger and my poor feline friend bounded upstairs in a snooty huff. Sighing, I fetched some cat food from the kitchen and went to find him.

My bedroom door was the only one open, so I knew he had to

be in there. Never mind the perfect memory of closing the door an hour earlier. I tip-toed inside, searched the corners for him, checked under my bed, and then banged the tin can with a fork. "Tigger," I said slowly and playfully. I heard his meow come from the wardrobe, which as I got closer realised was shut. Yanking the doors open, Tigger shot past and out of the room as fast as lightning. My heartbeat slowed, but I grew uneasy and checked inside the wardrobe. How had he managed to lock himself in there?

It was all in my head, I assured myself, but that curiosity expanded as I spotted what was in the darkness in front of me. The clay head, which I'd forgotten about. Mom had brought it in here last night and asked me if I'd made it in art class. All I could do to make any sense out of it, for her, was to say yes. So she'd put it there and left the door open a crack. Now it sat between my sneakers and flip-flops, gaping at me like a jack-o-lantern.

Waiting for me to unravel its mysteries.

9
CHILD OF CRUX

It was a great relief when my family came home. First it was Brendan and Mom, who weren't in their usual festive moods. I think it was because of me. They trundled in with sour faces, and barely said hello to me when they spotted me on the sofa in the kitchroom. I was watching the news, having given up on the chores after dealing with my wardrobe. Mom made us afternoon tea, something we'd not been treated to in years. Crackers with cheese, dried apricots (which apparently matched my brother's fat ears), and apple slices.

Brendan had his indecisive hands on the remote control. *"Which-one-of-these-shows-will-I-tune-in-to?"* he said with each channel change. "Ooh, Casey Degan!"

I snatched the remote off him and flicked back to the news network. I soon noticed he was staring at me and not the TV. I could see him out of the corner of my eye. Without moving I said: "What?" and he looked away.

"Are you normal again?"

"Uh… yes.."

"Good, because I have a favour to ask you," he said. "Will you take me into the woods one day to find that blue stuff that made you hallucinate?"

I must've mentioned the blue moss the night before, delirious.

"No!" I whined.

"I just want to trip, woman. I'm not asking for your ovaries," he snapped back, and he turned away with crossed arms.

Finding myself now aggravated by their presence, I stormed upstairs to be on my own. Still, as I busied myself around my room, I felt antsy and restless. I wanted the next day to arrive as quickly as possible. Not for the chore of school, but for the pleasure of company. I deconstructed one of Brendan's many fortune-tellers I'd found in the lounge, and then tried my hand at the Rubik's cube my Aunt Rachael had gifted me for my sixteenth birthday. Eventually I gave up, as I always did. I collapsed back on my bed and allowed the silence to wash over me. I needed a break from everything. Mental exhaustion was prevalent.

As I turned my head to land on my second pillow, I reeled as the tip of my nose brushed against the clay head. Jumping up in shock, I stared at it and tried to figure out how it had moved from my wardrobe to my pillow. I rubbed my eyes for a moment, and then massaged my temples. I checked the closed door, and then picked it up. Huffing in admiration, turning it around, examining its dimensions. It sure was basic. Vibrantly orange, it wasn't even well done. The features were too sharp. I grabbed a marker from my bedside table, drawing a curly moustache on it underneath the nose area. For a while I stared at it in boredom, thinking nothing of it, and eventually I laughed at myself. Then, of its own accord, the terracotta lid leapt into the air and landed by my side.

I jumped in fright and slunk to the end of the bed, curling into a ball on the floor. I could hear monstrous cries of despair from very far away, like trapped ghouls in hell. A boy's voice rose clear as day, panting and gasping for air. He was on my bed.

I took a chance and peeked over the top to see him outstretched on my duvet like a starfish, staring up at the ceiling and catching his breath. It was him. The boy from the woods with the pinched ears, in the very same blue pyjamas. All the memories of that afternoon came flooding back stronger than ever, but I found myself more curious than disturbed. I was calm. Shock had faded quickly.

I stood up to get a better look. "You're *real*."

He had flat features. An upturned nose, freckled, baby buck teeth and bright, light blue eyes. His short red hair, almost orange, stuck out of his blue night cap, and upon looking at me, he blushed.

"*You're* real," he retaliated, staring down bashfully. He placed the lid back on top of the clay head. When at last he saw the moustache I'd drawn, he allowed his gaze to meet mine. "Did you do this?" he asked.

I nodded, not sure what to say.

"Don't do *that*," he licked his right thumb and worked at cleaning it off. "I've seen this thing through hundreds of accidents. Smashed to pieces, spaghettified, turned inside out, shot at... But *you!*" He pointed at the poorly marker-induced moustache that was very steadily fading. "You're the first person to ever graffiti it. That was really *rude!*"

"Who are you?" I asked.

"I'm Zag. Who're you?"

"Cassie," I said.

My eyes lifted to his pinched ears.

"*What* are you?"

"I'm a Crux."

"A what?"

He'd finished cleaning the clay head. He turned to look at me, paused in thought for a moment, and then shuffled his butt across the bedspread to get closer to me. "I'm a Child of Crux. What are you?"

"I'm a human," I told him, assuming it was the most obvious thing in the world.

"Oh. You must be a local." He didn't sound overly impressed.

I scrunched up my nose. "Where are you from, *Alaska?*"

"Well, I can't say."

I shook my head in confusion. "And where are your parents?"

"*Parents?*" he said. It was as if I'd asked an eighty-year-old the same question. He smirked and bit his finger gently. "I don't know. Dead, I suppose. I'm an orphan."

"Oh. I'm sorry."

"Are you one, too?"

"No, my parents are downstairs."

"Do they look like you?"

"Yeah, sort of."

I stared down at the clay head, noticing it had the base of the same shackles that were around the boy's wrists. He'd been attached to it like a prisoner at some point. I looked up at him, down at the shackles, twice, hoping he'd divulge, but he didn't. Instead, he jumped off the bed and walked over to my window and looked out at the clear blue sky. "There's still no snow! We have lots of it where I come from." He came back to me, holding a Rubik's cube he'd found on my computer desk. He fiddled with it nonchalantly. "Y'see, it's always snowing where I come from. It's never light either, because the planet spins strangely. Not like here. You have a wobbly rotation, so you get night and day. I know," he said, sounding impressed with himself. "I've been here for about a week now. We've got a few hours left till night time. Then it's seven hours until daylight again. I've worked it out."

His fingers went here and there — blue square, white square, green square, while I watched him steadily, taking in what he'd said... All of a sudden, it was done. He'd completed the Rubik's cube. I took it off him to see if he'd cheated.

"Are you going to take care of me now?" he asked.

"*What?*" I cried in disbelief. "No! I'm sixteen."

"*Sixteen?*" he said with a laugh, and he wiped his left eye the way children do. He seemed to believe I was older.

"I'm sorry. I can't look after you... Zag. You're just a child, you need to be in a..." I thought about what I was saying. Foster home? For a kid who *obviously* wasn't a regular kid? I'd seen way too many shows about aliens to be stupid enough to take him to the police station. "Zag, the thing is..." I started slowly, and I handed the Rubik's cube back to him, "I don't think I can look after you, because I'm a kid myself. It's not normal here to look after a kid who isn't your own. You need to register them, like with animals. Somebody needs to know you're here, so you can be looked after properly."

Zag's face dropped, and he put the cube down so he could clutch at his clay head. "No, you can't tell anyone I'm here. I shouldn't even be out of the wooden wardrobe. They're probably already coming for me."

My stomach tensed.

"They can't track me when I'm hiding in something wooden. It's just a thing. That's why I was hiding in that tree. I don't know how *you* found me."

"I wasn't looking for you," I said, raising my eyebrows. I shot a paranoid look out the window as a bird flew past. "Who's after you?"

"I'm a Child of Crux," he said to me slowly, angrily.

"I don't know what that means."

"Orphans who can grant wishes. I'm one of them. We're wanted. I have a spell put on me that forbids me from granting any wishes until somebody agrees to take care of me."

"Like a foster parent?" I said.

"Yes, probably. My last owner got rid of me, and the chains that kept me attached to the clay head broke apart. As soon as I get another owner, they'll join back together. Will you be my owner?"

"Your *owner?*" I said in disbelief. "No, I can't be your owner!"

"You don't have to do anything, you just have to agree and let me live in your wardrobe."

I peered behind me at the closed door. If anybody was overhearing this conversation... I wouldn't know how to explain it. Maybe I was hallucinating again, so they would only hear me talking to myself.

"Okay, I need you to back up a bit. And take it slow. I need to..." I felt myself beginning to panic, so I forced myself to breath deeply. "First of all, explain who you are."

Zag hopped off the bed and stood tall, putting his right hand to his heart. "My full name is Zagreus Wendig the Three-Hundredth. But I usually go by Zag. My greatest-father would be spinning in his faucet if he knew what had become of his name. I was born in Summers City on the planet Danube."

I stopped. My eyes bulged at the news. I *knew* it. I'd suspected, but to hear it, to verify it. He was an *alien*. He stared at me, concerned at my loose jaw.

"Summers City is at the bottom of Danube, and it's always daytime there. Danube is on the top of Danube and is always nighttime and very cold."

"Danube is... on the top of... Danube?"

"Danube City. The planet is called Danube... The city was named after the planet."

"Right. Sorry, go on."

"I was auctioned off at a market when I was a baby, and the King of Danube City became my owner and looked after me until... well, until he died a week ago." He gazed down in melancholy. "So when I was let go by his daughter, I made it to this place and hid in the woods until you found me. I don't have any living relatives left.

Which is why I have to go from owner to owner until either one settles or I become legally able to take care of myself. As soon as I hit puberty, these chains will disappear and I'll be able to grant myself wishes, and nobody else."

"What's with the clay head?" I asked.

"It's the only thing left that belonged to my parents. I'm only allowed to keep it if I do everything my owner tells me. If I don't, it'll disappear."

"So it's a bargaining tool."

He shrugged. He didn't seem bothered. "I guess. That's what I was told. I don't know if it's true or not, but I don't want to risk it."

Then came more silence. I thought about what he'd told me, letting it sink in. He soon stretched his arms back, and something cracked. He grunted, and looked around.

"Have you got any food? I haven't eaten in a few days."

"A few *days*?"

"I usually keep a few bits and pieces in the head but I've run out." He took the beret off the clay head to show me. To my surprise, a fierce green and yellow light shone from within. A whole other world sat inside: stars and galaxies, tables and chairs, flower patches and explosions — they all floated around in what looked like the purple vacuum of space. However, what caught my attention the most was what sat close to the surface. It was a machine made of giant silver gears that moved and churned at great speeds.

I leaned closer to the brim to get a better look.

"Wow," I said, and I closed my jaw just as a bit of drool left my lips. I slurped it up and giggled. I giggled again, and tried to stop myself, but found I couldn't.

Zag closed the lid quickly and waved his hands around in the air. "That world's teeming with nitrous oxide. On the plus side, it'll help your nerves."

I stared at him calmly. He was right. I felt much better.

"Are you impressed?" he asked.

I nodded giddily.

"So you'll be my owner?"

I shrugged, blinked a few more times, and couldn't help myself from laughing. "Whatever," I chuckled.

Instantly, a fierce crack sounded from above me. I jolted in fright, and it snapped me out of my silly state. I watched in disbelief as a thousand tiny pieces of glowing strings appeared out of the air, weaving themselves around each other until they made a gigantic long line that stretched from the base of the clay head, right up to Zag's hands. His wrists were violently bolted together, and he let out a gasp of pain. Scolding hot chains had formed from the clay head to the shackles around his wrists, and for a moment they glowed red, burning him until they cooled into cold, grey metal. They, along with the shackles, promptly vanished from sight.

"Ouch. Are you OK?"

Zag nodded, although his face said otherwise. A moment later he fished a parchment out of thin air and handed it to me.

"Welcome note," he managed, before devoting his full attention to the fresh welts on his wrists.

Hesitantly, I read the parchment aloud:

"*Congratulations, Cassandra Lillian Gellar the First on your recent purchase of Zagreus Wendig the Three-Hundredth, commonly referred to as a Child of Crux, but hereby known as the Crux of Horn-Horn. As with all of these 'Crux' children, they are chained by the universal order to an object of theirs that is important to them to dissuade such subordinates from disobedience. Also put in place by the universal order, such a child is only considered a 'Crux' if they are without parent, namely an orphan. They are often considered cursed, as most who take them under their wing meet an unfortunate end...*"

I put the parchment down in horror.

"Unfortunate end? They *die?*"

"Sometimes," said Zag, and a pot labelled 'aloe-vera' appeared next to him. He dipped his fingers in and began nursing his wounds.

"You could have told me that earlier."

"It's not something I tend to remember."

I sat perfectly still as I pondered over the parchment's details.

"Relax," Zag chirped up, and I noticed his wounds were healed. "I have a good feeling about you. My bad-luck elbow isn't popping. Why don't you make your first wish? It'll show you what it's all about. No trickery, I swear."

Hesitating for the briefest of moments, I thought one up and said quietly: "I wish for a sherbet ice-cream."

Zag clapped his hands in delight and he watched my mouth in anticipation. I felt something rise in my throat, and before I knew it I'd choked up a big wad of something slimy and prickly. I coughed it onto my bed-spread and, gasping, could only make it out as a wad of golden, wet glitter. Before I knew it, I was holding a sherbet ice-cream cone in my left hand. I began eating it, hoping to get rid of the strange, metallic taste left in my mouth.

"That happens every time you make a wish," said Zag. "The phlegm, that is. There's a few other things you need to know, too. Don't rub the clay head. It's not a genie's lamp. You're just turning it on. If you want a wish from now on, all you have to do is wish for it. No matter where you are. You don't need the clay head with you, just as long as it's in your care, in your house, in your bag, whatever."

I nodded.

"And what are the catches? There's got to be a few of them."

"There are none."

I wished to know what ramifications there were. A spiral of golden glitter shot out of my mouth as I finished the sentence, and it disappeared as unexpectedly as it had come. This would take some getting used to.

Zag breathed in deeply, thinking about what he should say next. He chewed on his left thumb.

"Let's go for a walk," he suggested finally.

"Alright. Where?"

The room around me peeled away like a newspaper caught on fire, and a cold wind hit me. We had somehow ended up on the top of a hill, on a dirt track, amidst a wide open field. Stunned, I gasped in as much air as I could, and grabbed onto Zag's hand beside me. The sky was a dark hum of busy cloud-work, white, green and grey, zooming by at great speeds.

"Where are we?"

"It doesn't matter," said Zag, and we began to walk.

The wind, though cold, was refreshing after the heat of the day. My shoes became muddy, and the heads of daffodils jutting out from the borders of the path were wet against my bare legs.

"What were we talking about?" said Zag quietly. The clay head was under his free arm.

"The catches."

"Oh, right," he said sheepishly. He must have been hoping I'd forget. "Well… There is the *slight* chance that a past owner of mine will come looking for me. The odds of that happening are astronom-ical, though. First off you would need someone who actually regret-ted leaving me or selling me, and if my memory serves, I don't think that's happened yet. Everybody tends to hate me by the end. Or dies. My last owner was a Viking Princess and she never wants to see me again. Usually in the brief periods between ownerships, hundreds of sadistic vagabonds scour the universe like madmen trying to claim Crux children. But as soon as one is officially owned by someone, it's over. One fact you might find comforting: You can't claim a Child of Crux if you kill its last owner."

That's comforting, I thought. Still, there was a far-off nagging voice in my head telling me I'd made a deal with the devil. Wishing was overrated. It couldn't possibly be that great to have anything you ever wanted. What were the dangers if you wished to know your future, or other more macabre notions? If you were vague about wishing to live forever, for example, you could be turned into a vampire. The possibilities were endless. My throat tensed up, in part due to the glittery congestion, and I gulped in frustration.

"Um… I don't think I'll make any more wishes today."

I could tell by the look on his face that Zag found this absurd. Maybe all of his previous owners had been self-centred freaks who'd used his powers to rule the world. Why would I want to *rule* the world when I spent most of my time *avoiding* it?

"You're worried. I can tell by your sweaty armpits."

"I'm sorry this isn't going as you'd hoped," I said, trying to finish what I had to say before running out of breath. The wind got stronger and I raised my voice. "I'm not used to a *child* coming up to me in the woods and telling me he can grant wishes. Last week, I was sitting in my old house watching Sailor Moon repeats. I'm scared, and this isn't TV, this is real life. Nothing up to this point has ever included *magic* being apart of everyday living." I was breathing heavily, wondering where the nearest paper bag was. Zag opened the clay head again and wafted some of the air towards me, and I calmed down a little bit.

"I think I understand. We've both been sheltered. And I keep having to remind myself that you're just a human. But I know," Zag said, and he pulled my arm to lead me further down the slope. "Let's distract from the fact. Now it's your turn to tell me something. I'm entering new territory as well, you know. Is there anything I should be made aware of? What's the deetz on your crib? What town is it in? Are there any ghosts? Curses? Bad history? Monsters under the bed?"

The wind was definitely getting stronger. It knocked us back momentarily. "We just moved in, so I don't know," I said. "The town is named Horn-Horn."

"Horn-Horn?" said Zag, stupefied.

"Yeah. And I live with my parents Ichabod & Lesley, my younger brother Brendan and older sister Annie, and we have a dog called Pigsworth and a cat called Tigger. I just started a new school and I'm trying to fit in." The other reality, which I'd go back to as soon as I made sure I wasn't losing my mind.

Zag pointed ahead. "Look at that," he said, over the wind.

To my astonishment, the clouds seemed to almost melt down to the horizon, and a dark moving funnel disrupted the ground. A tornado. As soon as I spotted it, the wind intensified frighteningly.

"We should go!" I turned to him in panic.

"Why? It can't hurt us." He let go of my hand and grabbed a loose clump of dirt from the ground. He threw it as hard as he could, but it only went about three feet before it seemed to explode against something invisible. He turned to see my expression, and grinned, revealing his buck teeth. "Protective bubble. Have you never seen a tornado?"

I shook my head. "Only on TV."

"Come on, we'll keep walking and I'll show you. It's *terrifying!*"

We trundled past a battered lot of woods to our right, and forced our way closer to the confronting storm. The wind was fierce, but had stopped intensifying, I'm guessing, through Zag's magic. The landscape was changing dramatically. Unkempt grass battered, flattened as the tornado approached. The sky above seemed to almost be clearing, making way for it. And then, before I could prepare myself any further, the storm threw itself upon us as if pouncing unexpectedly on its prey. The brown dust surrounded us, and I could finally see the bubble Zag had mentioned, all around us, saving us from destruction. The winds still hit us, the sound still raged, but it was bearable. I still grabbed onto Zag's free hand with both of mine, and we stood still where we were on the path. Suddenly, we were thrown into darkness. I squinted at Zag's silhouette, and followed his line of sight just in time to see the clouds disappear. A clear blue sky emerged. The sound of the winds ceased a few moments later, and everything went still. Above us, I could see what looked like a few trees and a metal roof gently floating by as if stuck in outerspace. There was no sound at all, except for the gentleness of large stalks floating to the battered ground nearby.

"The eye," said Zag.

I jumped in fright as it ended and a smack of warm wind washed through our bubble. Disturbed and scared, I said firmly: "I wish we were back in my bedroom."

Sure enough, just as we'd arrived, we returned to my room. The silence was almost deafening, and the warm summer air of upstairs pinched at every pore in my body. We were sitting on the floor by the wardrobe. As I hopped up I noticed in my vanity mirror that my hair was evidently windswept. It had created a perfectly cool fringe, which I ran my hands through. I smiled, and looked back. "I'd love to do that again some time," I told him.

"You can do that whenever you like. There's always a storm somewhere. Next we should try a *tsunami*."

I frowned at the thought. No thanks.

Our ears popped on their own with time, and my hair fell flat, but we sat together discussing matters further. He had this indelible charm about him, a youthful innocence that made no sense given the nature of his ways. Still, he was well-spoken and deeply intelligent, more so than I. It was one suggestion, however jokingly made, of coming with me to school one day that made me put my foot down.

"If I'm your owner, that means I can tell you what to do. I don't want you leaving this house. You have to lay low."

"Oh, bother. There go my Mardi Gras plans."

"You told me that as long as you're protected by wood, nobody can find you, right? So you shouldn't leave the house." I stopped, thinking. "Do any other *humans* know you exist?"

"Nobody knows."

"At all? On Earth?"

"Not that *I've* been told."

"Alright…" I gazed down.

Spotting a daffodil that must have been pulled away from the tornado, I bent over to pick it up. It had been ripped directly from its roots. "What am I supposed to do with you? I can't just let you roam around the house. And you can't stay outside, like… in the dog kennel… Can you?" It was made of wood, after all.

"I am a *child*," he reminded me.

"Yeah, but can't you turn into things, like animals and all that? You're magic."

Zag's face bristled, and a moment later his dog fur disappeared quicker than it came. "That is beside the point. I don't want to live outside. Owner or not, I'm still wanted."

"I thought you said they couldn't kill me to get to you?"

"Directly they can't, sure," he rubbed his hands, and a vase with water in it appeared on my bedside table. "But inadvertently is another accident… I mean, story." He took the daffodil away from me and placed it in the vase.

"*Accidentally* kill me? So if somebody slips my bus driver a sleeping pill, and we crash, that's *accidental?*"

"Yeah."

"You think this will be a problem?"

"Definitely. It always is. My past owner had this creepy man who was always trying to do her in… Although she could never prove it. Nobody else believed her, but *I* always thought it was obvious, watching from the mantle. It just goes to show what you miss when you're not looking."

I suddenly imagined Eleanore Parker accidentally killing me at school by throwing a ball in the air and having it strike me in the temple, and then claiming Zag and taking over the world, and wearing jackets made of my friends.

"This wardrobe is made of wood, yes?" he asked, and he knocked on its side gently. "As long as I stay in there, I'll be alright. That's why I was sheltering in the woods to begin with. Those strange fallen trees were the perfect hiding place for me."

"You didn't knock them over?"

"No, and I don't know who did. But I would leave them at night to get water and food, so I was only free of their protection for ten minutes at a time. Ever since you brought me home and hid me in that wardrobe, I've been safe again."

People were looking for him in the woods, I realised. Aghast, I remembered the uncertain feeling I'd gotten during my day out on Sunday with the Saviours. Trampling all over those woods, innocently dodging dangerous villains without realising.

"I think I heard a few of them," said Zag. "But, you know, I went from tree to tree whenever one came nearby. And then that *moose* found me."

"That was one of them?" I said. *Of course it was*, I realised.

"I thought you were one, too. But then it tried to kill you."

I preferred not to dwell on the what-ifs of a near death experience. Eventually, noticing the soft amber glow of sunset hitting the wardrobe, he told me how late it was for him. We said our goodnights, and I struggled off my knees to get up. Zag opened the wardrobe doors and disappeared behind them. For a moment I stood in the middle of my room, staring at my bare feet, feeling dazed, charmed, wonderful…

Some time later, when darkness had enveloped the entire town, I ventured downstairs. I needed to slip gently back into the depths of regular, calm reality for a while. Mom, Dad, Annie and Brendan were on the couches in the lounge-room watching a repeat of the previous night's season opener of my favourite show: *'The Prefect Family'*. I slipped into the kitchen, hoping to find bits and pieces of food for our upstairs guest without anybody noticing. I searched the cupboards for food, and utensils. Their placements were still foreign to me. Finally, I gave up and called out my mother's name and asked: "Have we got any healthy food? Like bananas, or apples, or oranges or prunes and cheese with crackers?"

Mom turned to face me, seeming distracted. "Yes, all of those are scattered around somewhere. I would be more motherly and get them for you, but I'm quite comfortable, sweetie."

I humphed. "I thought having a daughter involved in an accident would trump comfort."

"And I thought you weren't going to milk that."

"I'm not," I said sternly, and I found the food myself and put everything on a plate. It was not one of my better ideas, as a plate literally teetering to the edges with food looked eerily suspicious.

"What, are you hiding a stray in your wardrobe?" asked Dad.

"Yeah, his name's Zag."

"You're going to spoil your appetite. Dinner won't be long."

I glanced at the noodles on the stove. "I'll manage both."

"Honey," he said with a sigh.

"Oh, let her eat what she wants," muttered Mom.

"She'll hardly touch her dinner, trust me."

"I think this week we should let her do what she wants…"

"You can't use that excuse!"

I ran upstairs. My parents were always going off on crazy argumentative tangents of late. I hated it. It was like they sucked the soul from the house. The atmosphere became dank, restless and exhausting, and it made me clammy from anxiety. In my room, I opened the wardrobe door and pushed the plate of food into the darkness for Zag. Gently, I closed the door again, and looked around my bedroom. Everything was exactly how I'd left it. But now there was something else to it.

A secret.

10

THE HOUSE-GUEST

A storm blew through Horn-Horn that night, taking with it the last remains of the dilapidated billboards district. A fair distance across town, where the brunt of the storm was taking place, Beverly Berry (once Hamilton) sat cosily with her grey cat on her lap in her sitting room reading a very old book she had found in the basement that night. The discovery of said book was quite unexpected, and she felt compelled to read it, for the main character's name was Hamilton. Seventy pages in she stopped for a minute as her cat, who looked like Hitler, dug its claws into her thighs to get comfy. She took a sip of her elderflower tea on the table beside her. Soon she would head off to bed, since she would have to rise at six-thirty to let in the cleaners. For you see, she did not live in a house. 727 Lovely Lane was her residence. Her mail was sent here, her daily newspaper arrived every dawn without fail, but it was not a *house* that sat on her property. It was a mansion. A very, very large mansion. Four storeys tall, constructed in 1910, painted grey in the sixties, and of Edwardian design. It had been a mental institution once upon a time, before the new one on the edge of town had opened up. It then became a hotel and remained as one until 1990 when newlyweds Mr. & Mrs. Rosemont Hamilton purchased the property and had been blind to the immense duties required to uphold. Soon it was deemed an unfit place of business, and rather than sell and move on, the rich couple decided they would simply keep it as a place to live. By 1995 however, after many deals were tempted in front of them, Rosemont Hamilton decided to offer the use of the mansion as headquarters for the town's immense golf course that rested on the adjacent property (and went all the way to the cliffs of the Horn-Horn eastern border). Horn-Horn was a town known for its wealthy inhabitants, and kind and overly-generous ones at that, most of whom were on the board put in place by locals for the town's welfare. The deal was made with the golf club owners, the Sheppards, and so it was that the Hamiltons would receive rent for the use of their mansion. Now, after the divorce of Rosemont and Bev, and with Rosemont long gone, Bev had resumed small duties since she remained: Letting gardeners in, and other staff, the long-distance travellers, the chefs, while at the same time taking care of little things herself such as maintaining the garden beds, cleaning windows, vacuuming and general cleaning. In turn, she had eighty percent of the mansion to herself, something she didn't particularly care for. But she was trapped in the comfort of ritual. She was a very lonely woman who had never come to terms with, nor accepted her husband's dishonesty. The arrival of the cleaners so early in the morning brightened her spirits enough to get her out of bed each day.

So it came as a surprise when she tackled the last chapter for the night, and somebody rang the front doorbell. The cat disappeared as quick as a flash, and Ms. Bev Berry's defunct instincts to never trust a stranger in the night were vastly AWOL. She rushed through the elegant rooms, into the giant foyer, and in the darkness saw a very tall shadow through the front windows outside. Her ears hadn't deceived her, and it wasn't another ghost pranking her. Somebody was physically there, waiting for her to answer.

"Hello?" she said shyly, although she was terribly excited.

"I'm inquiring about a place to stay," said the person, and it was most definitely a woman. "You are Ms. *Berry*, aren't you?"

The cat, who was hiding under a table nearby, paused and looked at its owner. Ms. Berry smiled and opened the door swiftly.

She was met with the tallest woman she had ever seen, dressed in a giant black cloak and hat with an extremely wide brim. Her wavy, long blonde hair was soaking wet, although Bev failed to notice at the time that her clothes were completely dry.

"I am. Please, come in!"

As soon as the orphan entered the foyer, Berry rushed to the nearest wall and turned on the light. Awash, she could see now that the woman in front of her was a middle-aged one with long blonde hair, crow's feet and thinning lips.

"I saw the sign outside and thought to inquire. I'm awfully sorry it's so late."

Berry was beaming. "Not at all, it's a pleasure! Although… this place hasn't been a hotel for quite a few years." She pushed her thick glasses to the top of her nose and laughed.

"Oh. I didn't realise… The sign outside indicates…"

"Don't worry about it. I've been meaning to get rid of that for ages. Serves me right for being so lazy! You can stay here the night."

"As long as it won't be any trouble."

"No, of course not. I *insist*." She held out her hand. "Beverly Hamilton. But you can call me Bev."

"Bev," the orphan repeated the name to remember it, and she shook her hand. "My name is Hermione Purplewink. *Dame* Hermione Purplewink, actually." She gave a short laugh, hoping she sounded as formal as the Dames around here usually did. Of course, this wasn't her real name. And she was not a Dame.

Bev reached for her shoulder and guided her up the nearest staircase to the second floor. "I'm guessing you're pretty tired so I won't keep you up talking. Follow me — I always keep a room prepared in case of visitors. Oh, it's just wonderful to have you here, Hermione. We don't get many people around this area of town. Not after the cyclone, you know. No, things have been quiet here. Unless you enjoy golf. Have you ever tried your hand at golf?"

"When I'm angry."

She kept grinning. "You're not from around here, are you?"

Upon reaching the second landing, Ms. Berry showed her to one of the biggest, most luxurious rooms on offer. Hermione, as she called herself, was immediately treated to a brief tour which didn't require any leg movement, for all they did was turn this way and that as Bev displayed with a point of a finger: the bathroom, the bed, the television, the window, and the mini-fridge and kettle underneath the air-con. Then she showed the diagram of the emergency exits on the back of the door. Hermione plopped herself down on the King-sized bed. She stroked the covers, becoming lost in her thoughts of home and the similar mattress upon which her father had met his maker…

"Is there anything you need?" asked Bev coyly.

The bed groaned under Hermione's abnormal weight. "No. You've done enough already."

Bev leaned her elbow against the door. She cupped the back of her head with the rested hand. "Cup of tea?"

Hermione kept her smile, but was growing agitated. "I'm just very tired and have a big day ahead of me."

"Oh, wonderful! Business or pleasure?"

"Business, I'm afraid."

"Are you in town long?"

"No, just a couple of days, with a little bit of luck," she pulled a few bed-time items from her black bag. "I've come to collect something that was taken from me."

Bev nodded in understanding. A normal woman would be deeply intrigued and suspicious of this stranger's arrival and vague answers. Desperation, though, has a funny way of veiling the truth. "Trust funds?" she guessed stupidly.

There was a silence between them, and Hermione desperately raised her eyebrows, to no avail.

"I work at the local high school," Bev continued. "The number's in the book if you need me. I'm a gym teacher. I've been there for nine years now. Next year I get long service leave, but I'm working on delaying it. When you wake up in the morning, I'll be gone. School starts at nine. Unless you're up that early."

"I will be, but if I miss you, how and when will I pay you? I may not stay another night."

"First night's on the house."

"You're too kind. Well… I think I'll hit the hay."

Bev was disappointed that the chatter hadn't lasted into the wee hours of the morning, but she knew when to quit and she left with little fuss. Once she was gone, Hermione spread herself across the bed and kicked off her tightly bound shoes. Her feet were throbbing. She had travelled all the way to this ridiculous place after pinpointing *him* to this district, and now he had disappeared. All because somebody else had gotten to him first. She knew perfectly well she was too late, but she couldn't just let it go without a fight.

There was a quick knock at the door.

Hermione barked: "WHAT?" before correcting her speech into a sugary sweet tea-cup sized call. *"Yes?"*

Bev's head was the only thing to show through the door. Her voice was lisped from her night-time retainer. "I just realised. Your car?... And your... Where's your luggage?"

Hermione sat straight up. She'd nearly forgotten. "Oh. It's outside, in my carriage. Yes, I'm a Dame and I came in a carriage. It's all inside that. Shouldn't take you long to bring it all up."

"You came in a carriage? A *horse* and carriage? You have a horse waiting out in the rain?"

Thunder shook the house.

"He'll be fine!" insisted Ursula, not giving Timothy a second thought as he shivered throughout the storm. She headed for the bathroom to cut the conversation short: "Oh, and he's not a horse. He's a moose."

PART
TWO

CAT
AND
MOOSE

11
STALLED

Ursula woke up late, or so it seemed. Her confusion began when she arose from her slumbers to find that it was sunny outside. She'd set her body clock to rise at five, so she could have a bit of time searching in the comfort of darkness. Unfortunately, it wasn't meant to be. She'd gotten up, had a shower as best she could in the tiny hold of the bathroom, dressed in her most expensive white daywear, and ventured downstairs to the kitchen for breakfast. To her astonishment, the microwave clock read as quarter to seven.

Ursula found a note on the fridge from Bev Berry, addressed to somebody called Dame Hermione Purplewink — a name which was foreign to her in her early-morning daze, but she soon remembered. Bev had scribbled down information about the town, along with phone numbers, and where she was. In case she'd forgotten. Ursula scrunched up the note and made herself eat and drink something. She was on her way out the door when she spotted a cat running down the stairs. It stopped in the foyer and looked at her.

"I suppose you didn't stay out there for too long?" she said.

It didn't respond.

"Well? Nobody's around. You can talk."

"Actually, I'm over here."

Ursula turned in the direction of the voice, and saw Timothy in the next room. He was in his human form, that of a black-haired boy, wearing brown pyjamas borrowed from the nearest linen closet. He was sitting in a mahogany chair, his skin half-covered in dried mud.

Ursula shut the front door and walked back in, dropping her handbag angrily. "When I agreed to take you with me on this trip, I assumed you understood we had to fly under the radar. Stop looking like a boy. If someone sees another human with me, questions will be asked. Now for goodness sake, go upstairs and have a shower. You're disgusting. Where have you *been?*"

"I stood out in the rain for an hour last night, in the form of a moose. That woman who lives here stood at her bedroom window watching me for an *age*. I know why, too. She was wondering what sort of a person has a moose and cart."

"Hmmm... I suppose people aren't used to moose around here, so you'd better try being a horse for a while," said Ursula quietly. She leaned back into the foyer to see the cat she had initially started the conversation with. "Oh, you're a real cat. Shoo!" She clicked her fingers and a gust of sharp wind smacked into the grey feline. It set off into another room.

"Are you going to look for Zag now?" asked Timothy.

"I'll try. Those woods, of course."

"You shouldn't have thrown him away to begin with."

"And you should keep your opinions to yourself until we are King and Queen." She clicked her fingers once more, and Timothy was assaulted by an array of rainbows until he was completely engulfed by them. When they disappeared, he stood there clean as a whistle. Satisfied with her work, she said: "I'm also going to hunt the west side of town this morning. You focus on hitting puberty."

Ursula left through the door quickly. Timothy watched her strut down the long gravel driveway, until the lush green of the oak trees and fern-plants lining the estate engulfed her completely.

———— · · · ————

When I woke up that morning, my mind sharply focused in on the wardrobe. Rather than checking on the little boy inside, I instead made sure that the clay head was still actually there. I was shy of Zag for some reason, and I wasn't sure why. I promptly got dressed for school, and as I brushed my hair in the mirror, I decided bravely to wish for its colour to change to blonde. My mouth filled with glitter, and when I wiped it away I glanced up to find that my hair was indeed lighter. I quickly wished for it to go back to brown, and it did. So that answered that, then. I was definitely not going insane.

"Okay," I said, steadily breathing in and out to calm my nerves. It was time to venture out into the real world. Past the safety of my own front door, towards the unknown.

Mom offered to drive Annie and I to school. I think it was mainly because of the moose attack, but she also happened to be going to the far west side of town to visit Brendan's school, Far West Elementary. This suited me because I was set to catch the bus for the first time that day. Maybe my mother understood how hard it would be for me, with all the gossiping of my disastrous walk home two days earlier sure to spread down the aisles like wildfire.

I was in such a state; I forgot about the havoc the previous night's storm caused. Fallen branches and loose outdoor furniture had been tossed around everywhere. Somebody's colourful patio umbrella was resting comfortably on the bonnet of our four-wheel drive. Annie and I sat in the back of the car. Earphones raging, I tried to ignore the constant glances in the rear-view mirror from my concerned mother as we drove away. Perhaps she was surprised at how normal I seemed. I was surprised myself.

Brendan sat in the front next to Mom. He was playing a video game, taking his frustrations of God-knows-what out on it. Halfway down Spasms Road, he purposely turned the volume up.

"Honey, don't. I'm trying to concentrate on the traffic."

Brendan retaliated by turning it up.

"What is wrong with you?"

Maybe she'd forgotten what it was like to be a kid, so I took my earphones out to remind her. "Did Grandma ever come into school with you?"

"I was home schooled, you know that."

Brendan continued with his noisy game.

"Honey, *please.*"

"Mom, *please,*" said Brendan.

Our mother slammed on the brakes and pulled over. We stared up at her in wonder. She was tilting her head from side to side pretending to be simple. "Gee, you know, all that beeping could have caused an accident. I sure am glad I stopped before I got to that intersection up ahead. We could have been killed just like *Tristan TyreStomach!*" She glared down at her son like a creep, and he gasped dramatically.

Last year while visiting the oldies for the holidays in Canada, Grandma Helen in all her perverted weirdness made us watch a children's educational VHS she'd purchased from the black markets about a boy called Tristan who distracted his parents while they were driving. They had a car crash and Tristan was thrown out of the open window and was run over by the longest truck in the world. Then the truck reversed to see what it had hit. To say it was unrealistic in every sense is an insult to humanity. The icing on the cake came when coy little Tristan uttered his final words in hospital before dying: 'I sure hope no other kids in the world do what I did and distract their parents while they are driving.' After seeing it, Brendan ran upstairs to his folded cot, crying. Apparently every kid who saw it reacted in the same way when it was released in the eighties, so the non-useful program was deleted from existence by the government. Except, of course, they weren't privy to the information that Grandma Helen had a copy hidden in her bunker. She would make kids watch it when they came trick-or-treating each year, to give them a genuine Halloween fright.

"Okay, bad example," said Mom, regretting bringing it up.

Brendan was shaky. "I could report you."

Knowing when to let things go, he turned down the volume without further mention. We set off again and all seemed fine, until I watched out the window as our school zoomed by. "Uh… Mom?"

She screeched to a halt once more, and a car swerved to go around us. Annie and I exchanged tired looks and we hopped out. We gladly bade farewell and walked back the way we came.

At the front gate, Annie wished me good luck. I stared at the ground, my stomach gurgling, and started biting my fingernails. I made my way into B Block, and spotted Hayley just outside our homeroom. She was leaning against the last locker in one particular row and I noticed she had on a sky blue army jacket. Her long, straight blonde hair dangled over the front of it.

"Hello," she said loudly, over the chattering kids walking by.

Oh good, she still wanted to be my friend. I checked for the second-hand science book in my new backpack. "Hey."

"Nice clothes," she said, checking out my regular wardrobe. A blue flannel top, jeans and sneakers did wonders.

"Thanks."

"We totally thought of ringing you yesterday to see what you were up to after school, but then Jonathan reminded me. You were attacked?"

I looked on in disbelief.

"Souffléd? Help us out. Which one of the rumours is true?"

I shook my head and got out a scrunchy to tie my hair back. "I don't want to talk about it."

"The way I figure," said Hayley, crinkling up her nose and closing one eye. "Tanya Tanner... this girl in our class, total Saviour... Well, her sister was in an accident in Italy and now she's going to be all incapacitated for like eight weeks or something. Whereas you only had one day off. So obviously you didn't fall off a cliff like she did."

"Indoor rock-climbing accident, actually."

"Whatever. You know what I mean."

I couldn't tell her the truth. She wouldn't believe me anyway.

"So, you were attacked by a moose," she said.

Her words totally threw me, and I must have given it away with my reaction. She smiled and said: "Hey, it's cool if you don't want to talk about it. Being felt up by an animal with horns must be fairly embarrassing. Especially in a town called Horn-Horn. I can see the headlines now: *'Horn-Hornian Honed by Horny Horned Creature.'* I won't say anything," she promised. Then she looked puzzled. "Wait... Do moose have horns, or antlers? And are they moose, or meese?"

I shrugged. "How did you know about the moose part?"

"Your sister told me yesterday."

"That bitch."

I jumped in fright at a pair of eyes watching from the corner of the row of lockers. Greg moved forward and smiled, then looked down. I did the same, while Hayley rolled her eyes.

"Greg, don't be weird."

At the same time, a hand pressed against my right shoulder. I turned to find Principal Eric Parker standing there in a purple suit, with not a spec of dust or hair on it. He gazed down at me sternly. I immediately felt like I was eight again, in trouble for something, not knowing what, or why, but knowing that there had to be something, *anything* I'd done to warrant it, surely, for he was an adult and I was a child. Besides, I'd barely met the man. He could be the meanest

Principal in the world for all I knew. My poor nervous stomach was not having a good start to the day.

"Good morning, Principal Parker," I said.

Parker didn't say anything for the longest time, and I wondered why. Had he seen me in the woods? Did he know everything? Since his daughter could look into my room through her window, perhaps he could too. That was it. He knew what really happened to me in the woods, he knew what I'd taken home, and he knew everything because he was in on it. Whatever it was.

"My office at nine-thirty, please."

With that, he left down the busy hall. Now it was my turn to gaze. A meeting? That didn't sound very much like he knew everything. Of course he didn't, I realised. He was just calling me into his office because I was a new student, his neighbour, and he wanted to see how I was fitting in.

Hayley's mouth was a perfect O shape when I focussed back into reality. "What did you do?" she asked me.

"I didn't do anything."

"You must have done something. Did you see his face? He never looks that seriously at someone unless they... I dunno... stole school equipment or something." She checked her surroundings. Something told me *she* had stolen school equipment or something.

I was going to act blasé about it, maybe laugh, to show off to my new friends. After all, I'd nearly been mauled by the Godzilla of meese, so getting into trouble at school should have been the least of my concerns. Yet strangely, it was right up there. I felt like the world was going to end, that a comet was heading straight for us.

I clutched at my gut. "Where are the nearest bathrooms?"

———— · · · ————

When I finally found the bathrooms down near E Block, I was reluctant to go in there. At my old school, the girls' toilets were mucky and smelly. You really did just go in there, do your business, and leave. Contrary to Salem, however, I was dumbfounded to find this place in mint condition. Blue tiles lined around three large mirrors. The lights on the ceiling were clean, devoid of trapped bugs long since dead, and they were actually working. When I reached one of the seven currently engaged cubicles, I examined the doors in wonder. They weren't hanging off their hinges. It was amazing.

A high voice spoke to me from one of the middle cubicles.

"Sorry, these are all taken. We're having a little get-together before class starts."

I shrugged. After a good twenty seconds of standing in there, I hadn't realised the silence was because of my presence.

"It's okay," said someone from another stall. "I'll move. I'm done anyway. Here you go." She flushed and opened the door.

I was greeted by a small girl with long blonde hair, who smiled friendlily. She was wearing pink clothes that were much like the ones I'd gotten from my ex-pals the other day. I couldn't help but notice that she was almost illegally beautiful. Her features weren't flawless though, as she had a scar on her nose.

"Thank you," I managed in a very quiet voice.

"Oh, here," the girl fumbled around with her handbag before I locked myself in. She pulled out a little piece of pink paper and handed it to me. "It's an invitation to Eleanore Parker's Annual Back to School Party. Everyone will be there."

I looked down at the paper, which was the size of a movie stub, and laminated. I squinted to read what was written:

Dear friends and school buddies,

It's that time of year again! The first weekend of the first term for the new school year. As a way to celebrate, I'm having my annual back-to-school party at my place. No need to BYO, just BYS and your S.O.

TTFN! P.S.: RSVPBF

Time: This Saturday, 7:30pm – 1am

Place: 10 Phillips Drive, Horn-Horn

Full parental supervision will be in action, just like school. LOL.

Warmest, most heart-wrenchingly authentic regards,

♡xoxo♡ Eleanore Parker ♡xoxo♡

The girl watched me intensely as I read it. She must have spotted my confusion, for she said: *"BYS is Bring Yourself... and your Significant Other. Ta-Ta for now. Postscript: Response please by Friday."* She kept my gaze. *"By which she means the day..."* She looked serious. *"To Friday. The person."*

"Thanks." My bowels were on their way to evacuating.

"Oh, and here's one for your S.O.," she handed me another. "Now if you have any troubles involving what to bring, *who* to bring, what to wear, just ask around for me. I'm Tanya Tanner, from 10W."

I stopped in my tracks. This was the girl Eleanore had mentioned the other day... *And* the girl Hayley mentioned not ten minutes earlier. She'd gone to Italy with her family to retrieve her injured sister. She must have returned yesterday when I was home sick.

"Okay, thanks," was all I said to her. I locked myself in the cubicle, and watched through the crack in the door as she inspected herself in the mirror. I pulled down my knickers and clenched my muscles so I wouldn't make any unflattering noises.

The cubicle to my right opened, and all of the others followed. A very sharp clicking of heels echoed off the walls and I shuddered as I realised how close I'd come to another face-off with the Saviours.

"Nice work, Tanya," said Eleanore. She put her hand on the nice blonde girl's shoulder. Surrounded by half a dozen other girls, most of whom I didn't know yet, none were taller than Wednesday and Friday.

Tanya began washing her hands. "Don't mention it."

"Okay, I won't," Eleanore uttered in her snooty way. "Can't be too careful when handing out invites these days. Such larger populations than when we were in elementary. So much harder to control everything. I blame the minorities."

"I don't," said Wednesday coldly, absorbing her own reflection.

Eleanore ignored her. "Listen, Tanya..." Her eyes locked onto mine and I backed away from the door. I realised immediately how silly I was, for she couldn't actually see me through the tiny gap. "I must warn you of someone. There is a new girl in our class. You haven't met her yet because you didn't come to school until yesterday. I would have mentioned it to you then, but you know how flustered I was after that mid-morning call from the party caterers. Can't make croissants in the shape of my torso? What plebs. It's a travesty. Just like this girl. She is trouble, Tanya. You must *not* give an invitation to her."

"What's her name?"

"Her name is Cassie Gellar. She's with the losers."

Tanya seemed surprised by this. "No way. Those guys actually let someone else into their group? That's unheard of."

Eleanore's grin deceived the fury in her eyes. "I know, so you see what a destructive force she has the potential to become, right? When you see her in class, toss her a cold one."

"What's that?"

"It's a dirty look."

"Oh. Yeah, okay, I will. How come she wasn't here yesterday?"

"I can't remember exactly. Her sister told me something about being attacked in the woods. I was too preoccupied at the time by her ugliness to pay attention.

"Cassie's, or her sister's?"

"Oh no, her sister's. Cassie, unfortunately, isn't ugly. So we don't have the usual attack methods to work with."

"The sad thing is, she *was* a Saviour," said Friday. "She was an actual Saviour, officially. For, like, a day and a half. Then she dumped us for the back-seaters. Can you believe it? *Us.* She dumped *us*. For them. *Them.* She dumped *us* for *them*." Apparently Friday couldn't grasp the concept.

"She stole clothes from us, too," said Wednesday.

My cheeks flushed at the accusation.

"She took them home with her, then dumped us."

"So... they were a present?" said Tanya.

"Initially, but then she..."

"But then nothing, once you give something to someone, they..."

"Oh, who cares about the precise nature of the situation, point is she's a loser and you've got to let her know it!" roared Eleanore. She turned to her other minions, clearly in much lower grades, and waited for them to stop chattering amongst themselves. They finally did, and they stared up at her tyrannical face. *"GO!"* she roared. They rushed out, leaving the Saviours alone with me.

All was quiet on the western front. During their conversation, I'd strenuously relieved myself as slowly and tediously as possible, without making a single noise. I was nearly done, and I pulled my knickers up very quietly. The elastic snapped against my skin and I held my breath.

"You in there!" Eleanore knocked fiercely on my door. "Forget everything you just heard or I will make life for you a living hell."

"Leave her alone, Eleanore, she's cool," said Tanya.

Eleanore moved away. "Well, if you say so. Come on, let's go sit in class early so Ms. Weiss will look favourably upon us."

They left in an endless array of chatter, their voices reverberating down the hallway until they were mixed into obscurity amongst the passersby outside.

I put my hands to my cheeks to cool myself down.

———— · · · ————

"My parents made me go last year," said Greg. It was five to nine and nearly everybody was in the homeroom opposite us. The only people to remain outside were my friends and I. "Principal Parker insisted I go, too. Not really sure why. I hated it."

"Why?" I asked.

Hayley put her hands up in defence. "Granted when I went a few years back, forced though I was, Mr. and Mrs. Parker had some fairly decent alco-ma-hol in the basement. I swiped a few bottles of wine and since then have had quite some fun nights home alone. But I'm not condoning her parties."

I nodded. I handed her the other ticket. "Think we should photocopy it on pink paper, or something?"

"What for?" mumbled JT, leaning over my shoulder to read one.

Hayley answered for me. "Obviously you need a pass to get in, so if we photocopy them like a dozen times on pink paper, and maybe pass them out to all sorts of nerd-burgers, it's the perfect opportunity to sabotage her life. Paper-cut her where it hurts."

"You're not invited this year?" I asked Greg. I'd been building up to asking him for the last few moments, and because of that, it came out in a sort of retarded mumble.

"Huh?" he said.

I repeated myself, in English this time.

"Nope, definitely not invited. She's sixteen now; her father says she can invite whoever she wants since she's a responsible adult."

"Responsible like a dog serving a birthday cake at a kid's party," said Hayley bitterly. "Crap, if we're going to do this, we'll have to laminate all the copies too."

"Are there any laminators at this school?"

"Only in the science lab. Sucks we don't know anyone in there."

"My sister joined the science club."

"She's a dork, right?" said JT. "Maybe... she could hand out some invites to all her dorky friends."

Hayley piped up and clapped her hands. "Oh, that's amazing. Oh! That's brilliant! I can't wait. We have to start this thing today."

It was three minutes to nine. Ms. Weiss was at the doorway,

leaning against it, tapping her wrist-watch impatiently at us. She strutted back into the room, expecting us to follow, but I noticed that none of the others moved. So I remained leaning against a locker with them, sheep that I was.

"She thinks we're losers too," Hayley whispered to me.

"She does not," said JT. "Losers. Pfft. That's such a hateful word, Hayles. You're so *hateful*."

"What *would* she call us, Jonathan? The socially challenged?"

"Of course not. She thinks we're *doibs*."

"What's that?" I asked.

Hayley snorted. "He made it up. It means: Damn Oafish Illiterate Boobs. But I'm telling you, boy, it'll never catch on."

"Yes, mein Mutter."

I smiled. "Well, Eleanore is a *doib*."

"No, she's a *lash*. Lost Alien Soul from Hell."

When we finally entered the classroom, I noticed the Saviours were chatting to themselves in the second last row. But one person was missing. Tanya rushed into the room, her head in her handbag searching for something. She quickly smiled at Ms. Weiss, who looked down judgmentally, and followed behind us to get to her seat.

"Oh gosh, quick. Hayley, give me your jacket," I whispered.

Without further ado, Hayley took off her blue jacket and I put it on. I dove into my seat, sunk as low as I could, and put the collar up to my crown so nobody could really see me. Unfortunately, we were talking about pure evil here.

"Hello, *Cassie!*" Eleanore turned around to eye me.

I was trapped.

"Have you met Tanya Tanner yet? I'm sorry you didn't get to meet her on Sunday, but you'll see her now. Around town, or at the pound. She works there."

"What's that sound, you clown?" Hayley turned to JT.

They clasped hands merrily.

"Don't frown. Pull up that gown, before you drown!"

Eleanore didn't get it.

"Cassie, say hello to Tanya," she said, ignoring them. "Tanya, say hello to Cassie Gellar."

Tanya said hello vaguely, having heard all about me. I reluctantly poked my head out from the blue safety of Hayley's jacket, and said hello back. Of course, her face drained of colour right away. Her brown eyes bulged. *"You're* Cassie Gellar?"

Eleanore spun her head a good one-hundred and eighty degrees to examine her tiny friend. "Have you met her before?"

"No, no certainly not," lied Tanya, looking to the ground.

Eleanore's eyes were locked on her for an excruciating period of time. Soon enough, Ms. Weiss started the class so she stopped scrutinising and faced the front. But I knew she knew something was up. I sincerely doubted Tanya would tell her it was me in the bathroom. I hoped she wouldn't, too. Not only would it ruin our plans to gatecrash, it would also make Tanya look bad. I had no idea why I really cared about that last bit, but for some reason I did. I was so overwhelmed with such thoughts, that it took me a while to realise my scary appointment with Principal Parker was a mere half an hour away.

My stomach tsunami revved up again.

12

THE LADY EMERGES

Horn-Horn Far West Elementary was for some reason on what locals referred to as 'the bad side of town'. Nobody had ever approved of the school being in this district, it just sort of happened. The school itself was quite well kept, looking more than respectable, but was unfortunately locked behind a security of metal gates and barbed-wired fences. It was more like a prison than a school, a notion many of the students agreed wholeheartedly with.

Mom and Brendan sat in the car across the street, tardy. Brendan had hoped her visit would go undetected by his classmates. He figured they would get there early, before class, which was exactly why he'd stolen the wheel five minutes earlier and forced them down a dirt track. Now here they were, late because the short-cut sported an inconveniently slow road-works crew. Their car was also quite dirty as a result.

"Why do you have to do this *now?*" Brendan complained yet again. "You could wait until school is finished. Teachers stay back until five, y'know."

"I have to go to the Mayor's office this afternoon to fill out some forms about my complaint."

"Oh, how very convenient for you."

"It won't take long. Your teachers sent home one of your papers last night with a message to come in as soon as I can. So I'm here. You say that there are two of them. One can stay with the class while the other talks to me. Nobody will even notice."

"I keep telling you, *no*," said Brendan, hands to his head as he tried to wrap his mind around her obvious stupidity. *"They have to stay in the same room."*

Mom undid her seatbelt and started getting out of the car. "Oh, you know, I don't think what you told me last night is even possible. And I don't appreciate you lying to me. Come on, let's get this over and done with."

She jumped back in upon hearing a gun shot in the distance.

"Right, you wait here while I go in and find your classroom." She slid out of the car and locked him inside. "I'll be back soon."

"Why can't I come in with you and show you?"

"No, no. You stay here," she said, half concentrating on what she was saying. She was glancing this way and that, expecting an hysteric crowd of angry zombie rapists to charge around the corner.

"Don't lock me in here! What if the trunk catches alight?"

"It won't happen."

"What if someone tries to steal the hubcaps?"

"Let them."

"What if my tongue tries to suffocate me?"

"Just wait! I'll be back in a couple of minutes to bring you in."

Mom crossed the empty street to get to the front gates. She had to undo a chain and put it back in order to get through, and then she was met with a tired looking security guard who scanned her and let her in to the main building. She soon disappeared into the jungle beyond.

Bored already, Brendan sulkily placed his arm against the window and pressed his hand against his head. What did his teachers want to say to her, anyway? He hadn't been bad like he'd been at his old school. There had been no detergent bombs placed in any school kitchen dishwashers. No old schoolmarms needing their smelling salts after falling victim to his fake decapitations. He'd kept quiet the past two days because he didn't know anyone and hadn't gained the confidence he was used to. He was actually doing his work, for Pete's sake.

A very tall woman in a white cloak appeared to stride out of the bushes in front of him. The school was across the road from a very small section of woods. The woman was the tallest person Brendan had ever seen, too. She wiped herself down and looked at the school, pensive, until she noticed him watching her from the car. She looked to see if anyone else was around, then quickly hotfooted it over. Brendan's heart raced. Maybe murderers wore heels.

Ursula knocked gently on the window and smiled at him. She held up a polaroid of what looked to be a hollow clay statue in the shape of a head.

"Hello, I'm looking for this. Somebody has stolen it from my... *art* factory, and it's worth a great deal. There's a copious... That is, there's a great big award for information on its wh… Have you seen it, little boy?"

Brendan shook his head and said: "Regrettably, your ample reward for its whereabouts is redundant since I have freshly relocated to this idiosyncratic hamlet."

Ursula shrugged miserably, placing her hands against the small of her back to crack it. "Well, do you suppose they'll let me inside that school across the road and interrogate the children?"

Brendan shook his head.

Giving up easily, she turned to leave, but quickly heard the sound of the car window sliding down. He'd only lowered it enough to speak easily to her.

"If anyone is likely to steal something that ugly, teenagers might be your best bet. I can show you how to get to the high school on my GPS if you want."

Ursula inspected him closely. "Is this your car?"

"Yes."

"You're not a dwarf, are you?"

"No..."

"Then where are your parents?"

"My Dad's at work, but my Mom's in there."

He pointed to the school, then set to opening the GPS on his dashboard. Ursula waited patiently. After a few moments of reading what was on the screen, Brendan turned to her and said: "Okay, the high school is on the far east side of town. So you need to go to the beach and then follow the main road until you get to those woods. Those big woods, you know the ones? In the centre of town."

Ursula felt a great sense of relief as the universe seemed to guide her in the right direction. She opened her bag and raked out a one hundred dollar bill.

"This is yours if you tell me how many high school students you figure walk home through the woods each day."

Brendan eyed the money. "What the heck is that?"

Ursula laughed. "It's bigger than any amount you've ever seen, I'm sure. Now, tell me. How many, do you suppose?"

"I don't think anyone does anymore."

"Yes. Kids and their damn cars."

"Not that. There's a crazy moose roaming around out there."

Ursula grabbed onto the door-handle to open it. Just then, a woman began yelling at her. Startled into her right mind, she backed away from the car and smiled at the blonde rushing towards them.

Mom stood by the bonnet, nerves on edge.

"Can I help you?" she asked.

Ursula showed her the polaroid from the curb.

"No, I haven't seen it," Mom replied, barely glancing at it. She unlocked her door, hopped in, and sat there waiting for the other woman to leave. Ursula stared hopelessly for a few moments, then wandered back into the woods.

Brendan noticed the money now on his lap. The strange woman must have slipped the note through the crack in the window without his noticing.

"Mom, what's this?" he asked, holding it up for her to examine.

"I don't know... One hundred dollars... Must be foreign."

"So it's *useless?*" he said in disgust. He tossed it aside. "Give it to Annie. She likes garbage."

Mom shoved it in her pocket mindlessly. "Trust you to talk to strangers in the two minutes I leave you alone."

"It was a woman, and she was dressed nicely."

"Doesn't mean she's not a psycho, honey. Come on, let's go in."

13
CASHEWS AND CARRIE

I anxiously watched the clock as it went from nine-ten… to nine-twenty. Why did time always seem to go faster when you didn't want it to?

We were in the middle of a short, not-so-official maths quiz, so the entire room was as quiet as a mouse. When it got to nine twenty-five, I begrudgingly stood up and went to the front desk where Ms. Weiss was sitting. As I loomed over her, I noticed she was drawing two naked stick figures kissing, grossly oversized groins and all.

"Ms. Weiss?"

She jumped, crumpled the piece of paper up and threw it into the bin by her side. She put on a laugh.

"Cassie? Why aren't you in your seat?"

"I have an appointment with Principal Parker."

"Alright, you may go," she told me, waving her hand gently.

As I walked out the door, I looked back to see her hand slipping into the bin beside her. When she spotted me looking, she sat back up in her seat.

It took me a very long time to find Principal Parker's office. As if this school wasn't already a maze, its maps were equally confronting. It was like one of those kids puzzles you find in restaurants where you have to draw a line from one end of a maze to the other.

"Enter at your own will," Principal Parker called from inside, once I'd knocked on the door.

It was a very small, dry looking office. The walls were a light brown colour, and everything else seemed to be left over from the eighties. Brown here, brown there. Here a brown, there a brown, everywhere a brown-brown. I had a sneaking suspicion the interior decorator was Old MacDonald. A potted cactus sat in one corner, while a painting of a frowning man hung in the other. The only nice thing to look at in the entire room was Parker's purple suit, which looked vibrant in comparison.

"Sit down, Carrie," he told me.

I looked at the cushiony brown chairs lining the wall to my right. I began to sit down on one, when he turned and gave me a look.

"Not here. In *there*." He pointed to a door near the cactus. To my surprise, there was another room beyond this one. I hopped up, apologised, and slipped through. Parker followed me in, and shut the door behind him. Now this was better. It was a large room, filled with bookshelves and a terrific pine desk with papers scattered across it. On the edge sat a black globe of the Earth, and in the corner on the wall I saw a very large, detailed painting of the entire Parker family (minus Eleanore for some reason).

Upon his request, I sat down in a rather uncomfortable leather chair on the opposite side of his desk. He sat down across from me, putting a hand against his chin pensively. I smiled at him. He didn't smile back. He rubbed his temples for a moment, breathing heavily.

"Carrie..." he said, and the smell of cashews wafted over me.

I corrected him bitterly. I was beginning to think that maybe people were getting my name wrong on purpose. Hoping my anger wasn't obvious, I trained my focus on a metal ash-tray which seemed to be resting perilously close to the edge of the desk.

"I wanted to check up on you. See how you are settling in."

"Oh," I said, relieved. "Everything's fine."

"... I also wanted to ask if your escapades on Monday night need any form of legal attention at all?"

I knew there was a catch. "Escapades?"

"Whatever happened to you after school that day is, quite

frankly, a mystery to most of us here since your parents refuse to answer any questions about it. As your Principal I was hoping I could get the information straight from the horse's mouth. Or moose's, as it would seem."

I kept staring at the ash-tray. "I don't remember. If I wasn't okay I don't think my Mom and Dad would let me come to school. And I kinda sorta don't wanna talk about it..." I rubbed my right arm nervously.

"We understand," said Parker, pushing a box of tissues my way.

I took one but didn't use it.

"Cassie, I'm afraid we have to report this to the school-board as an incident that took place on school grounds."

"What? But it didn't."

"We know. Unfortunately, since you are underage, we take re-sponsibility for you from the time school finishes to the moment you get home."

"It wasn't even within the first hour after school. Principal Parker, my sister and I got lost in the woods and..."

"We know, we know. We're sorry. This is the only state we're liable like this. You understand that we will be sending a letter home to your parents and bringing in a new school psychologist to help you. You will need to have allotted times to talk with them each week."

I was blushing. I was furious. I kept my gaze on the ash-tray.

"You understand, this isn't up to us."

"I understand *all*," I said venomously, and I reeled. I'd never spoken to an adult with such attitude before. At least not outside of my immediate family.

Eric Parker clearly sensed my angst, and he opened his drawer and pulled out a packet of opened cashews to chew on. "Alright, al-right. Is there anything less prickly you'd like to say to me before I send you back to class?"

I shrugged, keeping my head down. "No."

"Are you sure?"

I shook my head, then rotated it into a nod. "Yep."

"Eleanore came to me last night. She seems very concerned about you. Did you know that?"

I couldn't stand it. The fury was bubbling up inside of me.

"Expressed an interest in you, which I'm honestly very pleased about. She has nothing but good words to say."

"Really?"

"She also told me that you have been mixing with the wrong crowd," he continued, and it started to make sense. "Hanging around with those... you know... *back-seaters*, as I believe everyone calls them. Or something along those lines." He smirked and brushed his nose subtly. "The poor kids, you know what I mean."

I stared, breathless. "*Doib.*"

"Beg your pardon?"

I shook my head and looked away.

"Eleanore is concerned because she is not sure whether you actually want to spend time with them, or if they are *forcing* you to. Naturally kids of all ages, adults at times, are often forced into undesirable social situations, but find they can't break free because they haven't got anyone else to talk to about it. The only reason I ask is because… it's actually quite hard to tell right now which group you belong to."

He might as well have slapped me in the face with a codfish. His tone was irrefutably suggestive.

"Tell me, Carrie, are you really *happy* hanging around with Hayley Gauche? Or do you feel pressured? I bet you secretly want to be spending your time with Eleanore, am I right? No matter what you say here, I promise you it will remain partially confidential."

Well, it was all I could do to stop myself from laughing at the sheer absurdity. I needed to walk somewhere until I stopped. I opened my mouth to say... something, but nothing came out. So I tried again... Nope, nothing. One more time...

"Enough said," Parker stood up. "Just by the look on your face I can tell that you want to mingle endlessly with Eleanore, and leave the excess baggage where you found them. I'll talk to Ms. Weiss immediately and..."

"No, stop, please." I stood up and kept my gaze on the ash-tray. "I *do* want to hang out with Hayley. I really do. But I don't want that to mean I have to be enemies with Eleanore." I looked around in bewilderment. "Has the whole world gone mad, Principal Parker? If I didn't want to hang out with them, I wouldn't."

It was clear that I was dead to him. "As you wish," he said, and he walked to the door and opened it. "We'll let sleeping dogs lie. I'll sort out your counselling as soon as my brother Josh is done removing those darn magnetic pipes from underneath my office floorboards. Shouldn't take too long, but thank you very much paranoid war veterans. I'll see you later, Carrie."

"It's *Cassie!*" I snapped.

The metal ash tray on his desk flipped upside-down by itself and fell to the floor. I covered my mouth in wonder. Parker, however, didn't give it the time of day.

"Josh!" he yelled to the floor.

I walked back to class, my nerves a wreck. I sat in my seat and smiled when Ms. Weiss looked up at me. The maths test was over. We'd all moved on to what she called: 'Silent Working Hour', which took place every Wednesday so our teacher could do her correcting.

Yeah, right.

If you took the first 'C' out of 'correcting' and replaced the 'or' with an 'e', you'd get what she was *really* doing.

14
THE LEGEND OF TWO HORN

With lunchtime came a tremendous shock.

It all began on our way to the Vineyard. Greg stopped in his tracks and held his hands up. I was mid-chew of my sandwich so I didn't ask what was wrong.

"Guys…" he said slowly. "You know how I'm the only one here with twenty-twenty vision?"

We nodded, as it was something discussed briefly in class.

"I see something ahead."

Hayley laughed sceptically, but she joined JT and I in glancing about the schoolyard with the fiercest wonder this side of the equator.

Our eyes landed upon a strange spot at the back of the school. I squinted, and then covered my mouth. The Vineyard was gone. Just gone. As if it had never existed. Now all that stood against the back fence was a black cat, and it was licking itself with one of its back legs up.

"Son of a *Principal!*" shouted Hayley, not realising her error, and she tore for the back fence with haste.

"There's nothing left," said JT sadly, kicking at the red dirt.

"That crazy bitch did it. She threatened to, and she did it!"

"She wouldn't. It was there this morning. You don't think..?"

"Oh, I does think. I does think well!" Hayley's gasps turned into yells. Kids nearby looked over to see what all the commotion was about. Spit flung from her mouth like a rabid dog. It was the colour of grape juice. "That's it. If Eleanore Crapface Parker wants a war, let's send our troops out."

With that, she tipped her head back and roared like a dinosaur. I didn't dare touch her to try and calm her down. That was JT's mistake, and she grabbed his arm and swung him around. He fell onto a passing snail. When he stood up, he wiped his butt.

"You could have at least spared the snail. It didn't do anything."

"Oh, can it," muttered Hayley. She had a pained look in her eyes. "I need to be alone. Come on, Jonathan."

As Greg and I watched them disappear around a corner, an acute sense of sound came my way and I realised that we were alone for the first time ever. Far from a Rodgers and Hammerstein moment, paralysis claimed the both of us. I couldn't move my arms or my legs, and certainly not my mouth or my vocal cords. And neither could he. I finally turned to him, but all I could manage was one word: "Wow."

Greg laughed nervously, scratching the back of his neck. Unfortunately, we didn't really evolve much in our company for the next five minutes, which stretched like molasses on that damn January morn everybody talks about. We slowly wandered throughout the schoolyard, as if in a dream. Then we trundled down some hallways I hadn't been through before. I tried to seem really invested in the structure of the buildings, even going so far as to nod and make an impressed sound as I examined a nearby light switch at the end of a hall. Out of boredom, I flicked it to see what would happen. Of course, it sent the student body into near pitch black. Panicking, I swiftly turned it back on. Most people had stopped, glaring at me. Greg turned, bursting into laughter, and we ran away. We didn't stop until we reached the technical building. Greg was staring up at it, pondering. I followed his eyes to see what he was seeing, but there was nothing out of the ordinary. Finally, he spoke: "The science lab is in there. We could ask about the laminator."

"Of *course*."

— . . . —

Inside was what you'd expect from a science lab. I stifled about eight yawns in the first minute. Science was definitely not for me. The walls and benches seemed to be painted the exact same brown colour Parker's office was painted in.

"Cassie," my sister walked up to me from a corner, and I was so stunned I could only warble inanely for a few seconds. In my own way I'd forgotten she went here, as we barely crossed paths during the day. She was dressed in her white science lab coat and protective yellow goggles, and she suffered quite a concerned squint.

"Annie, what are you doing here? It's lunch time."

"I don't like to mingle with the rodents," she said aggressively, seemingly referring to her fellow classmates. "I prefer instead to experiment on them in here." She pointed to a nearby work bench. On it was a beaker full of bubbling blue liquid, some strangely curvy measuring equipment, a bunsen burner emitting an eerie hissing sound, and a wooden maze with an albino rat running around inside. I moved closer to inspect it as it tried to find its way to the cheese in the middle.

"This is Greg," I said, and the two of them acknowledged each other strangely by stretching their necks far back and ogling. "Annie, we need to use the lab's laminator and I was wondering if I could use you as a way to get to it."

"Why?" said Annie, her eyes still squinted in deep suspicion.

"Is it really that big a deal?"

"No, I mean, why are you asking to use it? Anybody can."

"Then why are you squinting at me like that?"

"I'm *not*." Fed up, she grabbed onto her goggles and pulled with great might until they ripped away from her eyes with a huge suctioned explosion. "Mom bought me safety goggles for five year olds, so they don't fit properly. On the plus side when I wear them, they pinch my eyes so tight that I can see clearly! I should wear them instead of my glasses."

I ignored her stupidity again. "Where's the laminator?"

Annie rushed to the nearest chalkboard, and read something on it. "Getting fixed. It'll be in the library for the next week."

"Great," said Greg.

I waved to my sister and told her to have a nice day. Put off by my company, she smiled so widely that her braces blinded us.

She's so weird, I thought momentarily, but got distracted as the white rat jumped from its maze prison into the bubbling beaker.

"We've got another suicide here!"

Annie called to her fellow science club members for help.

— • • • —

"Where did you move from?" Greg asked me not long after, as we rounded the front of the school. We criss-crossed between some very tall pine trees by Reception.

"Salem."

"Oh yeah," he looked down, recalling my introduction to the class. "Must be a pretty creepy place to live, yeah?"

I shrugged. "Not really. It's not like that when you live there."

Greg smiled at the thought. "I guess you're right. This town is creepier if you ask me. We've got *scientists*."

"What do you mean?"

"They're always coming here because of the earthquakes."

"We have earthquakes?"

He looked sideways at me, smirking. "Surprised your parents didn't look into that before moving here."

"Lovely!" I said, stabbing the dirt with my left foot.

"We get maybe two a year. You don't really feel them."

"I guess that's okay, then."

"There's an underground fire in Alexandria, the town next to us, from when they used to mine there. My dad reckons it'll be a ghost town in a century. The fumes don't get us though, don't worry, but everyone seems to think it's made a fault line under Horn-Horn."

I kicked another pile of red rocks as we walked.

"Why is it called Horn-Horn, anyway?"

It was hard to explain, insisted Greg. In 1802, a group of travellers happened upon an abandoned seaside landscape that had centuries ago been occupied by the Native Indians. Devoid of all human life, the area didn't even have a name. So one of the traveller's wives, Mrs. Henry Cornwall, decided to trek about the beach one day by herself. Her fellow companions were set up in tents a mile or so away. According to documentation, she went missing, and after a tiresome week of searching they found her body on top of a cliff. Mutilated. Sewn to her crown was a set of ox horns. *Two horns.*

What caused her death is unknown, but it was suspected to be a ritual killing of sorts. The only problem was that nobody from the nearby towns ever stepped foot in the region she was found in — it was, after all, cursed (according to them). So Henry, her husband, was convicted purely out of the fearful assumptions that gathered amongst his troop. Today's town members debated this, of course. And, as a grim reminder of the origin of the town's name (originally called Two Horn by the spooked villagers), a large wooden sign with *Horn-Horn* carved into its front was erected by the side of the highway. Right near the cliff where Mrs. Cornwall was found. It even had two ox horns fixed to the sides. I myself had seen the sign the night we moved in, but failed to notice the horns.

"They're there," Greg said surely, and he insisted they were the original horns from the killing.

"That's macabre. How come nobody's ever stolen them?"

"People have tried. But legend has it anybody who touches them is struck by lightning." He gave a spooky *'ooh'* sound and tried to tickle me. I laughed, and then he laughed. I didn't believe that one bit, and neither did he. Obviously the town board just kept putting new horns back up. Probably. That's what I decided in my mind was the truth, anyway.

15
MANILATOR

The day wore on tiredly, and the heat picked up with more strength than I thought was possible. The afternoon class was as boring as the first day's. It seemed to never end. We sweltered in the classroom, which tragically lacked air-conditioning, and even the usually perky Ms. Weiss ended up collapsing into her chair and muttering roman numerals to us. As if this wasn't enough to bear, Hayley was unresponsive and mad as hell. Perhaps it was her steaming rage giving off this unbearable heat. She barely moved her gaze away from the back of Eleanore's lopsided head. I became concerned that her hair was going to catch fire. Eleanore herself touched her neck at one point and looked at us worriedly.

"Conversion tables, combined to signify the sum…" Ms. Weiss had her arms draped over her head, and her eyes were closed. "I'm sorry, I can't go on."

Tanya yawned. "I'm so tired I could coma…"

The bell eventually rang. As the class made their escape, Ms.

Weiss sprawled her arms across the desk and admitted she was considering sleeping there. Then she reminded us to hand in our assignments on Roman numerals, which was something I knew perfectly well wasn't due until the end of the month.

Outside the classroom wasn't as hot. I made a quick call home to inform Mom that my friends would walk me home (far away from the woods). She didn't sound delighted at the idea, but agreed to it nonetheless. Then the four of us headed to the cafeteria, and bought ourselves some drinks. We sat down at one of the tables, waiting for everybody to go home. Our plan in class that afternoon had formed fairly well, although our brains weren't invested so much: After school we would go to the library when only a sparse few teachers and students were left, and use the laminator to copy a few dozen of Eleanore's invites. Then the next day, we would surreptitiously hand them out to the unpopular students, aka: the ones Eleanore would be mortified to find at her exclusive party.

"Hey, look!" JT said out of nowhere. "There's a cat."

I thought nothing special of it until I turned around. There was a black cat sitting by the opened doors on the other side of the cafeteria, bathed in the afternoon sunlight. It was like it had some sort of vendetta, for it wasn't moving away and its sights were set squarely on us.

"That cat's been stalking me all day," said Greg. "It was outside my house this morning, then it was in the parking lot."

"Maybe it was a different black cat?" said JT in a dumb voice.

"Well, two cats in one day is fine, but two *black* cats?"

"Racist."

Hayley grabbed the eating tray from JT, and threw it like a frisbee at it. Somehow, it missed. It clattered noisily around the cusps of the entrance and eventually settled by the cat's feet, who looked down at it with perfect contentment. JT and Greg laughed at Hayley's poor throwing skills, and she hit the both of them in turn. She grabbed an apple core from the ground and gave it another go, grunting as she hurled it. It missed, yet again. JT decided to have a turn. He waltzed over to the nearest bin, and fished out a mouldy orange. He threw it. Predictably, it missed. He ogled stupidly.

"That is one lucky black cat," he said.

Evidently tired of it all, Hayley heaved herself up from the table. "Alright, let's go before the racoon mariachi band shows up."

In hot anticipation of our arrival a week earlier, Annie had briefed me on the school's library, which I gladly avoided on my first hectic day. Looming ominously above, one of few buildings not painted purple, it lay almost in the exact centre of the school. It had been left there from a time long before the more modern constructions formed around it. Outside the slowly dilapidating walls, we stopped and stared at the wooden entrance that towered above us.

"What've they got in there, T-Rex?"

After a gentle push, the doors opened with a tremendous creak. Inside, it was really just a traditional, run-of-the-mill library that seemed to stretch on longer than the building allowed. We made our way through to the middle section which sported giant work desks that were tidily arranged with encyclopaedias, papers, chained pens, lamps, the odd student, and of course its most loyal compadre, dust. It also seemed to me that noise wasn't permitted in here. Aside from quiet breathing and pages turning, I felt like a single fly buzz would emulate and emanate in on itself until its echo was deafening.

"Air-conditioning!" Hayley put my fears to the test loudly. It was indeed cooler in here. A tyrannical woman, one of the librarians, shushed her rudely from the front.

I couldn't see the laminator anywhere, but I noticed a closed-off seated section near the very back. A sign above read:

'*STUDY AREA* - *DO NOT DISTURB*'.

I nudged JT, and we made our way over. Quite a few people turned to look at us, four or five of which looked stunned. Maybe my new friends had a reputation.

"What are you doing here?" said a man in his forties, as he appeared out of the shadows. He was wearing a suit minus the jacket, and had long brown hair tied back in a ponytail.

Hayley had lost her wits, responding with a guilty swallow.

"I'm just looking... uh, for the, uh, manilator. The laminator."

"Yeah?"

I piped up. "We heard it was being fixed, but we need to use it."

"What for?" the teacher asked, raising his eyebrows.

"School work."

"Show me the work."

"I don't have it... I mean, I... It's for a social thing?"

"Students aren't permitted to use the laminator unless it's for school work."

I thought for a moment in distress, and I quickly grabbed the two passes for the party.

"These are for Eleanore Parker's annual back-to-school gala. I'm supposed to photocopy and laminate, like, one hundred of these before the weekend!" I put on my best Saviour parody, and pretended I was chewing on gum.

The man's attitude immediately changed. Still, there was some doubt left in his eyes. "Oh. You're friends with Miss. Parker. That's right. I saw you with her on Monday. Well, what about these two?"

He pointed at the boys standing behind me. I turned to Greg and JT and thought quickly. I could feel the sweat slowly trickling down my scalp towards my temples. So I flinched, as if I hadn't been aware of their presence. "Are you two stalking me? God, you ask one weirdo for directions and they follow you like a puppy dog. *Thank you, you can go away now.*" I flicked my hand at them to leave, and they walked away in confusion.

"Yeah!" said Hayley, and she grabbed a piece of scrunched up paper from a nearby waste-basket and chucked it at JT.

I turned to the man. "Mr...?"

"Jackson," he said.

"Mr. Jackson," I kept my persona, lips quivering, nerves shot to hell. "Eleanore doesn't usually rely on her friends to do this, as it is a very important job. All I need is one hundred more of these, and to laminate them. Then I can relax, go home, do my homework, have my prayer half-hour, and Eleanore won't bother me again until the party. Can you please help me out? I'm quite stressed." I finished just as the first beads of sweat surfaced. I wiped them away and worked it like an award-winning actress.

Of course, knowing who Eleanore was, and what power she somehow held over this bizarre school, Mr. Jackson was more than willing to help me out. In fact he basically completed the task for me. Hayley and I sat tiredly, googling on one of the free computers, while he waited for the laminator to warm up. I watched out of the corner of my eye as he photocopied one of the passes, four times onto one sheet of pink paper. Then he did it again, and again, and again.

JT and Greg were sitting on some reading couches near the front, checking out books and quietly laughing at what I could only imagine were educational nude pictures. The tyranny lady was scowling at them from her perch by the front desk, preparing to squawk at any moment. Mr. Jackson finally brought over a thick fold-er, which contained all one hundred copies of the invites. He apolo-gised, as the laminator wasn't completely fixed yet, but I didn't care. I logged off the computer and thanked him, then we left in a hurry.

By the time we'd escaped up the nearest hill across the road, all four of us collapsed to the ground and caught our breaths.

"After hours…" Greg muttered by my side.

A car horn beeped, and we hopped off the road.

With that, I said goodbye and we parted ways to walk home.

* * *

Half way up the steep Doowhacky Road, I gazed upon the sky and wiped my forehead of sweat. Good Lord. Living up in the Hills was all well and good if you had a car, but *walking* home was an en-tirely different matter. I didn't notice the black cat until I came with-in a metre of it. I stopped in my tracks, stunned. It was sitting there on the pavement in front of me, as placid as could be. It *had* to be the same cat from the cafeteria.

"Are you following me?" I muttered. After a moment, I rolled my eyes at my own stupidity. "Of course not. You're just a cat."

I moved forward, but it refused to budge.

Maybe it's not real, I thought seriously, noticing it hadn't moved. *Maybe it's a stuffed cat. Eleanore's playing a trick on me.*

I grabbed a handful of dirt and threw it, blanketing its head. It blinked ferociously in disbelief and, when recovered, it hissed at me.

"Hey!" someone called out.

It was Tanya Tanner, and she was in a dark blue four wheel drive stopped across the road. She was on the passenger side, and a chubby man with a moustache sat behind the wheel. I turned back, but the cat was gone.

Feeling awful for throwing dirt at it, I forced a smile at the Sav-iour and said merrily: "Hello!"

"Do you want a lift? I live up in the Hills, too. It's no hassle."

I looked down, thinking. Saviour trap? No, not with an adult there. I shrugged my shoulders and jumped into the back seat, push-ing a dozen shopping bags aside. The AC was on, and I pulled my collar out to let the air in.

"This is my dad, Robert," said Tanya, pointing to the man in the driver's seat. The father shook my hand awkwardly from the front, but didn't say a word. "He's deaf," she told me. I nodded and then wondered if I should attempt sign language. The only sign I knew was for '*I love you*'. That might be inappropriate.

As we drove away, the *Hottest 100* played gently on the radio.

"How are you liking Horn-Horn?"

I pondered. "Oh, you know. I've had good moments and bad."

Tanya turned around in her seat to face me. "It's a pretty weird town, huh? I mean, *you* obviously know that. Especially after that thing… with the… well, y'know. The mayor said once that 'something weird happens every single *second* day in Horn-Horn'. I'd wager she's right, too."

"The horns on the cliff probably cemented its fate."

Tanya tried to keep up. "Oh, with the lightning? I reckon. Well, you know, if you want, I could always show you around the town. There's lots of cool places to go. I *think* we're on a good day today. A non-weird day."

I remembered Principal Parker's talk with me, and how he frowned upon my attempt to keep both friendship groups. "Thank you, that would be nice," I said.

Without a second to spare, she changed the subject. "You're friends with Hayley, huh?" She tried to seem carefree about the question, but my loins were suddenly moist with deep suspicion.

"Yeah…"

"She's hard to get along with. I guess I'm just surprised."

"Once you get to know her, she's okay."

Tanya laughed again, forcefully this time, with a hint of anger. "We've grown up with Hayley. We know exactly how she works."

"We?"

"Don't get me wrong. I don't care. Just…"

She laughed once more, but stopped herself. It was an annoying habit. "Never mind. There are worse things in the world than being friends with her."

"Like being friends with Eleanore?"

I hadn't wanted to say anything offensive given she was kind enough to give me a ride, but her Dad was deaf so I didn't care.

It didn't seem to bother her. She was probably used to people asking why she was sleeping with the devil. The same way John Lennon must have. She smiled so warmly that I suddenly felt bad about myself.

"I know everything's a bit daunting now, but that's only because you're new. Once you get used to this place, you'll like it. Has El... Did Eleanore show you the town when you were friends?" She twirled a strand of hair around her index finger with intrigue.

"Just a little."

"Oh, that's nice," said Tanya. "I've lived here for *years*. Longer than most people in our class."

I was waiting for more, but that seemed to be it. She faced the front and went quiet for the rest of the ride home. I pretended I was very curious with the lines going past on the road, just to make it look like I wasn't bothered. I realised soon enough how silly my feelings were, given silence was something her family was probably used to. Then, as we turned onto Philips Street, she begged a question from me as sheepishly as one could:

"So, um... Did you *really* steal those clothes from Eleanore?"

"What? *No!*" I blurted out. "They *gave* me those clothes. They did, and they know it. You can tell them that if you want."

I crossed my arms.

"No, no, I wasn't asking for that reason," insisted Tanya quickly, reddening. "I was just wondering. I didn't know if you were like Hayley, or if you..."

"It's not like she robs banks and pushes prams down hills. You should give her a chance, she's just like you and me."

Tanya twisted around and grabbed onto the head-rest so she could face me properly. "You may think she's cool, but just be careful because you don't want to end up like her *old* best friend. Hayley did something to her when..." she looked down, "....when she told her that she didn't want to be friends anymore."

Hayley had another female friend besides from me? Of course. She must have. It never even crossed my mind. How silly of me: I'd imagined Hayley had been friends with *only* JT and Greg since they were born. Heck, somewhere inside I'd even imagined they were born all at once, strung together like paper cut-out figures.

"What did she do to her?" I asked.

"She threw her out of the classroom window and dumped a bin on her head."

Of course she did. I could picture Hayley doing it.

The car stopped in my driveway. Before I hopped out, Mr. Tanner turned to face his daughter and spoke in a mumble, his hands moving up and down, from side to side in sign language. I could barely understand him when he said: "Honey, she didn't *throw* you out of the window. She only pushed you."

"Dad, thank you! Stop lip-reading. *Jeez*. Privacy much?"

Amused, I said: "*You* were Hayley's best friend? *You?*"

"You say that like it's so hard to believe..."

"It *is*. No offence, but you are not..."

I stopped myself, realising how little I knew either of them.

"I shouldn't have mentioned it. You should be careful around her, that's all I meant."

"Okay... Thanks."

I said goodbye to the two of them and hopped out, accidentally slamming the door as I did. Heart in my throat, I violently opened it again and retrieved the pink folder I'd placed on the seat.

That would have been bad.

The humidity hit me front on and I squinted down at the dried grass. By the time I got to the frail letterbox, the Tanner car had reversed out of my driveway and was heading off down the road. To my surprise, it pulled into the driveway a few doors down, and the two passengers hopped out. I blinked in confusion, and then it dawned on me. They were Eleanore's other neighbours.

"But of course," I remarked.

16
A WELL-KEPT SECRET

Annie discovered Zag during dinner.

She'd excused herself for a long period of time, and finally as Dad finished his second serving she came back into the dining room, pale as a ghost.

"What on earth took you so long?" asked Mom.

"Probably her wheat diet," said Brendan, with a guffaw.

Usually my sister would have snarked back, but she ate a few more strands of pasta and then told everybody she was going to lie down for a while.

With Zagreus stowed away quietly in my wardrobe, I soon went upstairs myself, feeling rather tense. Things were *too* quiet in here. I ventured into the darkness a few times and called out his name, and each time he would appear out of nowhere to see what was up. But he looked sheepish, like a guilty dog. Finally, I pulled him out one last time and wished to know if Annie had been in my room during dinner. Compelled to spill the beans, he did, and I covered my mouth and sat down on the floor beside him. Damn that girl. She'd been suspicious of me taking food up the night before, and she wanted to know where I'd gotten the clay head from. Eventually she pieced it all together and out came the Child of Crux, blowing my cover and blowing her mind.

"She's fine, trust me," Zag insisted. "I made her inhale some of that nitrous oxide, and it relaxed her. Or knocked her senseless. She's in her room now, probably tripping balls."

When I finally mustered up the courage to knock on Annie's door, I did so quietly. She told me to enter. There she was, putting on a night-mask to help with her acne. Without her glasses on, she squinted at me in the mirror.

"You know," I said.

"Yes, I do. Thanks for telling me."

This was not the reaction I'd been expecting. I chortled to myself, glad that she wasn't pulling out her hair at least.

"My deepest apologies," I said with tremendous sarcasm.

"I suppose you'll want to keep this between us?"

"Obviously. Annie… are we talking about the same thing here?"

Annie turned around to see me better.

"The Child of Crux in the wardrobe. He told me everything."

"Such as…?"

"He's from a planet called Danube and can grant us unlimited wishes. I'm not a simpleton, you know. Besides, I always suspected this sort of stuff was possible. I knew there was most likely life beyond this planet, and now that I know, it doesn't bother me. I don't mean to rub it in, Cassie, but I'm a *lot* smarter than you."

"Annie, you remind me every day."

"I'll admit, I was perturbed at first. Zag showed me what he could do, and I was frightened. But then I got over it."

I stared at her, wondering if she actually *had* lost her mind.

"Sorry if my reaction is strange," she said with a shrug.

I wasn't sure why I was so surprised. Come to think of it, she'd never been normal.

"What about Brendan?"

"Oh, no," I muttered. "We're not telling him. He's eleven."

"I think he would take it really well. Clearly we're not telling Mom and Dad, because I just know they'll spill to *someone*. I don't want us getting kidnapped and tested on by the government. Or worse. *Scientologists.*"

"We're not telling anyone else."

"That's perfectly reasonable. But I have to ask you something now, Cassie. And you're going to get offended, but I want you to think of it in a constructive way. You are about to take care of a child. He may be from another world, but you're his guardian. Do you realise how immense this responsibility is?"

I hadn't given it a great deal of thought, but I wasn't about to let her know that. "Of course I have!"

"Maybe I should become his owner instead. I'm not comfortable with this current arrangement. You're the troglodyte of the family, after all."

"Oh yeah? Well… you're the Sasquatch of the family."

"I'm much smarter than you. I have the ability to gauge situations better. I worry that you haven't quite come to terms with it yet, which is not something to be ashamed of given the immensity of it, but you could become overwhelmed at some point and make a mistake out of fear."

I crossed my arms and checked the hallway. Nobody was there. "Alright, I'm not mad. I promise you I'll sleep on it. But the answer will still be no, Annie. I am not handing him over to you."

Annie stretched and pulled back the covers on her bed. "Think about him, not you. Who we are, what our situation is. You're not mature enough yet, Cassie."

"Oh, bite me," I said, and I slammed the door as I left.

Wow, way to prove her point, I thought.

I'd planned to keep Zag a secret, and it had lasted all of one day.

One day!

Maybe I *wasn't* right for the job after all.

17

AN ONSLAUGHT OF PINK

Morning came far too quickly, of course, but as my head roamed from one pillow to the next in my mission for comfort, my mind set about panic as I realised something I'd forgotten. It jumped so nastily into the front of my brain that it nearly hit my nasal cavity.

"Homework!" I gasped, and I stared up at the ceiling fan.

It was due first thing. I was pressed for time, exhausted, and definitely not in the mood to get into trouble first thing in the morning for not having completed it.

Zag can help, I realised.

I looked up at my Exorcist alarm clock. It was seven-thirty. I hopped out of bed, fretting, and grabbed my duffle bag from the corner of my room. I fished out the pink folder with all of the faux laminated passes to Eleanore's party, and was about to toss them to the side when one of them fell out. It was crinkled and half-torn. Suss, I took a few of them out and glanced them over for the first

123

time. Worried, I tipped the folder upside down and emptied them onto my bed-spread. To my disgust, some of them were only half laminated. Others were so badly done by that they had burn marks on the corners (obviously the laminator was in repair for a reason). A few weren't even in their laminated casings: just clutching onto the corners of the plastic by their tips. What was that Mr. Jackson *think-ing*? What were my friends going to think of me *now*? I thought about how disappointed they were at the destruction of the Vine-yard. After this, they'd probably stop being friends with me.

Curiously, I poked my head into the wardrobe. The clay head sat still between my shoes. *"Pssst!* Zag… Wakey-wakey."

Zag walked into my room from the main door, frightening the life out of me. He had a toothbrush sticking out the side of his foamy mouth. "Hey, I'm up."

I grabbed him and pushed him back into the wardrobe. "Jeez, what are you doing? Don't walk around the house."

He spit into the clay head and threw his toothbrush in for good measure. "Relax, nobody is up yet except for Annie. Plus, I took the liberty of putting a silencer on your mother and father's bedroom door, so they can't hear anything."

"Well… alright. Listen, I need your help. See these pink pass-es? I wish to have one hundred more of them, perfectly laminated." I choked on a wad of golden glitter, but it remained this time, and I wiped some from my mouth.

Zag grinned widely, showing all of his teeth. "There you go."

Despite his words, nothing had happened. I checked the folder again, and I was certain there was nothing new. Then I noticed a strange lump under my bed cover. Suspicious and not in the mood, I swiftly flicked the covers back and was smacked in the face by a rush of pink. I had to close my eyes, and I curled into a ball on the floor as something whooshed all around me, and attacked my body.

"I said one *hundred!*"

The millions of tiny laminated invites were coming out of nowhere so fast and so thick that it spread right across the room and started to fill it up like water. I soon found myself swimming in a pool of Eleanore Parker's laminated party passes.

Zag was nowhere in sight. Keeping my composure, I swam over to the front of the bed and grabbed onto the posts for support. Just in time, too, as Brendan knocked on the closed door from the other side, and called out my name.

"No, Brendan! Don't open it!" I yelled.

Whoosh! again went the sound of propelled paper and plastic. The surge spilled out of my bedroom, knocking Brendan flat. He was quickly spotted bobbing past like driftwood, paralysed in sheer terror.

Something clawed at my right leg. I fished underneath the surface and pulled Zag up to my level. He didn't look surprised.

"Why are you doing this? I wished for one *hundred* invites!"

He put a finger in his ear and scratched inside hurriedly. "What's that? We'll fish for some what?"

"Are you freaking kidding me? I wish you'd clean out your ears!"

More golden glitter filled up my mouth. I spat it out angrily, and wiped it off with one of his sleeves. I watched as two toothbrushes appeared in front of us and shoved themselves deeply into his ear canals. He moaned in discomfort, and when they removed themselves they were covered in thick, yellow wax. They vanished into thin air.

"I wished for one *hundred* invites," I said calmly. "What's this?"

Zag covered his mouth with a hand that emerged from the swirl. "This is one *thundred* invites."

"There's no such number."

"Yes, there is. It's big! Don't worry, I'll sort it."

A moment later the river of invitations disappeared. Brendan and I fell to the ground violently, and Zag somehow levitated where he was near the ceiling for a moment before gently gliding down like a feather. He clapped his hands and pointed back to my bedroom, where the one hundred passes sat innocently on top of my bedspread. "Thy invitations await thee, m'la… Oh, who's this?"

I sat up and rubbed my head. I'd clipped Annie's doorknob on the way down. Brendan sat by Mom and Dad's door, his legs outstretched, his hands covering his groin for some reason. He was staring at Zag, stupefied.

"Want me to smother him with the nitrous oxide?"

"No, please. Let me handle it."

Brendan was staring at Zag, but there was nothing going on behind his eyes. He was catatonic. I wanted to slap some sense into him. What sense would that be, though? The fact that he'd been swept away by an overflowing river of paper in his own house? Not likely there *was* any sense to smack into him.

Locked in her own room during the commotion, Annie finally peaked an eye through a crack in the door. Seeing the three of us on the floor, she rushed out.

"Oh my goodness, what was all of that noise!?"

"It was nothing," I said quickly, shooting my eyes back and forth to my brother. "I didn't see anything, did you, Annie?"

Annie caught on immediately, then cricked her neck. "No, of course not. Brendan, you were just dreaming."

The hallway now had an eerie calmness to it, and Brendan eyed his surroundings in suspicion. At least he was back among the living. I hopped up, grabbed Zag by the shoulders, and marched back into my bedroom. As I shut the door, Zag turned to me with a big grin on his face and said with a chortle: "That was fun!"

"You shouldn't have done that," I muttered, and I went to my chest of drawers to pick out some clean underwear for the day. "You scared my brother half to death. Now what are we going to tell him?"

"I often find it's best to start with the truth," said Zag. "He looks smart enough to handle everything. And if he can't, oh well. Nitrous oxide him until he's okay."

I shook my head. He couldn't seem to empathise with me. Then I realised why. He wasn't human.

"Alright..." said Zag, catching on to my attitude. "You're not even going to thank me for putting everything back to how it was before the pink tsunami?"

I looked around my room, only now noticing it was perfectly half-cleaned, just the way I liked it.

"I've got to get ready for school. Oh..."

I grabbed my duffle bag and shook it at him.

"I wish you'd do my homework while I'm in the shower."

18

MORNING COFFEE

The bus stop, a simple pole by the side of the road, was five houses down from where we lived. Eleanore and her three friends were waiting there, dressed in their best. None of them looked over at us as we stopped nearby to wait. Annie and I carefully muttered this and that about Zagreus Wendig, until finally Eleanore turned to face us.

"What are you ladies talking about?"

I shrugged. "Nothing."

She scowled at me and turned back to face her friends, and they giggled amongst themselves. Annie gave me a mime of her blowing her own brains out.

The bus came not long after, but it didn't stop in time. It smacked noisily into the pole and sent it bending ferociously backwards. For some reason it didn't faze the Saviours. They pushed it back up and hopped onto the bus, resuming their chatter. My sister and I jumped on after them, and Annie handed the female driver a note to say who I was. She was an odd woman. Quite ugly, middle-aged, and she had gigantic shoulders. Like, *huge*. Her long ginger hair was platted fiercely into two segments, and her eyes were wide and possibly crazed.

I stopped by the front and scoped the seats. There weren't many spare. Eleanore and her crones were sitting directly behind the driver's seat, challenging everything a normal high school student was brought up to believe in. On the opposite side of the bus, in the other front seat, sat a very tall woman in white. She dwarfed Ms. Berry, who sat by her side. It was so weird seeing teachers on the bus, almost as if they were trying to spoil our fun or something.

"Good morning, Cassie," Ms. Berry said to me.

"Good morning. How are you, Ms. Berry?"

For a moment the chatter around me ground to a halt.

"I'm good, thank you," she said sweetly.

The chatter resumed, and I went and sat next to Annie halfway down the rows. We arrived at school twenty minutes before class was due to start, and I avoided the Saviours by walking the long way around to get to B Block. Halfway across the Teacher's Parking Lot, Ms. Weiss almost ran me over in her red convertible as she zoomed into the parking space I was crossing. I tumbled backwards, but didn't fall to the ground. I watched as she put her car into neutral, and pulled up the handbrake. She was wearing funky sunglasses, and was talking on her car phone.

"So sorry, Cassie," she said briefly, then continued to the person on the other line. "Genevieve, you jest. What do you mean, it's not only for children? It's hosted by a child. Really? Well in that case, I'm there. Good. I'll pick you up at the Old Folks Home at seven-thirty." Ms. Weiss had half a dozen miniature garden gnomes propped up on her dashboard, most likely held on by blue-tack.

I went on my way, curious as to what I'd heard Ms. Weiss say on the phone. Was she referring to Eleanore's party? How odd. *Teachers* excited about *parties*, and riding *buses* to school. It was all very strange. I was almost tempted to search the mulch in the nearby garden bed for an earthworm chasing a robin.

In my classroom, I shoved my duffle bag inside my desk, lost in deep thought. Out in the quiet hallway, I bumped into Hayley near her locker.

"Listen," she pulled me into the nearest corner. "I think that Mr. Jackson squealed. I've been hearing things through the grape..." She closed her eyes for a moment, composed herself, and continued,

"... *around*, about a mysterious new Saviour who's putting in favours. It's going to lead back to you eventually. Plus, Eleanore is bound to find out sooner or later, if she hasn't already. Oh yeah." She thumped the locker next to us with her fist and it sprung open. "This is yours. Now you're next to me. I bribed the kid who used to have it. Or threatened him. Well, anyway, he was a ginger so he did what I said."

"Thanks," I muttered, noticing some of my books were already in there. How had she...? "I'll get my stuff to put in it."

I walked into the deserted classroom on my own once more, and reached my desk. I pulled my duffle bag out. I noticed right away that it was covered in weird blue slime. I wiped some of it onto the sides of my jeans, wondering if it was the same blue goo that I'd spotted in the woods the other day. My stomach tightened, and when a dab of the slime dropped onto the desk from above, curiosity got the better of me and I looked up. I nearly screamed at what I saw. A fuchsia, slime-covered *thing* shaped like a half-melted ice-cream was rolling around on the ceiling quite merrily. It had four tentacles sticking out of its sloshy torso, and two of them were dangling down towards me.

I shrunk under my desk in grief.

"Hello. I'm looking for Zag," it said.

The disgust stuck in my throat. I looked up, unsure of what to make of it. It was, for all intents and purposes, a *monster*. It had funny little black dots for eyes, like a shrimp's, and blunt little yellow teeth in its wide, red mouth. Its voice was gurgled and gravelly at the same time.

"Zag, please?"

I shivered in disgust. I could barely talk, but knew I had to. I also knew that somebody was bound to walk in at any second, so I'd have to hurry. "He – he's not here. Do you want to leave a message?" My knees were wobbling so much that I knew it was best if I sat down in my seat.

"No, that's alright," the creature said, seemingly tired. "You *are* his new caretaker, aren't you?"

"Uh-huh," I said, my mouth loosely open. "But I just met him."

"Good," the monster dropped down to the ground and stood next to me. He really wasn't very tall, just wide with his tentacles. "We don't want too many people knowing where he is. My name is Coffee, by the way. Like the prisoner, only spelled different. I was a companion of Zag's a long while ago. He and I keep in touch from time to time. I knew his uncle, before she ate herself." He jumped back up to the ceiling with a large splat.

I nodded and smiled to be polite.

"I need to tell him something, and it's of extreme importance," he said, sloshing about in a pace above. "When can I see him? *Where* can I see him?"

Close to the edge of insanity, I was also rightly paranoid.

"He's on a trip somewhere," I lied. "Not too far away. Some business, you see. I could tell him you called."

"You tell him from me to watch out."

"Why?"

"His last owner has come to this planet. She wants him back."

"Oh?"

"Word is she's on the hunt. Awful things happened after she sent him away. She abandoned her Kingdom. Zag is quite a bit of trouble, you know. Not worth keeping around if I were you. He told you he's a... *Child of Crux*... didn't he?"

"Yes."

"Bad sort, those ones. Cursed. You'll probably end up dead soon. I wouldn't... Well, you'll see. Keep your head down. You don't want *her* finding you, that's for sure."

"Oh, okay," I said politely. "Thank you for letting me know."

"Tell you what. I'm feeling generous. You seem like a dandy sort of creature. I can look after the clay head if you want. To throw her off your track. Just to hold onto until things blow over." He glanced around the classroom, then eyed my desk rather curiously.

"Oh. I don't have the clay head *on* me," I told him.

"You don't? Where is it?"

I looked down at my bag, and the blue slime covering it. "It was you. Wasn't it? You left this blue goo in the woods the other day. You were looking for Zag. And just now... You were looking in my bag before I got here. You were looking for the clay head."

He stuck his tongue out, and spittled. "That's preposterous!"

"You *were*. You're not a friend of Zag's. You just want to be his owner. It'll happen over my dead bod—" My voiced petered out like a stalled engine. I cursed myself for giving him the idea.

The creature named Coffee frowned. His body darkened to a deep ocean blue, and his teeth appeared to grow larger, thicker. He wriggled to-and-fro on the spot above me. "Stupid. Humans are always *stupid*. You tell him what I told you, stupid human. That part, at least, is true. His last owner *is* looking for him."

"Fine."

"And we never met."

"Fine," I repeated myself.

"Good luck, Cassandra Gellar the First. I must leave now. I can hear your teacher coming down the hallway, and your friend is planning on beating her to class to show her up."

I nodded at him and then he twirled around with as much might as his tentacles could allow, and suctioned himself again to the ceiling. With that, a tremendous but silent array of yellow sparks lit up the ceiling. They quickly fizzled out, showing he'd vanished.

Dazed by my encounter, I waved lazily, staring into thin air.

"Bye..."

Hayley was at the door. "What?"

I pretended to arrange the contents in my desk. "Uh, I meant to say *hi*. I got mixed up." I waved to her and laughed. "Hi!"

Hayley looked at me oddly for a moment. "Why are you sitting in your seat? Class hasn't started yet."

"I... I guess I'm a nerd!"

She came over and dabbed at the surrounding goo. "What the hell is this sh–"

"It's not nice to swear, dear," Ms. Weiss walked into the room.

"Oh, good morning, Ms. Weiss," said Hayley aggressively. "How nice of you to join us. I see that I am earlier than you today."

Weiss dumped her bag on her desk. "That's nice, dear. Now out, you two. Class hasn't started, and I need to do some... personal stuff before we begin." She had a large paper bag tucked under her right arm. When she sat down and placed it on the ground, the contents inside clinked around. So I assumed our teacher here was not only a sex artist, but also an alcoholic. How nice.

"Ms. Weiss is such a hypocrite," Hayley muttered as we left the classroom. "You should have heard her when I accidentally knocked over a gnome in her garden last year. Forget cursing up a black storm. She was cursing up a black *tsunami*."

I hadn't been paying attention, but I caught up. "Oh. Well, people get wrong impressions of others all the time." I thought about what Tanya had told me on the drive home yesterday. How Hayley cracked it and threw her out of the window. As we rummaged in our lockers, I think my ruffian friend could tell I was sizing her up, and she kept huffing in disapproval. I smiled at her finally and pretended everything was fine, even though it wasn't. I was beginning to realise that Tanya was right. I didn't know Hayley at all, not really. I didn't know anybody in this town.

19

LESLEY AND ERIC, TRANSFORMED

The office was grimly neat. The blinds were half-drawn. The desert surrounding the uncared for playground sat beyond the large windows. The sound of a gentle wind whistled above in the vents. Eric Parker sat with Ms. Berry and Ursula. He sat back for a moment, eclipsed.

"Well, this is awkward," he said, and he stood up to skirt about them. "I'm afraid Horn-Horn High-High has already invested in a school counsellor."

"Who is this invader?" said Ursula furiously, with little care for her stature. "I will hunt him down and make loaves out of his elbow skin."

Parker strangely thought her words to be harmless. "Her name is Dr. Lesley Gellar. She is a well-regarded psychologist from Salem. Very smart. Really we're quite lucky to have her. Moved in next-door to me with her family, actually. She'll be a part-timer, of course. Just while we sort out our finances for the remaining year. She will be working at the Horn-Horn Looney Bin come this October, but I'm not looking at hiring anyone new until I see her work in practice."

"Gellar. Is that Cassie Gellar's mother?" said Berry.

"Yes," said Parker. "I'm ashamed to admit it, but Cassie's case has brought to light our underlying neglect for student mental welfare."

"Is it legal to have your own daughter as a patient?"

"Honestly, I don't know. Honestly, the board doesn't care. This whole matter with Cassie has been a bit of a burden on our clean slate as a school. We haven't had a death here since 1991."

"Nobody died this week," Bev assured them, laughing grimly at the absurdity of his comment. "Principal Parker, consider it a personal favour to me, will you? Just look over Dame Hermione's credentials, that's all I ask."

Eric stopped and looked on. "Dame, you say?"

"That's right."

"And you have decent credentials?"

Ursula nodded assuredly. "*Credentials* of credentials."

"Perhaps if the board sees you hiring two psychologists for the school, they will lessen their death-grip a little," said Bev carefully. "Dame Purplewink here has *assured* me that she has worked many years with children, as *well* as adults. The perfect blend for a high school. Not to mention if any teachers might need to talk to someone. She even took care of the royals. I mean…" She laughed again, showing her snaggleteeth. "The *royals*, Eric…"

Ursula could see the man was weakening with every persuasive comment. She took the reins with fierce determination. "Look. Parker. Ignore all that. This Gellar woman. She's not right for the part. Already committed to her job at the Looney Bin. Me? I work alone. I stand alone. I tackle each student individually and manage the best way to sort them out. How many therapists have you heard say that?"

"Eight. All previously having worked here."

"Oh goody. The point is, Principal Parker, I understand students. I know what goes on inside their swollen, egotistical heads. I know what they think, I know what they feel, and I feel that you will benefit from my being here because you know I am not working anywhere else."

"Yes, why is that? Is it because of the economy?"

Ursula frowned at the seemingly obvious question. "No. Because I am a *Dame*."

Parker sat back down. "I'm sorry. First off, I've only just met you. I can't simply take Bev Berry's word on it. I need proof of your place of birth, your working with children checks, your history; your resume would also be useful... And all that takes time. I need someone to work immediately. That is why Dr. Gellar is best suited for this position."

Ursula gazed intently at him, head down, eyes up. For the first time, he sensed something disturbing about her. An unnatural inhibition. He felt like she wanted his power. A coldness ran through him, and he shuddered just as the door opened. It was only the janitor, an old man with a grey moustache, who wanted to know where the nearest storage room was.

"Ah, Oakley. I'll show you in a moment," said Eric, and he stood up. "I'm very sorry, Dame Hermione Purplenurple... urple..." He shook her hand. "I'm afraid we can't help you today. Sorry, Bev."

Ms. Berry shook her head in carefree dismissal, and checked her watch. "I've got to be in the gym in five minutes. Hermione..."

Ursula smiled. "I understand. I'll let myself out. See you at home. And goodbye, Mr. Parker."

Eric Parker guided her to the hallway, and he ran off with Oakley the janitor. As everybody else appeared to be rushing off to attend to something, Ursula took her chance and snuck back into the office. She went around his desk to the filing cabinet, and searched through the folders inside as quickly as her magic would allow. The folder of Dr. Lesley Gellar appeared, and she opened it, checking her photo immediately. The blonde woman seemed vaguely familiar to her, but she couldn't place her. It didn't matter really, because now she knew who to mimic later.

Outside in the hallway, none of the passing students seemed to notice as the Principal walked out of his office for the second time in as many minutes. Nobody realised that there were now two Eric Parkers walking down the halls. The one Dr. Lesley Gellar bumped into as she made her way to see him was, in fact, not the real one.

"Oh, Eric! Hello, there you are," she said, laughing. She was dressed up and had lipstick on, with pearls strung around her neck, and sported a work-bag under her shoulder. "Sorry I'm late. I had to drop my youngest off at school on the other side of town and the traffic would not let up."

Ursula smiled her Eric Parker smile. "Lesley, how good to see you. I'm afraid there's been a change of plans."

"Oh?"

"Yes, you see, when we hired you, it was because our previous psychiatric associate quit unexpectedly. A lovely Dame of a woman, you might have read about her in the newspapers. She was used to travelling for her sick child, and needed to leave immediately."

"Oh, how awful."

"Well, not really. The son has made a full recovery so she is returning today to fill her post. Unfortunately, we won't be requiring your efforts any more. But we would like to thank you very much for all of your concerns, and hope that we can count on you for any future... uh... substitutionary... assistance..."

"Am I fired?" Mom stood in the hallway and put a hand on her hip as she tried to understand.

Ursula collected her wits and wiped her head of sweat. For a moment she was violently alarmed, until remembering that Parker was actually quite bald on top. "What I mean is, if it were up to me, I would be all over it. You're a fantastic resource to this school, but the board is quite bothered when it comes to this Dame Hermione. I think it comes down to her donating a certain amount to the school each year."

"Oh, I see..." said Mom, fiddling sadly with her handbag.

"So sorry, once again," said Ursula, and she tried to get Parker's tone down-pat. "I'll see you at parent teacher interviews, or at the Looney Bin? My wife works there, you know!"

The fake Parker led Mom down the hallway and out into the sun, where 'he' bid her farewell towards the parking lot. A moment later, out of sight, Ursula's take on Parker ended and she transformed back into herself in the safety of the shadows outside the library.

She immediately transformed again, this time into the figure of the woman she'd just fired. And it was just in time.

"Mom, what are you doing here?" said Annie, and she grabbed her arm as her class walked by to go to the library.

Ursula panicked. "Let go of me, you blistering freak!"

Annie pouted sadly and touched the acne on her cheeks.

"What I mean is, I have to go. I was, I am, I mean I..."

She shrugged out of her apparent daughter's grasp and fled dramatically. Now she was paranoid. How many other rotten miniature human beings did her doppelgänger have roaming these schoolyards? Suddenly every person who passed her didn't seem so hellbent on reaching their classroom on time. They seemed more fixed on staring her down, as if they knew her, as if they were her child waiting for her to say 'hello, sweetie', or 'get to class, sweetie'. To roam on the cautious side, she gave some students a ferocious: *"Get to class!"* just for good measure.

When Ursula reached Parker's office once more, she could see through the blinds on the door that he'd returned, flicking through papers on his desk. She had prepared what to say before her encounter with the daughter, but now she was fed up and just wanted the plan to work, so as she pushed her way into the room she said efficiently:

"Eric! It's Lesley Gellar. Good to see you. I'm afraid I have to quit. Other responsibilities. Can't have my own daughter as a client. You understand. Please don't ever bring this up again. Goodbye!"

With that, she left the office. Running for the hills in exhaustion, shedding her plump faux-figure on the way.

20
SHIPS
PASSING

After a devastatingly tedious morning, where I sat lifeless like a whale carcass and thought only of the boy locked in my wardrobe, the bell rang for lunch and everybody stood up. That was, of course, until Eleanore ran to the front and shouted politely for us to sit back down again.

"Fellow classmates," the queen said, smiling like an innocent child. "As some of you know, my Annual School-Semester-Opener-Gala is this Saturday night. Addressing those of you with invitations only, I am expecting you to bring along any delicacies you might consider worthy for such a party. Think punches, crab cakes, loin of venison en croute, spotted dick, caramelised blood oranges... Not that I'm suggesting!" She laughed falsely and flicked her hair back, which highly suggested she was.

"Oh yeah," JT whispered in my ear. "I'll bring some punches and loins... I don't think I have a spotted dick, though."

Easily amused, I grinned with my hand over my mouth.

"...Or any other fine delicacies you have lying around your large and expensive homes..." Eleanore eyed JT. "Thank you so much, and see you there!" She smiled and twisted her arms around very cutely.

Hayley put her hand up. Eleanore tried to ignore her, but then muttered: "Go ahead."

"Why are you telling us this now? It's Thursday."

"It's called heads up, duh."

"The term is bottoms up, cheers!"

Hayley, JT, Greg and I walked around really slowly that lunchtime, heading towards a large pole in the back lot for shade. It didn't really do the trick, except for Hayley's eyes, as that was all it covered from the harsh sun. We didn't have anywhere else to go, thanks to Eleanore and her Vineyard revenge.

"This is so lame," Hayley muttered, lying down on JT's jacket to avoid getting covered in the weird red dirt surrounding us. She sat up and squinted off into the distance. "Look at the sniper over there, watching us from her vantage point. This is exactly what she wanted all along. Us sitting in dirt."

I looked over as I opened my packed lunch, and noticed Eleanore, Wednesday, Friday and Tanya sitting on the lower branches of a very large oak tree near a drinking fountain. They were covered by the beautiful shade of one of the only decent trees around. Somehow, the grass under it was a luminous green. Almost vicious to the eyes. It sat like a mirage.

"Ah well, wait until Saturday," I snickered.

A strange whooshing sound came from nearby and then a beautiful shadow cast over the sky. I looked up to find a very, *very* tall woman looming over me, smiling and holding her hands out. She was dressed all in white. I wondered if I'd passed out from the heat.

"Cassie?" she said.

I sat up, paranoid after this morning's visitor, and wiped my butt of red dirt.

"I'm Ms. Purplewink. Come with me to the Principal's office."

I recognised her from the bus ride that morning.

"Am I in trouble?" I asked.

"No, of course not. You're my trial run."

"*Ms. Purplewink?*" said Hayley obnoxiously, trying not to laugh. "That's your real name?"

"Yes," Ursula lied.

"But you're not from around here."

"No."

"Are you an illegal alien?" asked JT.

"Yes," Ursula chortled.

I walked with her around the side of the school to get to Principal Parker's office. In that time, she told me about herself. She was the new school counsellor from far away, and thought she'd acquaint herself with the students who were listed for future sessions with her. This made sense, since Parker informed me of my impending mandatory obligations.

"I thought my mother was the new counsellor."

"No, not at the moment," Ms. Purplewink said serenely. She sounded like her vocal cords had been doused in Bio-Oil. "I thought you might appreciate attending these during the obscurity of lunch hour when nobody notices."

"I don't really need counselling, though," I said.

"I know, I know," said Ursula. But in fact, she didn't know. She didn't know who I was, and why I was here. When Principal Parker had called her back into his office to give her the job earlier that morning, she paid little attention to him as she sat there. Her mind was conjuring spells across the country so that when the right person looked up *Dame Hermione Purplewink*, they would find the appropriate papers on her. She knew little to nothing about me, other than the fact I was Lesley Gellar's daughter. In turn, at the time, I knew absolutely nothing about her, except that she was close to seven feet tall.

"I hear you're new in town?"

We passed by my block and I stared longingly into my empty classroom. "Yes."

"I'm new myself. I've come to reclaim my position, so to speak."

"At the school?"

"No, well, but... Yes. It's a long story. You wouldn't believe me."

"Try me," I muttered.

Into the Principal's office we went, the door shutting us off from the noises of the outside world. Ursula told me to sit down in one of the comfortable armchairs in the corner, and she soon joined me after venturing in Parker's desk for a box of tissues. I declined politely to take one.

"So," she said.

I kept straight.

"Cassie, have you ever asked yourself, who am I?"

I thought for a moment. "No. I mean, maybe. Yes, have you?"

"Oh my yes, dozens of times. But what I want to know is, what makes you, *you?*"

I let out a laugh, one that I'd tried to hide, but it was just too funny to pass up. Once it flowed out of me I couldn't pretend it hadn't happened. "Sorry. That sounds like a clichéd question on a sheet of paper."

Ursula panicked. This was exactly the case, only she'd used Berry's computer the previous night to look up questions to ask, and how to tackle the answers. This was rudimentary thinking, she realised.

Calm yourself, woman, she thought. *Just talk with each student that walks through that door until you find out which one stole your Child of Crux. It doesn't matter how authentic you are. Then, everything will piece together like the world's most complicated jigsaw puzzle after being blown up in a silo explosion.*

She giggled to herself at the idea, then restored her Dame-like posture and glanced down at the papers on her lap. "Cassie. What's got you so down?"

I shrugged, certain I was turning red. "I don't know. Stuff. You should know. You were a teenager once, right?"

"Apparently."

We both knew why I was here. Things weren't about to get easier if I kept my feelings on the moose subject truncated. I took a quiet breath and said: "It wasn't a major thing, right? I mean, I'm over it. I don't care, anyway. I don't even remember it. I'm fine now."

Ursula nodded, sucked in her lips, and tried to resist the urge to recheck the papers.

"Let's face it. If anybody needs counselling, it's my sister. She was awake the whole time."

Ursula searched rabidly. *Good grief, what is her major trauma?*

Suddenly, a different bell rang. It was one I'd never heard before. It sounded like a siren.

"What's that?" I said.

Ursula looked up, distracted, and tilted her head to one side to listen better. "Fire alarm?… Oh, that's not good."

We stood up, and I left without another word. I slowly made my way down the hall, following the crowd. Everybody from the nearby cafeteria was being guided out by loud, demanding and stern teachers. I ran as fast as I could for the back lot and spotted my friends almost exactly where I'd left them. They were trundling towards the giant oak tree now, as were most students. Mr. Jackson was guiding a lot of nearby students there. It was a safe spot. I kept my head down as I passed him, and he didn't seem to notice me.

"What's going on?" I asked JT upon reaching him.

No one replied.

Eleanore and her friends looked absolutely livid as we sat below them. Friday tipped her black sunglasses and looked down at us. Eleanore purposely dropped a straw from a milk drink she had in her hands, and it landed on Greg's head. He picked it up and flicked it at her.

"Why on earth must this tree be a safe haven during a fire?" sighed Wednesday.

"Because it's so green and *moist*," said JT.

"Don't speak to us, you mealy-mouthed pheasants."

"Hey, you're the ones clucking in a tree."

The landscape was like a scene from a zombie movie. Brainless students, all of them, and their tired heat-worn teachers were slowly heading our way. They looked as impressed as we were.

"What's going on?" I asked again.

Eleanore sighed above me, and I looked up. Clearly she'd heard me the first time. Now she was kind enough to point at the sky beyond the many green oak leaves. I followed her direction and noticed smoke amidst the endless blue.

"They're *he-ere*," Friday sang sombrely.

I felt the unease all around me. Ms. Weiss was running towards us, wearing a strange white and tight uniform. It was like an Olympian's body suit that tucked every bit of her body in, and covered all but her hands, feet and face. Even her hair was tucked away under a hood which was tight like a swimming cap. She looked remarkably like a deformed sperm. "Don't worry!" she was screaming to students. "It's alright! The fires aren't here yet! Nobody turn irrational, and we'll be fine!" She grabbed a girl who was texting from her phone and shook her. "Stop it, you stupid girl!"

When she turned to face us, she was met with little eye contact.

"Ms. Weiss," I dared. "What's going to happen?"

"Oh, I imagine it'll burn things, a couple of horses, and—"

"No, I mean, with us. We can't just stay under this tree."

"Well, dear, I suggest it's time you face the obvious. I imagine you'll get to go home."

I was struck by her rudeness. Everyone else who heard started to cheer. Eleanore, on the other hand, found it all rather distasteful.

"Children," she snarled at us.

She lost her balance and fell, landing on the soft grass below.

"Ow! Ms. Weiss, I broke a nail!"

"Oh, you poor girl. Let me get my broken nail kit."

All the students and all the faculty were surrounding the tree now. Nearby onlookers would suspect a religious undertone to what they saw. Eventually, Principal Parker emerged. He stood on the roof of the nearest building, which was a rather creative art room. The roof was tilted instead of straight, so he struggled to stay on top.

"People!" he cried, clutching a red mega-phone. "Students, teachers, workers, disadvantaged apprentices. Stay calm. We've gotten note that the out-of-control fires are heading straight for Horn-Horn. The Horn-Horn Fire Brigade are doing everything they can to control it."

"Way to state the obvious," Hayley muttered.

The library woman behind the tree shushed at her.

"So, we've made a plan," Parker said. "For the safety of our students, we have decided to let you all go home. In an orderly fashion, of course… *STARTING NOW!!!*"

He jumped off the roof and landed in some bushes. Many students started running away. We stayed where we were, stunned.

Ms. Weiss tossed her head to look here and there.

"This is highly unorthodox. My word, children! Didn't you learn anything in the first grade? Don't run in school!" She turned to us and stretched, cracking her back as she did. "I bought this fireproof uniform down at the Horn-Horn Mall II. I suggest you all do the same and *run like the wind!*"

She jumped over my head like a hurdle, and darted for her car. She was pretty flexible for an ageing lady. As she sped away in her snazzy little convertible, I noticed one of her beloved gnomes slide off the dash board and land on the pavement nearby. I quickly ran to pick it up, and waved for her to come back. She saw me in her rearview mirror and promptly gave me a hearty wave in return, misunderstanding.

Tired of how many strange things were plaguing me of late, I walked back to my friends miserably, and placed the gnome on the grass. Above me I noticed Tanya, perched high up in the tree with the other Saviours. She was calmly reading *To Kill A Mockingbird* by Harper Lee. One of my favourites.

"My party..." sobbed Eleanore, nursing her sore arm. She hadn't bothered to climb back up. She was on our level for once.

"It's not 'til Saturday," Friday assured her.

"There's no way in hell I am cancelling it just because of bush-fires. I'll stand on my roof and wee at it if I have to!"

Hayley snorted. "Please send out invites if you do."

"This is no laughing matter, you fool! My party is a time hon-oured tradition, passed down from generation to generation!"

"From tadpole to tadpole," muttered JT.

"This is all your fault!" Eleanore snapped at me. "I *know* you wanted my party to be cancelled, deep down."

I waited. "And?"

"Well... you come from Salem. So... you must have some eerie witch powers. You've probably put a curse on me!"

Friday and Wednesday screamed and fell from the tree.

"Eleanore, please," said Tanya quietly, still reading. "Don't you think you're getting a little bit carried away?"

"No-I-*don't!*" Eleanore said each word on its own. "Stop being so judicious. Ever since you started reading that book, you've been all icky and nice."

Tanya faced her for a moment.

"Seriously? Cassie does not have any cosmical powers in her, or around her, so stop being so paranoid." She closed the book and hopped out of the tree. "I'm going home to watch some television and to pack some things up, just in case."

Greg and JT checked their watches.

"We'd better go home too," they said together.

We parted ways, being some of the last people to leave the schoolyard. The bus wasn't back from its day trips yet, as it was only lunchtime. I was quite happy that the day had wrapped up early, be-cause I definitely needed a break. Plus, the weekend was just that little bit too far away. Hayley and I walked away together as JT and Greg headed off on their own. Hayley wanted to come round to mine because, as she told me, that's what friends do. She failed to mention any future trips to her house, though.

To our great surprise, the counsellor I'd just met with came riding around the corner on a horse-and-carriage. She smiled down at us from her seat on top of the carriage, reins in her hands. Her horse was of a pleasing light-brown colour, almost caramel, and Hayley immediately went to stroke its head. "This isn't weird at all," she said, glancing up at the woman.

"Cassie, I'm so sorry our conversation was cut short, but I think I ought to drive you home, given the circumstances! And you too, child…"

Something about the way she looked at Hayley sat strangely with me. Still, she was the school counsellor, psychiatrist, therapist, whatever. She couldn't be that bad. It wasn't like I was taking a ride with a stranger.

We opened the door to the carriage and hopped inside. Hayley immediately sniffed the air and made a disgusted sound. I pushed open the window and said thank-you to Dame Purplewink above. Then, I told her my street address.

Something thumped against the door, startling me half to death. It was Tanya, and she looked exhausted.

"Cassie, can you go to my place? I live on the other side of Eleanore. It's important." She was glancing over her shoulder every few seconds. "Really important."

"Okay."

She looked at Hayley. "You can come too if you want."

Hayley humphed in mild approval. It seemed Tanya suddenly became very aware of how odd it was that we were in a carriage. She looked up at Dame Purplewink, and then ran off, keeping her eyes peeled like a paranoid schizophrenic. With that, the horse pepped up and began lazily trotting out of the school grounds.

The carriage was a very old one at that. Its interior was definitely influenced by the late eighteen-hundreds, at least. The walls were padded with purple silk, and the cushiony seats felt like real brown leather. To add to the ancient feel, resting in front of us was a wooden walking cane with an orange diamond-knob. Did Dame Purplewink need this? She hadn't been using it for support on her long journey through the school-grounds to fetch me.

"This is better than sitting in red dirt," said Hayley happily.

I looked out of the window as we went up one of the rising nearby hills alongside the woods. The sky was slowly filling up with smoke.

"What an odd thing Tanya said before," my friend remarked. "I wonder why she wants you to go to her house? Are you guys friends or something?"

I turned at last and she eyed me, waiting for me to slip up. I didn't say anything, yet somehow this answered for me. Her jaw dropped and she whacked my arm.

"You know what happened. I knew it."

I whacked her back. "So what? Big deal. Who cares?" I'd watched too many episodes of *The View* during summer break. "Does it really matter?"

"You can bet your brother's left nut it matters," said Hayley angrily. "I can't believe you talked behind my back like that. And with her, of all people! I would rather you do that with Eleanore than with her. *Anyone* but Tanya."

"I don't know the full story. She told me one small thing and that was it, okay?" I retaliated spitefully, and I went red at the confrontation. "Besides, she wasn't ragging on you that much."

"You know she likes to rag. I know you know she likes to rag, so don't pretend you don't! And what was with that whole inviting me over thing? Like I could avoid it at this point. Thanks a lot."

"She lives a few houses down from me."

"I know that! I've been there before, *as you well know*."

We sat there in silence; it was a fairly awkward ride because of it. Thankfully it wasn't a very long one.

"How are you going to get home later?" I finally ventured.

"I was hoping your parents would drop me off, but now I'm not so sure I want to ask!"

I'd have to put my bag in my room before I went over to Tanya's, but that meant Hayley would still have to come in. So when the carriage turned into my driveway and drove all the way through the oaks, down the winding path and parked itself right outside my front door, I whispered in my quietest voice: *I wish to keep Zag locked in the wardrobe, just in case.*

The overwhelming need to sneeze made its debut, and with the release came an alarmingly substantial amount of golden glitter, shooting from my mouth and nose. It nearly suffocated me, spraying across the front window of the carriage, narrowly missing that expensive looking walking cane. It was force enough to cause the cane to jump to-and-fro for a second, as if it had a mind of its own and was excited by what had happened.

"You're a freak," said Hayley.

I hopped out of the carriage and waited for her to exit before I shut the door. I looked up at my counsellor. "Thank you, Ms. Purplewink. We really appreciate the ride."

Dame Purplewink looked up at my house serenely. After a moment, Hayley waved her arms and said: *'Helloooo'*; the woman on the horse-and-cart quickly collected herself.

"Not a problem. I couldn't leave you two stranded at the school alone when you've clearly got a lot of emergency planning to do."

Hayley snickered. "Right."

Ms. Purplewink waited for a clearer explanation.

"I don't live here," said Hayley.

"Oh, I thought you two were sisters?"

"No, this is my friend Hayley," I said.

Ms. Purplewink bit her lip. "Sorry, I thought you had a sister."

"I do."

"Oh. She's blonde as well. You have the same hair."

Hayley frowned. I couldn't tell if she was offended or not.

"You two go inside, and call your parents immediately."

Hayley pushed me towards the front door. "No point. My mother is passed out at the kitchen table. My father is long gone, and my step-father is only thirteen years older than me, and he's a fireman at the moment so he can't come get me."

"If ever there was an excuse," said the Dame. She snapped the reins in her hands and the horse became alert. It whinnied quietly at the disturbance, and started to trot down the driveway again.

We entered the house. Nobody else was home yet.

"I didn't know your step-father was a fireman."

"He's not," said Hayley, and she kicked off her shoes.

"But you said..."

"That was just a white lie. He isn't *technically* a fireman, but right now, he *is* a fireman."

"Oh..." I said slowly, possibly catching on. "Volunteer?"

"No, he gets paid."

"Part-time?"

"What?"

"Part-time."

"What are you *talking* about?"

"I don't think I know anymore."

"He dresses up as a fireman, for money. You figure it out."

I stood there, thinking.

"*God,* he's a *stripper,* alright?"

I focused on the drink I was making, and blushed.

After that, I went and showed her my room, eyeing the shut wardrobe intensely. As she checked out all of my flash gizmos, she grew increasingly amazed.

"You're so rich," she laughed deeply. Suddenly, she frowned. "Why aren't you a snot-face like the rest of them?"

"I don't have a car," I said enthusiastically for the first time. "Or a credit card! What you see in this room is all I have."

"Oh, boo-hoo, poor baby," said Hayley. "Because, you know, what you've got here isn't a lot or anything." She tinkled on my tiny electric piano in the corner. "I have the weirdest memory of being in this house when I was tiny. We didn't live in Horn-Horn back then, but we came here a lot since my mother's family lives here. And we came to this house because the owners were friends of my mother's gypsy hairdresser, and she invited us with her to a party here, and I remember being in the foyer near the door, where they had this *huge* grand piano... and I hit a few of the keys. Isn't it funny how you remember little things like that?"

"Here, here? As in, *here?*"

"Yes. And I see you're taking on the town's habit of repeating everything twice."

"Who were the owners?"

"Then? No idea." She brushed past me. "It was seriously back in the eighties. I need to pee." She turned without fault and went into the bathroom. It seemed like she knew this place better than I did.

I sat fidgeting on the end of my bed as I waited for her to finish. After quite a long time, I became curious and knocked on the bathroom door. There was no sound, and when I checked, no soul inside. Intrigued, I searched the house for her and found her in the foyer downstairs, sitting delicately at our own grand piano.

"There you are. Do you play, Hayley?"

"My dad used to teach me," she muttered.

"So play me something."

Hayley started playing the right-hand side of *Good King Wenceslas*. When she finally stopped, I clapped to be polite and forced a smile. I wasn't that good of an actor, so she turned a bit sour.

"My dad left when I was five, alright? Jeez. Look, I'll try again. Better this time."

I sat by her side as she played with great difficulty, and for a moment I watched her fingers point with unfamiliarity and strike the ivory. Finally, I moved to her other side and joined in with the left hand of *Good King Wenceslas*. The corners of her mouth hooked upwards in a grateful smile, and she bumped my shoulder.

So this is friendship, I thought to myself.

21
THE OTHER SIDE
OF ELEANORE

Once we were well-refreshed, we left my house and walked down the sidewalk until we got to Tanya's property. Instead of dozens of oak trees cluttering up the front garden like ours, they had a huge array of giant hedges and conifers, and some dark kind of tree lush with foliage that also sported little red berries. They hid the house from street view. We walked down the driveway, past those initial trees, and were greeted with their home in front of us: a giant red brick house with freshly painted white windows and doors, with an equally white gazebo sitting to the left-hand side. It was a double storey just like mine, but was not of the French persuasion when it came to design. Nonetheless, it was a gorgeous property and stretched all the way back to a lake. The roof towered perhaps too far above, almost making it seem like it was in fact a triple storey without any windows to see out of. The chimney sat even higher still, where the antenna claimed top prize by positioning itself quaintly near one of the cowls.

"Hasn't changed," muttered Hayley, and we walked up the front steps. To our right sat a secluded outside eating area that was paved in orange bricks. I spotted a barbecue and next to that, a swimming pool. A garden hose was rolled up by the nearest french windows, too.

When we got to the giant wooden front door, I noticed a tiny window at eye level in the middle of it. The glass was made of wavy amber and was extremely thick, so you couldn't really see in or out of it. I knocked on the door, but it made absolutely no sound and it absolutely killed my knuckles. Hayley pressed the doorbell instead.

"*Hello,*" a cheesy voice came out of a speaker next to the doorbell. "*Welcome to the front doorstep of Robert, Shelby, Cindy and Tanya Tanner's house!*"

Hayley crossed her arms in embarrassment for them. "God, I would've thought they'd get rid of that by now."

A moment later, the door opened to reveal a tiny shrieking rat at eye level, hissing and yapping at us as if we were its worst enemy. It took me a moment to realise it was actually a tiny Brussels Griffon, being held up by a young woman. She was probably in her early twenties, with short blonde hair tied up in a bun. Wearing a tiny pink t-shirt with a dead kitten on the front, it stretched across her perky breasts. Next to that and her skimpy pale blue panties, she was all but nude. She could have easily belonged in a teen movie if it wasn't for the cast wrapped around her entire left leg, the crutches, the scars and the general beat up appearance solidifying her identity and back-story to me in an instant. I tried not to stare.

"For the love of everything that is non-PC," she said, dropping the dog, who scampered off. "Hayley, what do you want?"

Hayley backed away a bit, and pointed at me. "I'm with her."

The girl turned. "Okay, what do *you* want?" She lost her grip on the crutches and slipped over a little. I went in and helped her up. "*Scrutches...*" she muttered.

"What?" said Hayley with a quick laugh.

"It's a time saver. It means stupid crutches. *Scrutches.*"

"Right. Stupid," said Hayley.

I figured from the get-go that Cindy wasn't like her sister by the very fact that she allowed herself to get so messed up in Italy, as I recalled. Also by the fact that Tanya would never wear a t-shirt with such an upsetting image printed on it.

"My name's Cassie Gellar. I'm... I know Tanya. Is she here?"

The girl invited us in officially. "She sure is. She's busy making *another* useless mug. My name's Cindy, by the way. I'm her sister. I guess you heard what happened to me?"

I was going to answer, but Hayley did it for me. "All those years you dreamed of having fun in Italy. Worth it, Cindy?"

"Shut up, Whore-ley."

She guided us through the wonderfully pristine but lived-in hallway, past the white-as-white-can-be lounge-room, and into the kitchen, which was a mess. Still, they had a beautiful home. It was better than ours. I felt like I was in one of those rich beach houses. The walls of the kitchen were a dazzling yellow, and it suited the kitchen benches and floors. Like my house, it didn't have any walls between it and the lounge-room.

Tanya was sitting at the bench, moulding a mug out of clay, which was spinning slowly on her pottery wheel. It was obviously a machine she'd gotten when she was little, because it had Minnie Mouse stickers on its cheap red plastic frame. Clay was, unfortunately for whoever had to clean it up, everywhere. This must have been a hobby of hers. Along with reading, for a Saviour it was an impressive change from fashion-obsessing and being a cow.

"Hey," she said to us.

She stopped the machine and went to wash her hands in the sink. Cindy lazily hobbled around us.

"So, Tanya... Are you and Hayley back to being basic buddies?"

Tanya ignored her.

"Don't you have a pillow fight to get back to?" said Hayley.

Cindy scowled at her and headed for the hallway. "Well, the ogre dares. I'll leave you guys alone. I have a hell of a lot of insurance forms to fill out. Venus, get out from under my feet!" She limped around the small dog, and the two of them headed off together. I heard her slip in the hallway. *"Scrutches!"* she cursed.

Tanya had finished rinsing the dried clay off her hands, and she wiped them down with a tea-towel. "Oh, you guys, just chill out and watch some television while I clean up. I taped *The Prefect Family* from the other night. You can watch that if you want. I won't be two ticks."

"Tick, tick," said Hayley.

"You're funny."

Hayley eagerly rushed into the other room for the large widescreen television and found one of fifteen remote controls on the couch. She turned it on and pressed play. I joined her on the couch. She seemed perfectly at ease given she was enemies with Tanya. When *The Prefect Family* came on, the familiar theme song played and we sang along together:

'One o'clock, two o'clock,
Our prayers, our prayers, our prayers!
Three o'clock, four o'clock,
Affairs, affairs, affairs!
They're not perfect, but the lord says love thy
Preeeefect Family!'

By the end of it, Tanya had joined us and sat curled up on one of the armchairs. "I liked the old theme song better."

"You would," muttered Hayley.

"Yeah. I'd also pack when there's a bushfire coming," she said smoothly. "Crazy, huh? Have you guys packed anything yet?"

Hayley and I shook our heads at the same time.

"Well, you should. Just because we have automatic sprinklers attached to our gutters doesn't necessarily mean the fires can't get past them. Especially when the fire brigade exhausts the water supply for their own hoses."

"We have automatic sprinklers on our gutters?"

"I don't know if your house does any more. They probably took them down when the last owners left. But we do. Most of us on this street do, as well. Welcome to the 21st Century."

I laughed and Tanya laughed, and we forgot ourselves until Hayley, who was in between us, wriggled about. "Get on with it so we can leave."

Tanya held her breath for a moment and fiddled with her nails. "Oh, right. Well, you know, just to... I... Look, Cassie, I'm in a predicament. When I gave you those two invitations the other day, you realise it was because I thought you were cool, right?"

"I gathered."

"You know what I mean. I figured... I mean, you're pretty, so I just assumed that you were apart of the *in*-crowd."

"You guessed wrong, *lash*," said Hayley.

Tanya frowned at her. "I was the one who made that word up so don't use it on me."

Hayley rolled her eyes dramatically.

"You understand where I'm coming from, right, Cassie? I was just wondering if I could have them back."

Her gaze lingered on me. I didn't know what she was talking about for a moment. Then I realised. The tension was fierce like a lit cuban cigar in a non-smoker's section of an upper-class restaurant.

"Oh. Sorry. I can't give them back. I flushed them down the toilet after you gave them to me."

The lie made my soul die a little. Tanya was a little red in the face at this unexpected news. "Oh. Oh, well, okay. That's fine. I didn't want Eleanore to know that I'd given them to you, that's all. She would garrotte me if she found out. Can you imagine if you guys turned up with passes to her party?"

Just then, the doorbell greeting repeated itself once more. The house was so open and wide that you could see right outside, and to my horror I spotted the Saviours waiting at the front door. Eleanore was looking in at me.

Tanya jumped up. "Uh-oh, time to go."

We sat there for a moment, perplexed.

"Just hide under the table or something..."

I watched as she rushed around me, and I said: "Why don't we just leave?"

"*No*," she snapped, pulling Hayley up. "She hasn't seen you yet. If she finds out you're here, she'll know something's up. I can't tell her why. Not really, without letting on about those invites. Please do me a solid, and hide until she leaves. *Please?*"

I let out a tired moan, which was signal enough, and Hayley pushed me towards the dining table behind the couch. It sported a large white cloth that reached almost to the very ground. She shoved me underneath, and followed. Tanya went to answer the door. We sat there in silence, breathing quietly. I looked to Hayley and she looked to me, and she put a finger to her mouth.

"Eleanore, hi!" said Tanya, sounding a little out of breath.

We heard their clip-clopping as they cantered into the room. Their shadows appeared across the cloth in front of us. Then, a pair of heeled feet stood within arm's reach, and a thud sounded above us. One of them, or all of them, placed their handbags on the table.

"I saw Cassie. Where is she?" demanded Eleanore sternly. "If *she* is here, *Hayley* is here. That means you're conspiring against me. Where *are* they?"

My heart was racing a mile a minute, and I felt absurd for it.

"Eleanore, Eleanore, look..." Tanya said slowly. "They're not here. You must have been seeing things."

"Are you calling me crazy!?"

"Well, you *were* acting a little nutty today, accusing Cassie of being a witch."

"I know what I saw..." Eleanore was quiet now, and it was deeply unnerving. "She was sitting on that couch, and I saw a blond man's reflection in one of the mirrors, too. Big and burly."

Hayley could barely contain herself. I peered underneath the table cloth and saw Eleanore looking around the front of the couch. Friday and Wednesday were standing like soldiers near the front foyer. As I began to lower the cloth back down, I realised in horror that Wednesday was looking directly at me. My heart leapt into my throat and I froze. Then she winked at me. I stared blankly, trying to figure her out, and slowly slid the cloth back down to conceal us.

"You know," I heard Wednesday speak, "you have been a *little* bit crazy today, Eleanore. Remember when we were outside the classroom this morning, and you thought you saw a slimy creature on the ceiling?"

Such silence filled the room that I felt the urge to vomit. Hayley covered her mouth so she wouldn't laugh.

"Alright, I guess I am a bit overstuffed," said Eleanore. "I'll drop it. Anyway, Tanya, we came to ask your parents if we could take down your fence and use your backyard for the party on Saturday."

"Uh, sure, okay," said Tanya forcefully.

A sudden snap and a bang caused Hayley and I to jump. We whacked our heads on the top of the table, but nobody noticed.

The Saviours screamed.

We peeked out of our hiding place and saw Tanya's clay-maker in the kitchen promptly burst into flames. The fire spread across the kitchen bench and down onto the floor.

The Saviours rushed to the kitchen to find some water. I turned to Hayley, but she was long gone. She'd snuck out the other side and run out the back door. She was jumping over the fence into Eleanore's backyard by the time I noticed.

The fire on the carpet trailed away like a snake, darting with intent through the lounge-room. I escaped my veil and began crawling away, but the moment I moved the flames turned as if they'd spotted me. They stopped in their place. I gaped in astonishment. Then, as absurd as it seems, the fire rushed forward. I jumped back as fast as I could and rolled over the table to avoid it. It ran into the cloth. I spotted the girls, who were in plain sight, but they didn't notice me. I ran for the door and rushed out. The moment I was outside, I rested my hands on my knees for a moment to breathe. I noticed the hose-reel near the french windows, which were actually the windows near the television in the lounge room. From there, I could see the fire engulfing the table-cloth, and the girls' screams were even louder now. The smoke alarm went off, and Cindy collapsed against the open front door with her crutches. Smoke was pouring out with her. She saw me with the hose. I couldn't figure out how to unravel it. It was locked.

"Click the orange button!" she wheezed.

I did so, and the hose obeyed. I yanked it out of its roll as fast as I could and turned it on. The water exploded from it crazily, and then with my free hand I forced open the french windows and sprayed the lounge-room from head-to-toe. The fire died down immediately, almost too soon to be real, and all that was left was a surprisingly minimal amount of damage. I turned off the hose and ran back inside. As I checked the kitchen, Eleanore and I locked eyes. She gawked rather obviously at the hose in my hand. Cindy looked around the room. The smoke-alarm finally turned itself off. The girls stopped coughing and checked their surroundings.

"There's no more smoke. Where did it go?" said Friday.

Tanya looked over at her sister. She was on the verge of tears, and as pale as a ghost. "It was the pottery wheel. It caught on fire."

"Cassie put it out," said Cindy mindlessly, and she grabbed the nearest phone and started dialling. She left the room, but called out: "Dammit, Tanya! What did I say about leaving that stupid thing on all the time?"

I was left in the room with the four stunned girls. I couldn't help but think how shallow it was of Hayley to run off like that. Maybe Tanya was right. Hayley only looked out for Hayley.

"How did you get here so fast?" asked Eleanore.

"You could hear the alarm from my house," I said quickly.

"How did you get the fire to go out so easily?" asked Friday.

I shrugged. "Covalent bonds."

Eleanore hadn't taken her eyes off me. She was like a cheetah stalking its prey, or in my case, stalking a potential slip-up. "Why Cassie Gellar, I do believe you *are* a witch."

Cindy hobbled back into the room, and put the phone on the

hook. "Jesus, this town is horrendously unorganised. Fire Brigade's unavailable, for Christ's sake."

"That's because there's a bushfire nearby. And will you *please* stop taking the Lord's name in vain?" said Wednesday quietly. "A simple Holy Bean-Curds will suffice."

I was knocked to the side by Hayley, who burst through the open door with a giant bucket of water. Before she could assess the situation, she threw it at the Saviours in a panic. Drenching them completely, the four of them gaped like fish in disbelief. Then Eleanore screamed. "My dress! My beautiful, new dress! Look what you've done! I'm... I'm..."

"Let me guess. You're melting," said Cindy in amusement.

Now who's the witch? I thought wickedly.

22

THE CRUX OF IT

Mom popped down to the Tanners' and introduced herself that night. She took with her the frozen lasagne she'd made the previous night. When she came home she spoon-fed the gossip: Tanya's pottery wheel was now in the bin, along with the family's Christmas vacation abroad. The damage to the house from the fire was next to nothing, but the very paranoid lady of the house was now planning to invest in some serious upgrade in electrical safety, and other products that would keep her family safe. Add to that the unexpected family trip to Italy to rescue the injured daughter, and the bill was well into the thousands. All I cared about was what the heck that fire *was*, and if it had anything to do with the Child of Crux upstairs that nobody was supposed to know about.

Zag was sitting on top of the fish tank in Annie's room. She was on her bed, and she sat up guiltily when I walked in. Then she relaxed. "Oh, I thought you were Brendan. He's been bursting in ever since the pink tsunami."

"Something very weird is going on," I told them.

"Have you met my friend Zag?"

I collapsed on her orthopaedic bed.

"When I was at Tanya's before, there was a fire."

"I know," Annie rested on her elbows next to me. "I heard their smoke alarm, but I thought it was just a ringing in my ears from the school's one."

"Well, it *sounds* crazy, but... I could have sworn the fire reacted to my presence, or something."

Annie's jaw dropped. "You mean you got burnt?"

"No. When I moved, it sort of... I don't know... *flinched*, I guess. And then it chased me."

"You're right, that does sound crazy. But then again… have you met my friend Zag?"

I couldn't help but feel that there was something here I was missing. The impossible task of accepting the supernatural into my life was daunting enough. Now that it was evident something else supernatural, seemingly unrelated to Zag, was at hand, I found myself turning to Eleanore's favourite emotion for support: paranoia.

"Will you protect me if I get into trouble?" I asked Zag.

"Of course! Wish pending."

"What about the sneezing?"

"Oh, that. You know, it really depends on the individual, and the humidity. Some days are better than others. If you've sneezed glue, you've reached the worst."

At least that was one less thing to worry about.

"I have a message for you," I said, suddenly remembering. "The very fact I forgot about this is testament to what that glitter is doing to my insides."

Zag smirked at me playfully. "I knew someone from Danube would find me eventually. Who was it?"

"A clump of something named Coffee."

"Is caffeine alive now?" asked Annie, confused.

"*Coffee!* Oh, I miss him. Tell me, did he wildly scare you with his unusual appearance?"

"Sure did. What scared me more, though, was the message he wanted me to pass on. He said that your last owner wants to reclaim you, or something…"

The weight of the air suddenly became very thick and heavy. Zag was frozen. His skin turned lily white. Then, he imploded in on himself, disappearing into a tiny black hole. I looked at Annie, and she looked back, and we figured this was the end to our jolly old time spent with a creature from another world. Of course, he reappeared moments later and simply stood in front of the fish tank, teetering gently, gazing into space as if he'd been whacked with an iron baseball bat.

"People, it's okay. I will fake my own death and live on a deserted island for the first million years. By then, she'll be gone."

"Is it really that bad? What's her name?"

He propped himself back up on top the fish tank. "Oh boy. Her name is Ursula, and she was that Viking Empress I told you about. She blames me for killing her father. I don't know. One moment I was cleaning her toilet, the next she came and started accusing me, and she sent me away, and that was it. Haven't seen or heard from her since. She wished not to be my owner any more, so she can never have me back. I won't allow it, anyway. The woman's a psychopath. She has this bizarre glowing crystal ball on a staff. I heard that it sucks your age from you."

"The universe is a deeply disturbing dwelling if someone can do that," muttered Annie.

"Hold on. Does this mean Ursula is here, looking for you?"

Zag nodded.

"Does she know who *I* am?"

Zag shook his head. "No. How could she? And the only reason Coffee knows who you are is because he works on his own. Doesn't trust a soul and yet somehow is always ahead of the game. I know for a fact he would *never* tell Ursula, either. Ever! Did he say whether she was in *Horn-Horn*, or simply on this planet?"

I couldn't remember the conversation that well. I didn't think he was that specific. But then a rather obvious thought popped into my head.

"Maybe she had something to do with that moose in the woods!"

Zag scratched under his chin in thought. He knew she wasn't able to transform into animals. Humans, yes, but not animals. That was Timothy's foray, but to explain that would be far too complicated. "Yes, of course. It was Ursula," he said.

I calmed down and sat on the edge of the bed, the bottom of my back a little damp from sweat. "This town is gigantic," I assured myself out loud. "The odds of crossing paths let alone *meeting* her are astronomical. Just to be safe, I wish this Ursula woman would leave Earth and never come back."

This time, I didn't sneeze up a glitter storm. An oddly distant, vibrating boom ran along the corners of the room. Zag sighed with apparent boredom. "If only it were that simple. See, she's a Royal Empress. A *Viking* Empress. She has roots here, dating back thousands of years to her seafarer ancestors. Blood runs thicker than wishes. To cut her out of her right to be on a planet that is, by lineage, her own, is an impossible task. Unless the planet was destroyed."

"Well, let's not wish for *that*."

"Ursula is a walk in the park. She's not very bright. She's selfish. She won't see anything more than two feet in front of her. I didn't know her for very long, but what I learnt about her is that she is generally weak. She won't stick to this for very long. She'll get bored and probably want to go back and govern Danube. So act normal out in public, don't let me leave the house, and *don't* let strangers in."

"I wish that anybody with bad intentions was unable to enter this house," said Annie smugly. She appeared to be quite pleased with herself, until she started to cough and wheeze. A tremendous golden slime exploded from her mouth and her nostrils. "Oh," she groaned, recovering. "That didn't feel nice at all. Does that happen all the time?"

"No," said Zag. "I just don't like you."

Feeling a little bit safer, the conversation ran dry and I became awfully sleepy. The security I felt was also met with an ulterior emotion: suspicion against the very same security. By the time I went to bed, I'd convinced myself that it was all in my head, and that I was as safe as money in a bank vault. Something I stupidly should have realised was not a possibility anymore.

XXIII
ROMAN NUMERALS

The weather was quite cool the next morning. I woke up with a bit of a headache and a great need to crawl back into bed. It was one of those days. My fingers were aching for no apparent reason, and I had a creepy taste in my mouth that just wouldn't go away.

JT, Hayley and Greg boarded the bus somewhere in the lower parts of Horn-Horn. I was glad for their company, as the continuous whispers, giggles and glares from the Saviours was getting to me. Had my saving them yesterday meant absolutely nothing to them?

Hopping off in the parking lot, I heard a different kind of clip-clopping for once. The sound of horse hooves. We turned in time to see the school counsellor riding atop her carriage. People turned, of course, since a horse-and-carriage was out of the ordinary. Dame Hermione, or whatever her name was, waved upon seeing me, and I quickened my pace.

The hallways were abuzz with chatter about the previous day's fire scare. In our homeroom, Ms. Weiss was standing by the door with a cup of coffee in her hands.

"Morning, people," she said. We were in a long line of slowly trundling students, and we muttered inane comments in response. "Oh, cheer up, it's Friday. Papers on my desk, please."

I looked up from my stupor and nudged JT. "We handed that homework in yesterday."

"No, no, the Roman *numerals* paper," said JT. "She told us about it ages ago."

I was getting all sweaty and panicky. "When did she say this?"

"On Tuesday, when... Oh right, you weren't here."

I put my hand up. Ms. Weiss looked at me and I told her of my predicament. She sighed in distress.

"It's not my responsibility, Cassie. You should have asked one of your friends what you missed on Tuesday."

I felt rotten. The blood rushed to my cheeks like never before.

"Did anybody else fail to write it?" asked Ms. Weiss. "You might as well confess now, gang, or I'll whittle away the suspects later."

The only other person in the thirty or so class of students to put their hand up was Greg, and he too went bright red.

"I'm feeling very lenient," said Ms. Weiss, sipping her coffee casually. "Perhaps it's because the impending doom of flames has postponed its trip to sunny old Horn-Horn. Or perhaps it's because it is Friday. But here's what we'll do. Cassie, Greg, I'll give you until tomorrow."

The class laughed. Greg frowned, not quite understanding. "But... tomorrow is *Saturday*."

"Very good, Mr. Cooper. I'm giving you until tomorrow to write those papers and hand them in to me. You can drop them by my house before five o'clock, or else you'll start losing end-of-year points."

"Where do you live?" I asked.

"1045 Flavour Street," said Ms. Weiss, and she sat down at her desk to get ready for class "It's three streets down from yours, Cassie. The giant double storey wooden house with two brick chimneys. Look for the garden gnomes. They swarm the front garden."

I looked at Greg. He obviously didn't know where it was, either.

"Miss. Parker, would you escort them at some point tomorrow?"

Eleanore hadn't been listening for once, but she straightened up and caught on. "NO!" she declared venomously. She regained her stature as soon as her teacher's right eyebrow raised. "I mean, I'm sorry. I can't, Ms. Weiss. Party preparations and all."

"I'm sure half an hour's break from blowing up balloons will do you good," said Weiss. "And not tarnish your record."

"My record?" Eleanore looked around angrily.

"I'll take that as a yes! Perfect. You three sort it out amongst yourselves, and I'll see you some time tomorrow."

This day wasn't starting out very well. Like it was my fault nobody told me about the stupid paper. I'd been home sick, or… whatever. Well, for all they knew I was sick. It was her job to tell me about it the next day, not my own.

What was this, the twelfth grade?

24
MYSTERY IN
THE FACULTY LOUNGE

Ursula finally had her own office. It was a recently vacated space that had been painted an unfortunately grotesque shade of pink. The previous counsellor had painted it this colour to encourage comfort and emotions in the students, which she personally thought was daft.

The day drifted on tiresomely. She saw student after student, whom often gave detailed explanations as to why they were depressed, emotionally fragile, homosexual, asexual, dysfunctional, gender-fluid, suicidal, and what-not. Ursula tried very hard to pretend she was interested in what they had to say, while at the same time trying to bestow a sense of camaraderie with them so they might feel okay in letting her know about their secret encounter with a strange moose in the woods.

The bell rang, and soon she heard the familiar sounds of those pretentious young humans scouring the hallways outside. She stood up, pondering what she would eat for lunch. She was larger than everyone here, and ate like the size that she was. Rather than gorge herself like a beast in front of everybody, she would hide somewhere and inhale the tiny sandwiches they made in the cafeteria. She was always lonely, she realised, no matter the circumstances.

Somebody knocked on her door and opened it. Bev Berry poked her head in gingerly and looked around. "Garish," she giggled. "The last person who had this office is now in the Looney Bin. I wonder why?"

"So that's what happened. It's the colour, the colour, I tell you!"

"You know," Bev walked in and skirted the desk placidly, "When I was little, my mother always used to tell me that pink was the *evil* colour. I know it sounds silly, but her reasoning was this: When you first see the colour, you find it innocent and beguiling. It's light, the colour of flowers, gentle on the eyes. But at its core it is red, the devil's colour. As white is added to it, it becomes so pretty and alluring, you can't pry your eyes away. Then as it outstays its welcome, you find that it digs its nails into you, and becomes harsher and harsher until you can't stand it any more. You suddenly find it cruel and manipulative, and devoid of wonder or sympathy. At least, that's what mother would say."

"Actually," said Ursula, "white isn't a colour. It's a combination of all colours. But I like your mother's theory. Is she…?"

Bev Berry smiled half-heartedly and stroked the wall. "Oh, no, she died a long time ago. She suffered from mental problems. One time she told me that if I got a perm, the curls would attract birds. She was worried they'd mistake it for a nest. But it went deeper than that, though. She was paranoid by the end. Thought there was a curse on our family. Feared if I kept my eyes, I'd have triplets, or something along those lines…" She laughed sadly.

Ursula stared in wonder.

Bev caught the look and waved it off. "Because every few generations in our family we have twins or triplets. I'd always say to her: Now *who* would consider that a curse?"

Ursula remained disdained for a mere moment, but then she saw the lost, brown deer eyes in front of her, enlarged by that giant eyewear prescription. *Why is she here?* she suddenly wondered.

Bev answered her gently.

"Some of the faculty and I were wondering if you would like to have lunch with us in the teacher's lounge?"

Ursula felt bizarrely human as she agreed.

———— . . . ————

Inside, the lounge was not the expected smoke haze, nor were there tattered couches and ancient coffee machines that sent out individual, rank odours. Instead it was a calm, clean, well-lit space much like a classroom, with black chairs and white circular tables to sit and eat at. A television was on in the corner, playing the local news network with the promise of something called '*The Prefect Family*' after the next break.

Ursula followed Bev through the familiar faces of the adult population, until they sat down at one half-empty communal table. A small, frumpy woman with short black hair sat there, along with the tenth grade teacher, Ms. Weiss. They were in a heavy argument about something.

"A reflection my *ass*," said the small frumpy one, who's name was Ms. Winch. "It was a fluke of nature, an assembly of lights in the sky that are made up from the aurora borealis."

She gulped down some coffee.

"What are we talking about?" said Bev, scooting her chair in.

Ms. Weiss pointed upward. "Last night people near the beach claimed to see a reflection of the Earth in the sky." She skidded that day's newspaper across the table for them to read. "Different continents. See? It was another world."

"That's science fiction!"

Ursula stared at the giant black & white photograph that took up almost the entire front page, and squinted in disbelief. Scoping down the article, little caught her attention, but the *photograph*. It showed as clear as could be the night sky in downtown Horn-Horn, a few gatherers around the shore pointing towards the giant, unmistakeable presence in the sky above. With the aurora borealis masking most of it and taking its credibility with it, it hosted a shimmery, out-of-focus reflection of the very Earth they stood on, except slightly different somehow. But as it edged further into the sky, the reflective planet vanished into the darkness. It was too heavily masked by the aurora to be perfectly plausible.

Ms. Weiss pointed an arthritic finger at the other Earth. "It's not a reflection, because what are they? Huh? Those continents. What are they?"

The weight of something awry sat heavily on Ursula's chest.

She'd never seen anything like it. A planet reflecting itself? Couldn't be. *She* would know. Chalking it up to a fluke of nature, a secret this planet would probably never share, she relaxed in her seat and tried to look as unconcerned as her innocent friend sitting next to her.

Bev saw her look, and faced the others. "Everyone, this is Dame Hermione Purplewink, the new school counsellor. Hermione, this is Jacqueline Weiss, the tenth grade teacher of all basic classes; and Maggie Winch, who teaches art for all grades."

"It's Dorchester now," said Maggie Winch angrily. "I divorced Brian, remember? His stupid turd of a surname can go to hell."

Bev sat with her hands coyly tucked between her legs. "You shouldn't say such things, Maggie."

Ursula's stomach exploded from hunger pains. The growl that emitted almost shook the table, and the three fellow teachers looked over at her. Ursula excused herself to go and look for food. Flustered and overcome, she was barely out of the door when she bumped into Eric Parker, who grabbed her arm.

"Glad I caught you, Hermione. Are you alright? You look sick."

"I'm hungry, what is it?"

"I looked at your report for Cassie Gellar yesterday," said Parker. "The school system's breathing down our necks about her case, as I mentioned, and it seems you only had a very small meeting with her due to that embarrassing false alarm." He blushed.

Ursula waited for him to continue.

"Well, I'd really prefer not to pull her from any more classes, as her teacher told me earlier that she didn't hand a paper in today, and I'm concerned that all of this nonsense with her situation and missing school on Tuesday is going to interfere. So perhaps just this week you could talk to her parents instead?"

"Yes, fine, I will," she said dismissively.

"Oh, and come back to my office after you're done."

Ursula forced her attention on him. "Done what?"

"Given Cassie's mother a call, of course. She's at home all this week; I don't know why she couldn't have simply come in and helped us with... Well, never mind. You're here now, which is good. Give her a call and see if you can brief her on your plan of approach."

Ursula started to walk away slowly. "Yes, alright, I will."

Best to get it out of the way, she thought. *Besides, this Cassie girl may very well be the one I'm after.*

Of course, she thought this with little hope.

25

STARVED AND LABOURED

nother lunch spent in the dusty desert of the back lot of the school yard. I sat eating my sandwich with little desire to finish it. All four of us were together, huddled in a circle, discussing the plan to sabotage Eleanore's party. We'd actually gone to the library at recess and spent fifteen minutes handing out some of Eleanore's fake party invitations. Today was the last day of school for the week, ergo, last contact with less-popular kids before the party the following night.

The Saviours waved at us as they ran across the grounds for their favourite oak tree setting. JT flipped them the bird. Was this how every lunch-time was going to be from now on, without the Vineyard?

"Why don't we just find somewhere else?" I suggested.

"No," said Hayley bitterly. "We don't fit in anywhere else. This is the one place nobody ever bothers to go. It's perfect. And magic."

"But it's a wasteland," I said.

"To you, maybe, but it's also where Jonathan and I first met," she punched the earth with her fists. "I'm standing my ground until I die. Or graduate. Whichever comes first."

Greg waited for me to look at him before he said: "I'm just here on principle."

We shrugged together.

———— · · · ————

By the time lunch break neared its end, Ursula found herself sitting in her office quite starved, having not had a moment to eat. When Eric Parker barged in, smelling of cashews, her stomach grumbled terribly. He put some more papers on her desk, as if expecting her to know what to do with them. Working sure was hard.

"What are these?" she asked, staring down at them in distaste.

Parker stopped on his way out. "Dated stuff. Student files, reports. Sociological and cognitive components mostly. Oh, and a scholarly article about the royals I thought you'd like."

"What royals?"

"The ones you told me you used to tend."

"Oh. Yes."

"How did you go with your phone call to Lesley Gellar?"

Ursula nodded. "Quite good. She seems fearful now."

"Fearful?" said Parker, frowning. "Does she wish to speak to us more about the situation?"

"She requested we meet to discuss it, but I'm fully booked with..." she sighed loudly, "...*more* students this afternoon. I suggested Monday. I suppose I can fit her in somewhere."

Ursula shuffled through the mounds of papers on her desk for a moment, but noticed that Parker had gently closed the door. For the first time on this planet she felt a sudden, intense sense of dread. Eric's lips were thin and he was evidently upset about something.

"I should not have to tell you that leaving parents in the dark is profoundly unprofessional. Not to mention the woman is as qualified as you are! I suggest you call back right now or... or..."

He paid attention to his surroundings.

"Let's get someone in on the weekend to repaint."

Ursula was quick to the phone, with Parker over her shoulder. She was half tempted to set her giant crystal ball on him, to turn him into a heavily decaying corpse, but she'd left her staff under her bed that morning for safe keeping.

Nobody answered on the other end. The line was engaged.

"There's a strange, alternate beeping sound emitting from this communicator. What does that mean?"

Parker hung up the phone for her.

"It means that you need to drive up there and have a one-on-one with her, before she complains about us to the school board. Have I mentioned they don't like me lately? Goodness!"

He stormed out. Ursula rushed to her filing cabinet and pulled out the address folder marked A-M, and dug out the Gellar residence. It was next door to Eric Parker's.

Suddenly, she remembered the house from the day before.

With one quick click of her fingers, she disappeared into thin air.

26
THE LADY EMERGES,
AGAIN

Lesley Gellar, mother dearest, lonesome and bordering on displacement, had long finished the odd task of dropping random items across the house in order to give it that 'lived-in' feel. The house was *too* clean. The real estate agency must have vacuumed with the suction of a thousand black holes. She was about to get started on one of her lazy-man's Pilates work-outs, when there came an unexpected knock at the door. Answering it, she was met with a tall woman, distractingly so in fact. She looked strangely familiar, dressed in a white power-suit. She had a black handbag strung over one shoulder. Reaching a hand out to shake, she said: "Dr. Lesley Gellar?"

"Yes," said Mom, accepting the hand gesture.

"My name is Ur... Dame Hermione Purplewink. I believe we spoke on the phone earlier? I am the new counsellor at Horn-Horn High-High. May I come in?"

Mom looked her up and down, and obliged. Ursula strode forward and took in her surroundings. Large entrance, cold tiled floors, wide spiralling staircase. She'd wanted to take a peek inside yesterday afternoon, for curiosity's sake. Now inside, she felt a strange electrical energy buzz about her. Mom offered her a drink and a seat in the kitchroom, distracting her from the currents, and she joined her on the couch.

"I'm here to talk about Cassie," Ursula said, once comfortable.

"Of course."

"I had my first session with her yesterday but it was cut short due to those fire scares. I gave her and her friend a lift home but unfortunately due to my current transport I was unable to talk with her more. Eric Parker insisted I speak with you and your husband instead to make up for lost time. My next appointment with her isn't until next week."

"Well, I happen to be a counsellor myself, specialising in child psychology, and I can assure you she is fine. Better than I would be, anyway."

"She's fine?"

"Oh yes."

Ursula smiled. There was no use pretending any more. She had to know what happened. Rather get the information straight from the source's mother than back at the school and get yelled at again by the Principal, who she was starting to dislike.

"I must admit, due to such little time I've spent with her... I'm not entirely clear on the details of what Cassie went through. Are you able to bring me up to speed?"

"It was nothing, she says. She was attacked in the woods this Monday, but she doesn't seem to remember anything."

It took a moment for the words to sink in. It was as if somebody had poked holes into Ursula's eardrums, and blood flowed noisily throughout her ear canals.

"Oh?" was all she could muster. She was sitting unnaturally upright, her jaw clenched.

"Yes. Consensus seems to be that she blacked out during the attack and has forced herself to forget," said Mom.

"Now when you say attacked..."

"Oh, not by a person. No. The doctor came to make sure of all of that. And it couldn't have happened at a worse time. She has had such a hard time fitting in in the past, it breaks my heart to think this could affect her social life. I know she was really hoping for a clean slate here."

"Who attacked her if not a human— a person, I mean?"

"All we've gotten from her is that she was attacked by a moose. A *moose*, of all things. At first I thought she was hallucinating, but then I did some research, and it turns out rabid moose collect in small wooded areas along coastal spots at the end of summer. The sea-breeze and the heat confuses them, you see, and…"

Her voice faded into white noise.

Ursula's grasp on her half consumed glass of water became so tight she felt the glass beneath her fingers crack.

"You say, a moose? That is interesting. Perhaps she…" Her mind was elsewhere, looking up, but she knew she had to stay present. "Often people in circumstances that are traumatising, uh, hallucinate solutions that are beyond their comprehension, but are far kinder to the… uh… You know, I'm feeling a little green suddenly."

"Oh. Would you like something to eat?"

It was finally dawning on her. This was the mother Ursula had met outside the elementary school, with the boy in the car who gave her the information on the moose attack. She knew, at last, that her Child of Crux was either at the school with his new owner, or in this very house.

"No, I don't need anything to eat. May I use your bathroom?"

"Of course, down the hall and to your left."

Ursula tip-toed into the foyer. As she made her way past closed doors, she sniffed the air. Where was he? Behind this door? No. Behind that door? No. *How am I going to do this?* she thought hopelessly. She could rip apart the house, destroy the mother and anybody who tried to get in her way. But that would require noise and would be a fair warning for Zag, who would then likely pack up his things and disappear as fast as lightning. She had to be quick about this, and silent. If he was sleeping right now, he would be doing so in his clay head. She could easily snatch him away without stirring him.

She went about her business, fake urinating in the downstairs bathroom, and then she washed her hands and looked at herself in the mirror. All this could have been avoided if Timothy hadn't scared Zag out of the woods on Monday afternoon. Why her soon-to-be husband would take the form of a moose and attack anybody was beyond comprehension. Panic, maybe? He didn't do well with conflict, she'd noticed. He hadn't used his senses, but then again he had never received any form of training either, so rushing to explosive judgements to capture Zag was likely his only logical strategy.

"Mrs. Gellar!" Ursula said as she strode through the foyer. "I've seen you before."

"Funny, I was wondering why you looked so familiar."

"I was outside your son's school recently, speaking to him at your car window. I showed you a polaroid of my missing art piece."

Mom frowned as she thought, and put a hand to her cheek. "I'm sorry I was so short."

Ursula laughed and walked head-strong to the front door. Her confidence regained, she stood taller than she had ever stood before.

"I understand. I was a bit preoccupied myself. See…"

She scrounged through her handbag and conjured the polaroid.

"My father gifted me this clay head shortly before he died, so you can understand its value. Since moving here, somebody has stolen it. I left it in the school art classroom on Monday for five minutes and while I was gone it went missing."

Mom inspected the polaroid closer.

"Hold on one second, will you?"

Ursula did so and Mom raced upstairs. A few moments later she came rushing back down, holding something familiar. Ursula's heart leapt into her throat. As if in a perfect dream, the clay head was handed to her without a fuss.

"I'm so sorry. It was in Cassie's bedroom. She brought it home with her after she was attacked in the woods. I don't think she would have stolen it, though. Intentionally that is. She's not like that. She's a good girl…"

"It's okay…" said Ursula, beaming from ear-to-ear.

"She told us she'd found it…"

"Really, it's fine," said Ursula.

"I'll have a word with her when she gets home tonight. This has been such an unusual week —"

"I said don't *bother!*" Ursula bellowed.

It echoed across the foyer, and a cat pranced nervously along the corridor behind them. She collected herself and started for the door again.

"Really, Mrs. Gellar, don't worry her any more. But when she brings it up, which I'm sure she will, tell her I said thank you."

"You want me to thank my daughter for *stealing* from you?"

"No, thank her for taking *care* of it. You must treat these things with the most positive light you *can*, Mrs. Gellar. For the child's sake…"

Ursula waved goodbye as she left the house.

With the door shut behind her, she leapt into the air excitedly, bathed in the afternoon sun. Now she could go home, take over the throne, make a wish to send her fiancé deep into puberty, then marry him and live happily ever after. She walked slowly, carefree, to her waiting horse-and-carriage near the end of the driveway.

"Oh father," she spoke to the branches above her. "Thank you."

"Are you talking to me?" the horse spoke.

"Don't be silly, Timothy. I'm talking to this."

Ursula held up the clay head for him to see. He whinnied in approval and wiggled in his constraints, but kept his head low as a car drove past.

"I suppose this means we can finally go home? And I can live with you in the Palace instead of that decrepit cabin far away?"

"Indeed, my love."

"Good. I must say though, I will miss this climate."

Ursula thought back to Danube's icy rotation, and squirmed.

"Yes, so will I. Perhaps we can stay here another night and relax by the beach. To celebrate. You can even take your human form if you like. We'll pretend you're the sick child I have been telling everybody about."

Timothy whinnied again in approval.

"How did you get a hold of the clay head? You didn't know it was here when you went in, did you?"

"No," said Ursula, stroking its sides tenderly. "Serendipity played a larger part in this. And when I found out it was here, I was smart about it. Which is more than I can say for you."

There was a subtle grievance to her tone.

"Me?"

"Monday afternoon when we were scouting the woods. I wasn't going to say anything, but if you're to live in my Kingdom you must at least know the basic rights and wrongs to battle decrees. You *never* attack before you assess the situation!"

"I have absolutely no idea what you're talking about."

"You attacked the blasted girl with the clay head when you were in the form of a moose! Damn near killed her, and the child from what I imagine. Now she is going around telling everybody how she was attacked! I'm surprised Bev Berry hasn't connected the dots."

The horse turned his head to stare at her directly.

"I never saw any girl in the woods that day. I would have told you. I'm sure you know that."

Ursula laughed for a moment, unsure of a retort, but as she pressed the thought harder a decent enough reason didn't seem to come to her as to why he would be lying.

"If it wasn't you, who was it?"

The carriage behind them shook violently and it splintered apart, each side falling onto the road with a terrible piercing. The purple lining flopped heartlessly to the gravel below, and the entire contraption seemed to steam up. Ursula pointed a finger at the harness holding the horse and they snapped off, freeing him. The two of them backed away together and watched as the carriage erupted in fire, and quickly burnt into a pile of ash. The strange and wooden walking cane that had been inside, however, remained intact, its orange diamond glimmering in the daylight. It was standing rigidly upright on the pathway, as if being held by a ghost.

Ursula squinted at it in wonder, trying to decipher its ability, until finally she realised. She let out a terrible moan.

"*van Pan!*"

The cane transformed before their eyes. Now a man stood there, gaunt and middle aged, with sharp features, and burns across his cheeks. Black, thinning hair slicked back, he wore a red waistcoat with golden lace, and his beige shirt was lined with ruffles.

Ursula immediately grabbed hold of Timothy in urgency, and they disappeared as subtly as a shadow at twilight. Rudnick van Pan stared at the spot they'd vanished from on the sidewalk. He creakily turned his head to the house through the trees, for a moment contemplating, and then went on his way.

27
DOWN-TOWN

The last class consumed my soul. At least, that's how it felt. The bell rang and our dear friend Friday demanded the last RSVP's be handed to her, and then we all fled for our lives.

"Another week down. How many to go, Jonathan?"

JT pulled out a notebook from his bag and flipped through it. Amongst some amazing sketches, he landed on a calendar of this year and he started counting. By the time we were inside the bus and had found our seats, he'd come to an answer:

"One hundred and five days left until Christmas break."

Hayley gave him a treat as a reward.

Eleanore and her tribe came on just as the crazy bus lady did, and for the first time they joined us near the middle, although with a few seats between. They began talking quite loudly about the party the next day. Obviously a ruse to try and make us jealous. I eyed them with intrigue. Eleanore was clearly put-off by my stares, and she jumped into the seat behind her to get closer.

"Cassie and Greg. Look. About tomorrow. I hope you realise that I am extremely busy for the whole day and that I simply cannot afford the time, effort or charm to whisk you about the countryside searching for the Weiss residence. I'm sure you understand. I mean, it *is* the night of the gala."

"Party," Greg corrected her, and he frowned. "You know exactly where Ms. Weiss lives. I know you've been to her house before."

I nodded. "Even I do. You told me about the gnomes on my first day here."

She shot her hand up to silence us. "I was merely lying to politely get you off my back. Can't you take a hint?"

"Nothing about that was polite," said Greg.

Eleanore sighed in exhaustion — for that's clearly what this conversation was: exhausting. "Fine, meet at mine at eleven in the morning, on the dot. No earlier, no later, or else the deal is off. I'll walk you down there and back but that's it. Alright?"

Greg and I nodded.

"Come to think of it, this will be good for my rep with Weiss. I don't think she likes me anymore."

Friday was eavesdropping, and she perked up. "Oh Eleanore, don't say that. Of course she does! She's just on her period."

Our jaws dropped in appal.

"Ms. Weiss in her seventies," said a stunned Hayley.

Friday didn't cotton on.

"So's my mother..." she offered.

During the short bus ride home, our dear crazy driver was a menace to all society. She didn't stop for a duck crossing, which caused quite the many screams amongst us, but on inspection out the back it seemed all of the precious ducklings had managed to avoid the wheels and were running for their lives toward their mother on the other side of the road.

"Yishel is particularly eager to get home tonight," JT remarked. "She must have a date with *Frasier*."

"Who's Yishel?" I asked.

"*She's* Y.S.H.L.," said Hayley, regarding the driver. "We don't know her real name, because she never speaks, so we call her Yack Spit Hack Lady. *Yishel* for short."

"Why Yack Spit Hack?"

"Because she looks like a yak," said Greg.

I stared at the back of her head. Suddenly it was all I could see.

"Okay, and what about the other parts?"

As I asked this, Yishel wound down her window and snorted a great deal of phlegm and spat it out onto a passing car's windshield. With the bullseye hit, she laughed loudly, and then started to cough and wheeze and… sure enough… hack.

Case solved.

Soon enough, we reached Hayley and Greg's stop. They lived in a fairly dismal part of town. It was so flat and lame around here. Everything was concrete this, single storey houses that, probably formica, and feral dogs then.

"What are you doing tonight?" Hayley asked me as she got up.

"Not much," I said. I'd been planning on my usual Friday night *Frasier* marathon, but now I wasn't so sure.

"Give me a call if you want to do something. We were thinking of seeing a film at nine. Greg works at the movie complex, so he can get us in for half price and put extra butter on our popcorn."

"And in our drinks," said JT happily.

"You disgust me."

I shrugged. "I'll ask my parents. They should be okay, assuming they don't hang me out to dry for not doing my homework."

I thought for a moment. Crap, I had to do that too.

Well, socialising was more important.

— · · · —

Annie and I gasped as we entered the house. Brendan was on the couch wearing only boxers, and he was severely sunburnt. Mom came waltzing in from the foyer, carrying a basket full of lotions.

"Don't ask," she said angrily. "He went to work with your father today, and had to travel with him to *Meadowsfield*. For some reason he decided to spend most of the day shirtless."

"Meadowsfield… Isn't that the town where the rumoured ozone hole is located?" Annie piped in.

"I can't move," muttered Brendan, turning slowly to face us. "Ow, even my eyelids hurt."

"I'm taking him to see the doctor in twenty minutes," said Mom, and she started to put some of the lotion on his back and shoulders. "I'm lucky they could fit him in. Do you girls want to come into town with us?"

Reminiscent of a rhino stampede, Annie and I catapulted ourselves up the staircase as fast as lightning to get ready.

"I think that's a no. We should leave right now!" cried Brendan.

———— · · · ————

I called Hayley on my phone in the car. I was the first one in, and Annie was soon to follow. Excitement at the prospect of going to the mall with our mother was not your every day expectation, but it was a Friday night. Hayley was pleasantly eager to come and hang out, while JT couldn't because of some pressing family matters, and Greg had to work. I was sorely disappointed at that last bit of news, but didn't mind so much as long as Hayley was tagging along. When Mom and Brendan hopped in the car, I asked if we had enough time to pick Hayley up on the way. Luckily, we did. So we drove straight down to one of Horn-Horn's dodgiest residential areas and found 45 Dinklage Lane, a small wooden house painted an off-white. It was well kept with a hefty garden, surprising given the street it was on.

"No more than five minutes," said Mom.

I'd already run down the driveway, and I knocked on the front door. A tiny dog immediately started barking. I heard it scratch away on the other side. After a moment, Hayley told him to shut up and she opened the door. We said our hello's. She picked up the barking culprit. It was the most adorable thing I had ever seen. It looked like a cross between a Chihuahua and a Cocker-Spaniel.

"This is my dog, Scruffster. Steve found him abandoned on a porn set once."

Upon hearing his name, he turned and started licking her face. Hayley had dark-blue eye make-up on her bottom eyelids, and it must have been recently applied because Scruffster licked it all off. I didn't bother to tell her about it. Hayley laughed and relished the attention, until a certain point, when she said: "That's enough," and dropped him just like that. He yipped and ran off. "Whoops," she said with a laugh.

She let me in.

"My mom says we only have five minutes."

Her home was severely lacking in recent redecorating. In fact it looked like it was still in the early eighties. Brown, formica as ex-pected, amber glass.

"Cool house," I said.

"Cool house? You *are* polite. Come and meet my mother."

I followed her through the dinky lounge-room, and into the kitchen which was equally dismal. It was small, cramped even, and dirty. I held my breath at the smell of cat pee. There also seemed to be a big furry tumbleweed sitting on the round wooden table in front of us. It took me a moment to realise that it was actually the head of a woman with unkempt, fluffy brown hair.

"Mother."

The hair lifted up and I got a good look at the face underneath. A woman in her forties or possibly fifties with heavy make-up and a dead cigarette in between her lips rolled her eyes lazily and examined her surroundings.

"I missed work again," she muttered. "Why didn't you wake me?"

"I *did* wake you. When I got home from school. To tell you that you were six hours late."

The two of them bickered loudly, and I took to looking around the room to avoid eye contact. I noticed Scruffster was now at his drink bowl, lapping up the water which seemed to be a dark-blue colour. Clearly the eye make-up discolouring. That couldn't be good for him.

"This is Cassie," said Hayley, interrupting my thoughts.

I automatically looked to her mother and smiled politely. "Nice to meet you."

I held out my hand for her to shake, and she took it, and we shook, but when she let go I found three of her glittery green fingernails still attached to my palm. Horrified, I flicked them off.

"Look at that," she said, and she hickeldy-burped. "Last time I buy adhesive from the back of a van, that's for sure." She laughed and I smelt alcohol on her breath. "How are you, hun?"

I was about to say fine when I turned to the sound of Scruffster hacking on something. A moment later he coughed up two of the same glittery nails.

"Woman, are you breeding fingers in the basement?" said Hayley angrily, and she went to fill the dog's water bowl with clear water. A thick blue swirled down the drain. *What the hell is this stuff!?*" she screamed in frustration.

"I've heard a lot about you," her mother smiled at me, one eyelid half-mast. "I'm Bonita. You don't have to call me Hayley's mom."

"Alright, Bonita."

Suddenly she snarled. "I said call me Mrs. Gauche!"

Her head fell back onto the table and she started snoring.

"Ignore her," said Hayley, and she placed the bowl on the ground. "She's a drunk. Usually she's a funny drunk, but she hasn't had her period in a week so she thinks she's pregnant, even though it's probably just poo babies backed up again. Ready to go?"

———— · · · ————

Mom was kind enough to give Annie and I thirty whole dollars each. As the doctor's clinic was in the middle of the mall, this came in handy. Brendan was quite humiliated that he had to walk through the mall half-naked, but I reminded him of how I'd once had to limp through a similar shopping centre dripping blood from my foot when a kangaroo had bitten me. He didn't appreciate the comparison, and was glad when Hayley and I left to check out the session times at the movies.

"Great, nothing's on," said Hayley, munching on some popcorn.

"Why'd you buy that before checking?"

She shovelled a handful into her mouth. "I'm psychologically obsessed with movie popcorn. It's my only source of weakness. You dangle a bag of this in front of me while I'm in a cage fight, and I'll get K.O.'d."

I reached for some, and she snarled just like her mother.

"I thought I heard the sound of a freak," a voice called.

It was Greg. Emerging from behind the counter, he was missing an earring and wearing quite an adorable movie complex uniform: a bright red vest, black shirt, black ironed pants and a red dickie-bow.

"Eugene, *hello!*" said Hayley.

We walked back over to greet him. The complex was empty due to the fact that another movie wasn't scheduled to start for a good half-an-hour.

"What time do you get off?"

"Quarter to ten."

"Hear that, Cassie? Greg masturbates at nine forty-five."

"That's not what I meant," said Greg, and his cheeks flushed. He promptly went to changing topics. "What movie are you guys seeing?"

"We're not, because nothing's on."

"Ah. That would explain why we're open, then."

"And why she's got popcorn," I said.

Greg laughed, and I went red. A moment of silence followed.

"Okay," said Hayley very slowly. "We're going to get something to eat for dinner. See you tomorrow for the party. I'll text you."

Greg waved his right hand. "Bye, guys," he said, and then he waved his other hand at me before turning around, bumping into a bin, and leaving through one of the doors behind the counter.

Hayley and I walked in silence out of the complex and through the main mall, past the pet shop until we made it to the food court. She bought a chicken baguette and some falafels, while I bought a roti wrap with bacon and lettuce and decided this would suffice for an early dinner. We sat at a table.

"You like him," she said, chucking some popcorn pieces into her baguette.

I was flabbergasted. Had I done something that made it obvious? I'd tried to be nonchalant around him. Perhaps that was it. I was *too* blasé. I'd have to kick it up a notch, I realised.

"*What!... Who, Greg?... No!... Who's Greg?*"

I started to eat quickly, panicking. Hayley eyed me suspiciously.

"He's single," she said. "Of course, you know that. You're like the only other girl he hangs out with."

"I don't like him," I said firmly.

"You're single, right?"

I nodded.

"No long distance boyfriend? Girlfriend?"

"Boyfriend, and, uh, no."

With only the power of my mind, I tried to force my cheeks to cool down. I needed windshield wipers for my face.

"The thing you've got to know about Greg is that he's annoyingly mysterious..." she muttered, eating some falafels.

"I don't like him, Hayley. Not like that. He's just a friend."

"Good. Because he's not in the right head space for a girlfriend at the moment," Hayley eyed my half-eaten wrap with envy, as she'd finished her food like a wolf. "I know you're probably thinking I'm saying this because I have the hots for him or something, but that's not true. As slutty as Jonathan and I come across, we're pleasantly content with one another. Greg is my best friend, though."

"I know."

"And I think you're a keeper, but it's early days," she watched me cautiously. "Plus he's got family issues up to here, and then some."

"Okay."

Hayley put a hand out and touched my forearm with a tenderness that surprised me. Our eyes connected, and she pushed some of my hair behind my ear affectionately. I thought she was going to go full lesbian on me, but then she uttered in the softest tone imaginable: "If you mess with him, I will *ruin* you. You'll have to move again, I promise."

Surprised and offended, I thought about how she'd reacted to Tanya's betrayal. Through the window with her.

"You don't know me," I said.

Perhaps Hayley realised then that she'd gone too far. She clapped her hands and smirked.

"I know. Oh look, an extra falafel."

28
FAREWELL SUNSET

The orphan sat with her back against the open door, so when Bev Berry arrived, she didn't notice until the cup of tea brought in for her clinked on the bedside table. After a few sips Ursula decided that it wasn't very tasty, but instead of hurling it across the room in her usual fashion, she would pretend it was delicious to spare Bev's feelings.

"You seem a little quiet today, Hermione," said Bev, and she walked to the window and looked outside at the fading sun. "I went window shopping earlier and found a few vinyls on sale I think you'll like. I'll put them on in the sitting room a little later."

Ursula gazed down at the clay head in her lap. She placed the empty tea-cup to the side and stood up to join Bev at the window. She had to hunch to see at her eye level.

"Isn't the sun amazing?"

Bev pouted in thought. "Especially this time of year. I love the end of summer. I wish it was like this all year round. The days feel like they last forever when it's like this."

"It's winter all the time where I come from."

Bev curled her fingers around the edge of the door-frame, and rested her head against its wooden support. Sensing melancholy in her new friend, she desperately wanted to ask her if everything was alright. She was afraid to, however, because if Hermione was as depressed as she was, she wasn't sure she could handle it. As if sensing the question burning in her mind, Ursula faced her and felt a sudden emotion wash over her. Remorse... or pity, or... gratefulness. It overwhelmed her enough that she couldn't bring herself to speak. Instead, she started leaking from the eyes.

"This happens so often lately!" she gasped in dismay, wiping away the tears.

Bev went to her and hugged her and this somehow set the waterworks off even further. Ursula eventually regained her composure and backed away. In her emotional confusion, a magical bolt of electrical current exploded from her fingers and hit the ceiling. The power in the mansion shorted out and they were left in the dark, with the exception of the setting sun outside.

Bev was standing up straight now. All she could see of the woman was her silhouette, the window directly behind her. Tall and black as death.

"What was that?" she said, patting down her frizzed hair.

Ursula put a hand to her mouth and tried to understand. She wiped the tears from her cheeks.

"You've been a good friend to me while I've stayed here, Bev. You remind me of my step-mother. She... *appreciated* me. It's funny, I never realised until now. Nobody has given me the time of day since she died."

Bev's eyes caught a shadow sweep past her from the hallway. It was a black cat, and it jumped up onto Ursula's bed. It sat upright and stared at her, with strange piercing green eyes that glowed, somehow, as if taken from another realm. Ursula pulled something out from under the bed. A giant staff made of twisted wooden roots, with a large crystal ball on top. Ursula propped it up and a strange pink mist churned inside of it. She clutched the clay head under her free arm, and the cat shot up onto her left shoulder to rest. She stomped the staff three times and the mist inside turned red. Soon it was glowing enough to distract Bev, and she stared, unwavered, into the crystal ball's centre. It wasn't until they'd faded away that she realised she was now staring at the setting sun through the window. She blinked a few times and glanced about the empty room in confusion, trying to see around the sun-spots in front of her vision.

"*Pink...*" she muttered, gently putting a hand to her lips.

29
THE
UGLY TRUTH

I arrived home that night feeling sick. My throat was quite itchy and I kept trying to cough up something that must have been a phantom hair or piece of dust. We'd dropped Hayley home after Brendan had seen the doctor. He was now being treated upstairs in a bath full of baking soda (apparently helpful). He was prescribed Lidocaine and benzocaine anyway.

I hadn't given Zag any food today. I popped my head into the wardrobe, hoping if I wished him a plate instead of making one downstairs, he would lighten up after being left alone yet again all day.

There was no sign of the clay head, though. I checked in and around several shoe-boxes I'd kept, and tried to remember where I'd last put it. Maybe he was with my sister again.

"Annie," I said, opening her bedroom door. "I need Zag."

"I haven't got him," she said, feeding her piranha named Chafe.

"Give it a rest, he's not in my wardrobe and you're the only other person in this house who knows about him. I need to make a wish."

"I'm telling you, I haven't gone into your room at all. I have a life, you know. Now go away. I'm busy."

With that, I went and knocked on the bathroom door. Mom answered inside. "What is it honey? We're busy."

"We?"

"I'm helping your brother out of the tub."

"Gross. Remember the clay head in my wardrobe? Did you move it?"

She didn't say anything, but a moment later the door opened narrowly and she snuck out. She stood with me in the hall, her arms crossed, a few water stains here and there on her purple top. Her eyebrows were raised expectantly. "I gave it back to that woman from the school."

My mind was extremely confused, but most of all I'd set into a mini-stroke, or at least the highest level of panic one can suffer from. *"What?"*

"It was hers, so I gave it back to her."

"That was *my* clay head! *My* property!" I yelled.

Mom winced at my raised voice. "You *stole* that clay head from *her*. She told me."

"Who?" I demanded.

"I don't know, the psychologist. Your psychologist. It doesn't matter. Frankly, I'm disappointed. Given the week you've had I think I've been very understanding."

My cheeks were ablaze. I had to start walking down the hallway to stop from passing out. "You don't understand... *Don't you see what you've done?"*

Startled by my outburst, she collected herself quickly. "Wait until your father gets home, young lady!" she yelled back.

Annie snuck out of her room, curious, but I didn't need an audience for this. I rushed into my room, holding back the tears. I grabbed my handbag, afraid, and walked down the hall, determined.

"Where are you going?" said Mom, following me.

"The woods," I said.

Annie pushed past her, catching on. "Why the woods?"

"Mom gave the clay head away."

Now it was Annie's time to shriek. "Oh mother, how *could* you?"

I was downstairs now, and the two of them were following behind me very closely as I made my way for the hall table.

"It wasn't *yours*," our mother declared defensively, and she swiped the four-wheel-drive keys from the kitchen bench before I could grab them. She faced Annie, and our frustration said it all. "What are you girls not telling me?"

I held out my hand. "Please give me the keys."

She withheld them.

"Mom!"

A split second later, Annie snatched them from her grip and bolted for the door. "Run, Cassie!" she screamed.

I did just that. We skidded through the door and ran down the gravel driveway for the four-wheeler which was parked near the open garage. Mom gave chase, yelling at us, but we hopped in and locked the doors just in time. She tried my door-handle twice, and then slapped the windows and yelled my name.

I watched as Annie started the engine, reversed a little bit, and drove off. We clipped the letter box, spinning the top around on the base. Down Philips Street we went, the darkness confusing Annie until she realised she hadn't turned the lights on yet.

"We're grounded for life," she said.

I placed my arm against the door and pressed my hand against my forehead. "I couldn't care less. She told me that someone from school took the clay head. My *psychologist*." I squinted as I tried to figure it out.

"The one at school? Why would she want the clay head?"

"I don't know! I barely know her!"

Annie forgot to slow down and we hit some speed bumps with ferocity. "Why would a *psychologist* from our school take it? Why was she even in our house?"

I think I had it figured out. I didn't want it to be true, but I knew it was. "Maybe it was Ursula," I said quietly.

Annie's gaze was right ahead. She blinked a few times. "The one who came for Zag? But she's… I think she's an *alien*."

I bit my nails. "I hope Zag is okay."

"Don't worry. He's fine. We're fine… Which way are we going?"

We were stopped at an intersection. I looked both ways, at the signs, realising we were near the school. Where did I want to go? Where should we go? The woods were to the left, and the school was to the right.

"Let's go to the woods," I said.

I couldn't even bring myself to look at the school right now.

30
WHITE IN THE WOODS

It was bitterly cold outside. I could see my breath as I stepped out of the car. My feet landed in mud. We were parked on an embankment, the woods outstretched in front of us. Annie had a torch in her hands, and she locked the doors behind us.

"Let's stay together," she said.

An owl flew past right above me, scaring me half to death. "I wasn't planning on leaving you."

A few moments later we were hand in hand, amongst the giant pine trees that made up most of the area. Flashlight ahead, shaking in my sister's grip, I looked from one side to the other, paranoid we were going to be attacked by a wolf, a bear, a moose.

"Those fallen trees have got to be around here somewhere," Annie muttered.

We went over a few slopes, climbed over some rocks. Soon enough, up ahead, we could see a different light, white and shimmering. We waited, wondering. It was far ahead, through the trees.

"Maybe that's her. Does she glow?"

"I don't know. Turn the light off," I said, and I did it for her.

Covered in darkness, we waited for our eyes to adjust. With a deep breath, I started walking forward. Annie followed, her free hand on my left shoulder. I pushed through some low branches, hid behind some of the trunks, until we were close enough to see what it was.

I let out a sigh of relief. "It's just the moonlight on a lake."

"Gosh, how big *are* these woods?"

I started walking towards it, taking my steps carefully as we were on higher ground, and I had to steady myself to walk down the steep descent. It wasn't until Annie clutched the back of my shirt that I saw it. I stopped. A moose was a few yards ahead of us, drinking from the body of water. It was gigantic. It had to be the same one I'd seen last time. The one that had almost taken my life.

My breath was caught in my throat. I was frozen. I couldn't move. It hadn't seen us yet, its head down, lapping up water. A chill fog had seeped out of the branches from around us and was weaving itself through the trees. The temperature was steadily dropping with each minute. I slowly reached around for my sister, and tapped her side to make her go back. As I faced her, a fierce white light lit up her face, and she squealed at what she saw. I turned back in horror.

The moose had its head turned, and was looking right at us. Its eyes were glowing white. I pushed into my sister, and we shakily crept backwards as fast as we could. The moose remained, forbidden to move, its glowing eyes squarely set in our direction. I finally turned my back on it, and we began to run away. As fast as we could through the woods, tripping over anything that got in the way. I thought after a few minutes that we had to be going the wrong way, that in a wild run it wouldn't possibly take this long to get back to the car on the embankment. Just as I was about to give up hope, Annie cried out: "There it is!" and we almost flew through the air as we rushed up the slope and hopped back inside. We collapsed in our seats, locked the doors, and panted.

"What were we thinking?" Annie said over and over. She gulped, breathing heavily again. She pulled her asthma pump from her jacket pocket.

I looked out into the darkness. "Was Zag there?" I said.

"I don't care. I just want to go home."

I couldn't see anything outside. The moonlight seemed to have vanished. I felt rather odd, like I was in an elevator going up. I closed my eyes and rubbed my knuckles against my eyebrows.

"Fine. Just fine. Forget it."

In a fit of rage, I punched the dashboard.

"Why do you care?"

"Because I saved him!" I yelled.

"You heard him though, he's not just any child. He's a Child of Crux. He's bad luck! And this week certainly hasn't been a *good* one."

Annie put the key in the ignition. The engine revved.

"I'm too shaken by that moose to argue with you, Cassie, but I will tell you one thing. We're going home. *Now.*" She turned on the lights and put the car into reverse.

To our confusion the lights met with nothing. We stared blankly, trying to figure it out. Sparkly little white things sat in front of us in the darkness, and they were moving. It took us a moment to realise they were stars. Then the moon spun into view and disappeared above. The tops of the pine trees were suddenly illuminated, and then it dawned on me. Our car was high in the air.

We were flying.

Annie and I screamed. I clutched at the door handle to steady my mind, and fastened my seatbelt. I wretched as we began to fall. At the last second the car swerved on its own and started on its way back up into the sky, as if we were on a demented roller-coaster ride. Without thinking, I grabbed the wheel and tried to steer. It did nothing. Finally the car slammed into the gravel road below. Uninjured, I grabbed my sister's shoulder. The car started to drive on its own. Annie and I could do nothing but sit there, shaking. Clueless and at its mercy, it seemed we were driving towards town again. The lights of passing cars came and went, as did streets and buildings. It wasn't until the car turned into our street that I realised what was happening.

It pulled into our driveway and drove all the way into the open garage, where it stopped in the darkness and turned itself off, lights and all. The radio had been playing the entire time, and now that the engine was off, the silence felt deafening. We didn't move. We couldn't move. I stared ahead at some unpacked boxes by the wall.

A pair of green eyes were peering at me through the rear-view mirror. I gasped and turned around. There, in the back-seat, sat a livid little man. Fifty or so, skinny, dressed strangely. His wicked green eyes seemed to sparkle in the darkness.

"*I urge you to stay out of this,*" he said, thin lips barely moving.

The door from inside the house lit up the garage, shadows prancing across the tarp covering Dad's old motorcycle. We spotted Mom's silhouette in the doorway, hands on hips.

I turned back, but the man was gone.

"*Get* inside!" our mother yelled.

31
THE DARK SIDE
OF DANUBE

The planet loomed closer and closer. What started out a tiny spec gradually emerged as a giant ball of light, glowing blue and sparkling white. From the outside it looked as peaceful as ever, a home which she'd spent almost her entire life living upon. Ursula rode Timothy's body as it galloped through the deep void of space, at an indescribable speed, powered by her magical travelling bubble. In her hands she held the clay head tightly.

"Next time, I think we should just take the Carl Sagan subway."

It was finally close enough now that the ice sheets were coming into focus through the clean and sparkling atmosphere. The protective travelling bubble slowed down, and they descended through the clouds until they landed gently in a field of snow amongst the frozen landscape. Nearby, rising high in the air above them, stood the mighty ice dome that protected the great Palace of Danube from outside forces. The bubble popped, and Ursula hopped off Timothy and commanded him to return to his human state. The crisp air shocked him for a moment, and she put her arms around his naked torso. She clicked the fingers on her free hand and conjured up a fur coat to protect him. With that, Ursula walked up to one of the hundreds of the dome's giant ice doors that allowed entrance to the Palace inside. She knocked twice. Almost immediately, a purple cloud of fog appeared above her head, and inside it she could see the face of her father's good friend, Duke Wilson of Elmer. His secret shame had been painted over yet again; this was definitely his best attempt yet.

"Ursula," he said, his lips barely moving in stunned disbelief.

The orphan smiled tiredly. "Let me in please, Wilson, I need to lie down for a few days."

Wilson seemed apprehensive, even perturbed. "Just a minute."

The giant door before them opened and the fog containing Duke Wilson's face vanished into the crisp air. Ursula could finally see the large sparkling city clearly before her, and she found herself momentarily pining for the warmth of Horn-Horn. Before she stepped forward, two large guards in armour and elephant boots emerged and grabbed onto her and Timothy. Alarmed, Ursula demanded they let her go. But they ignored her orders, lifted them into the air and flew down the main streets of Danube. Around her she could see the buildings, apartments filled with people who were watching from their balconies. Suddenly, there was a cry from her left. Then there was one from the right. They were cheering! Pointing and crying with delight.

They like me, they really like me! thought Ursula.

But then, why did they seem so devilish in their cheers? With a sinking feeling in her chest she realised that they were not cheering for her return. They were cheering for her capture.

"She's handed herself in!" somebody called out.

A terrible dread washed over her, and she watched fearfully as the castle loomed closer.

Duke Wilson of Elmer's barracks sat directly beside the late King's headquarters. It was a small office, lavish though it were. Ursula had never been in there until now, but as she found herself dragged through the iron doors she saw how it was full of wooden bookshelves, art, couches, with a desk, a bed, a window, and a moose carpet.

"What is going on?" Ursula snapped at the guards holding onto her. "Unhand me! Unhand *us*."

Timothy transformed into a tiger and batted the guards away, just as Duke Wilson walked in from a side door.

He was an elderly man, scrawny, white as porcelain, with no hair on his head whatsoever. He was of no royal blood, but had grown up with King Frederick. The two were practically brothers, although Wilson himself wasn't even of the same race. He'd been found on another planet, very long ago, and back then he was but the corner of a golden mountain. When Frederick's parents chiselled some away and took it home with them to put on their mantel, they were flabbergasted to discover it contained traces of life. They nursed it, sculpted it into the form of a man, until it learned to act, think and grow like a man. To fit in, he had continually paid top quality artists to paint his body the colours of a typical man, but the truth was: as human, or Danubian as he seemed, everything about him was fake. A secret nobody outside of the royal family knew about. If you were to wipe away all of the paint, you would find a man-shaped, golden chunk of rock beneath.

"Ursula," said Duke Wilson, dressed in a suit, and sporting his favourite green cloak. He sat down at his desk. "This is quite unexpected and unusual. Why have you handed yourself in? We've been trying to find you ever since… Well, we thought we were close, but it turns out we were quite off the mark. We're sending troops back from the middle of Boomfarc-Nuweres right now."

Ursula paced the room, her head held high, and she kept the clay head firmly in front of her. "My treatment since I have returned has been beyond astonishing. Disrespectful to say the least. I hope you are planning on a quick dismissal of whoever organised such horrid treatment against their new Queen."

"Ah, but you are not the Queen of Danube."

"Not yet, this is true."

"Not ever."

"How dare you!" she cried.

"You don't seem to quite understand the circumstances of your case," said Wilson. "As soon as you killed your father, you ran off with your little man servant there… or tiger servant, as he appears… without a single explanation as to why you left, or why you killed your only living relative."

Ursula's jaw was set. "I did not kill my father."

"You most certainly did. The evidence was quite clear to everybody in that auditorium, and the autopsy confirmed what little doubt we had..." He said this all rather quickly as he placed his eyeglasses on and studied a document in front of him. "Torso crushed into the shape of one Diamond of Amber... which has since gone missing... Along with the obvious curvature of your breasts." He looked up. "Witnesses reported seeing you flee from the scene. The last anybody saw of you. Until now. So what I want to know is, why have you returned?"

"I have returned because I left the planet to retrieve my Child of Crux," said Ursula solemnly, and she took the clay head's lid off, revealing a giant rush of light. She closed it quickly. "Being the last present my father gave to me, I regretted dismissing him immediately. I had to have him back. So I went after him."

Duke Wilson laughed.

"A clever story from a clever woman. You've managed to avoid the press and authorities on previous occasions with your 'accidental' murders, Ursula, but not when it comes to regicide."

Numb with shock, she sat down in one of the mahogany chairs offered. Timothy transformed back into his human state, and put his hand on her shoulder. This caused her to weep openly.

"This is how it's going to be, then? After all this time. Wilson, you are *family*. You helped raise me. I haven't intentionally caused harm. I didn't intentionally kill anybody. I am your Queen by *right*. You can't do this to me!"

"There's still hope for you yet. There's the trial. As I'm aware, Rudnick van Pan has stepped forward out of the goodness of his heart and offered to represent you."

Ursula stopped her crying and bared her teeth in fury. "Oh, he has, has he? Has he? He has. Well. A little something you might wish to know about Rudnick van Pan, Duke Wilson. He's been tailing me this past week."

"I imagine he was joining the cause in tracking you down."

"Oh, Wilson, you know his vendetta perfectly well. For forty years he has been trying his best to undermine me, to destroy my reputation, my power."

"van Pan is a staple in our community, a godsend to the people of Danube. Now get over yourself, woman. Guards, take her to the unused gas chambers until we can find a big enough holding cell for her. And for goodness sake, Ursula, don't strike the top of the doorframe on your way out!"

He looked up at her for a moment longer, then shook his head and studied his papers some more. Ursula and Timothy were grabbed by the guards, and found themselves yanked away.

"I want to go home…" she muttered sadly.

It was by a tremendous fluke that Duke Wilson heard this, and the Almighty powers that be must have allowed his hearing such a chance that day, for she'd said it very much under her breath.

Wilson became aggravated. "You are home, you simpleton."

"No," she replied. "Horn-Horn…"

Duke Wilson stood up in such a rush that his joints ground and crumbled. He stared at her a long while as the guards dragged them to the door; finally he demanded they stop. With that, he clicked his fingers to the desk, and they forced the duo back into their chairs.

"What do you know about that place?" he asked.

Ursula could barely answer. A few mutters and mumbles of incoherency later, she finally uttered: "I was there."

"*Why* were you there?"

"No reason."

"Interesting. You liked it?"

Ursula nodded slowly. "Yes."

"What convenient news, then. You are to be punished for your crimes of homicide and abandoning your people by spending the remainder of your life in Horn-Horn. Case solved. No further trials needed. Guards, take these two out of my sight immediately and dispose of them."

Ursula was picked up under the arms and flung away. As the world spun before her, she spotted Timothy the cat spring through the air and clutch onto the back of her own fur coat. Not long after, they were greeted with the same entrance they had come through twenty minutes earlier, only now as an exit. The door opened automatically and with that the guards threw them out into the cold, outside of the dome, banished from Danube forever.

Ursula picked herself up out of the snow and watched as the heavy-set men stepped back through the doorway. One of the guards had taken its armoured mask off, and she was faced with a man much younger than her. Surely he'd only recently hit puberty. He was too young to know what he was doing. Still, he frowned and with fierce determination said:

"By orders of the Duke, you are forbidden to ever return to the Planet of Danube, or its demented moons. If for whatever reason you do, you will be treated as a traitor and will be destroyed. If you leave the town of Horn-Horn for any reason, you will be sent to trial. Is this understood?"

Ursula chose to ignore, turning away instead. She spotted her crystal ball and staff buried under a mound of new snow nearby, which she'd dropped when the guards had grabbed her earlier. Without further ado, the door closed and she found herself shut out from her own Kingdom, with only her future husband, her cat, by her side.

Timothy turned back into a human, bare naked, and quickly resumed hugging her fur coat for warmth.

"What do we do?" he asked through chattering teeth.

Ursula could not bring herself to answer.

PART
THREE

A
FRIGHTFUL
SATURDAY NIGHTFUL

32
GNOWING GNOMES

I was in no mood the next morning.

The night before had been a terror. As Mom and Dad yelled at us for running off like that, all we could do was sit there, not really taking any of their words in. Annie didn't sleep. I could hear her TV on all night. I didn't sleep much either. I drifted off, on edge of course, at about five. I was woken by my phone ringing on my bedside table a few hours later. I jumped in fright and checked it. It was an unknown number, which I usually never answered, but I was in such a desperate state that I didn't care.

"Hello?" I said, hoping stupidly for it to be Zag.

It was Greg. "Hey, what time do you want to go to Ms. Weiss's this morning? Eleanore just called my home number and told my Dad. Now I'm in trouble and he wants me to go as early as possible."

"Oh…" my brain wasn't able to cope with normal life yet. I crawled out of bed, went to the mirror by the door and saw my horrible reflection. Maybe a little walk around town would be good for me. "Give me half an hour. Where do you want to meet?"

"How about at yours?" he suggested.

"Good idea."

"Thanks, but it wasn't mine. Eleanore thought of it."

"Congratulations to Eleanore, then," I muttered, walking down the hall. My throat was dry. "I haven't even finished the paper yet, but at least if I hand it in I won't fail."

"Didn't you have all night to do it?"

"I was distracted."

He laughed. "Cool."

I laughed too, even though it wasn't cool. At all.

Thoughts about the man in the backseat weighed on me as I hopped out of the shower, dried my hair, and chose my clothes from the cold wardrobe. I turned my computer on and printed off what I'd written on Roman Numerals. Shortly after, the doorbell rang and I jumped around with my paper rolled up in my hand.

"Going out," I declared to the empty foyer.

Before I'd reached the door, Dad called out and thundered down the stairs like the giant boulder from Indiana Jones. "You're grounded," he said quickly. "You're not going anywhere until school on Monday."

I gasped as I realised what this meant. "But the party."

"You're *grounded!*" he stressed.

"Look, I'm only going with a few people to my teacher's house. I need to hand in this paper because it was due yesterday. Dad, if I don't go, I'll fail."

Dad bit his bottom lip as he thought about it. "Why didn't you hand it in yesterday?"

"Somebody's at the door. I have to go."

Caught on the spot, he waved his hand for me to leave, and I slunk out of the front door. Greg was outside, with Eleanore and Jack Frost.

"Hello, Cassie!" said Eleanore, frowning.

Her arms were crossed and she was wearing a pink jacket over her usual summer wear. I reached back inside to the coat rack and grabbed my own black jacket. Greg smiled, and I noticed he had his earring back in. It was odd seeing him without it last night at the movie complex. I mean it's not like you could see it that well anyway, under his shaggy black curly hair, but you could catch glimpses of it here and there and it was cool. Really cool. I smiled back at him and we went on our way.

The street that Ms. Weiss lived on was on a slightly lower street to ours, but not many away. It was a historic street in the town, for it was lined with large cherry blossoms that were bursting with colour. It was odd that they were blossoming in Autumn, but given the state of the planet these days when it came to global warming and what-not, was it really that major? Dad had told me once that sometimes plants get confused when the weather isn't matching to the season for long periods of time.

Sadly, it wasn't enough to distract me from Eleanore's jabberwocking. Since we left my house she'd found it impossible to stop blabbering on about her party that night, adding in subtle reminders of how Greg and I weren't invited. There was something about an ice-sculpture of a nude baby, a portable outhouse, and a dingo. I kept looking over to Greg, hoping he would share in my silent amusement at how lame she was, but every time I did it seemed like he was really paying attention to her. Didn't he hate her like the rest of us?

When we turned into a driveway at last, I looked up to see our teacher's house. It was a lovely double storey, made of wood, painted white, with black shutters on the windows. A large verandah with potted plants and a wooden swing was perched at the front, with a wonderfully full front garden filled with the most amazingly rich blue flowers you'd ever seen. Around the property were a few tall oak trees, with one very young maple tree growing by the side of the house. Here and there I could see little garden gnomes parked in peculiar places. Some were fishing, some were holding little tools, some were simply smiling up at the sky. They weren't creepy to me at all, but Eleanore was having a difficult time.

"Just don't look at them," muttered Greg, guiding her up the steps until we reached the front door.

I rang the doorbell, and a very upbeat trumpet version of *The Mary Tyler Moore Show* sounded from inside.

"Doesn't anyone in this town have a normal doorbell?"

Ms. Weiss called from somewhere outside, for her voice echoed. We wondered where she was looking at us from, until we saw through the front windows all the way to the backyard through the house. She seemed to be in some kind of a chicken coop at the very back of the property, waving to us with a trowel in her raised hand. "Come through the house!"

We wiped our feet and opened the front door. The inside was

very neatly kept, but everything was made of the same radiata pine. It gave off a sort of nineties snow-cabin vibe, despite being decorated in flowered curtains, flowered cushions and flowered table-cloths. And, of course, more gnomes.

"I told you," muttered Eleanore.

We walked through the dining room, through the kitchen and out the back door into what was a spectacular garden. Not just your normal one, that is. It was like something out of *Better Homes and Gardens*. How she found the time to keep it as spectacular as it sat before us simply was beyond me. Yet even from here, I could spot the gnomes. Dozens of them. Upon dozens. All hidden amongst bushes, some sitting up in branches of trees, a few of them watching from high-hung baskets. It was, as Eleanore had warned, starting to get a little bit creepy.

"Good morning, Ms. Weiss!" the one and only piped up in her best naughty schoolgirl impression. "Your garden is looking wonderful as always!"

Ms. Weiss never seemed to care for her choice of words. She didn't smile at her but still said thank you, and moved on to Greg and I. "I'm glad to see that you both have actually bothered to do your work. Let's see them, shall we?" We gave her our papers, and she smiled at us warmly. "Stay right here. I've got a surprise for you for making the effort."

With that, she stabbed her trowel into the ground right by the Saviour's foot. Eleanore flinched. Then, she made her way inside, leaving us alone again with the gnomes.

"Look at them," said Greg. The one up in the basket had somehow made it swing gently, although I suspected it was the breeze that passed by moments before.

"There's more of them this time," said Eleanore in a hush. "They're breeding. I swear on my mother's grave."

"She's not dead, you creep."

Ms. Weiss came out again with a picnic basket under her right arm. She seemed to be quite excited. "My sister was here last week and she made too many chocolate chip cookies, so I thought you three would like to share them amongst yourselves."

We did what anybody would do when faced with a kind gesture from a teacher: We smiled and said thank you, while our butt cheeks clenched awkwardly. I took the basket and peered inside. I'd been expecting a full load, but there were only three in there.

I met my teacher's gaze.

"Please return the basket when you've finished," she said nicely.

Either Greg or Eleanore poked me in the back.

"I've got to go home," I told her. "I'm grounded... For not handing in my work."

Ms. Weiss was the first to head back inside. Greg followed her, then Eleanore, and I walked behind still with the basket in my hands. I purposely kept my eyes straight as the garden gnomes seemed to peer at me from my peripherals. What was it about these garden statues? I was halfway up the back steps when I found out. Something caught on the bottom of my jeans. I turned to see one garden gnome clutching at my hems, its giant painted eyes looking right into mine. I froze in place and stared in disbelief.

"Don't give up on Zag," it said in a pleading whisper.

I flinched out of its grip and ran to catch up to the others.

"I'll see you both bright and early on Monday morning; no hangovers," Weiss said to Greg and I. "And with your grades for these." She tossed the papers around from hand to hand. Then she turned to Eleanore. "I'll see *you* tonight."

"Yes, you will!" said Eleanore excitedly.

With that, we said goodbye and left. Once around the corner and out of sight, Eleanore snatched the basket off me and opened it up to grab a handful. She was equally surprised by the little amount inside. "That woman is insufferable. How rude! And especially with me, since I had nothing to gain out of today's exercise. We might as well toss the basket! Say a bird stole it. The birds in this town are abnormally pesky."

Greg rolled his eyes and stopped in his tracks, and grabbed my arm so I would, too. When Eleanore stopped as well, he gave her a slightly pleading stare and she gave a tremendous sigh and walked off. With that, I forgot all about the garden gnome. Greg stood in front of me, very close, but not too close. We'd never shared much eye contact. And we had never been this particularly up front. His eyes were green. I'd thought they were blue, but no. Very green. He had a few blemishes on his face but no pimples. Not like my three eyesores clustered around the corners of my nose. He had shaved this morning, too. I noticed the difference from the previous night. Shaving for me over shaving for work.

That must mean something, I thought.

"Hey, do you want to get breakfast?" he asked.

I looked down the road at Eleanore walking away. Her head was held high, clearly not pleased at being dumped yet again. The familiar emotions of guilt and pity set in. I'd known her for six whole days now, but it felt like a lifetime.

"As long as I can invite Eleanore."

He didn't look thrilled. It was something in the way he tilted his head, but he covered his tracks and smiled as genuinely as before.

"Sure!"

I called out to Eleanore. She stopped at once and faced us, lifting her arms up in irritated concern. Greg and I ran to the spot she stood at, near a stop sign by the last cherry blossom tree. When I invited her, she scowled suspiciously, scrutinising my motives, but one look at Greg and she sighed at what a clear inconvenience this was to her.

"Alright. But *only* because we're already out, and being the first week of school my responsibilities as the Principal's daughter still apply."

"Great. Where should we go?"

"There are *so* many options," she told me merrily. "But there's one particular restaurant called the Pop Shop that makes the most amazing waffles. Either that, or Eggs Benedict."

As we walked downhill, it started to drizzle. The weather was abysmal. Greg and Eleanore started talking as if the hierarchy in school had never existed. I wasn't paying attention, though. Thoughts of Zag seeped their way to the front of my mind. The gnome, was it an alien too? Is that how it knew him? Were all gnomes aliens in disguise? A clever disguise it was, but unnerving for sure. I pitied all of the humans throughout history who had gone outside in what was assumed to be the privacy of their own backyard, only to have sex in front of one. Or, pity be for the poor gnome's soul, atop.

— · · · —

The Pop Shop wasn't open on Saturday mornings, the two of them soon recalled. With that we hot-footed it down the road a little more until we were way past the school and heading towards the beach. About fifteen minutes later we were on the busy side of town, away from the woods, surrounded by in-town apartments, businesses, and the Mayor's office right ahead. It was a grand building with giant sophisticated marble stairs out the front, and was one of the biggest and oldest buildings in town, a fact I'd actually picked up in school that week during History class.

We turned left, though, down Nightmare on Elm Parade, until Greg and Eleanore both entered a door to a tiny café called *Spliffany's*. Greg kept it open for me to go through before him. Inside was small and cramped, and the floors and walls were made of the same concrete slabs. As small as it was, there seemed to be enough room for seven tables. Eleanore went and grabbed one in the back corner, and I joined her promptly, sitting in one of the circular shaped wicker chairs.

"Breakfast at Spliffany's?" I said to the both of them as I undid my jacket. They nodded tiresomely. Obviously this joke had passed its use-by date many eons ago.

A woman came over to take our orders that didn't look much older than us, although apparently she was. She was a skinny little thing, petite, with blonde hair, and she sported a baby bulge. It turns out, this was the owner, and her name was Tiffany. Eleanore was chummy with her because when she'd been in the seventh grade, Tiffany had been in the twelfth, and Tiffany had been a very popular girl. Naturally, the story that unfolded can be easily predicted. Turns out the name of the café was derived from an experience Tiffany had gone through in high school when she and her friends were busted with marijuana.

"See, clearly everybody grows out of the juvenile behavioural cycle that comes with being in high school," said Eleanore, pouring herself a glass of water. "Tiffany is a prime example; the only difference between her and myself is that while I'm only sixteen, I would never be stupid enough to get busted with drugs..." She checked over her shoulder. "Plus, Tiffany doesn't have an adoring father like I do. Hers died in a plane crash, or a buggy-ride. One of the two, I've forgotten. So her wayward ways are way worse than anything I would do, because she has no father."

"You really think fathers are what keep girls together growing up?" Greg sounded like he was amusing her.

"Yes, and the other way around for boys; without their mothers they turn rebellious."

"That's not true. My father is raising me just fine."

"Um… correct me if I'm wrong, but aren't you the one who had a pet spider not so long ago? Plus, those other things, Mr. James

Dean? That shan't ever be mentioned again?"

Greg gave her a look that seemed to suggest they had some sort of history, and a flare of jealousy erupted inside me.

"Where's your mother?" I asked him.

He hesitated, and Eleanore looked down. Greg smiled at me.

"She's here. Just not... all there."

I nodded in understanding, but didn't understand at all.

The conversation after that was tepid at best. There was no more natural flow. I had to think up conversation starters, mostly about school and the fires, and even went so far as to bring up what was happening on the news, and the weather if you can believe it. The two of them kept it going, probably with as much hope as I had, but it wasn't until our breakfasts arrived that we finally had something genuine to keep us occupied.

Twenty minutes later, Greg's phone rang. He didn't sound too pleased when he replied. I guessed in this case, it was his father whom I knew nothing about. Maybe it had something to do with his mother, who was here but not all there.

When he hung up, he said: "I've got to go home."

My world crumbled. What did I have to look forward to now? A day home alone locked in my room, punishments abounding.

"That's okay!" I said to him, laughing it off. "No worries!"

"It was nice to see you outside the confines of school again, Gregory," said Eleanore rather formally, and she placed her cutlery in the middle of the plate.

At the front counter as we paid, Greg turned to me and tilted his head from side to side for a moment, and held out his hands. He smiled, but painfully.

"Well, bye!" he said.

I got the hint, said: "Oh," and gave him the hug that he'd been hinting at. It was a gentle hug, where I was too afraid to really properly touch him, but I noticed he smelled of coconut. I let go first, and then watched as he walked out of the establishment.

"I'm feeling generous today," spoke Eleanore from my side, and she took her debit card off the cashier. She grabbed my arm in that all too familiar dominative style of hers. We headed into the chilled street, the bell above the door jingling as we left.

"You are?"

"Yes, and therefore I may regret this later, but out of the goodness of my heart this fine day I am personally inviting you to attend my fabulous gala tonight."

I stopped in the street and paid her full attention, irrevocably suspicious down to the very marrow in my bones. She held two of the laminated pink tickets in her left hand, spread apart like the smallest deck of cards.

"Who's the second one for?"

"Your boyfriend, of course."

"Greg is not my boyfriend," I insisted, clenching my jaw.

"No, but something tells me he will be. If you play your cards right. I get you, Cassie. I don't particularly like it, but I know what you're doing now. You see a boy you like so you befriend *his* friends, ditching us while you get your man. It's very clever."

I tried to keep up with her. "You're saying...?"

"You know what I'm saying," she winked at me, and placed the tickets into one of my palms. "I figured it out during breakfast. You can stand Hayley Gauche just as much as I can. But you're willing to put up with her while you woo Greg. Then, once you've got him under your womanly spell, you'll ditch his yeti friends and take him with you. He'll be too caught up in your romance to object. A proper Saviour couldn't even pull it off, but here you are."

I crossed my arms and arched one of my eyebrows. "That's not how it is at all."

"No, of course not," she giggled. She refused the return. "I'll see you two tonight. *TTFN!*"

Eleanore blew me a kiss and walked off in the other direction, leaving me on the pebbled sidewalk.

Compelled to scream in frustration, I spun around to head back home, but didn't get two steps before I bumped into Hayley. Quite literally, I might add. She was standing there on her own, her arms squarely on her hips, completely still, with the face of a peeved bulldog. I collected myself, and crammed the tickets into my jacket pocket for some reason.

"You scared the crap out of me," I said nervously, and then shook it off. "How cold is it today..?"

I couldn't pretend I didn't notice any more. I met her eye-line, and for a few moments we said nothing.

"So, you're having secret meetings with Eleanore Parker now?"

I shook my head. "It's not quite like that. Look, she..."

"I know about the homework. But you see, a little birdie told me you were grounded and only taking your homework to Ms.

Weiss's house, then going straight home. Since that little birdie was your mother, and she's coming around the corner, I'd love to hear the conversation you have to see if it matches up. But I won't bother."

The words sunk in and I peered behind me just in time to witness my mother and brother trotting around the nearest corner. When I turned back, I was stunned to find Hayley barely an inch away, her face beetroot red with rage.

"Do this town a favour, and go back to Salem," she said.

I watched as she ran across the street without causing a scene. Flustered, I undid a few buttons to breathe easier, and turned just as my mother caught sight of me. She stopped in her tracks, and huffed in displeasure.

"Mom," I called out.

Striding angrily, she pointed a finger before reaching me.

"In the future, when your father tells you to come home right away, you do it. Don't mess with me today, Cassie, I mean it. Come on, we're going to the shops and then straight home. *Do you understand me!?*"

People turned at the commotion. I submitted with a tiny nod, and she grabbed my arm with one hand and my brother's with the other. We were pulled away in a rush.

Brendan declared immediately: "Let me go; I didn't do anything. *My sunburn, woman!*"

33
BROTHER KNOWS BEST

It was the grocery trip from hell. Brendan and I kept our distance from Mom as she smelled fruits, weighed them, inspected milk expiry dates, checked the racks for cheap items of food, tried to find spiced chai for her precious coffees, and scoped the medicine section for aloe vera. It was clear to both of us that we were meddling with a woman who had recently been pushed to her limits. Uncharacteristically, she complained to one of the teen employees when she noticed all but the red hair dyes had sold out (which was apparently a very common occurrence in town). We watched in horror as the poor clerk blushed at the confrontation.

"This is all your fault," muttered Brendan, scowling at me.

It was only now that it was dawning on me what a week it must have been for my mother, too. Losing her place at the school to that... well... woman from another planet, moving to a new town, trying to find her bearings, having one of her daughters involved in some mysterious attack in the woods. I yearned to spill the beans, but I knew I would be sent off to the Looney Bin. And that would be awkward, since she'd be starting work there soon.

———— · · · ————

Once we arrived home, I was ordered straight to my room. I collapsed on my Legs of Luxury, smothered my face into my pillow, and muttered to myself nonsensically to try and alleviate the nasty headache I'd developed.

Did Eleanore *really* think I was some sort of a Saviour spy? Hayley seemed to be convinced of the same thing, too. I couldn't wrap my head around it. This wasn't a friggin' Scooby-Doo mystery.

A sudden deep throbbing started pulsating throughout the house. I sat up curiously, annoyed even, thinking it to be the end of the world, or my heart-beat flowing through my ears. I quickly discovered it to be mundane trance music playing very loudly from nearby. I assumed it was the sound guys testing out the speakers for Eleanore's party.

Brendan opened my door without even a courteous knock. He was wearing a singlet and shorts, his sunburn still very evident. He had walked with caution at the shops, but now without the confines of a jacket and pants he seemed to manoeuvre with a touch more freedom.

"I wish you didn't have sunburn," I said in pity.

An off-handed comment, really. No intention behind it. But something glittery caught in my throat like an unexpected belch, and I covered my mouth in disbelief.

I could still make wishes!

Brendan's skin changed like a chameleon before my very eyes, from red to his usual lily-white. His head tipped back and moaned in pleasure. He quickly examined his arms and legs.

"Wow, that sulfadiazine works fast."

I cleared my throat nervously. "Feeling better?"

"It's like a summer breeze is mating with my genitals."

I nodded and blocked the mental image forever. "What's up?"

"Why did you and Annie run away last night?"

I didn't like this, and became defensive again.

"It's complicated."

"The Pythagorean Theorem is complicated," he said, giving me a frown. "I heard the commotion from the bathtub. It's obviously got something to do with what happened the other day. That pink rush of paper in the hallway? I only thought I was going crazy for about *three* minutes. Ever since then I've been snooping around listening to you guys."

I shook my head and tried in exhaustion to cover my tracks.

"Nothing... went..."

"Knock it off!" he yelled. "Mom made me come up here to ask if you were in any trouble, then report back to her with whatever you told me. But she didn't see what I saw the other day, so anything you do tell me is going to stay right here." He pointed to his head.

I laughed at the absurd idea of confiding in my little brother. He was four and a half years younger than me. That wouldn't be much difference in the same amount of years, but at the age we were now it seemed radical.

"Give me a few more days to wrap my head around everything. Then maybe I'll tell you."

Brendan threw me an icy stare. He turned to go back downstairs to 'report' to Mom, but before he did, he said something that stirred me a little:

"I'll find out. You know I will."

As he disappeared down the hallway, I sat there cross-legged on my bed and tried to assess my emotions with little success.

34

THE FATE OF HORN-HORN

Mid-afternoon came with a mysterious gale from the east. Upon the cliffs of Horn-Horn, directly behind the town sign with the two ancient animal horns perched atop, Ursula sat plaintively and watched as the storm front bulged and rolled across the oceanic horizon in front of her. Lightning struck far off at sea, but no sound was heard. She placed her powerful staff onto the ground. The crystal ball, overwrought with its connection to her emotions, turned the grass in contact with it yellow, until it rotted. A large circle of dirt now supported it instead. Timothy, in his favourite cat form, emerged from some nearby shrubs with a dead mouse hanging from his clenched jaw, and he played with it a moment before seemingly realising what he was doing. Disgusted in himself, he batted it away, and watched with surprise as a seagull swooped down and carried it away. He then looked up at his future wife and they shared a moment of understanding. Doom was setting in.

On her way back to the planet, Ursula had busied herself scrounging up information, using her crystal ball as source. In it she saw the planet Earth, and discovered a disturbing fact. The decision had been made many weeks before. Now, forbidden to leave Horn-Horn for the rest of their lives, Timothy and Ursula had unwittingly signed their own death warrants.

"Go on, wake him up," said Timothy, and he stroked the clay head with a paw and watched as the golden and aqua lights shone from inside the ancient hollow piece of art.

Zag emerged and lay down on the grass in front of them, fast asleep as he had been since long before his abduction from the comfort of ownership. He was non-the-wiser, until the moment he opened his eyes and saw a cat in front of him. He turned in confusion, seeing Ursula, and yelped. He jumped to his feet and examined his surroundings feverishly. The busy highway exit was just behind them, the heavy shrubbery and the town sign being the only protection from passing humans in their vehicles. He deduced with great sadness that Ursula had the clay head in her possession once more. His luck was up.

"Tell me you didn't hurt them," he said to her.

Ursula blinked, taking in these unexpected words of desperation. "Of course not. Sit down, Zag. I need to tell you something."

Ursula thought of how to begin, and once she pinpointed the right place, it soon flowed from her lips like the news reels she'd conjured just hours before. "The powers that be have decided that this planet is very special. For years now, as you know, there have been experiments going on in the far reaches of the galaxy to tamper with flipping dimensions around, twisting them, like twisting a balloon. Many organisations feared that meddling with such intricate, intimate depths would destroy the entire universe, so it was never fully explored as a credible scientific breakthrough when we discovered the multiple, nay endless amounts of dimensions that exist beyond our own. Millions of them very closely resembling ours, with the possibility of there being one for each different spec of matter in the universe. Then recently, somebody discovered one that had the exact same timeline as the very one *we* live in. Bar a planet. A very *important* planet."

Zag sat on his knees. He listened intently.

"There were arguments for months. I recall most of them now, but hardly ever paid attention to universal events as they bored me so; but this one stood out because of its significant threat.

"As you know, a comet has been heading straight towards Earth, a fact known by Danubians for many years. The final trajectory has in recent weeks been discovered. It is going to hit New York City in May of next year. Smack dab in the middle of it. Now, you can understand the predicament. Not only the notion of losing this important hub for its history, but also losing the millions of residents. Given the city's notoriety, it's an event that will be nothing short of a global disaster, perhaps the biggest this planet's population has ever seen.

"You know Danube is on good terms with all the continents and nations of this planet. And you know the common human does not and will not know life exists beyond this planet for a very long time. But Zag, everybody involved has already commissioned the plan. To flip the Earth with another. Until the comet has come and gone."

Zag could only gulp, stupefied. "They'll flip what, exactly?"

Ursula looked warily at Timothy, and he urged her to continue with a gentle nod. "They will flip this Earth with another Earth. The one from the other dimension they found, where the similarities in culture were close, but the evolution of the continents and social history are drastically different."

"What has this got to do with us?"

Ursula grabbed a handful of grass. "We are on that Earth, Zag. The other one contains seven continents. They are named: Africa, Antarctica, Asia, Australia, Europe, North America, and South America. Countries are divided amongst these seven."

"I can't imagine more than four, as it is on this planet."

"The positioning there is different, too. Which is why they chose it over millions of others. The governments of this Earth agreed with the governments of that Earth, and all contracts have been signed. The comet will instead strike a small town on *our* Earth, instead of New York on *their* Earth."

A slight tingle ran down the child's spine. It spread across his shoulders and over his scalp.

"Millions of lives will be spared, and the western world will not crumble with the natural destruction of one of the most powerful cities in the world… Which happens to be going through its own crisis at the moment, on the other side at least."

Ursula admired the sun as it began to set prematurely behind the cumulus clouds. Thunder clapped in the distance at last and a fresh warm wind danced about them.

"You understand, don't you, that…"

"Yes, I understand."

Zag thought it through, curiously, until Ursula clicked her fingers and a globe of the Earth appeared in front of them, transparent in nature like the memory of a ghost. He squinted and leaned in, examining it, and noticed the drastic differences. As she said, there was a vastly different face to this planet. Similarities, yes, but so very different in geography. He went searching immediately. The disturbing thought had plagued his mind, and he scanned above the equator for the place where New York sat. Up he went, past unfamiliar or misplaced towns, cities, until New York appeared. On that version, it was located higher, closer to the border. And it sat exactly where he'd hoped it *wouldn't* be. In its original place, the small town Ursula mentioned that would take the impact instead, was…

Zag tossed his head to-and-fro as he battled with the raped morals of what was planned. "No. *No, you can't be serious!*"

Ursula didn't want to say it, but knew she had to.

"The comet is only a quarter the size of Horn-Horn, but come May, it will annihilate everything you see around you."

Bereft, Zag turned in near madness to the scenery about him. The cliffs, the lighthouse, the ocean. He watched a pair of seagulls glide together on a pocket of air above, until a strong gust swept them further away.

"Rather the loss of a small town like this than the millions in New York, don't you think? No matter how you look at it."

They would evacuate. That's what they would do, Zag realised. He would help, too. The governments would flock in around April or so, order everybody out, and it would be done. It had to be done. They would get everybody out safely, as well as the surrounding towns. In New York if such a scenario were to happen, they would never truly get everybody out, he knew that. At least here, the certainty was that unless something very bad happened on the day, they could all be saved. Still, the town would be gone, lost forever. Its history, its foundation. Just a crater in the ground.

"Funny," he said, more to himself. "I choose to look at it as the barbaric act that it is."

"Barbaric or not, it will happen. Horn-Horn will cease to exist. And so will we."

"We?"

"I've been punished to spend the remainder of my life imprisoned in this town. Therefore my time is short. But truthfully I'm not very woebegone about the whole matter. I mean really, Danube has never loved me. I've been a horrid boil on their backs for decades. They were simply putting up with me. They never cared about me in the first place. The only one that cared about me was my father, and he's gone. At least I'm stuck in the one town where somebody was genuinely kind to me... Even though I've probably scared her away." She wiped a tear from her eye, and stood up. "So we shall stay with her. I'll hold onto that job at the school, and eventually learn my way to being competent. Then we will die."

Zag doubled in an uproar.

"You can do what you want, but *we're* not staying here! Cassie and her family, we're gone. You may have taken the clay head away from her, but Cassie Gellar is still my owner."

"The Heads of the Universe must realise that I didn't mean to give you up. It was a moment of weakness. I'm still your owner, rightfully so. Not that *teenager*."

"You know the rules," said Zag angrily, pointing a finger at her. "Once you give up a Child of Crux, you can never get them back. Even if you *steal them*. Plus, you have to explicitly give orders of dismissal, and she never gave that to me. She's still my owner and she probably doesn't even realise it."

He stood up at once. Ursula grabbed her staff and pointed it at him, her eyes watering.

"Don't you *dare* do this to me, Zagreus! You have *no idea* what I've been through in this town. You're the last gift given to me by my father. You are too important."

"You're right, I am important," said Zag, and he scooped up his clay head in preparation to leave.

"Please!" screamed Ursula desperately. *"I have no one left!"*

Green envy and loneliness eclipsed her better judgement. As her cheeks flushed and her breast heaved, the pointed staff began to vibrate. Timothy backed away. The clouds inside the crystal ball turned purple. With that, she jerked her head to the side as the crystal ball exploded with light.

An energy blast spat from its tip with the power of a thousand volts of lightning, and they gutted Zag from inside to out. The deafening roar was covered from the outside world by the coincidental roll of thunder moving in from the sea. When the energy stopped, Ursula found herself in a nearby bush. The force was so strong that it had lifted her off her feet. Timothy was under her, not injured. He meowed and slunk out carefully. The light had been so powerful that even with their eyes closed the entire time they could still see spots in front of their vision.

Ursula looked around for any sign of Zag, but could only see his clothes in a mess on the ground. Her heart leapt at the thought of him in a pile of cinders. She ran forward, devastated, but as she grabbed his clothes she noticed that the clay head was nowhere in sight. There were no shackles either. Which meant he was still holding onto it somewhere. *Somewhere.*

Ursula looked up just in time to see an infant with pointy ears clinging to the clay head as it rose like a balloon into the sky. The naked baby was crying in fright, whinging as it disappeared into the clouds above.

"Damn that mysterious clay head!" she screamed.

35
STRANGER DANGER

I got a text at some point in the afternoon from an unknown number. I was quite sick of these unknown numbers calling and texting me, but being new to town I guess it was to be expected. Except for the fact that this number sent quite a disturbing piece of advice:

'Watch your back – Hayley's fuming.'

I read the words over and over again, then placed my phone down and turned the television on instead.

Dad swooped through the door, causing me to jump. He watched with raised eyebrows as I quickly switched the TV off again. I stayed perfectly still, clearly busted.

He humphed.

"God. What do you want me to do, sit here and stare at the wall all day?"

"Do your homework," he said grumpily.

I equalled his grumpiness: "I didn't get any. I handed it in to-day, remember?"

Dad put his arms up. "I'm tired of fighting with you. I'm just here to let you know that your mother and I are going out to see a movie. We need a few hours away from… whatever all of this sud-den angst is. Alright? It starts in half an hour so we have to leave right away. We'll bring you guys back some pizza for dinner, alright? What do you feel like?"

"Margherita," I said as usual.

"Fine. In the meantime, do not leave this house. One, you're grounded. Two, there's a big storm coming."

I looked out the window and saw a flash of lightning. "I bet Eleanore will be thrilled."

"No going to any parties, either, no matter how loud and entic-ing they may be."

I threw a sock at him. "I wasn't planning to!"

I waited until he had left and then got up and went into An-nie's room to sneak a peek at what they were doing next door. Annie was already at her window and she had the blinds wide open. From where I stood behind her, through the trees and over the fence, there were big electrical speakers on each side of the back fence, and a giant flood-light that thankfully wasn't turned on yet, even if it was getting dark early due to the bad weather.

"Exciting stuff. I can't wait to go."

"We're grounded," I reminded her.

She pouted sadly. "I wish Zag was here. It feels like a dream now. Did you wish for him to come back?"

"Yeah, about ten minutes ago, but it didn't do anything…"

She made an 'uh-huh' sound in her throat. Without another word, I went back into my own room where I lay on my bed and stared out at the grey sky, trying not to think of him. I instead set my mind on Eleanore's party. Maybe she'd get the hint that I wasn't ma-nipulating Hayley when I didn't actually turn up. Even though Hay-ley would think that I *was* manipulating her by not turning up to sabotage. Either way, I couldn't go. Unless I snuck out. But I had never done that before. It was something I'd only seen in the movies, and it never worked out. I wasn't any good at climbing ropes, let alone bed-sheets.

It was at that moment a strange sort of box emerged from the clouds above and made its way very gently through the sky until I was absolutely certain it was floating right down into our own front garden. Of course, I couldn't see the front of our property from my room, but I sat up in wonder and put some socks on to go and check. A second later the doorbell rang and I froze in place at my bedroom door.

"I'll get it," said Brendan from the lounge-room.

Panicking, I fled from my room faster than the lightning that struck nearby as I did, and I tumbled down the stairs and raced for the open door. I rammed into Brendan, who was holding the box. It had landed on our doorstep quite literally, it seemed.

"Give it to me," I said.

Brendan backed away, leaving the door open. He ran into the lounge, and behind the couch with the box in his hands. When he was sure he was safe, he rested it on the top of the couch and opened the lid. I immediately saw that my name was written on one of the cardboard flaps. I pointed at it, but he told me to hush, and he dug inside. First he pulled out the clay head. He examined it with intrigue, then tossed it onto the nearby sofa. I ran to it and clutched it, relieved. By then I'd left Brendan alone with whatever else lay inside. I watched as he pulled out a mound of wrapped blankets. His face lit up, delighted astonishment glimmering in his eyes.

"It's a baby brother!"

The cherubic face of a sleeping baby poked out of a gap in the blankets. Upon pressing it against his chest, I noticed the red hair and pointy ears. It was Zag, alright. Only... younger.

"Brendan! DROP IT!" I shouted as sternly as I could.

My brother was about to abide when he glanced at the open doorway, and jumped in fright. I turned and saw the man from the backseat, standing in the door frame. He was wearing the same peculiar attire from our previous engagement.

"Hello, children. I see you've found the Child of Crux." His voice was gentle and high and sweet, but in turn it had a certain curl to it, like the almost inaudible growl of a lion.

Brendan was speechless, as this man looked terrifying. His skin was ravaged by small scars, looking like wrinkles.

"What do you want?"

Upon hearing my voice, the man very gradually moved his gaze from my brother over to me, a humoured look in his crescent-shaped eyes. "Aha. You must be Cassie Gellar. Won't you let me in?"

"You are in," I said, looking him up and down.

"In fact, I am not," he laughed curtly. He looked down to show he was on the outer side of the doorframe. "It's impolite to leave someone out in the cold. Weren't you taught manners?"

"Our parents taught us never to invite strangers in," I said, and noticed Annie at the top of the staircase, peering down from a safer distance.

"I was nearby and I noticed this delightful little box float down from the heavens, and I knew it had to be Zagreus. May I take a look?"

Brendan watched me curiously, and then Annie walked down the stairs. "You look familiar…" she said. She squinted for a moment, and then her face dropped as she recognised him.

"Allow me to introduce myself," the man spoke through a grin that was somewhat growing so wide it looked like somebody had sliced through the meat in his face. "My name is Rudnick van Pan. I have been following you for the past week. Everywhere you have gone, I have been watching."

"Why?" I said.

"To protect you from evil forces, of course," he said. "I came here hunting a very dangerous woman, and I took an oath to protect whoever got in her way."

"Ursula?" I guessed.

He stroked the sides of the door with his hands in an unconventional manner. "Yes. Exiled from her own planet, she came here to capture that Child of Crux, but until yesterday she'd failed to locate him. I for one knew where he was the entire time, but distracted her from finding you for as long as I could, hoping the authorities would reach her first. I controlled that fire in your friend's house the other day. I initiated the bush-fires to break apart your session with her in school. Now I'm afraid she has slipped through the system once again and is on her way back here to claim that child. Which is why I am here, and that is why I must come in."

To all of our surprises, the baby started to cry. A second later, thunder shook everything in the room. The storm was getting very close now. A gust of wind entered through the open door.

"Please, let me in," said van Pan.

I looked at him one last time, then at the baby that seemed to be clawing with desperation at the sides of Brendan's shirt. Rudnick van Pan was here to help us ward off Ursula. If what he said was true, she was still in town, and now that Zag was back in this house she was surely on her way here.

"The leaves..." said Annie behind me.

I'd forgotten she was there. I faced her, taking in her confounded and wary look, as she was staring at the entrance. I turned to see what she was talking about and noticed right away. The wind was coming in through the door, where Rudnick van Pan stood, and with the wind came scattered early autumn leaves. Only, the leaves didn't enter the house. They pressed up against something invisible, like a sheet of glass. A forcefield. Something was stopping them from entering the house. Something was stopping *him*.

"The wish I made!" Annie hushed in my ear. "To stop bad people from entering the house."

I lifted my head to confront the stranger. He knew I knew, and something dark appeared in his eyes. I felt giddy with shock. Without another word, Annie ran to the door and closed it in his face. The wind stopped, the eerie impossible foliage vanished. She locked it in good measure, then shrugged herself off and came back over to us. "Spooky. Just like in those vampire stories."

I looked at Brendan, whose eyes were still focussed on the front door. I grabbed his cheeks and turned him to face me. "I told you not to get involved in this. Now please, give me the baby."

I tucked my arm under it to get a better grip. But before I could go any further, he snatched it back to his chest and ran upstairs, sobbing as he did. I gave chase. Annie followed in hot pursuit. He'd shut his bedroom door and placed something in front of it. I banged hard. "Let me in," I demanded.

Fed up, Annie and I stomped into my room and I placed the clay head on my bed.

"Make a wish," said Annie.

I thought for a moment. What could I wish for? Anything, really. But more importantly: "I wish Brendan's door would open."

I heard a dramatic smash from inside his room. Annie and I jumped in fright, heard our little brother cry out, and we desperately raced for his door. We didn't have to push at it to open it. Brendan opened it himself and came running out with the baby still in his arms. It seemed my wish had caused his window to break inwards. I looked at Annie. Well, the wish had worked, sort of. Brendan's door *was* open, one way or another. I grabbed my little brother's shoulders and pushed him into my room with my sister.

"*What is going on!?*" he screamed, half afraid, half angry.

Now was the time, I realised. I plopped him down on my bed and stood in front of him.

"Okay, here's the deal. You're holding an alien. A magical wishing alien. It sounds stupid, I know, but he's not a toy, Brendan, and he's not a baby. I don't know why he... why he *is* a baby, but he's not normally. He's a kid, like you. That man out there wants him, and we don't know why. But he threatened us last night, so he's bad. Also, there's this..." I looked up at Annie, searching for the words, "there's this lady from school who wants him, and she's an alien as well. I don't know what else to tell you. This little guy's name is Zag, and I found him in the woods on Monday and brought him home and now I can make wishes with him; but most importantly these people out to get him will probably want to hurt us, or Mom and Dad if they get inside. So don't let anybody in. Alright?" I grabbed at Annie's waist. "Oh God, do you think Mom and Dad are alright?"

Annie didn't answer. Brendan wiped the baby's right cheek of tears. It was for once a good thing we were grounded.

Somebody knocked on my window. Upon seeing Rudnick van Pan's lurking, pale figure lit up by the inside lights, the three of us backed against the furthest wall in fright. Brendan ran with the baby down the hall, into our parents bedroom, insane from shock.

"*Shut the blinds!*" screamed Annie.

I rushed over, trying not to look at him. He was as close to me as I would ever get to a bathroom mirror to inspect myself. He was smiling, too. Always smiling.

"*What do we do, what do we do!?*" cried Annie in a panic, once the blinds were closed. "*We have a madman outside, from another world, and he can fly! And make cars fly!*"

"*I don't know! I don't know!*" I yelled back.

Brendan came walking back in, pale as a ghost, baby in one hand, phone in the other. He looked up at me, ashamed. "I called Mom. They're coming home now."

My eyes widened. I looked from him, to the baby.

"Try wishing him away again," said Annie quickly.

"Forget it! The wishes aren't working properly. I'll probably make him explode, after that last try."

"You've got to do something. Anything. *Try.*"

I smiled at Brendan calmly for a moment, and then wrestled fiercely with him to claim the baby. When I succeeded, I plopped him on the bed. My first wish was to make him stop crying. It didn't work, and I looked around, preparing for something much worse to happen. It was then, as my head was turned inspecting the room, that I saw the baby's shadow on the wall begin to rise. I looked back and caught him just in time. He'd started floating into the air by himself. I pulled him down, then let him go to test him. Without supports, he would slowly float to the ceiling, as if he were a helium balloon.

"This is ridiculous. You two, help me find some kind of bags or something to tie him to the bed with."

Within a few minutes we'd taped together four coat-hangers, stabbed them into the sides of the mattress, and used elastic bands to tie around the baby's wrists and ankles, attaching them to the coat-hangers. It worked, sort of. He was still crying, though.

"Now try practice wishing," said Annie, and she grabbed a bottle of my rose-scented deodorant from the bedside table. "Wish it was invisible."

I did as she said. It instead split the object inside out, crumpling the metal and sending the powdered ingredients all over the wooden floor.

"What's the good in having unlimited wishes if they don't work!?"

"It must be because he's a baby," said Annie. "Maybe they don't get powers until they're older. Look, Mom and Dad will be home soon. We've got to think of something." She raced around the room for inspiration. "Oh, there! A mirror. Wish that he could hide in the mirror for now. He could hide in there until Mom and Dad go to bed, at least."

"Alright, I wish for Zag to be on the other side of the mirror."

I covered my eyes with my hands, afraid of the outcome. I knew right away that something was different, though. No more sound. Zag's cries had disappeared. I opened my eyes, and flinched in major confusion. The confusion remained and I kept flinching until I clutched at my bed to support my spinning head. I was in my room, alone. Only, it wasn't my room. Yet it was. I glanced at the mirror on the back of my door to make sure I wasn't merely mistaken, and that's when I saw them. Standing there, on the inside of my mirror, looking in at me. My siblings, their hands pressed on the glass, crying out at me. I couldn't hear them.

They were locked in the mirror.

No.

Wait.

I examined everything behind them, the reflection of the room I was in now. The reflection was how my room normally looked. Curiously, I turned to examine my own surroundings.

They weren't the ones in the mirror.

I was.

36
NROH-NROH
OT EMOCLEW

I paced with intensity. I scrutinised the mirror from afar as I made laps around my bedroom. Annie and Brendan had now moved away at the obvious sound of something in their own realm. Mom and Dad were home, I knew it. Brendan had called them and now they were back and they would find the baby in a panic and something would happen with Zag and van Pan would grab him and kill my family.

I leaned into my mirror to get a better look. There was nobody there. I tried calling out, but only once. The sound of my voice was unnerving in this world of absolute loneliness. I eventually gave up and sat down on the bed. What was there to do, other than sleep at a time like this? Wait for something, anything. Hopefully I wasn't to spend the remainder of my life like this, punished by fate to age gracefully but completely isolated from any human contact on the other side of the mirror. How very Ozma.

I sat up quickly, realising there was a baby behind the throw pillow I was resting against. I scooped Zag up and examined him. He had a note attached to him.

I read it out loud: "I wished for the same thing you did, but instead of wishing the baby into the mirror, I wished myself into the mirror. By this point you either have him or you have me…" I sighed and crumpled up the paper. "Annie…"

OK, so, I said to myself in a get-to-it-manner. If the first wish was to wish the baby Zag into the mirror, and it sent me… And the second wish was to wish Annie into the mirror, and it sent Zag… Then to get us both back to the other side, I would have to…

I sat back down on the end of the bed, grabbed the throw pillow, and pressed it against a part of Zag's arm-flesh.

"Zag and I wish that this pillow could be banished into the real world until we say otherwise."

There was a pop in my ears and a strange shimmering of items around my room, and I stared at it all happening until I realised that somehow, subtly, it had reversed. My room was back to normal, and I was back on the right side of the mirror. With a great sigh of relief, I noticed baby Zag was in my arms, too.

"Let's not do that again," I smiled down at him.

A rushing of footsteps had me in a panic, and I carelessly dropped the baby. As Mom raced into the room, my eyeballs felt like they were going to roll back into my head from shock.

I'd dropped a baby! *A baby!*

To add insult to injury, I kicked him under the bed.

"How *dare* you leave the house!" was the first thing my mother yelled as she came in, and with that she grabbed the TV remote off my table, stole the cable for the TV, went to my computer and ripped out the keyboard and mouse, and stormed into her own bedroom with them. For a moment I thought it was over, but then she came barging back in and took my phone from my bedside table, and tucked it under her arm. "I don't know *what's* gotten into you, Cassie, but you're really starting to get on my nerves. This is the last time. Do you hear me? The last time you…" She stopped on her rampage and stared at me strangely. "Why are you sweating?"

I wiped my forehead and shrugged, but it was too late. My skin was an eerie shade of lily-white, almost green; my lips pale, pupils dilated.

"We'll discuss this tomorrow," she said quietly.

With that she pulled out a giant bronze key from her pocket.

"You're locking me in?" I spoke at last.

"Give me another choice."

Expecting the secrets to pour out like the golden glitter from my mouth, she waited for an answer. I remained silent, my mouth hung open in delay. She shook her head regrettably, and shut the door behind her. I listened as the key turned and clicked and was then removed. She stayed on the other side for a moment: I could see her shadow on the floor; but then she walked off, and I was as trapped now as I had been in that mirror.

37
URSULA'S NEW PLAN

The preparations for Eleanore's party were utterly absurd. Tanya was overwhelmed just thinking about what she'd accomplished. At three-thirty she had arrived with her bag of decorations, which had set her pocket-money back a few weeks. No mention of Eleanore ever reimbursing her. Plus, she had brought over a dozen mixed CD's with music she assumed and hoped Eleanore would approve of. Also, despite the fact that it was not her birthday, the hostess had demanded at some point that the attention be focused squarely on her while she blew out candles on what was deemed the 'back to school' cake: a gigantic chocolate covered heart-attack-in-the-making with raspberry jam and lemon curd throughout. It was placed on Tanya's shoulders not only to order it days earlier, but also to pick it up, store it in her family's fridge, and bring it over on the day. So as she set up the Parker family living room, which was a pristine valley of china dolls in display cases, uncomfortable Victorian-era furniture, and Parisian shutters, she took it upon herself to up her slowly dwindling ante by drinking an un-scrupulous amount of soft drinks and red cordial. The streamers were up by the time Eric, Ella-May, Eleanore, Elliot and Eliza sat down for an early dinner. The balloons, however, were not.

"Honey, perhaps you'd like to ask your friend if she would care to sit down with us while we eat?" suggested Ella-May.

"Mother, don't make things awkward."

Eleanore turned to the red-faced girl, who was struggling to blow up a packet of balloons on the carpet across from them.

"Don't forget to distribute them evenly colour-wise, and also... Rub them on your head for static, since you forgot to get the helium ones like I asked." She shot her a look and then turned back to eat her Moroccan lamb.

After wolfing down their meals, Eleanore excused herself to get ready, and the twins headed out to play in the backyard before it got dark. Tanya awkwardly continued straining with the balloons while Eric and Ella-May remained sitting at the table in front of her, acting as if she wasn't there, discussing all sorts of private matters. It was the final comment of Ella-May refusing to take any items of clothing off for her gynaecologist that made Tanya forget she was nearing the end of a very large balloon. With a big pop, the world around her disappeared in a haze of white, and when she regained consciousness, Mr. and Mrs. Parker were watching her with the blankest of looks on their faces.

"Tanya, maybe you'd better stop that and... do something else," suggested Eric.

Gladly, she stood up and went upstairs. She found Eleanore in her own personal en suite, about to get undressed to have a shower.

"What happened, did you finish the balloons already?"

Tanya's eyes were droopy.

"I got light headed. I need to lie down. Just... right... here..."

She flopped down on Eleanore's water-bed. It took a while for it to stop moving, but the bronzed beauty was not having it; she strode over and heaved her back up.

"No. Unacceptable. What is this, some sort of a pheasant party? This is my Annual Back-to-School Gala. It has to be perfect!"

Tanya grabbed her cheeks as they flushed.

"*Peasant*. Not pheasant. You guys have *got* to differentiate be-tween the two. Eleanore, I really can't right now. I want to go home and crash before the party starts. I think I've had an unhealthy sugar intake."

She belched before she had a chance to control it.

"Fine. Be that way. See if I care. I'll just hand the responsibilities and ribbons to Wednesday and Friday instead."

"What ribbons?"

Eleanore ignored her and went into the bathroom, locking the door. A few moments later, Tanya could hear the sound of water running, but not from a shower-head. A bath-tap. She was having a bath. So, she was particularly mad, then.

Tanya let out a sigh before going back downstairs to continue.

In a way, being locked up for the first time in my life was actually alright. It meant Zag couldn't get out either. After fishing him out from under my bed and making sure he was fine, I sat and burped him. I noticed he had more hair sprouting from his head than before.

"You're not so bad," I told him honestly.

It didn't take him long to fall asleep in my arms, and I found myself also lulling into a slight doze, until there was a knock on my door. I rushed right over and pressed against it.

It was Annie. "I still really want to go next door."

Naturally, it was the furthest thing from my mind, and I told her.

"Oh, Zag *is* safe as long as he's in there, and you can't get out, so what's the harm?"

"The harm, if anything, is that you have no friends to hang out with even if you do go."

"I don't need friends. I have my brain, and its other personalities. Besides, I can see it all happening from my window and it looks like fun."

"Annie," I reminded her, "your idea of fun is staying home and watching *The Cosby Show*."

"Hey. Don't drag on Vanessa again. Look, I'll keep a low profile."

"You're not actually serious. Annie, come on."

"I've made up my mind," she said in a high voice.

"What if van Pan kills you as soon as you step foot out the front door? What am I supposed to do then?"

There was silence on the other side.

Then she muttered: "He didn't kill Mom and Dad when they

came home. I can't take this, alright? I'm more scared now than I was last night when the car lifted into the air. I need to get out of here. Please understand."

"I do, but it's dangerous! Promise me you won't go?"

I waited for an answer, but didn't get one. She'd wandered off, unable to tell me what I wanted to hear.

Suddenly my window smashed in with a hurricane force of wind. I fell sideways, landing against the wall, and I instinctively cradled the baby in my arms. The shutter collapsed onto my computer, pushing everything on the desk to the floor. I watched helplessly, expecting Rudnick van Pan to defy the laws preventing him from entering, but instead I was greeted with a familiar giant of a woman with bright blonde hair, sporting a giant staff and a cat on her shoulder.

It was Dame Hermione Purplewink.

Ursula.

"Go away!" I screamed.

The cat jumped off her shoulder and landed on my cluttered desk. A moment later Ursula floated through the window frame and came to land gently on the floor in front of me. She was so tall her head nearly touched the ceiling. She was gazing down at me mercilessly, protected from the night air by a giant white fur coat that hid whatever else she wore beneath. She opened her mouth to say something, but the sound of a key in the door caused her to stop. Before I could blink, she and the cat vanished, along with Zag, and the window was fitted perfectly back into its frame, with the shutter fixed perfectly. It was as if nothing had happened. A phantom picked me up by the left leg and flung me onto my bed carelessly, and a magazine from the corner smacked into my face and landed lazily on my chest. All of this happened in the space of two seconds, just in time as Dad burst through the door, closely followed by Mom. Their eyes were wide in panic.

"Is everything alright?" said Dad.

"I don't know!" I cried in shock, but then I collected myself and frowned at them. "You tell me. You're the ones rushing in here for no reason."

"We heard a bang, and you screamed…" said Mom.

"Must have been next-door," I said, and I sighed.

A great flash of lightning lit up the room, and ten seconds later thunder vibrated everything. My parents glared at me, and I could tell that they weren't entirely sure whether they could trust me, but since nothing on the surface appeared out of place there wasn't much they could do. I crossed my arms and huffed to appear as normal as possible. They left, shutting the door behind them, and I heard the inconceivably irritating sound of the key turning once more in the lock.

Ursula burst from my wardrobe immediately, the cat on her shoulder again. She was carrying Zag in her arms. At least it looked like Zag, except he was no longer a baby. He was a toddler. He was sucking his thumb innocently, and looking at me with wet eyes. She'd conjured some blue summer pyjamas for him.

"Here," she thrust the toddler at me. "Take him. I don't want him anymore."

I grabbed him greedily, grateful but astonished.

"You didn't come here to hurt me?" I asked. That would explain how she got into the house.

She went and sat down in the swivel chair by my desk. "Of course not, I'm not a sadist. Zag, he *clearly* wants to be with you. Who am I to get in the way? Besides, I can't access his abilities. Or his lack of at the moment."

"Don't you think you could have knocked on the front door? Instead of barging in through the window?"

"I'm not a fan of doors."

"Alright. And who are you? Really?"

"I am Ursula, Viking Empress of the planet Danube," she said, standing up. She stared at me for a moment, perhaps waiting for me to bow, but I didn't, so she sat back down again. "At least I *was.*"

"Where's Danube?"

"It is far, far away. Forever hidden behind Pluto, always in Earth's blind-spot. Although you can't see us from here, we have kept our eye on your planet for millions of years. You are our descendants, after all."

I was dumbfounded. "We came from you?"

"Some people on our planet don't like to think so. They look at Earth humans as barbaric animals, not to be associated with. But evolution begs to differ."

"And you came all this way for Zag, only to change your mind..." I held him closer than before. "Why is he a baby now?"

"That's my fault, actually. I was angry, so I used this on him." She stroked the giant tree roots shaped in the form of a staff, and I watched the giant crystal ball that sat on top as it hummed with green energy. "I have the power to transform a person's age forward or backwards. I only used my temporary spell this time, which is why he has since grown to a toddler. Unfortunately, a Child of Crux doesn't gain his wishing abilities properly until he's a little older. If you've made any wishes in the past few hours, I imagine they'd have come out... demented. But all looks fine here. Give it until the end of the night and he will be back to his normal physical age. He'll be able to talk again soon."

Her eyes widened in panic as she realised what this meant.

"Which is why I need to borrow him again and cast a spell to... uh... quicken the pace. Here."

She held out her spare arm, and Zag was whisked out of my grip and back into hers. He started whining and crying immediately, trying desperately to get out of her grasp. She ran back into my wardrobe and shut the doors behind her. Waiting, I sat blinking in wonder, and stared at the black cat on my desk. He stared right back. I didn't look away, wondering if this was the same one I'd thrown dirt at earlier in the week.

"What are you looking at?" he said suddenly.

Ursula came back out with Zag, who was no longer protesting. He looked quite vacant, as if he'd gone in for a lobotomy.

"What did you do to him?" I asked suspiciously.

"I sped up the ageing process," she lied. "That way you can use his wishes however you please. You know the general rules of using wishes, don't you?"

"A bit."

"If I'm going to let him stay with you, I'll have to know you can take care of him. Don't give him up, don't cast him away. Because once you do, you can't get him back. Not rightfully. You can steal him like I tried, but he'll always find a way back to his owner."

"I won't give him up," I said. Not in a million years.

"Good."

As she blew raspberry kisses on Zag's stomach, and he squealed with delight, I took her in. She was dressed in a business woman's black power-suit. It suddenly struck me how odd this was.

"If you're an alien, why are you dressed like a human?"

"I need to learn to fit into this town more easily, that's why," she replied. "Your people survive on sex appeal. Now, I've been banished here. I can't leave Horn-Horn ever again. By order of the mutinied government of Danube. I am no longer a Viking Empress. I have to keep reminding myself that my power on this planet must not be any different from yours or your other teachers. As far as anybody else is concerned, I am an average human. And I'm single." She ran a hand down her thigh.

Still, I pressed her for more information. I couldn't wrap my head around such a valiant effort to win Zag back, only for her to throw it away at the last second.

"Sometimes, when one is born into a life of luxury, it turns them rotten. They lack any experience with juxtaposition; as a result they're more susceptible to inconvenience. I'm the first to admit that due to my upbringing, I've grown into an incredibly selfish woman."

With her spare hand, Ursula picked a bent coat-hanger from the floor and played with it mindlessly.

"I'm not proud of it, of course. And perhaps if I weren't so selfish, I might not have been so hasty to send Zagreus away when I did. Eventually, after some stern lectures from those in my palace, I realised what a terrible mistake I'd made. After all, Zagreus was the last gift my father ever gave to me before he died. So, I left Danube to track him down again. But my disappearance from the Kingdom at the time of the King's death was looked upon as shady abandonment; they thought I was deserting my Empire. So I in turn was cast away.

"Since I am powerless to escape this town... until my death... I don't need a Child of Crux. I still have my magical powers, and they do me a great service. If Zagreus chooses to be with you, I won't bother you any more."

I held out my arms to hold Zag, and she passed his slowly growing body back to me. I sat him on my lap. He was likely to be four years old now, and his milk teeth were coming through perfectly. It was strange to see a creature grow like that, just barely visible to the naked eye. It was like watching one of those plants grow in fast-motion, in the nature documentaries my sister would watch from time to time.

"What do we do now?" I asked.

"I stay where I can and make a home for myself," said Ursula. "My job at your school will serve us weekly opportunities to discuss how things are going for you as an owner. It can be very stressful work. Almost like a job itself."

"Can't you just leave me alone?"

Ursula sucked at her top lip as she considered it.

"No. I want to make sure he's fine, living with someone as powerless as you. Sometimes wishing orphans are sought after by outsiders. Rogue employers, who defy the universal laws, wanting one for their own reasons. Once word gets out that there is one in Horn-Horn, and word will get out eventually to the masses, you'll be ripe for the picking. They can't kill you, but they can arrange your death in other ways, and swoop in to claim Zag. Which is why it's good that you know me."

"Can't I just wish them away?"

Ursula walked over to the door and inspected herself in the mirror with a sigh before saying: "Sometimes they are protected from wishes themselves. It's only people like you, with your lack of powers, that can fall prey to a real wish. The naïveté of the average human brain is your biggest weakness."

I combed Zag's hair with my fingers. It was soft, lacking the wiry texture from many years of life.

"I don't know if I can do this," I said quietly. "I'm only sixteen. I have school on Monday."

"Trust me. If somebody can write a Curry Bible, you can look after a Child of Crux."

There was a knock at my door again. Ursula and the cat tensed, but I put my hand up. It couldn't be my parents. They wouldn't knock. I went over to the door and pressed my ear against it.

It was my brother, his voice high and tense.

"Annie's gone!" he whispered harshly.

The party. Gosh, she was so stupid. A genius, but stupid.

"Thanks, Brendan," I said, and he left for his bedroom again.

"Has your sister gone missing?" asked Ursula.

"No, she's gone to a party next door, because of..." I turned around and looked the Viking square in the face. "I can't let her go on her own."

"Then go to this festivity you speak of."

"I'm not supposed to... I'm grounded..."

Ursula tipped her head back and laughed heavily. Then she looked at me in earnest. "What does that mean?"

"It means I'm not allowed to leave the house. It's just a law of, like, childhood, I guess." I went to the window and pulled up the blinds. I then opened the sliding window and poked my head out, and looked around. No sight of van Pan.

"I can help you," said Ursula.

I turned to face her to ask her how, and nearly fell out of the window in shock. I wasn't looking at Ursula any more. It was me. A doppelgänger, at least. Wearing exactly what I was wearing, except she had a staff by her side.

"Whoa," I said, holding tightly to the gutters above.

"It pains me to exercise this trickery, so you'd better hurry up," said Ursula, jumping onto my bed to try and perfect the art of being Cassie Gellar. "My nemesis can turn into all kinds of people, animals, even objects. But like my special age altering power, transforming is *his* birth gift and he is natural at it."

"I'm sure in another life I'll know what that means."

"Well, it means that it took me a long time to work this out, so I might be likely to slip up somehow." As she said this, her hair went from my natural dark brown to her natural bright blonde. She noticed and shook her head, and it returned to normal. "See?"

"How long until *he's* back to normal?" I asked her, pointing to Zag sitting on the floor, now playing curiously with his doodle.

The end of the night, she told me. The wishes would become more solid the older he got. She warned me not to make any more tonight if possible, and only when necessary.

"Unless van Pan gets me, I won't," I said. I edged my way down the nearby gutter. "Anyway, he'll be too busy floating by this window to bother with me."

Ursula giggled to herself as I disappeared from sight, and she grabbed a newspaper off the floor. After reading a few lines from *Dear Abby*, she bolted upright in disbelief. Zag stopped fiddling and he stared at her.

"*van Pan?*" she roared.

38
INCOGNITO

From the highest window that faced the front of the Parker property, which just happened to be the parental bedroom, one would have seen an eerie sight had there been someone there to witness it. It wasn't supernatural, but it wasn't exactly normal. People were walking, as if in a trance, down the road. None of them particularly banded together, mainly keeping to themselves. One thing was for certain though: they were all heading towards the giant Parker residence.

The first to arrive was a chubby boy with slicked-back hair. He was only in his teens, but dressed much like a well-established man of business might. The automatic iron gates opened and he headed into the vast front yard, eagerly watching the red door where people were entering and chatting amongst themselves, mostly pretty young girls. He licked his lips in anticipation, but everything changed when two men in black jumped out from behind a jacaranda tree and blocked his way.

"Pass," said one of them.

The boy, frightened of authority and everybody in general, quivered in his thoroughly polished black boots.

"I can't. You're blocking my way."

"*Pass*," said the other, rubbing index finger and thumb together.

The young boy with very little spine fished about his pockets and pulled out the laminated ticket, the fake pass. One of the men pulled out a stamp and rolled up the boy's right sleeve. He soon entered the house, excited as ever, now with a temporary mark on the back of his arm in the shape of Eleanore Parker's smiling face.

This same event took place time and time again over the coming hour, as nerd after geek after pipsqueak after sleeve after misunderstood youth came piling into the property. Not invited, but appearing so.

"Brains…" remarked one security guard, making a witty observation of the cluster's slow moving nature, and their intelligence.

I was one of the last to make my way over there, sneaking my way from my heavily shadowed front yard to theirs. Of course, of all the moments to do this, I had to pick the moment my friends arrived. Or ex-friends, as they'd prefer. Inhaling silently in frustration, I didn't approach them, for upon seeing me Hayley muttered something to JT and fixed her vision ahead. They were impossible to avoid completely, though, as we got to the closed gates at the same time. We waited as they slowly split down the middle to allow us through.

"Hi, guys," I offered gently.

"Don't talk to us, faker," said Hayley, and she grabbed onto Greg and JT with both arms, and jetted forward.

I tailed them, making sure I was behind enough that I couldn't hear what they said. When they were bombarded by two men who jumped from behind some trees, I was momentarily startled as much as they were, and I stopped. Once they showed their tickets, got stamps and moved on, I walked ahead and encountered the same routine. I looked at the red mark on my arm in disbelief. Only Eleanore would have a stamp made of her own face.

I snuck in the front door as inconspicuously as possible. I wasn't here for the socialising, I was only here to check up on Annie and that was it. There were a few people congregating contently inside, just enough of them to sneak past without getting noticed. I went through to the kitchen, a long white and pristine palace of tiles and cabinets that looked more like a royal bathroom than a kitchen. Giant windows sat opposite me, and they looked out upon the vast backyard, which was lit up by giant stage lights. Quite possibly hundreds of people were out there, chatting, dancing, running, drinking and eating, playing games. A lot of them I recognised, but only vaguely from school and around town.

Somebody tapped me on the shoulder. I turned around in fright, but it was only Tanya. However, my stress refused to flounder.

"What are you doing here?" she said in a high voice. "You weren't invited, were you?"

She looked down anxiously, spotting the pass in my right hand.

"I was, actually, last minute. Have you seen my sister?"

"She's probably out there with your other friends," she said coldly. "I guess you're the reason all of these uninvited guests are here. Eleanore's in her room crying because of you."

I stared, speechless and confused.

"I was the only one she gave the duties to, handing out all of those invites." She bumped my hand. "The real ones, that is. And to cool kids only, she said. She entrusted me, and you've ruined it. Like I needed this, they're already..." She sighed and put a hand to her forehead. "What did I ever do to you, Cassie? Actually, don't answer that. Do me a favour and don't ever speak to me again." With that she whisked off up the nearest lavish staircase, most likely to comfort Eleanore and to make everything better again.

Trying not to think about it, deciding to do so tomorrow in Tara, I moved past the alcoholic-free drinking hoards to the back door, and went outside. The house must have been sound-proofed, because as soon as the back door opened a rush of sound and warm air hit me, and I almost fell backwards. It was too loud. You couldn't possibly have a conversation out here. I blocked my ears and made my way through the crowd, pushing past William from my class, a girl in a wheelchair, and a nerdy theatre geek with his tongue stuck to a slowly melting giant ice sculpture of a baby. I spotted Ms. Weiss and smiled. She tilted her head curiously, but collected herself and smiled back. Then, I saw my sister in the nearest corner talking to a tall blond boy with huge black-rimmed glasses. I made my way over. As soon as she saw me, her face dropped and she looked up at our house, then back down at me.

"*Let's go out the front!*" I shouted.

"*What!?*" she yelled, cupping one of her ears.

I leaned into it. "*Out the front!*"

The bass shook my heart. She grabbed me by the elbow and we made our way through the side-gate and into the front yard, where it was possible to hear again. "What did you say?"

"I said let's go out the front, and here we are!"

"Oh. What's wrong? Is it Zag? Brendan? The... What?"

"I just came to check up on you. It's not safe here."

"He's not going to do anything with so many people around!"

I shrugged. "I guess."

"Good. Are you staying?"

"No, Annie, I'm not."

My sister gazed lovingly into my eyes, but I saw a pang of sadness and pity reflected. "Cassie, you don't have to look out for me. *I'm* the older sister. I'll be fine. I know this will sound crazy, but... I feel safer here. Please understand."

I was tired, and my mind was too congested to argue with her anymore. "Alright, Annie, alright."

"Good. Now go away."

She ran off. Then she came back, smiling.

"By the way, I met a boy!"

She gave me the thumbs up and ran away again.

Before I could get any more bothered by her erratic behaviour, I heard a rustling in one of the giant jacarandas above me. I ran inside as quickly as possible.

— • • • —

The key was turning the lock. The door was opening. Ursula watched from the bed as Zag and her cat disappeared from sight, and she smiled contently at her 'mother' as she came in.

"Where's your sister?" said Mom.

Ursula flicked the long borrowed locks out of her eyes and shrugged as perfectly as I would have. "Tried her room?"

"She's not there..." Mom muttered. "You know, I might have to lock her in, too."

Ursula laughed. "Oh, Mom. You and your paranoia. Just chill."

Mom frowned and stared.

"Or don't. *Whateverrrr.*"

Mom leaned against the door, and her eyes filled with tears. "Why are you acting so strangely? I'd guess it was because of the moose, but you and your sister acted so strangely last night, and now Brendan is... Oh, please tell me what's going on, honey."

Ursula shrugged, knowing when best to keep out of things, and it was at this moment she saw the other side of the open door be-hind Mom's head. A large, distinct crack that almost ran from the top to the bottom. She covered her mouth in astonishment.

"What's wrong?" said Mom.

Ursula jumped off the bed and went to the wardrobe. She pulled Timothy out and made her way for the exit.

"Get out of my way."

Mom looked down at the cat in shock.

"No," she said firmly.

Intolerant, Ursula slammed her against the door with her free arm, pinning the woman's shoulders back. She didn't notice her hair returning to its natural colour. Her face slowly started contorting back to its original state.

"*Cassie!*" cried Mom, panicking.

Ursula could feel the effects wearing off.

"I'm *leaving!*" she declared.

She let go and stormed down the hallway, leaving nothing but a bruised and disoriented mother behind on the floor.

39

THE CONFRONTATIONAL TYPE

Inside the Parker home, I edged around the party-goers. I was too afraid to sneak back home after hearing something in the trees. *He* was probably watching me from afar. I snuck to a window on the right side of the house and peered out, but all I could see was the top of the oak trees in my own backyard, and our guttering. Beyond that was utter darkness, as the storm blotted out the moon and the stars.

I soon took a chance and braved the outdoors, not daring to go any further than the Parker family's back patio cover. Ms. Berry was standing nearby in casual clothes, cross-armed, with a glass of near-empty Merlot in one hand. She seemed more forlorn than usual, and rocked to-and-fro. Suddenly, she spotted me and pepped up.

"Cassie," she said in a drawl, and she looked at me with her gigantic green eyes, glazed and enlarged by her hideous glasses. "You know, I now bereave in mirror-kills, if *you* were in-vide. She says inthe Jim that she doesn't lie you, but then*WHYYY*… isshee or ways *torken* a-bow you? Maybe sheen *love* wiyeu!" She laughed and then cried. "May *everyone's* in love wiyeu. Maybe *Rosemont* irrine love wiyeu. Hey, where my wine gh?"

I wasn't sure what to say. Drunk teachers made me uncomfortable.

"Do you bereave in masczh sick?"

"Yes," I said immediately.

"I didn't until… and then she… Just like that! Mayb I should buy a 1-orrery ticket to-more. Because why not? Ah, I donut it, though. I don't need *more*. I lah being your teash-uh. High-lie, or, ma… life. I'm happy as lawn essay can teash."

I smiled at her sentiments. The truth really did come out when you were drunk. "Thanks, Ms. Berry."

Her eyes grew wider still, and through her magnified glasses I spotted something different. She tossed her empty wine glass to the grass and shouted: *"IT'S HAMILTON!"* Grunting as she did, she pushed me aside violently and stormed off into the crowd.

A few of the other teachers nearby watched as she plodded off, and Ms. Weiss came over to me.

"There, there, dear," she said, patting me on the back. "I'm sure she didn't mean it. You know how she can be about her name. It must be awful, not knowing who you are."

— · · · —

van Pan pricked his bat-like ears, his eyes set firmly on the new owner of the child from his position on top of the Tanner roof. He became distracted upon noticing an angry woman storming off, tripping over the garden hose on her way. Soon she was in a dance with it, convinced it was trying to kill her. She cried out for a snake charmer, and as two security guards ran to assist she finally untangled and went on her way again.

For some reason van Pan became drawn to her. He glided from roof to roof until he landed in the front lawn of the Parker property, settling in the top branches of one of the giant jacaranda trees. She was walking down the street, muttering to herself, and he thought she seemed beautiful. Not in a sexual way, for she was far from out-standing, but in another way. An admirable way. He couldn't under-stand what he was feeling. Jealousy?

It was in that moment something out of the corner of his eye caught his attention. Somebody was leaving the Gellar house. To his great surprise, it was Ursula. She stormed along the driveway and down the road in the opposite direction, her feline giving chase.

"Where is she going?" van Pan muttered to himself.

As Ursula sped up and disappeared into the darkness of Philips Street, her cat suddenly stopped where it was, looked around, and then decided to run off in the opposite direction.

"Where is *he* going?"

———— · · · ————

I was inside now, leaning against the kitchen bench alone, keeping my eye on Annie outside. I looked up just in time to see Greg stopping by my side. He rested his arm against the same bench, stared right into my eyes for a moment, and then shrugged at me. I kept my eyes down and wondered if he hated me, too.

"Having fun?" I asked.

"Not really," he said, and he wiped a strand of hair from his face. "It's not much of a party when everyone's mad. Hayley's mad at you, JT's mad because she's mad, Eleanore's mad, so Wednesday and Friday are mad..."

"Remind me why we thought this was a good idea?"

Greg looked at me earnestly. "In my defence, I was against it."

His staring was usually so blank that it confused me as to what he was thinking, but now I knew exactly what he was thinking and it hardened my soul. I felt I had oil running through my veins and that I was some sort of slippery jinx to society. Well, maybe I was. I'd become a sneak upon arriving in this town, and I wasn't proud of it.

I turned to leave, but the Saviours came down the stairs behind me. I held my breath and prepared for the worst. And it came with a ferocious slap. I regained my composure and stared at Eleanore in disbelief, my mouth hung open. There were several people in the room and they all stopped what they were doing.

"Who do you think you are?" she said, her jaw clenched tightly.

I couldn't answer. I pushed myself away from the kitchen bench and left the house as fast as I could. I ran by the guards and clutched at the closed iron gates, whimpered when they wouldn't budge, and backed away.

"Cassie!" I heard someone whisper from nearby.

It had come from the bushes to my left, and as my eyes adjusted to the dark I saw my brother looking at me from the side fence. I forced the gates open with my strength and raced around into my property to meet him in the dark. Horrified when I spotted Zag in his arms, fast asleep, I put a hand to my astonished mouth.

"Have you lost your ever loving mind?"

"Mom and Dad are fighting; I was afraid they would go back into your room. I had to get him out of there."

"Good thinking."

"A blonde lady I met earlier this week was in our house, and she ran out a few minutes ago."

"That's Ursula, Zag's last owner. Where did she go?"

"How should I know?" he said, looking above in paranoia. "Cassie, I don't feel safe here."

I thought for a moment. I turned to look down the street. It was too dark. The street lights did nothing.

"Alright," I said, "we'll hide somewhere else for a while. Come on, I know just the spot."

40

UNTIL WE MEET AGAIN

The skies dark with dread, the wind barrelling through the low bushes and brambles, the ocean below spraying sharply against the rocks. Ursula sat with what little light she had from the nearby highway exit lights, and the lighthouse across the way. Its light came, then went, rushed over her, and left again and again. She was sitting cross-legged, staring out at the darkness, the gale battering her hair across her face, and she shed a tear.

"What are you doing here?" came a voice from behind her.

By the time she turned around it was too late to stand in defence. Rudnick waltzed cockily in front of her and teetered on the edge of the cliff.

Ursula remained where she sat, and wiped her face clean.

"I was going to ask you the same thing."

"Well, these sorts of places are all a part of the job," he said, and he turned back to her and grasped the edges of his frilled collar with his fingertips to stop it from billowing and slapping his face.

"You look almost human," said Ursula.

"You *do* look human," said Rudnick with a tsk. "Pity. Everybody is *very* interested in you at the moment. The news headlines are all about our fallen Princess. *'Ursula, the Viking Murderess'*, they're calling you."

"Do they know the truth?"

"Of course," Rudnick stared at her in mock disbelief. "Why, about how you killed your father? Of how you escaped the punishment by fleeing to Earth? Then upon your surrender, you were cast back to Earth as punishment with a set date of execution in the months to follow! A modern Greek tragedy, I believe they would've call it, in the other world."

"Nobody's mentioning *how* I will die."

"No, it's best not to worry the people of Danube with comets and such. They're a bit sensitive on the issue after that thing with Madonna. Your return to our fair planet followed by that *dramatic* exit is enough excitement to last until our extinction." He smiled winningly at her, then touched his chin pensively. "I do wish you hadn't done that, though. Gone back. Until then I was the head of the task force to find and annihilate you. I was stalking you. I took the form of a white moose in the woods that I knew your child was hiding in, so that you would mistake me for your own shape-shifting fiancé. At that point I was going to kill you, but a stupid human got in the way and someone stole that Crux right from under my nose. Then as you dug your heels into the girl's schooling location, I took form of many things, spying on you and her, and I learned what it was like to be such objects. More so, how humans and others act when they think nobody is watching. It was interesting. I became a cactus in one room, a painting in another. I hid the school janitor underground and took his place for a week, and I *even* sat as a walking cane in your very own carriage. But unfortunately, every moment of every day you were within the range of too many humans for me to do anything without risking exposure. I *couldn't* kill you. And now that you have been exiled to remain here until that comet hits, I'm bloody powerless to do so without it looking suspicious. So what am I to do?"

"Throw caution to the wind."

"No. I would never kill for fun. That's just so... non-constructive. I wanted an excuse. Now I won't have your head on a silver platter for public viewing."

"I've never understood your hate for me, Rudnick," said Ursula, and she pushed her staff subtly into the bushes behind her. "Is it because I was a better drawer than you as a child? I mean, it has to be *something*."

"Why do lifelong rivalries exist? There's always a logical explanation, a chain of events. Nothing comes from nothing. Ha! If you can't figure it out, then you haven't the right to learn why the very thought of you makes my skin crawl." His eyes stared at her, dead, their green fading strangely to a flat brown, almost orange. He squinted at her until they were nothing but despicable slits. "The only thing I seek is revenge."

Ursula laughed and sat up on her knees. "Revenge for *what?*"

"I shall speak no more of this. Instead, I'm going to leave. Trust me, it's all I can do to stop myself from ending you right now, in fact. But knowing how little a future you have is solace enough, I suppose, given the circumstances. To see the pain in your eyes as you remain in such close proximity to that boy, that Child of Crux, that *gift*, the last one your father gave to you before you killed him. That'll do."

Ursula rose to her feet and grabbed her staff.

"I did *not* kill him."

Rudnick eyed it cautiously and licked his lips.

"Well, for once you're absolutely right. I did."

As she inspected his eyes for a trace of mistruth, her arms fell numb to her sides, and she kept her mouth open gaping for a moment before muttering: "How?"

"That's the beauty of my particular metamorphosis abilities. Being able to turn into inanimate objects has helped me greatly in the past. You didn't think your *bosom* was enough to crush his neck, did you?"

As she replayed the night's events in her mind, she recalled distantly the concern she'd felt as she tried on the new amber necklace that the guards had brought to her, and the sudden feeling of heavy pressure on her neck. She'd thought it was from anxiety, the burden of having an ill father, the press, the boy in the cabin, the birthday guests, the expectations, the fear. It hadn't been any of those.

It was the necklace. *He was the amber necklace.*

"You... you..." she stuttered in disbelief.

Lightning struck across the seas behind him, and Rudnick turned his head in acknowledgement as he thought. He cracked his knuckles against his thigh, letting go of the white frills on his loose shirt. With a final, ugly smile, he waved at her.

"I hope you enjoy the rest of your stay in this town, Ursula," he said knowingly. *"Have the time of your life."*

His unbuttoned red jacket flapped ferociously about; she watched in confusion as it seemed to engulf him entirely. It wrapped around itself in a mystery of twirls, then devoured itself until there was nothing left of either of them.

Ursula was stunned She couldn't breathe or feel anything at all. No anger, no pain, or sadness — she was completely numb. Where the man in front of her had gone, she did not know. Where Timothy has disappeared to, she could not say. The only thing she knew for certain was that she was now finally, utterly, completely alone.

— · · · —

The poor soul was drunk and in the middle of the street, and as she plucked strand by strand of hair from her head, a very frustrated Bev Berry saw two black cats running down the empty road ahead of her.

"Here, kitties," she leaned down and clicked her fingers, but became deeply concerned as her four identical hands appeared before her. Soon her eyes uncrossed and she looked back up at the cats, which happened to only really be one cat, trotting silently towards her.

Instead of going around, it decided to stop and sit in front of her. Bev was so intoxicated at this point that she merely grinned when Timothy opened his feline mouth and uttered: "Run home."

"What!" she burst into a quick snort of laughter and looked him straight in the eye. "I *know* you. Now excuse me. But I have *never* been ordered around by a cat, and I'm schertttainly not about to start now."

Timothy hissed at her and flung one of his claws up.

"I am serious! You've involved yourself in an extremely intimate argument between two very dangerous individuals. You are lucky to be alive. Go home now, and forget about Hermione and I, and whatever else you've seen."

Truth was, Bev Berry had felt she was losing her mind ever since her only friend had disappeared right in front of her eyes. She'd tried drinking, but it did not blanket the fierce curiosity of everything she wondered. She had little regard for any sorts of rules now, and when it came to the laws of society, or even that of physics she would simply stick out her tongue, as if *she* knew *they* knew that she wasn't meant to know. The puzzles within her mind were now overshadowing what was right and wrong, so she stuck her tongue out right on queue.

"You are like a belligerent school child," he told her quietly. "Do you want to die?"

Bev Berry continued on her way, but the cat turned to follow her. She giggled in her throat.

"Do *you?*" she asked.

Timothy was taken aback, and he muttered: "No."

"Then why do you do the things you do?"

"You're intoxicated, and you aren't concentrating."

"Who are you, my mother?" laughed Bev.

When she received no response, she lazily turned around. The cat was no longer there. Instead, her long-dead mother stood as clear as day, eyes deeply set on her. Any affect the alcohol had over Bev was now long gone. She stared in the utmost disbelief at her mother, and the colour drained from her face. Timothy pursed his wrinkled female lips and pointed one of his newly arthritic fingers at her and found himself speaking in a stern, throaty female voice:

"*Go home, Bev.*"

Naturally, she didn't need telling twice. She twirled around and jogged off the same way she'd come, heading up the hill once more for Philips Street, which led directly down the road to her mansion.

— · · · —

Brendan and I had taken to hiding in the garage, and it wasn't until we were getting comfortable in the leather seats that I recalled van Pan had been in the car, in our garage, so the garage mustn't have counted as the house. We very quickly escaped and ran to the side door. I turned the door-knob as quietly as I could, and looked around the dimly-lit foyer. There was nobody in sight. The clay head snuggled safely under my right arm, I turned to give Brendan the heads up, and he pushed past me, struggling with the much larger Zag in his arms.

Just as we made it to the staircase, a bold shadow skimmed jaggedly across the wall above us, and before we could make a dash for it they emerged. Our parents' bore down on us, and Brendan let out a shrill scream.

"IwishZagwasinatreeoutthefront!" I cried without thinking.

Brendan's grip on him shattered and we watched as Zag's body flew across the room, out the open door, and disappeared above.

"CASSIE!" shouted Mom and Dad, running down the stairs.

I was doubled over after the worst glitter congestion so far. Before I could recover, Dad grabbed my wrists tight.

"Ow, you're hurting me!"

He loosened his grip. "Where have you two been?"

I noticed Mom keeping her distance, her eyes watching me strangely from behind his shoulder.

"Out," I said nervously. A thought came to mind. "At the party. We couldn't help it. We just really wanted to go."

"Where's my daughter?" cried Mom suddenly, and then she shrunk back, and whispered: "Where's Annie?"

A rather unnatural tension stood between us. I opened my mouth like a stupid fish and blurted it out: "She's next door, too."

Suddenly she rushed forward and grabbed me by the throat. I felt myself pushed backwards until my back hit the nearest wall. For a moment I couldn't breathe. I grabbed at her forceful hands to try and pry them away. My mind was numb with panic.

"Lesley, for God's sake…" said Dad quietly.

Brendan tore at Mom's purple sweater, and beat at her thighs, but he couldn't move her.

"Stop it! *Mom!*" he screeched, then turned to Dad. "Make her stop! Please! I'll tell you everything!"

Mom let go of me and I fell heavily to the ground. Catching my breath, I curled into a ball and started to cry. Brendan had tears running down his cheeks, too. He was hyperventilating, but Dad grabbed him by the shoulders to face him properly.

"Tell us," he demanded.

Brendan looked from one parent to the next, and he barely got through the story without passing out from sobs. There it was, all laid out on the table for the world to hear. The hideous truth of how I was attacked in the woods by a moose that had tried to kill me, and how I'd found Zag, and how the school counsellor was really from another world and was just trying to get him back, but how a horrible man from her own world was out to kill us because of our association with her. It didn't even cross my mind that perhaps they would think he was lying, but for some reason the looks on their faces told me they believed every word of it. Their white cheeks went terribly sagged, and their eyes drained. I could see the fear build up inside them.

Mom came over to me, made me stand up, and then she hugged me. I pushed her away and for a moment we were all silent, just standing there. I took a chance and looked over at the open door, and before they knew it I'd made a run for it. Brendan was on my heels and we raced outside to find Zag.

"No, wait," cried Mom, her voice hoarse and cracked.

We searched all of the oak trees until we found him in one near the front of the property. He was crying too, clinging to one of the branches. He couldn't seem to speak yet. I grabbed onto Brendan and hoisted him up onto my shoulders. He reached as high as he could and managed, standing on my shoulders, to grab Zag's bare feet.

"Got him!"

Before another second passed, Brendan screamed out my name in warning and I jerked my head up just in time to see the devilish face of Rudnick van Pan in the tree, grinning as his claws wrapped around Zag's torso and pulled him up. Courage melted into fear effortlessly, and I almost let go. I grabbed onto my brother's legs tightly, and pulled us back, but van Pan started to fly into the air and I found myself rising off the ground. We rose above the lowest branch and I grabbed it with my feet. I locked onto it, and found that somehow much like everybody who could climb that rope at school, my feet were able to hold onto the branch well enough to stop us from going any higher.

"Let *go* of him!" I shouted mechanically.

The menacing face above snarled and spat at our efforts to thwart him. I could do nothing but grasp with my hands and feet, at my brother and at the branch, and I felt my body stretching uncomfortably. I was almost too distracted to notice the woman walking by on the sidewalk below.

"Help!" I screamed.

Ms. Berry spread her legs and grabbed onto our broken letterbox immediately, frozen in place, and then she looked up at me. Recognition came; she saw what was happening and leapt back in shock. A moment later, she heaved and scowled.

"Get away from them…" she demanded crossly to the man in the sky, and she walked determined towards us. "Get away from those *children!*"

My father had been with my mother at the doorstep, afraid to venture further out, but at last he began to run quite willingly towards us. By the time he and Ms. Berry got to us, my grip on Brendan's legs was loosening quicker than my own legs around the branch. Then they did something very foolish. They took to unravelling my legs. For a moment I felt myself rise like a helium balloon, and in that moment of panic I let go of Brendan. I fell immediately, past the last branch and onto the bodies of my gym teacher and father.

We stood up immediately and raced to the letterbox to get a proper view. Rudnick van Pan flew slowly above us, carrying Brendan and Zag with him. Brendan's echoing screams cut through the party music and thunder, and it chilled me to the bone, so my knees buckled. I collapsed to the ground, but kept watching in horror.

On the other hand, Dad, with a furious growl, ripped the half-loose letterbox out of the ground and tossed it as high as he could into the air. It somehow struck van Pan in the side of the head, and he stopped, injured. He glanced back at us. I saw the anger in his eyes as they glowed a gentle ruby. At the last moment I remembered the same glow in the moose's eyes in the woods that first day.

Two unholy red energy beams shot out of Rudnick's eyes and struck Dad and Ms. Berry directly. I watched from my place on the ground as Dad was lifted into the sky as fast as a cannon and disappeared into the clouds above. Mom screamed from her vantage point by the door. Ms. Berry, struck by the second beam, simply erupted into a pink explosion, disintegrating beside me.

They were dead.

"Au revoir," van Pan chuckled.

I rolled over on the ground, and tiny pink electrical currents shimmied across my body and into the air. As I clawed at the grass I wondered if he was watching me. I closed my eyes and waited. Waited for death, for the end, for a great pain, a strange blackness. I sat for a good spell, until I heard rushing footsteps on the gravel driveway. My mother's voice seeped through the ringing in my ears, and I opened my eyes as she grabbed me.

van Pan had spared me. Three guesses why.

41

ONE SAVIOUR DOWN

She was all but a puddle of tears amongst her duvet, and as she wiped her eyes for the twentieth time, Eleanore sat up furiously and listened for a moment. Were they the screams of a pug, or a frump-gump enjoying themselves outside? She just couldn't tell anymore.

"I'll ruin her," she honked furiously, and she blew her nose into her friend's expensive dress.

Friday, who had been resting against her on the bed, turned to the door and grimaced. She saw Tanya there, her arms crossed.

"I can't believe you hit her," said Tanya.

Eleanore sat up. Her eyes bore into the pretty blonde girl's head, and she said venomously: *"What's that, friend?"*

"You don't do that to people. It hurts them."

"I wasn't the one who invited her here in the first place," Eleanore punched her pillow. "Just shut up about it. I don't want to talk about it, or of her, and I don't want to see your face, either. My night is ruined, and it's all your fault."

"Your night wouldn't have *happened* if I hadn't done everything. I ironed your clothes, I baked your products, I hired the audio equipment, I organised the invitations. I even blew up your stupid balloons."

"And a lot of good any of them have done now! You might as well have thrown yoghurt over everything and called it art."

The offence Tanya took was unprecedented. Utterly vilified, she opened the door behind her, and snapped off her necklace. "You know what? I'm done. Take your stupid Saviours jewellery back."

Wednesday giggled at her through the dresser mirror she'd been inspecting herself in. "What are you doing? We all know you'll come crawling back. You can't live without us."

"I can too."

"Yeah, you wish!"

"I don't need to wish. God. I've... I've had the week from hell and none of you even noticed. Now, I realise this isn't very important to you and your pretty little existences, but friends don't treat other friends like crap. As if you care, though. Did you know, we came back from Italy last Saturday night? I didn't tell you guys because I could barely see straight, I was stressing so bad about school on Monday. I thought it was just a temporary exhaustion, but Sunday night I had heart palpitations, and my mother took me to the emergency room. She thought it was chronic fatigue but they just said I was anxious about something. And I knew what it was. I was anxious about you."

Friday and Wednesday giggled at each other. *"Anxiety girl!"*

"Oh, grow up," said Tanya, with a roll of her eyes. "I am tired. I'm tired because my sister nearly died. I'm tired because of school, of my dad's hospital bills, of the fire, of all the animals in the pound who aren't there when I go back the next day. But what I'm really tired of is the judgement, and the meanness, and... the *sadness*... that comes with being friends with you three. We're through."

Eleanore was in no mood to be meddled with. She slinked off the bed and rose to her feet. "I'll tell you when we're through."

"What's the matter? Two Saviours quitting in one week. Afraid you're losing your touch?"

"You're losing touch... of reality!" snapped Eleanore. "You're a loser just like them."

Tanya raised an eyebrow mockingly. "Oh yeah? Well, who's the one with nerds at her party, huh?"

Eleanore gasped. "Get out of my house, you feline!"

"You can't just throw random words as insults."

"Watch me, ankle paint! And don't ever come back, not for nothing, not for no-how."

She tried to toss a balloon at her, but it floated in front of them gently. She followed as Tanya walked down the hallway for the stairs.

"Let's get one thing straight," snapped Eleanore in a frenzy. "We were *never* friends. I don't befriend leeching whore-bags whose sisters are reckless enough to get messed up in alternative countries."

They were at the front door now. Tanya opened it wide to leave.

"Oh, and one word of advice…" said Eleanore.

Tanya turned to listen, her usual hunch vanished.

"Think ahead of where you'll sit at school on Monday."

Amused by such an anti-climactic threat, Tanya couldn't help but grin as she finally said what she'd been dying to for years.

"Here's some advice for you, Eleanore… Change the name of that stupid group. Calling yourselves the *'Saviours of Tomorrow'* is like broadcasting what massive wankers you all are."

42
CLIFFTOP SOLILOQUY

I don't know who came up with the idea, but before I could collect my senses I was being hauled back into my house, upstairs and into my bedroom. Who held me, I couldn't figure out. But as I was thrust down onto my bed, I became aware that the world was spinning. I focused on a sock in the corner and tried to contain myself. Eventually, I let out a great big cry of exhaustion.

Then, for the second time that night, I was slapped. I looked up at my mother, awakened from my self-absorbed anguish. She had tears in her eyes, her eyes which told of the horror she'd seen and what she'd learned. As she got down on her knees to come face-to-face with me, she grabbed my cheeks and said pleadingly:

"Find him."

How could I find Brendan? He was a goner. Abducted, and not by a person. We couldn't very well call the police for this one. I didn't even have my wishing friend to help us. I'd made a wish for them to come back, but it hadn't worked again. Who knew why this time? The only thing I had was my wits. My wits, which wasn't much to go by, my luck, and the knowledge of the universe tucked away in my tiny human brain. Ursula had bailed on us, and now Zag had been kidnapped by van Pan. They would not be returning. They were probably halfway to Danube by now.

"I can't," I told my mother honestly. "I wish I could, but I don't know how."

"Please, Cassie!"

Tears streamed down her cheeks. I stood up and pushed her away. I told her to leave me alone while I thought, but really I just wanted to be on my own. I had no answers. And as soon as she left I collapsed on the bed and closed my eyes and tried to block the world out. It was impossible, though. If I could find them, I would, but there was no use. It was over. Fatherless, brotherless, lifeless.

My eyes opened as soon as my head thumped against the wooden floor of my bedroom. I sat upright, perplexed, and for good reason. Something was tugging at my right foot, pulling me along the ground towards my door. I tried grabbing onto a bed-leg, and after that my chest of drawers; still it was no good. It was a gentle pull, but certainly a firm one. For some reason I wasn't afraid. It was the only thing even remotely close to helping me, and right now I was desperate. If it was taking me away, anywhere was better than here on my own with my thousand thoughts and guilts.

I was dragged along the hallway, down the stairs, through the lounge, and past Mom who was standing by the open front door. She tried to help, but I told her not to, and she watched as I left her sight and was lifted high into the night sky. I covered my eyes, dangling upside-down, rising higher and higher, and soon I felt a chill from the altitude. The storm had settled, and my face became moist with dew. I took a chance and opened my eyes, to find myself amidst dark gloomy fog, presumably clouds, with the tiniest moonlight getting through.

After a little while, I felt myself begin to descend, and I took as many deep breaths as I could to calm myself. The clouds parted below me and I saw the ocean. I tried to grab on to something, but there was nothing there. No sooner had I tried, a gentle wind guided me towards a cliff-top and I suddenly knew my bearings. I was being placed gently down near the main road into town, amidst some brambles and evergreens behind the town's welcome sign with the two horns.

Masked by the darkness, I couldn't make out what was there. Just some black, ominous figures standing near the cliff-edge. As if the invisible presence holding my foot knew I was getting presumptuous, I found myself the complete and utter slave to gravity once more and I fell into the bushes below. My body curled around and I landed on my back amongst the branches, fell through them, and crashed gently to the soft ground. I was completely unhurt.

"Grab her!" somebody yelled out very close by, and a pair of hands gripped my shoulders and hoisted me up. I stumbled to my feet and was forced around. In what little light I had, I could see who was holding me. It was Ursula. I peered at her hopelessly, and she shook her head before turning to the cliff-edge. Rudnick van Pan was standing there on his own, with his arms crossed. He was smiling in that disgusting, disturbing way he so often did. He clicked his fingers at a patch of grass near a bush, and Ursula pushed me over there with blunt force. I stumbled and fell to my knees, grazing my hands as I did. I turned back quickly.

"He made me do it," said Ursula, pointing up into the sky.

Behind van Pan, over the edge of the cliff and far above, Brendan and Zag were hovering in peril.

"How did she find us?" said van Pan to Ursula.

"The clay head has a way of connecting with its owner. We still don't understand it fully," said Ursula. "It must have pulled her here because she had no other way of finding it. Happened before, too."

I watched as a strange, curious expression crossed van Pan's face. He turned and beckoned for the bodies in the air, and Zag slowly glided back to safety. As soon as he was within grasp, he wriggled and writhed in discomfort, and van Pan grabbed him by an ear to keep him still.

"You *are* a wondrous little thing, aren't you?" he said. "I'm curious, how do you work, exactly? What are your mechanics?" He clicked his fingers behind him demandingly. I was thrust to his side and he said: "Make a wish. Any wish."

"I wish you'd die," I said immediately.

A strange dull sound moaned from around us, and then van Pan shared his distaste. "Poor form. I don't believe that sort of a wish is permitted. Wish for something else. And before you get any ideas, remember where I've placed your brother."

I could see Brendan watching everything unfold from high

above. He wasn't close enough to hear. I thought for a moment. My mind raced a thousand miles a minute. What could I say? What could I wish for that would end this, that could bring everything and everyone to safety?

"I wish..." I said slowly. "I wish... I wish you would tell us why you hate Ursula so much."

The smug grin on his face dropped. I could see the intense hatred return. He let go of Zag, and I felt the invisible push loosen its grip on me. I jumped backwards until I was standing by Ursula, and then I grabbed on to Zag and held him close. van Pan strode here and there, not saying a word, trying to fight off the impending wish with all his might. After a short moment, he stopped and spat at the ground furiously.

"The very idea of you makes me *spit*," he said, regarding Ursula. "Whenever your name pops into my mind, I have to spit. It's like a strange tick, to rid my mind of such filth. Since I'm being compelled by the laws of the universe to tell you why I hate you, I have to cleanse my mouth..." he spat again, "... as much as I can during the process." Once more, he spat.

Then he mushed some saliva up in his mouth for a moment, and spat as much as he could on the ground until he could produce no more. He turned back to us, eyed me, and laughed.

"The reason I hate Ursula is because she ruined my life."

Ursula chortled in disbelief.

"Be quiet," snapped van Pan, and he stared me down again. "Since you must know. I grew up in a very different time and place to you. *Any* of you. I never knew my mother, or my father. In fact I remember nothing from my childhood due to an accident I had once involving a strange electrical strike. I lost a chunk out of both an arm and a leg from the experience, and that's why I have so many scars on my face. I woke up on a snowy hill-top in Danube's ogre badlands, and was saved by the Prince. Ursula's father."

I turned to look. It seemed Ursula didn't know this.

"He took me in, cleaned me up, and was very kind to me. I had no one else, you see, and he cared for me as much as I cared for him. The people of the Kingdom didn't like our friendship. Many people thought I was taking advantage of him. But I didn't listen to those who made snide comments on the streets about me. They were urchins. He was my whole world. Soon enough, we fell in love."

"Oh, enough!" Ursula picked up her staff and pointed it at him.

"Not even the well-being of that Crux and human child can persuade me to stand here and listen to you desecrate my father's honour like that. He had his two wives and lived the rest of his life alone. And was not of that persuasion, as normal as it is."

"You wanted the truth; well by wish I'm afraid this *is* true and you shall hear it. Do you remember the experimental chambers your father granted to test on subjects? Mainly initiated to research and find a cure for the *Suffrolens* gene that terrifies all bound for puberty. It was a subject held very dear to your father, for obvious reasons. Well, they completed all sorts of experiments there, some good and some bad. They also held tests on orphaned children, those of whom had nobody to miss them. All of these were documented and then blacklisted, so that the public would never know of the atrocities, but they were carried out and still *are*, in fact. My plan, once I come to power on Danube, is to end the suffering, to keep those orphaned children alive and unharmed. Your father was a good man, Ursula, but he was also very bad in his own way. Perhaps a little crazy." He addressed me once more: "When I was first helped by King Frederick, he was a young Prince with high hopes for his future rise to power. He had an infant daughter to raise on his own, Ursula, for his first wife had died during childbirth. Perhaps it was that I resembled her in some way, with my brown hair and terrible eye-sight — Ursula's mother, Princess Octavia, had also grown up with *Suffrolens* – so it would have served as something of a challenge ahead of them to raise a child, whilst both blind. But the truth of the matter is, Prince Frederick took care of me and loved me because, at that time long ago, I was a woman."

We shared a silence, allowing the wind to whistle past us undisturbed. I sucked in my lips and I tried to understand.

"You had a sex change?" I asked.

"No," said van Pan, "I was born a woman. Wherever I had come from, however I'd been before the incident that knocked the memories from my mind, I had started my life as a female. And I was a woman until you were two, Ursula."

Her eyes were strained, her lips thin and tight, and when she gulped I noticed the muscles straining in her throat.

"Prince Frederick and I were wed when Ursula was nine months old. The people of the Kingdom still weren't fond of me, and I often wondered if it was due to my strange resemblance to the first Princess. They accepted me wholeheartedly only because they had to, and there was a strain, a begrudging nature I was only able to catch in their eyes. Oh, the way they looked at me. Then, from my powerful position, I was able to sneak out spies to see if my suspicions were right. They were talking about me when they thought nobody could hear. People *hated* me. I withdrew from the public eye, never letting anybody know why. Not even Prince Frederick.

"Then came a strange, wintery day I will never forget. I found out I was pregnant. It was, unfortunately, the same day that Frederick's father died. He had been sick for many months and the cold ended him. So, the joyous news that we were expecting was put on the back-burner and I wasn't allowed to let anybody know until we were crowned King and Queen. With the deafening of the city due to that rogue planet pelting our barrier, we couldn't hold the ceremony until our hearing was regained. By then, as you know, I was showing. Soon, it was revealed that I was carrying triplets."

"*Wallacia*," said Ursula grimly.

"I don't go by that name any more. I completely removed myself from your father's branding after the atrocities I faced in the years that followed." He, she, looked back at me. "Some time after, as Ursula grew into a toddler and she began calling me mother, she finally developed her magical powers. She'd remained without magic for two entire years of her life, so it came as a great relief to us when her staff lit up one night and she turned our ageing canine into a puppy again. But unfortunately, as we soon learned, this gift also had its repercussions. Not only could she wipe years off somebody's age, she could also add years. It was covered up when she accidentally killed one of her nannies. The crystal ball aged her so quickly that her body gave in and her bones turned into powder before her muscles and organs could even react. She sagged in her seat at dinner one night and it took us quite a while to realise she'd likely died mid-way through the first course."

Ursula silently stepped forward. It didn't seem she was afraid any more. Perhaps she was just stunned. "Mother... I mean, Wa..." She sighed, "*Rudnick*, why didn't you tell us? I can't believe I'm hearing this. You were the only mother I ever knew. I loved you dearly! We thought you'd died. You just vanished. And the triplets, they... they went mad."

"Lies, all lies," said Rudnick angrily. "*You* are the only one who didn't know. Your father knew everything that happened, and what happened next was all your fault."

"What did I *do?*"

"That night in the nursery. When I disappeared. You were too young. Of course you don't remember. I was reading you stories of your royal ancestors to get you sleepy for bed. Nothing I did would work. You were restless, and you got angry at me when I tried to force you to sleep. So you threatened me. You told me that if I didn't let you stay up, you would use your power on the triplets."

Ursula looked down, the memories flooding back.

"I told you that was enough, and I snatched your staff out from under the bed and took it away. You would be doing no such thing, I said. So you screamed at me, angry and in distress, for being far away from your staff makes you terribly uncomfortable. But it was punishment for threatening the triplets. And then, no sooner was I out the door, your crying stopped. I wondered why, and as I peeked a look back into the room, I saw you sitting up in bed with your eyes closed, brow furrowed, concentrating, and I knew immediately what you were doing. I felt this *searing* heat in my palms, and I dropped your staff quickly. But it was too late. You had set your spell on me. And by the time I ran down the hallway to get help, I was a child."

My heart was beating heavily. I glanced up at Brendan, fearing this distraction would cause him to fall. He was tipping back and forth with each gust of wind.

"Duke Wilson came out to see what all the noise was about. I was naked and crying, but for some reason I couldn't speak. I turned back and pointed so he would see my clothes in a pile, and connect the dots. But the clothes were gone."

"I took them and hid them in my room," said Ursula, and she frowned at her own wickedness.

Rudnick's eyes were watery, and he scowled deeply.

"Can you imagine what it's like being taken against your will from your own home? That was *my* Palace. A naked little girl, wild and crazy, trying desperately to explain in her own way how this had happened. Nobody knew it was me, and Frederick was blind. Even as I was carried out, past the nursery I saw my three little babies lined in a row in their cots. They didn't recognise me, either."

"That was the last time you saw them?" I asked.

"No. I was placed in an orphanage near the Palace, out of sight and out of mind as they dealt with the 'disappearance' of their Queen. They had no idea I was so close. But then... knowing the King's fondness for children, I had hopes that he would come to the orphanage one day, as we often would to see the orphans... Somehow he would notice me, realise, or perhaps by then I would be able to speak and tell somebody... But before any of this could happen one of the workers whisked me away at night in secret to another orphanage. The orphanage where they conducted those horrid experiments. I was terrified. I decided that I wouldn't allow myself to have those horrible things done to me. Those things I had heard while eavesdropping on my husband's meetings with city officials, governors, mayors, the like. I knew of the things they did there and it made me sick, but I was simply his caring wife. His *second* wife. I certainly wouldn't out his experiments to the public, for it would end us and our position. And if I had done anything else, such as divorce him for his crimes, it would not be doing any favours as I was already hated by the people. I'd had no power to do anything, and so I'd dropped it. For you see, it didn't affect me. Until then. Placed in one of those *chambers* with five other orphaned children. Six reeking, unkempt beds. We were scared, so we turned to each other for support. I made friends, but everything was very limited as I couldn't talk yet. I feel sad now as I realise, being so long since it happened, I can't remember their faces at all.

"Then one day while the six of us were in the eating hall for lunch, chained to the tables and to one another, we overheard the news that my triplets had gone and died from madness. I was... overcome. King Frederick was apparently quite composed, which they said was possible when struck by terrible news. And then, no sooner had nighttime come, we were greeted with three new children into our chamber, and they were chained to us as well. It took me a few days to recognise them as they were a bit older now, but it was them. It was definitely them. My triplets. Oh, how they'd grown. They were able to walk, to stumble. They were barely a year old, but their hair was golden and wonderful. My beautiful boys: Able, Chase, and Just. Here with me at last. In the worst place imaginable.

"I soon learned that they'd been brought here by King Frederick himself, that he'd fabricated their descent into madness as a cover-up. I turned feral when some women came to take them away. I couldn't sit by and watch as they were forced from me again, and for a fate surely worse than death. Soon enough, I think I myself went mad. I was crippled with the fury that overcame me. The pure betrayal of my family. I was still yet to speak, but the struggle I held with my tongue was loosening up and I knew that it would only be a matter of time before I would be able to reveal myself to the people around me.

"Unfortunately, that time never came. A week after they took the triplets away, a man came to me and unchained me from the others. He held my hand I recall, and for the first time I acted as calmly as when I was sedated, looking up at his unfamiliar face and admiring the kindness found in his eyes. I sensed my struggling was about to come to an end, that they had discovered the truth and I was to be reunited with my family. But I soon found out that he was taking me somewhere else. I was taken to a much darker chamber, deeper in the ground because of its coldness. The man placed me onto a steel gurney, and three other men crowded around me, checked the documents signed by the King himself, and proceeded to dissect me while I was still conscious. I wanted to writhe about in pain, but the leather straps prevented it. Soon it became too much and I believe I fell unconscious. When I awoke, I was too groggy to function properly. I found myself in a rather pleasant giant bed, in a room full of toys. I stayed there for a week as the wounds around my chest and thighs healed under their bandages. I only ever saw one person in there, and it was a nurse who never looked me in the eyes. She simply came in, silently, with food or injections, and often checked under the bandages for infections.

"On the last day, they told me I was to be released to another orphanage, and that the procedure was successful. I'd been working in the last week to speak, and had managed five words in very long intervals. I was happy. It was nearly over. But then they..." He gulped gently, "...When they removed the bandages, I saw what they had done. They'd turned me into a man. Or, rather, a boy. I screamed and could not be contained, and it took another few days for them to calm me down. Then, spooked I suppose, they didn't send me to the orphanage as planned. Instead, they threw me out into the snow. Just like that. Like a piece of rubbish.

"To cut a long story short, I was picked up by a pack of travelling folk, and was raised on their morals and practices. You know the story, Ursula. When I was a teenager again, I excelled in all my studies and went to the highest college in the Kingdom. Coincidentally, the same place a young girl 'roughly my age' was attending. Who I remembered from, you might say, another life.

"I thought of letting you know who I was, but how would you possibly react? Besides, I had a plan to kill you and I knew that if I rushed it, it wouldn't work. So I grew up as Rudnick van Pan, made my way into parliament, and on my apparent twenty-first birthday I was given the chance to meet the King at my birthday celebrations. It was there that I took him aside and revealed to him who I was."

"And?"

"He was stunned, of course; beside himself. Also, a little disgusted. I cursed his existence and threatened to ruin him if he didn't allow me the highest clearance throughout the Palace. In return the secret of his wife and children would remain under lock and key, and you would be kept in the dark."

"You should have told me."

"Never. But now you know why I hate you. You took my life from me. And I've been made to suffer throughout a new life. I may look younger, but my soul is old and tired. You stole my past. You destroyed three childhoods in order to give me another. *That* is why I want to kill you. Why you deserve, I think, to die."

Ursula pursed her lips and stepped forward. "Wallacia..."

"Nothing you say to me can undo the past, or make it better."

"They are alive."

van Pan looked puzzled, as if he was sure he'd misheard.

"What?"

"Wallacia, the triplets. Able, Just, Chase. They're *alive*."

van Pan turned immediately and covered his mouth, and for a moment I saw the female in him, and thought he was crying. He looked up. I don't know what he was staring at, perhaps it was my brother. I grabbed onto Zag's hand. I muttered something as quietly as I could, and a moment later I made a quiet wish. Just then, van Pan turned back. He had tears in his eyes, but he was smiling. He laughed happily, and I believed then that he really was mad after all.

"I know," he said. "I know they're alive. Who do you think has been helping me all these years?"

He clicked his fingers and three figures emerged from the nearest bushes. Three large men, all blond, with horrible scars on their faces, standing tall in front of us.

"These are my children. Able, Just and Chase," said van Pan.

It felt like the world went silent. The distant thunder and wind disappeared from my mind. I didn't even hear van Pan's next orders.

Upon nudging his shoulder, Zag and I held hands and ran as fast as we could for the triplets. Before we hit them, something invisible around us knocked them over like bowling pins. Brendan dropped from above like a weight had been tied to him.

Zag and I didn't have time to stop before we toppled over the edge of the cliff. I grabbed hold of Brendan's right arm, and the three of us fell to the rocks below.

43
TRIPLETS
WHO TAIL

I couldn't see or breathe. My grip had been severed from Zag and Brendan upon hitting the rocks, but due to the wishes I'd muttered we weren't injured for very long. My broken bones and shredded muscles, lacking in any form of pain, soon regrouped. My dislocated shoulder popped back into place, while my shattered skull inflated. My brain recovered and I soon became acutely tuned in to where I was, what we were doing, and what I had to do. My first wish when we'd been standing on top of the cliff, when I had muttered to myself, was to know how to escape. Upon discovering how, I furthermore wished that we could escape without any injury whatsoever. I'd had to put faith in the vagueness of my wishes, which seemed to be working perfectly again.

I was swimming successfully now, and I looked about me for the other two in the darkness. Lightning struck far off at sea, and I found Brendan in front of me. He clutched at me and sputtered. His eyes were half gouged out from impacting with some sharp rocks, and he moaned as I embraced him. A few moments later, his eyes regained perfection and he looked about in confusion.

"Where's Zag?" I demanded.

He looked up and screamed, and I jerked my head up to see the three brothers jumping off the cliff above. Before we could move out of the way, they slammed into us. I was blinded by flashes of light, but my grip on Brendan's arm didn't loosen. Panic rising in my throat, I kicked my way back up to the surface. Before I could even catch my breath, I cried out: *I wish we were somewhere else right now!* And then I felt the water surrounding me vanish.

We landed on a hardwood floor, and the water that had been caught in the wish spread across it. Soaking and choking, I opened my eyes and breathed in as deeply as I could. In a decadent, empty white bedroom, Zag lay by my side, but Brendan was not with us. Overwhelmed, I wiped the hair from my face.

"Brendan!" I screamed.

He rolled out from under the giant bed on the other side of the room, soaked from head to toe. Before he could say a word, the three triplets jumped out of a mahogany wardrobe next to him and tried to grab him. He must have used a magical power of his own, as he missed their grasp by the pure bend of his backbone, and we fled as fast as our reflexes allowed, out of the room and down the long, winding unfamiliar hallway.

"Zag, I wish you'd do something," I declared urgently, and I watched as he threw a cosmical blue and green fireball of sorts from his palm at the oncoming danger. Two of the brothers fell backwards, burning, but the other kept barrelling towards us.

We ran down some stairs and through an empty lounge-room until we were outside. It was a tiny property with hardly any front garden, and we made our way down the dark street, sprinting for our lives. We kept running, not even considering stopping until we reached a nearby park where we jumped into some bushes. Hidden in the blackness, we huddled together, shaking from fright and cold.

"What do we do?" said Brendan through chattered teeth.

"I don't know," I whispered back.

"Why did that wish bring *them* here?"

"I don't *know*," I repeated, and I poked my head out of the bushes, scouring the shadows with scrutiny. "Where is everyone?"

"Maybe they killed them."

"Don't be stupid, Brendan," I said.

The trees were completely still. Not a single car engine could be heard, here or in the distance. It was strange. Quiet.

Too quiet. No sound at all.

I paused for thought, and something came to mind.

I knew where we were.

<hr>

Ursula had her staff pointed at van Pan, and pushed him back with it towards the edge of the cliff.

"They *will* find them," he promised.

"Leave them alone. Deal with me."

"*No*," said van Pan, and the light from the billowing clouds in the crystal ball against his neck lit up his face from below, making him appear ghoulish. "If that boy is the only thing left you care about, I'll kill him myself, and that cat."

Without an ounce of forewarning, he smacked the staff aside and punched her in the jaw. She fell backwards into the bushes, quickly getting up to defend herself. He stole the staff from her and cracked her in the spine with it. She fell down again amongst the same shrubs. Dazed, she struggled. She clawed at the dirt, clutched at the branches around her. She stood up again, facing him, and made a feeble attempt to escape by numbly walking backwards, but upon doing so she slammed into the back of the town sign. She looked up at it, her forehead aching, and saw double of everything. *Four horns*. Her eyes uncrossed, and knowing she had to act quickly, she ripped the two horns off the top of the sign. They both felt ancient by touch. One of them was black faded to brown near the base, with a sharp tip at the end. The other, probably an ox horn, was curved and grey. She pointed this one at her opponent.

"A horn," he laughed. "Or, better yet. Two horns."

She threw the ox horn at him like a dart, and it flew through the air in a frenzied blur. It sank its sharp end deeply into van Pan's left shoulder, and he cried out in agony. Then Ursula threw the other horn, and it dug itself into his right shoulder. Furious at his impalement, he painfully pointed the staff at her and toppled forward, grunting in rage. With a fierce thud he landed on top of her, and they fell to the ground amongst the shrubbery. He placed the staff against her forehead and watched as the billowing clouds inside the crystal ball changed from purple to a dark and menacing red. Ursula screamed. She felt it. She felt it for the first time in her life. What she'd inflicted upon others. Her age started to quickly decrease. She felt her body contort and her bones shrink. Her breasts raised and her thighs shrank. She curled her toes and tipped her head back as her breath was taken away from her.

Ursula caught his eye. Her *step-mother*, somebody from her past who was killing her. Killing her with her own gift. As the last moments went by, the pain subsided and the details of the world sparkled and glowed in crisp perfection. She noticed something different about van Pan. It was a strange glimmering within the two horns embedded in his shoulders. Almost too subtle to spot with the naked eye, and impossibly precise, it was nothing more than a tiny speckle. A very tiny stream of what looked like mist trailed from them and up into the sky. Then, a great blinding jagged line of light shot down from above and struck van Pan in the top of the head. Suddenly the two of them were smeared from head-to-toe in deep, dark blue flames. They both let out their final harmonious death rattles before exploding outwards in a ferocious spectacle, leaving the once peaceful welcome sign in a giant shattered mess.

— · · · —

I made a wish that we could land safely in Philips Street. The wish went almost perfectly — we appeared one street down. I looked around in paranoia. Had the three brothers also appeared here? My last wish had included them, but the wishes on top of the cliff had worked perfectly. There was no sign of them though, so I rushed Zag, full-grown again, and Brendan and we made it to our darkened and quiet street safely. It was the empty Parker residence that proved my theory. The iron gate had been smashed for some reason, so it lay open in a half-bent fashion. We walked through and entered the barren house in a hush.

"Stay here, I have to check something," I told them.

I left them in the foyer, and ran up the stairs towards Eleanore's bedroom. I entered, and was surprised at the state of the room. Things had been thrown, probably in a temper, but not here. Not *really* here. I entered the bathroom and looked at the mirror. The only person to look back at me was Eleanore, not my own reflection. She had been wiping foundation off her cheeks and upon seeing me in front of her in her own mirror, she dropped her pad and went white. I slowly snuck out of the bathroom and back down the stairs, where the other two were waiting patiently.

"Yep. We're on the other side of the mirror again."

"Wish us out," said Brendan.

I did so, but yet again that strange dull noise erupted around us that suggested this was a forbidden rule. "Why is it doing that?" I said angrily to Zag. He shrugged. I pondered for a moment. I poked him in the shoulder. "Say something."

He coughed and opened his mouth, but a strange jumble of sounds came out instead of actual words. It then dawned on me. The power of Ursula's staff had long ago made van Pan a toddler and he... *she*... had been unable to speak for a very long time. Zag had been turned into a baby tonight. It was the same problem we were having. Well, we'd have to make do.

"Come on, let's go out the back. I have a feeling Annie's still here. I hope there are some mirrors somewhere."

The backyard was still and empty, like a wasteland with the fence knocked down between this yard and the Tanner yard. Unfortunately there *wasn't* a mirror out there, but it was understandable. It wasn't until Brendan suggested I bring one out that I realised this was entirely feasible. I found a compact in a drawer in the kitchen and ran back outside and opened it up. Through the mirror, people seemed to be partying all around me. I turned around just in case, but sure enough I was without company bar Zag and Brendan. In case in the real world it appeared as if a tiny make-up kit was floating in mid-air, I placed it near the ground and walked around with it like that, pointing upwards, until I found my sister chatting to a blond guy by the corner fence. I placed the compact on the ground and stood still, staring down at her and waiting. After a few moments she began to look about her uncomfortably, sensing someone watching. In an unusually short amount of time she had caught my eye. She turned to look for me nearby, but failed. She looked back, and I leaned into the mirror and breathed on it, then wrote the word 'GO' backwards. When my breath had cleared, I huffed on it again and wrote the word '*HOME*' backwards. I waited, and she patted the boy on the shoulder, shook her head, and walked away. I clicked the compact shut, kept it on my body, and then we walked back home.

Inside, which was difficult to comprehend in its backwards state, we stopped by the staircase.

"I have a bad feeling," said Brendan.

There was certainly an uncomfortable, heavy atmosphere around us. Perhaps it was left over from the terrible things that had happened tonight. It was awkward finding our way upstairs, as everything was in reverse, but we made it to my bedroom and stood waiting at the mirror on the back of my door. There was nobody on the other side. Where was she? I'd thought she would come straight here, as this was where my last trip into the mirror had taken place.

Finally, Annie appeared. Then Mom appeared behind her and covered her mouth in shock. Over the next minute, we sent each other breath messages again.

'*HELP*' I breathed.

'*WISH*' breathed Annie.

'*CANT*' I wrote, then: '*STAND BACK*'

Tired of messing around, I grabbed the chair from my desk and ran at the mirror with as much force as I could. I swung it fiercely and the glass smashed loudly. When it fell apart, Annie and Mom remained in front of us.

"Hello?" I said.

Annie jumped and I heard her squeal. With that, Brendan, Zag and I squeezed through the gap. Mom and Brendan embraced, and when she let go of him she turned to me. Her eyes puffy from crying, she hesitated to speak.

"What happened?" asked Annie.

"Long story. But we have to go and help Ursula."

Brendan pulled on my shirt and cried: "Are you crazy? I'm not going back!"

I pushed him off me.

"You don't have to," I said. "I'm going on my own."

Zag nudged me in the side. He wanted to come, too.

Mom gaped at the little boy in front of her, but had enough sense to actually acknowledge him with her next question.

"Who's Ursula?"

"Dame Purplewink," I eyeballed her knowingly.

Mom opened her mouth. I knew she was about to beg me not to go, but she stopped herself, then nodded her head. She grabbed Brendan by the shoulders and kept him close to her.

"Brendan stays," she said.

Annie began to cry. I wrapped her in a quick, assured hug, offering a silent promise of support. As I let go, my fingers found one of Zag's hands, gripping it tightly as if to anchor us both.

"Okay, here goes. I wish that Zag and I could find Ursula."

Mom, Brendan, and Annie found themselves enveloped in the stillness of the room, alone once more. Brendan, swaying slightly, his eyes drooping with fatigue, turned to his mother, gently guiding her to the bed's edge. As he shook his head, droplets of ocean water scattered, catching the light faintly like fleeting stars.

"It's strange," Mom murmured, almost dreamlike. "How brave you kids have been tonight. Where did you get it from?"

A smile flickered across Brendan's face as he met Annie's gaze, but it was short-lived. They lurched as a man stepped through the broken mirror frame, a tense rage emitting from his wide eyes.

It was one of the brothers.

"Great question," he said in a rumble. "Let's find out."

44
AMONGST THE PLASMA

There was a fire. That was the first thing I noticed when we appeared on the cliff-top. The town sign, parts of it at least, lay flat against the bitumen in the middle of the highway. The occasional car that drove past swerved around it, beeping their horns as if expecting the sign to react like a deer and run off. In front of us, dirt from one spot had been heaved from the ground, looking as if a tiny little meteorite had landed there. Around it, two or three remaining bushes were gently ablaze. In the distance, sirens were approaching.

"We should go. They're not here."

Zag huffed and tried to say something again, but failed. I quickly made a wish for him to speak. He tested his tongue first, and soon the words poured out:

"Took you long enough!" he said angrily.

"I wasn't sure if it would work. Besides, we haven't ended up where Ursula is."

"Yes you have."

A voice spoke from behind us, and we jumped in fright. From the shadows of a tree nearby, a figure emerged. It was too big to be van Pan or Ursula. It was one of the brothers. As he came closer, he put a hand up as a sign for peace. He had burn marks across one side of his body, and his clothes were in tatters. He'd been one of the brothers hit by Zag's fireball.

"They're over there," he said, and he pointed behind us.

We stared at him in confusion.

"Dead. Destroyed each other. I don't know what happened."

"How did you get here? You were with us in the mirror."

"My other brother is dead. Your fireball killed him. I wasn't hit as hard. My birth gift is to travel between this world and the mirror world. I've been in there all week, watching you and Ursula from a distance. I knew how to get back here, and I knew you would come back to help Ursula. But… when I got here I found them."

I pointed behind the triplet. "Can we see them?"

"I don't think you want to."

Zag insisted upon it. We were led through some thickets to a small eucalyptus tree. Some of its leaves near the top were burnt, glowing gently orange. In the dim light I saw something that my brain couldn't comprehend. By the trunk sat Ursula's staff, which was burnt and smelly, and the crystal ball was cracked and was oozing a glowing orange liquid that lit up the sight in front of us. Two tiny curled objects, strange in detail, almost like little sea-horses. I reeled in fright when I realised what they were.

"Why haven't you killed us yet?" asked Zag.

"Better judgement," a different man emerged from behind us. In the dim amber light seeping out of the crystal ball, I could see a tall man in a tight black suit walking towards us. "Zagreus," he said.

"Wilson?" said Zag, and he coughed. "That is, Duke Wilson."

"King Wilson now," he replied, and he eyed the triplet with distaste. "If only we'd arrived ten minutes earlier."

"What are you doing here?"

"Capturing the prisoners. But upon landing here we discovered an all-out *war* taking place."

"It had to be done."

"Hush up, Able," said Duke Wilson firmly, and he turned on me. "Who's this?"

"The Crux's new owner," said Able.

Wilson looked like he'd seen a ghost. "Well. An Earthling. I'm sorry to drag you into all of this."

I said 'that's okay' at about the volume a mouse would, if a mouse could talk. This king before me didn't quite seem real. I couldn't place it, but he was caked in make-up and his eyes moved differently than other people's eyes.

When he spoke, his voice came out gravelly: "I was cleaning out the late King's office yesterday, when I happened across something very interesting. Where are your brothers?"

Able hesitated.

"Dead," he muttered, and he wiped his matted blond hair away from his scarred face.

I piped up like an angry goose: "That's not true. There's one left; he was chasing us."

"That would be Just, then. Where is he now?" said Wilson.

I shrugged and looked at Zag.

"He needs to be caught before he does any more damage. You, Able, don't move. You're under arrest."

He walked to the edge of the cliff and gazed off into the darkened ocean. Strangely, he pulled a packet of cigarettes from his breast pocket and lit one up.

"You'll want to hear my news, too. Trust me, all of you will. It's a doozy," he said. He inhaled the smoke, paused, and breathed out. "Changes the *entire* game."

45
GREG AND ELEANORE...

Eleanore decided that it was time to end the disaster, and she went and pushed the DJ out of his temporary booth, then turned off the music.

"Dear guests and gatecrashers," she said into the microphone, "and whoever crashed their car into my gate, this party is over. Le finished. Parlez vous leave instante."

She waved to the side gates, and one by one the hoards began to leave. Many of them thanked her on their way out, but they were mostly nerds or smartly dressed people so she went on to pretend she couldn't see them.

"Next year, sweetheart, next year," said her father strangely, and he ushered the last guest through the back door, leaving her alone.

Except for Greg, who was lifting up the Tanner family's side fence as best he could. He struggled under the weight, and let it drop.

"Why are you still here? You bring your mangey friends to my party; the least you could do is mingle."

"You shouldn't have hit her."

Eleanore sucked in her lips and crossed her arms defensively. She glanced upward, seeing the first stars amongst the slowly separating clouds. "I can't believe I'm using this excuse, but... she started it."

"It was Hayley. You ripped down the Vineyard, and she wanted to get revenge."

"No freakin' dur. I figured it out the moment the first nerd stepped inside. It's *always* Hayley. But how dare that new girl sweep into town and..."

Greg was picking up empty red plastic cups, so he didn't notice as her eyes welled up with tears.

"I wanted *one* more good party. Just *one*," she whimpered. "Cassie Gellar ruined it. It's gone now. It's over. I *hate* her for that."

"She didn't know," repeated Greg, coming over and putting a gentle hand on her shoulder. Eleanore knew he was right.

Something smashed next-door. They both turned to look at the shrouded house amongst the heavy trees. A tiny, creeping sensation tingled down their spines. Someone was yelling in there. Greg edged closer to the fence, tilting his head to hear better over the incessant wind rustling in the trees around them.

Then the house shivered and convulsed, and the ground rumbled beneath their feet. The fence started to sink, and the two of them grabbed onto each other as one of the giant oak trees in the backyard began to fall over. They leapt out of the way in time, and narrowly missed being crushed by it. As they lay there in disbelief, they poked their heads up, curious. A body smashed through an upstairs window next-door and landed on the ground. A blond man stood up, uninjured. He wiped himself down and then, somehow, bounded like Peter Pan into the sky above. A moment later several people ran around the corner of the house and stopped in the backyard. Eleanore covered her mouth in surprise as one of them pointed a hand to the sky. A beam of golden energy shot off above, illuminating some departing storm clouds far away. A moment of silence passed. She and Greg held their breaths. Their heartbeats pulsed heavily in their eardrums.

"Did you get him?" I came running around the corner as King Wilson lowered his hand. He turned to me and shook his head. I sighed. "He has to know the truth. He'll hear it eventually, won't he?"

"He's likely to remain on this planet until he fulfils van P... I mean, his mother's duties to kill your Child. Since we don't broadcast Danube's news on Earth, I somehow doubt he'll pick up on it."

Wilson turned away from the clouds, puzzled, and grabbed hold of my shoulders urgently. "Protect the boy as best you can, and in turn we will protect you. Just will come back eventually, so we'll keep your house under close surveillance until he does. Then we'll be right there to nab him."

"What sort of powers does he have?"

"He can harness other powers, and keep them forever. Until yesterday, we didn't know who he was. He has travelled to many places in his years of freedom, so he could have *thousands* of powers from *thousands* of individuals."

I thought grimly about where he would go tonight, who he might cross paths with, what he might pick up.

"Surveillance, Cassie," said Wilson, as if reading my mind. "As I said, surveillance."

I nodded and turned back to see Zag coming to find us. It was dead quiet, and very dark. "The party is finished. Maybe we should just go inside and sleep. I need sleep. At least it looks like the worst of the storm is over."

Wilson inspected the tree that had fallen into the next-door neighbour's property, missing the two people as they ducked out of view. "Yes," he said, "it certainly does."

———— · · · ————

A good night's sleep, no matter how deep, was never going to be enough. Mom was still unable to grasp an understanding of where Dad had gone, and in the end she decided to manically busy herself with my Rubik's cube, as if that would solve all of her problems.

On the other side of the richly magical palette of devastation, van Pan had gotten his wish and ended Ursula. Even though he, or she, had died in the process. Still, as smart as he thought he was, there was one important fact he'd not known, and Duke Wilson told me that night:

Ursula's father never sent the triplets to that experimental lab.

It turns out that when they were little they'd gone to the physician and had been diagnosed, all three of them, with an early case of 'Suffrolens' — a dreaded disease of the eye that comes around puberty for some people on their planet. Dreading the idea of being a single, blind father taking care of three blind triplets, King Frederick ordered them to a special wing for entitled royals. Turns out, the scientists had told him they were incredibly close to a breakthrough in the cure for the disease. Of course, as history shows, they were nowhere near it. Frederick was so desperate for a cure, and with the recent disappearance of his wife he was driven to desperate measures. Any sort of possibility for a cure to their oncoming ailments was, in his mind, worth the risks. And what risks they were. In the end, the constant experiments they went through were so rugged and fierce and random that they actually worked. They recovered from their shrivelling eyes and regained full eyesight, but by then they were well into their teens and held in the chambers for so long that they were deemed retarded. When King Frederick went to get them, they'd formed their own special language with one another and rejected his approaches to bring them back to the castle as Princes. They instead went and stayed with Rudnick van Pan, who had visited them weekly upon leaving college. Soon enough, van Pan would go on to reveal his true identity to them, and they would then devise a way to bring down the one who'd caused their separation. Work Ursula into a tither, so that she would constantly be a nervous wreck. That was easier said than done. Little words whispered into her ear, rumours spread, embarrassing nods in published works. Being a Princess in this day and age, it was impossible to get by without glaring judgements and casual insults. You couldn't please everybody. So with patience and a bit of magic, they turned her into a mess, a royal mess, anxious and nervous forever to be.

Second on the list was to kill the King. After years of working in the experimental chambers, he inadvertently inhaled far too many dangerous fumes and in the end it was the cause of his many alien illnesses. But that wasn't how they killed him. van Pan's slithery talent to turn into anything came into power, as he declined the invite to Ursula's birthday celebrations in favour of sneaking into the Palace disguised as a rather flamboyant necklace which sat heavily on Ursula's neck. Upon her embrace with her father on stage, van Pan pressed his full concentrated weight as heavily as he could on the King's oesophagus, unchained himself from around Ursula's neck, and suffocated him. As van Pan had predicted, this sent Ursula over the edge. Her father was dead, and that meant one thing. She was Queen. But van Pan had his own ideas. He was about to reveal to the world that he was the long lost Queen Wallacia, and reclaim *her* title. All was going to plan, until Ursula disappeared, on her quest to track down the Child of Crux she'd just disowned. van Pan's intentions to send her to the barracks for the murder of the King didn't go so smoothly. Instead, the authorities went on the biggest manhunt the planet had ever organised, but they didn't know where. He of course volunteered to lead the mission, taking along his three similarly looking work-hands, and so they arrived on Earth to find her, after tracking the location of Zag in the woods. van Pan would take Ursula back with the boy, and destroy her. Of course, delays occurred, as were revealed in time, and upon Ursula's return to Danube with her male animal acquaintance, the government instead punished her to life in Horn-Horn. Which, according to Duke Wilson, is apparently the end to *that* part of the story.

All of this would have gone down a treat, and who knows if any of those triplets would have killed us if Duke Wilson had not found some secret documents in the late King's locked desk the day before. They revealed the truth about who van Pan really was, why he was always on every government list, and why those triplets were forever employed by the Palace. Realising the danger Ursula was in, the Duke immediately rushed to our planet to try and stop van Pan.

As we sat in my living-room — Annie, Mom, Brendan, Zag, Wilson and I — the new King of Danube helped himself to a glass of whisky on the rocks. He twirled it around gently and reclined in his chair.

"I was too late," he confessed.

It was followed by the most regretful sigh I'd ever heard.

46

BY THE
LIGHT OF DAY

Early the next morning, as the sun streaked across the tops of the teenage oaks and filtered in through the Tanners' back garden, the orange rays sparkled merrily across the tiny ripples in the swimming pool. Tanya stood there, hose in hand. The morning was very warm, a sign of things to come. Hair tied up in a ponytail, pyjamas consisting of tank top and pink boxer shorts, she aimed the hose at the body lying asleep in their pool and turned it on. The man she knew only as Ichabod Gellar jumped in fright and looked around in such a rush that he lost his balance and fell off the floating pool couch. When he stood up in the shallow end, he wiped his face and looked up at the blonde girl. She had turned the hose off again and placed it on the ground by her side. She smiled at him.

"Big night?"

Ichabod gazed up at the sky. Like a drunk man, he struggled out of the pool and crossed into the Parker's messier backyard, then walked through the side fence, out the front gate and angrily down his own driveway. By the time he reached the front door, he was practically dry. He opened it, and was met by ten men standing about his foyer in navy-blue uniforms. They faced him quite serious-ly, as if *he* were the intruder.

"Dad!" yelled Brendan from the top of the staircase.

With a terrific bound, he made his way down the stairs and into his father's arms. Mom was next, after hearing Brendan's call, and then Annie and I made our way frantically from our places in the house. We clasped onto him tightly and cried.

"We thought you were dead," sobbed Annie.

Mom kissed him on the lips. I remained hugging him, fearing that if I let him go he would walk out the door and never return.

"Who are all these men?" he asked distantly.

Mom leaned away and looked about. Duke Wilson caught her eye and he came over. Upon reaching us, he smiled and held out his hand for Dad to shake.

"Ichabod Michael Gellar."

"Hello."

"Honey, this is King Wilson. He's a... It's a long story."

"Why are you in my house?" asked Dad, breathing heavily.

Mom tried her best to explain: "After you disappeared last night a man who turned out to be a woman tried to kill Cassie, or, well, the little boy... Oh, you remember. And then she was killed but her son is still on the loose, so all of these... *people*, here, are going to protect us."

"He's trying to kill Zag," said Brendan, doe-eyed.

"Which man?" asked Dad, confused.

"The *blond* man," I told him carelessly.

My father gently moved away. He turned in almost a full circle, inspecting everyone and everything around him.

"Are you hurt? Did you hit your head?" said Annie.

"No, I landed in... a pool," he replied, and he turned back to King Wilson. "Are you here to protect my family?"

Wilson nodded.

"Then let's get one thing clear. That's the *only* thing you're here for. Am I right? No tests on my family for being around... other creepy crawly creatures, or anything like that."

Wilson absorbed the words, chortled to himself, and crossed his arms as if perhaps he were slightly offended by these comments. "Sir, half of the people in this room *are* creepy crawly creatures."

On cue, five of the men around us shifted before our very eyes into strange animals, all of different colours, and like no other species we'd ever seen before. They quickly returned to their human forms.

"I know it's a lot to take in," said Wilson, and he guided Dad with a hand to his back through the hallway to the kitchen. "Living in a place where ignorance is bliss, the sun continuously shines in the morning and sets at night, with each day passing without question. You may find yourself in the weeks to come overwhelmed, and let me assure you we are here to help. However, our primary reason for being here is to capture a very dangerous individual who has one simple goal in life: to destroy that child." He pointed to the strange orange haired boy hiding by the banister above them. "He'll kill whoever gets in the way, which will most likely be your family."

"Easy solution. Let's get rid of the boy, then."

"Dad!" cried Annie and Brendan at once.

"Over my dead body," I told him.

"That's what we're afraid of," said Wilson, and he continued pushing Dad down the hallway. "Just, that's the maniac's name, he won't think twice. What we fear most is that he will sever the connection your daughter has with Zagreus, and then find that temptation gets the better of him and claim the child as his own. He'll abuse that newfound power, we know it. It's happened before, with terrible consequences."

Dad stopped and took the stranger's hand off his back. "I need to lie down for a while. Just..." He smiled falsely to show he was supportive. "Just keep her safe. Just keep them all safe."

"Stop saying Just," muttered Annie.

With that, he walked up the stairs towards his bedroom. He gave Zag a less than pleasant sideways glance before slamming his door.

— · · · —

For the rest of the day, men and women came storming through our house like it was a train station. They used my wardrobe as a transport hub at first, saying it was special. Special or not, it was a nuisance. I tried going to sleep a few times but then with a loud thud inside the wardrobe I'd be startled awake and forced to smile as the newest visitor would emerge, apologising for the inconvenience. Eventually, I asked King Wilson if he could change the arrivals' location, so he chose one of the spare rooms.

They put their own planet's version of cameras in every corner. Naturally, our concern of them witnessing our naked bodies during shower-time was the first thing to be brought up, but we were assured that with their own superior technology, we would become simple black shapes on the screens as soon as we took off our clothes. With great relief, I ended up having a midday shower, but I kept a close eye on each corner of the ceiling and had a towel close at hand.

We had a few visitors that day. It was quite the ordeal, too. Once the doorbell rang, the twenty or so continually growing visitors used some sort of witch devices disguised as necklaces and pressed themselves against the walls. All of a sudden they would vanish. The first human visitor to our home was a woman I'd never seen before, but Mom perked up as best she could. Her name was Chloe, and she was apparently from the mental hospital in town where Mom was scheduled to start. She'd brought over some forms, and was quite happy to chat at the door. Eventually, she got the hint and left.

The second visitor was Greg. We could see him ringing the doorbell on the giant screen they'd projected onto the foyer ceiling. I sucked in my lips and felt my cheeks blush. Brendan couldn't keep the smirk off his face, no matter how hard he tried. I pleaded at the walls as I turned the doorknob. "Give me a few minutes alone with him. Watch all you want, just..." I grunted in desperation. Wilson's face appeared like a ghost in our grandfather clock. He nodded.

I pushed past the door and smiled at Greg, who smiled back. I scoped the surroundings, wondering if Just would jump from a tree and kill me right there and then, in front of the boy I liked. It would be quite a Shakespearian end.

"Have fun last night?" I asked, not realising that my neck was strained and my eyes were wide.

"Oh. Not really. I wanted to.... Can we go for a walk?"

"*No*," I said firmly. I flung some of my long hair over one shoulder and smiled. "I mean, I'm grounded."

He walked over to our car by the open garage. He leaned against a door. "Are you okay?"

"Great," I lied.

He stared at me intently for a moment, and then laughed joyfully, baring his pearly white teeth. He nodded strangely, and then scratched his elbow. He could see how clueless I was to what he was trying to get at. But I wasn't clueless, I was distracted.

"I'm sorry about last night. That's what I really came here for, I guess. I should have stopped her. I should have done something."

He was looking at his own reflection in the car window now. Not in a vain way, either. His words sank in, and for a second it seemed as if he were telling me how I felt about Ursula.

I regained my composure and walked over to him. I opened my mouth to speak, breathed in, then paused awkwardly. I twisted my fingers around a strand of hair. "What are we talking about, again?"

He looked up, dumbfounded. "Eleanore slapped you."

I felt so stupid. I burst out in a brief laugh. "Greg, I've got other things on my mind." I stretched and allowed myself to yawn quite loudly. I hadn't realised it until now, but the fresh air was exactly what I'd needed.

"I feel terrible, and I just wanted to say I'm sorry. Next time, I'll defend your honour... or something."

He smiled at me. I smiled back, and looked down.

"That's okay. I can take care of myself. Anyway, I deserved it."

"No," he started.

"Yes. Yes, I did." I thought back.

I didn't care to think about the events of the party. Be it embarrassment or lack of importance, it wasn't something my mind was willing to embrace. Greg and I were on good terms. At least he was talking to me. That made me feel good.

A crackle in the trees changed all that.

I pushed him against the car and looked up. Eagle eyed, on edge, I saw as the three men emerged from their hiding places against some oaks across from me. They'd seen me react to something, and were ready to protect.

Alas, it was but a bird changing locations.

I came back to reality, and realised that our faces were deliriously close. Greg's eyes had a touch of hazel in them today. They just never seemed to settle on one colour.

He smiled, then I smiled.

Before I knew it, he'd leaned forward and kissed me.

I pushed away and slapped him. I covered my mouth in shock, remembering something.

"I'm sorry," he said, and he went completely red.

I shook my head. Not now.

"I'm *sorry*," he couldn't get past the apology.

"No, no, no, no..." I forced myself to talk, and I had to cough to clear my throat. "Maybe you should go home, Greg."

"Okay," he turned and started to walk away.

This isn't happening.

I kept gazing at my feet as I walked quickly back to the house. My mind was racing. I opened the door and went inside. The visitors in the foyer revealed themselves, looking away from the ceiling video and down at me instead. Mom, Dad, Annie and Brendan joined them.

My first kiss.

Viewed by my entire family, and then some.

47
TIME MARCHES ON

The first day back at school was very strange.

As I boarded the bus with Annie on Monday morning, two 'new' kids hopped on with us. These were, of course, some of the 'protectors' that looked the part: youthful in appearance, down with the human lingo, the right size of a human. One of them was named Chelsea and the other was named Brad, according to their new documents. One of them was even put into our class, somehow. Apparently the Earth governments knew about van Pan's maniac son, and he was listed privately as Public Enemy No. 1. This didn't help my nerves, or my parents as we left the house. Brendan was the only one who got to stay home. As Mom rang the school, she thought of excuses as to why he would be absent for a while. She went through them all: he'd contracted a virus from travelling to another state, he still had severe sunburn and couldn't move, he'd been bitten by a dog... In the end she said that he'd broken both his legs, and then hung up the phone in a panic. Despite what stress we were under, we burst into uncontrollable laughter.

At school that morning, as we crowded into the classroom, I tried to ignore Brad sitting on his own in the front row. I then had to ignore everyone else as well. What a royal mess I'd made of my life in just one week. Tanya took one look at me and rolled her eyes. Eleanore came in and didn't even look in my direction, but her neck was as long as a giraffe's. Then Hayley and JT ran in laughing, saw me, and turned glum. They whispered in the back row, and called for Greg when he arrived. He, too, didn't look at me. I huffed quite loudly at the unfairness, and got out my books. I moved myself to the front row, a few desks across from Brad.

"You can hold my hand if that is an appropriate gesture."

I stared deeply at him in his grey hoodie, and shook my head slowly and deliberately.

Ms. Weiss soon came in, looking strange and glum. "Class, quieten down, I have some terrible news," she said, and we hushed in curiosity. She placed her handbag on her desk and sat down. She crossed her arms in front of her. "Usually we are not required to bring up details like this to students, but since you were meant to have gym class today, you should know. Your gym teacher Ms. Berry died on the weekend."

The room was silent. Every pair of eyes were focused on our elderly teacher, and we urged her with our beady expressions to go on.

"I'm sorry, I can't say any more, except that... Oh, it's just too..." With that, her trembling hands rushed to her trembling mouth and then covered her eyes as she cried.

Eleanore and, surprisingly, Hayley jumped up and ran to console her. Hayley reached into her drawer and got out a box of tissues, and Eleanore stroked her shoulders soothingly. I sat there dumbfounded, and shared a dark look with Brad.

Ms. Weiss finally looked up. Her mascara was staining her cheeks. "They found some of her arm in a field yesterday afternoon. They're saying it happened the night before. I'm sorry to break the news to you like this, children."

A few of the girls behind me started crying. I myself felt immediately sick. I'd seen Ms. Berry at the time of her death, exploding in an array of pink and red. I was a witness to her murder. The thought of her limbs surviving the explosion and landing nearby made my skin crawl.

I left to go to the bathroom without asking. The emotions began building up inside and soon they rose to the surface and expressed themselves with pools of tears. I burst into the empty bathroom and stared at my puffy face in the mirror.

Why did we have to move? I thought to myself.

I suddenly yearned for the bay windows and the broken chimney of my old house. There wasn't anything left here. Not one goddamn thing.

— · · · —

Tuesday was a little less troubling. I sat on my own in class, with the exception of Brad, who'd suggested I befriend him so he could be close at all times. I agreed and halfheartedly.

It was at lunch as I sat with him at a cafeteria table, admiring my plastic fork and wondering who actually invented forks, when Eleanore approached me.

"May we have a word?" she said rudely to my protector.

In the same hoodie as the day before, despite the heat, he shrugged. "Sure, go ahead."

I nudged him. "She was talking to you, but she meant me."

Brad stood up and nervously went to the other end of the cafeteria, where he stood in the corner near a bin and watched us with the eyes of a stalker. Eleanore sat down across from me and unpacked her wrapped sandwich.

"Okay, that new boy is freaking me out."

"What do you want?" I asked.

She looked up at me and took a sip of her carrot smoothie. "I have to apologise, and really mean it. It's going to take some time, you understand, because of that pole I've got up my butt."

I would have laughed, but I was tired.

"You know when you're so overwhelmed by things that you don't know where to turn and you feel like you're being pushed into a corner and the only form of defence is to bite and kick and scratch?"

I nodded.

"Well, I shouldn't have taken it out on you."

"No," I shook my head and put down the plastic fork. "You don't need to apologise. We purposely ruined your party to get back at you for ripping down the Vineyard. I'm the one who should be apologising. I'm not a four-year-old."

Eleanore kept her eye on me, inspecting me, and then she

smiled. Suddenly, she became very grim. It alarmed me a little, as the blood rushed from her face and then her smile did, too. It was so drastic that I could see the red under her bottom eyelids, like when you wake a dog from a deep sleep. She stood up and said: "Thank you. Now let's return to normal, shall we?"

"Okay."

"Good. Oh, *hi!*"

She waved at someone coming towards us. It didn't take me long to realise that it was Hayley. Eleanore shot me a sinister look and blew a mock kiss at me. Things truly were back to normal, then.

Hayley walked past without looking at me, but as she did she knocked my drink over. It landed on my lap and I gasped in disbelief as it stained my crotch orange. People around me laughed, and I couldn't help but feel like the world was out to get me. Brad came back and sat next to me and started eating. Deciding he needed to fit in better, he also pointed at my crotch and laughed.

"Who's next?" I said aggressively, raising my arms in preparation.

— · · · —

Wednesday afternoon, it came as quite a surprise when Mom insisted we take a trip to the mall together. I didn't really feel like going, but before I knew it I was in the back seat with my other siblings. Apparently, it was good to 'get out of the house' sometimes. Especially when you were being stalked by a serial killer. The ride downtown was silent, though. We all knew there was a camouflaged protector tied to the roof, and an alien equivalent of a camera in the rear-view mirror. It spoiled the conversation.

Annie, Brendan and I walked ahead of Mom and Dad in the mall, looking in a few CD shops for some new things. It was nearly five, so the staff were beginning to pack up.

"Look," said Annie. "Isn't that your friend?"

I looked up and saw him straight away. Greg. He was in his work uniform, dickie-bow and all. Heading towards the movie complex with great strides. I ducked my head down and whipped out my phone. There was nothing interesting on there, so I texted to myself: *'omg why really funny haha you maybe whatever music rake'*. Upon receiving it, I forced a laugh. That George Glass, what a prankster.

Brendan put on his best girly voice and called out his name. Greg naturally turned, seeing me, and waved.

Screw it, I thought. *I can deal with this. If I can jump off a cliff, I can certainly... No. No, this is much scarier than jumping off a cliff!*

"Hey, Cassie."

"Hey, Greg."

He was pink in the cheeks already, as I'm sure I was. He shuffled from one foot to the other, hands safely behind his back, staring at the ground. I did the same.

"Well, see you tomorrow," he said.

"Okay," I muttered, and we both walked off eagerly.

— • • • —

Come Thursday night, the protectors were well and truly outstaying their welcome. One of them, a dark skinned woman, kept tapping her foot loudly in the foyer. Being such an open space, it echoed off the walls and I could hear it from my Legs of Luxury as I sat reading a book, with Brendan lying on the floor by my side. He stood up angrily and slammed the door shut.

Zag slid out from under my bed. He was covered in cobwebs.

"Get them off me," he said shakily.

I brushed him off with a jacket from the corner of my room. Mood changing just like that, he hoisted himself merrily onto the end of my mattress.

"Thanks! Don't you ever clean under there?"

"We only moved in last week," I reminded him.

"Oh. Well then, you have a problem. *Hey!*"

He crossed his arms in front of him and blinked. Next thing I knew, he was dressed in a mini black tuxedo.

"I've been meaning to change my wardrobe for a while now. In honour of the new chapter in my life, I'm going for a Groucho Marx motif. No more of this Jack-Be-Nimble nonsense. You dig?"

I smiled. "It's very... *becoming.*"

I turned at a noise.

Zag heard it too. He morphed into a Jamaican.

"Speaking of becoming. Dey be comin', mahn."

He transformed back to himself and jumped under the covers, then he must have flattened himself to the width of a pancake because it seemed like he disappeared altogether.

Annie walked in, flustered.

"Any sign of Just?"

"No," I said with a sigh, blowing a strand of hair from my face.

"All those people down there. I'm sick of it. I can't wait to have my life back. To study in peace would be an awfully big adventure."

Zag showed himself, rolling off the bed and landing by Brendan's side. Brendan smirked, then took off his nightcap and playfully ruffled his hair.

"Dad's still on a rant about Toothy McPearl-Jones here."

"I resent that name," Zag replied, his pearly white buck-teeth McGlistening. "Anyway, I don't have anywhere else to go. And I really like your pogo stick, so I'm staying."

"Oh yeah? It's not so fun when you're only allowed to jump on it in the basement."

"You're not going anywhere, Zag," I promised him, and I noticed a few split ends which I attended to cross-eyed. "Besides… by the time they find Just, Dad will have calmed down. Anyway, you're family now."

"You're still my owner."

"You know what I mean. And Annie will be eighteen soon, so with all these new options, she'll probably need to make a few wishes."

"Travel," said Annie confidently. "That's what everyone else does. You just travel until you're bored."

We laughed together, the four of us sitting on my bed.

I knew we were all thinking the same thing.

It felt nice to belong.

PART FOUR

LAND IN THE SKY

48
WANNA TAKE A RIDE?

It had almost been a whole week. I'd distracted myself immensely with school-work, the only time in my life, and I was starting to get headaches from sitting in front of the computer for so long. Annie warned me against it, acknowledging her glasses tiredly. Thursday night, I was all alone in my room reading the work I'd jotted down off the board during the week. We had passed the roman numerals segment of our term, for now, and were basing our concentration on the wonders of John Steinbeck's epic *East of Eden*, among other things. Here and there I would underline a word in the book, write it down and highlight it.

Somebody knocked on my door. I gathered myself and allowed them to enter. To my surprise, it was Brad. I didn't know what his real name was. This was the name he'd been given while undercover. He came in slowly and shut the door behind him. He was still wearing the same grey hoodie with the top up.

"This room is wonderfully lit," he said in admiration.

I shrugged, not sure of how to respond. "Thanks. What's up?"

"I was flipping through the user's manual," he said, and for some reason I knew he meant his interaction guide. "I found an interesting phrase, and it applies very well to what I am thinking. I apologise if I say it wrong, but I shall try saying it anyway. I am wondering if you will date me?"

I thought for a moment. Heck, he was good-looking enough, and since everybody at school hated me, it would surely be a win-win on a social level. "Brad, that's perfect!"

"So, you will?"

"Yes," I said, and I laughed. "Good thinking."

He smiled back, keen as a beaver, and he bowed, which made me laugh even more. Then he said a few thank-you's and bowed out of the room. I turned over, lay on my back and stared at the ceiling. He'd put me in a good mood at least.

But a nagging thought plagued me for the rest of the night. He'd meant *undercover* dating, right?

——— · · · ———

Friday morning on the bus, Brad sat next to me. With the warmth of the day already muggy and unkind, he took to opening the window. My hair soon became a party of its own, flailing a good foot above me. Brad chatted non-stop, flawlessly maintaining his fake story about being raised on a farm east of here.

I barely said a word, and every time our elbows bumped I wondered if it was by accident. To anybody else I would have appeared melancholy, distracted. How had I just agreed, like a harlot? If he was any good at his job, he would act like a typical teenage guy and boast about how easy I was. Still, I was the only person he talked to at school. Chelsea was all over Annie, and she and Brad never acknowledged each other in fear of suspicion. Unless Just was to reappear, they would stay apart.

The school was still a bit uneasy and weird after the death of Ms. Berry. Her husband returned to town and was battling the Sheppard family for rights to the mansion. He and his 'girlfriend', who was blonde, young and newly busty, were considering living in it now that the 'old model' was no more. Sounded like he really loved her, once upon a time.

As I soon learned, a woman from the mental hospital was

coming down to speak to us in groups, all day, about how we were feeling, and how the death had affected us. Eleven in each group. If only she knew what she was dealing with. At ten to eleven, Ms. Weiss called out the names of who would be going to see her next. I was on that list, along with Greg, Hayley, JT, Eleanore, Tanya, Wednesday, Friday, Brad, Mary and William. I thanked my lucky stars Brad was there, and kept close to him as we walked down the halls in silence. Nobody wanted to say anything to anybody else, so long as I was there.

We were escorted by a twelfth grader to the auditorium, which had been vacated for these sessions. Besides, a gym teacher substitute had not been called into duty yet, out of respect.

I recognised Ms. Croxley immediately. She was the woman from Mom's work who had popped over to our house the morning after all hell broke loose. She was a hippie, it seemed. Or a sort of hippie, maybe a wannabe hippie. She had loose clothing on, looked to be in her early to mid-forties with scraggly short brown hair, a goofy smile and some very stressed out neck-muscles. She had a name-tag on and it said: *'Chloe'*.

"Hello, kids," she said in a soft voice, and she waved her arms for us to gather on the bleachers.

Once seated, spaced out in our vastly isolated groups, she hugged herself in typical hippie fashion and let out a great big sigh.

"What a beautiful morning. Isn't it *just?*"

I scowled at her choice of words. Nobody bothered to answer, either. Our stares could have frightened a ghoul back into its grave.

"What's the best thing you've done this morning? Huh?" said Chloe, and she strode around in a small circle in front of us. "Put your best thinking caps on and go to town."

"We know what this is about," said Wednesday, unenthused. "We're not twelve."

Chloe smiled at her for a moment and said: "You're snarky, ain't ya? Alright…" Her smile dropped and she pulled a cigarette from her top pocket, promptly lighting it up. "If you want to go back to class early, I'll tell you what I need from y'all." She counted on her fingers and muttered with the butt between her dry lips. "Your name, your age, your hopes and fears, your feelings about death, and where you hope to see yourself in ten years time. I've got paper over on that table…" she pointed to the rogue table behind her, "… along with pens. Like I said, you'll be out of here in no time. Since you're so adept at dealing with this."

"I don't want to go back early," said JT.

Chloe shrugged dismissively. "It's up to you guys."

"I'd rather talk about my feelings than go back to that pit of despair," said Friday rather ominously. She was staring at the ground, her face white with distaste.

"Then let's do this, okay?" Chloe spun on the spot and held out her hands. "Let's create a circle, sit, and start talking."

We formed a circle on the cold wooden and polished floorboards. I sat next to Brad, but unfortunately I was also next to JT, who scoped me pompously out of the corner of one eye. Chloe was directly across from me, sitting between Tanya and Greg, and she pointed at me as soon as we'd settled.

"Do I know you?" she asked.

"I'm Cassie Gellar."

Her eyes bulged for a moment, giveaway of recognition, and then she clasped her hands. "Okay. Cassie, you start. How does Ms. Berry's death make you feel?"

"Not good..."

Chloe rolled her eyes. "I know *that*."

"Why me first?"

"Why not? Someone's gotta start. Okay, you, the darkest one."

JT scoffed in disbelief. "Uh, that's *racist*."

"That's not racist, hun," Chloe took a long drag. "We're all the same. I pick on everyone. If I'd ignored you, *that* would've been racist."

"Let's agree it's a fine line," JT scowled.

His lips were zipped for good.

"And we're back on Cassie. Shoot."

"What was the question?" I asked.

"How does Ms. Berry's death feel to you?"

It was an odd phrasing, I felt. That was my first thought. Then, the truth came to the surface and I edged around the details and let it slip: "I feel disturbed... that somebody I once knew... *isn't*, anymore."

Chloe turned to the person next to me. "You?"

Brad shrugged. "I only started here last week."

We continued, and when we finally got to JT, he finally opened up. "I think it's the fact we don't know how she died that bothers me the most. I..." He edged back into his cool zone. "Anyway, whatever. I'm over it." He cracked his knuckles and grinned at nothing, as usual.

"Right. Blondie, what's your favourite thing in the world?"

Tanya hated attention, but answered with delight. "Puppies!"

"And why?"

"I don't know, I just do."

"Now if you died, is that something people would remember about you? That you liked puppies?"

"I guess."

"You guess, or you know?"

"I *know*. I work at the pound, and I'm gonna be a vet one day."

"There we go. I know something about you. Now tell me something you knew about Ms. Berry."

"I know she had a husband," said Tanya. "And I know that they got a divorce, and that she wasn't happy about it."

"Yes, but tell me something about *her*. What did you know about her personally?"

Tanya looked up at the ceiling, both thinking and also freaking out as expectations began to build. Eventually she looked down, trapped in fear, biting her bottom lip.

"I didn't know anything about her."

Chloe tapped the floor.

"And you, if you'd met Ms. Berry out in public, all on your own, would you have started up a conversation with her or just said hello and then kept walking?"

"Kept walking," answered Eleanore.

"My point exactly," said Chloe again.

Friday huffed. "What *is* your point, exactly?"

Chloe was about to answer, when Tanya cut in.

"Her point is that we didn't know anything about her, but she was still a person. I think it's a blessing that we didn't know her, or else we'd be up poo creek. More than we are now."

"I didn't ask for your opinion," snapped Friday.

"She didn't ask for *yours*," said Hayley, glaring.

"Shut up," said Tanya. "I don't need your help."

"Oh, blow it out your ass," muttered Hayley.

"Hey, don't be a dick," I told her.

"Coming from the queen of all dicks," said Wednesday, motioning a crude gesture with her hand.

"That's enough," said Brad, realising what this gesture meant.

"Don't talk to my friend that way!" cried Eleanore in defence.

"Leave him alone, you brat," said JT.

"Don't call her that, man," muttered Greg.

Within moments, each person was yelling at another, until we were all on our feet. Chloe was yelling too, at all of us, and it wasn't until she got out a whistle and blew on it that we stopped, red faced and furious.

"Sit *down!*" she demanded in a tremendous roar.

We did as we were told. Then Chloe followed her own orders.

"Don't you realise how much I *hate* using my rape whistle? Now, obviously this group has its own issues to resolve. We're clearly not going to get anywhere with our feelings if all this pent up anger keeps messing around. I suggest we get it all out in the open."

"No way," we all started, but she cut in.

"Listen very carefully. You've all suffered a serious shock to your systems. You need to vent, you just don't realise it yet. This is how our minds and bodies work. But we cannot do that until we clear the air. So here's what we'll do."

She wrote something down on a piece of paper.

"I'm thinking of a number between one and ten. All of you will guess a number, and whoever guesses the right one will have to tell us about their issue first. *No exceptions.* Okay? Go."

We kept tight-lipped.

"Start guessing or I'll send you back to class."

Eleanore was the first to guess correctly. The number had been eight. She cursed some religious figure, and Chloe turned on her fiercely to get it out of her.

"I'm just annoyed that my party was ruined. Plus, that was the last place anybody saw her, so I sort of feel like I'm to blame."

Everyone sat quiet, listening. Suddenly, I noticed a glint in her eyes. She looked up and water began to build around her tear-ducts.

"I'm just so un*happy!*"

She covered her eyes with her hands and cried openly. Friday quickly rubbed her back in support.

Greg sat up.

"I helped ruin her party. I feel bad. I'm sorry."

"Me too," said JT.

I piped in. "Me too."

We looked at Hayley. She caught her boyfriend's encouraging stare and rolled her eyes.

"Oh, please. I am not apologising for treating a crap person like crap. And that's what Eleanore is. She's like a piece of faeces you step on in a meadow. It ruins the experience."

Chloe went on to protest this comparison.

"But if you only *knew* the crap she's done," snapped Hayley. "She is trash. Eleanore Parker is trash. She's just... *trash!* She's trailer trash, with good genes."

Eleanore continued to cry, but uttered: "I hate you so much!"

"It's all an act," said Tanya, edging away from her position near the Saviour. "Everybody knows she hones in on the sympathy card for attention."

"What makes you say that?" asked Chloe.

"She's only upset because her party was ruined. I mean, look at her. She's a crazy person! She doesn't care that Ms. Berry is dead. She is *annoyed* that she died, because it distracted everybody from talking about her party."

"After everything I did for you," said Eleanore, and she took her hands away to meet Tanya's gaze. "How could you say that about me?"

"Because it's true," said Tanya.

Greg was frowning. "No, it's not."

Hayley laughed. "Oh, Greg. Are you..." She grabbed his arm sternly and muttered, "Are you on *her* side now? The Saviour? What is happening to the world? You're not..."

Greg pulled out of her grip with intent. "No. It's not like that."

"As if I would ever," said Eleanore, and she wiped her eyes and looked around in embarrassment. "Anyway, he's all hot for Cassie. I saw them kissing."

"*Cassie?*" said Chloe, annoyingly surprised at this piece.

I felt like I was sinking into the floor. I opened my mouth in surprise, but then glanced down. "I don't like Greg," I lied.

"Yes she does," said Wednesday venomously. "It's so obvious. That's why she was friends with Hayley, to get with him. I wish I'd..." She stopped and scratched her elbow.

"That's not true!" I yelled in astonishment. "I am so sick of this. Everybody's mad at *me*, when I haven't done anything wrong."

I stood up and the world starting buzzing around me. I felt the rage electrify all of my senses, and it gave me control, power.

I directed my anger at Wednesday: "You don't know half of what I'm going through. I can't be your scapegoat. Do you hear me? I didn't hang around Hayley because I liked Greg. I hung out with Hayley because she was my friend." I turned to Hayley. "Greg and I hung out with Eleanore that morning because we felt *sorry* for her."

Friday and Wednesday gasped, but I wasn't finished.

"And I helped ruin her party because..." I tried to think. "Because I wanted to belong."

"Well congratu-friggin'-lations on that revelation, Miss. Good-Intentions," said Eleanore, and she stood up to meet my line of vision. "You ruined my party, you ruined my life, now will you just do me a favour and *die?*"

She pushed me, only this time it was intentional. Chloe sprang to her feet and stood between us. Not that I was about to fight back. With that, I turned and ran out of the auditorium as fast as my legs would allow.

It was thickly humid outside, but I didn't want to go in yet. I went and sat by the back-fence, the wind howling around me, red dust getting in my eyes, and I cried. It wasn't even about the argument. It wasn't even about the past two weeks. It was about how much hatred there was aimed at me from the people I'd once considered friends. How had I managed this in such a short space of time? I was following in my sister's footsteps of leading a solitary existence, even if I didn't want it. Maybe I was destined to be alone.

"Tissue for your issue?"

I turned to see someone standing behind me, but the dust got in my eyes and I couldn't make out who it was. The voice sounded familiar, maybe Greg or JT. Whoever it was, he was kind enough to hold out a tissue for me. I took it off him and used it to wipe my eyes, and then my nose.

"Thanks," I said. I wiped my eyes of tears and smiled at him.

He grabbed me by the throat. I felt his thumb press into my larynx and I tried to cough, but nothing came out.

"Wish I was his owner, and I'll let you go."

Curly blond strands flew across Just's angry face, and I noticed the scars across his forehead and temples were patterned, like a secret map. Paralysed with fear, I wet myself and my legs gave way, but he kept me upright with his grip around my neck. I couldn't breathe.

Something smashed against the top of his head. Shards of clay, or plaster, fell around me. Another caught my eye as it whizzed past my face. It catapulted into his shoulder and exploded into white powder. Just let go of my throat but kept a tight grip on my right sleeve. To my astonishment, I saw a herd of tiny little people running towards us from across the school yard. The closer they got the stranger their appearance. They weren't little people. With tall red hats, some sporting miniature wheel-barrows and gardening utensils,

I realised they were *garden gnomes*. Some of them had the audacity to commit suicide by flinging themselves at the man holding onto me, shattering as they made contact. I knew immediately that they were there to help. I cried out once, and then as one more gnome leapt in the air to smash across Just's face, I had enough energy in me to pull away from him. I fell onto my back, winded. The mass of gnomes reached him. He kicked at them, flung his arms, stomped, killing many of them. But there had to be hundreds of them.

"Run and hide, Cassie Gellar!" one of them, with a white beard, blue eyes, and a gap in his teeth demanded of me. "Save Zag from a fate worse than death!" A second later he was crushed to powder.

A fierce whizzing of metal spun past my ears, and Just jumped up in the air. A whirling metal hook missed slicing through his shins by an inch. It exploded into the ground behind him and the impact shrouded us in dust. I started to choke as it swarmed my lungs. Just turned, and I saw Chelsea standing across the playground. She clapped her hands, and another strange metal hook barrelled past, catching Just in the shoulder. It wedged in, and started to pull him towards her. But he ripped it out as if it were only a splinter, and threw it at her. She ducked and it missed, and it spun off into the air with a mind of its own. Brad appeared out of thin air, and he grabbed hold of me and lifted me up.

"We have to get out of here," he told me.

We started running. But we weren't running away from the school, we were running towards it. Brad forced the doors to L Block open with a kick of his foot and we started in a sprint down the empty hallway. I turned back and spotted Chelsea chasing after us, eyes locked on mine, her face blank with focus.

"He's coming," she called informatively.

The doors ripped off their hinges and the structure of the building flew off into the air behind us. The sounds were unbelievable and shrill. The thunderous shrieks of metal and explosions all melded into the same tinny ringing in my ears, and I found myself blinded by debris. The ground left my feet, but I hadn't fallen. I was being lifted. By the time I was able to open my eyes, the wind was blowing my hair off my face. I looked around. Brad was holding me, and we were soaring into the sky. He was flying. I looked down, astonished. The whole school, the buildings in which my friends and sister sat in, were collapsing majestically amidst fierce explosions. The ground seemed to lift in places and then sink. A sole figure, that of

Just, stood near the back lot, his arms in the air, moving from side-to-side as they controlled the destruction of Horn-Horn High-High.

"What is happening?" I yelled, but my ears were still ringing.

Brad had his hood up, and he kept his gaze ahead. We rose through the clouds, and for a while there was a chill and a silence, then white blindness came once more. I hugged him tight and waited, fearful. When the clouds disappeared below us, I looked up in awe. A giant reflection of the ground startled me and I tried to crawl out of Brad's grip. It didn't make sense. It was the ground far below, yet above us.

"*HELP!*" I found myself screaming, and I scratched at him.

He tried to calm me down, and grabbed my hands together with one of his.

"It's not a reflection. It's not here. It's *there*."

I couldn't understand what he meant.

"We're going to hide there. Until they catch him."

The ground above started closing in.

"*Do something!*" I screamed.

The force of gravity disappeared and suddenly we were upside-down. The world above was now the world below, and we instantly began our speedy descent. The loud ruffling of clothes, the whistling of the air soaring past me. The turbulent new world we were entering was too much. Everything around me went black, and I passed out.

49
WANDERERS

To say I woke with a start would be an understatement. I jolted upright, horrified, and for a moment I figured it all to have been a dream, but as I opened my eyes I realised that I was in a meadow. The sky above was blue, and clouds were sparse now. The weather wasn't as humid as it had been earlier. In fact, it felt more like an autumn day.

Brad was sitting behind me, covered in soot and yellow dust. He helped me to stand, my legs wobbling like jelly. It was a vast place, a meadow that seemed to go on for miles. There were mountains far away, but really they were *far* away, and barely visible through the distant haze of the atmosphere.

I discovered that there were many other people nearby. In fact, they were sitting up too, just as I had. Gasping, crying out in confusion. The nearest to me, to my great surprise, was Annie. I rushed to her and tackled her to the ground and hugged her. She was as dirty as Brad. We all were.

"Where are we?" was the first thing she said.

"I don't know," I replied, and I cried into her shoulder.

Brad towered above us.

"Everybody is here from your school. We had to save them. Just was going mad. He was destroying everything. So, here we are."

His wording disturbed me. He spoke like a robot, a military officer with no afflictions or emotion to his response.

"Where *are* we?" my sister repeated herself, to Brad this time.

"Another world. It sits parallel to your own, and is very similar. A few places are in different spots, and the history is all over the place, but other than that..."

I spotted Hayley and Greg a few acres away, just as Tanya started running over to them. They were all so bewildered, scared, perturbed, and covered in dirt. I hopped off my sister and made my way as quickly as I could to them.

"We're dead!" sobbed Tanya, tears streaking her dust-covered face. "The roof ripped off and now we're here. It's limbo. We've *died!*" Her chest heaved in and out.

"We're not dead," I squinted in the harsh midday sun.

Ms. Weiss hobbled over to us, Friday tagging behind. Their hair everywhere, their clothes in tatters. They looked dazed and muddled.

"Oh, don't cry, dear," said Ms. Weiss. She wiped the tears from Tanya's face. "If we *are* dead, there's nothing we can do about it."

Chloe lit a cigarette and put it to her parched mouth.

"Really helping there, Jacqui."

Brad came over and whispered gently in my ear. "The less they know, the better." He tapped his nose for some reason, and shot a look at Eleanore and Principal Parker nearby.

"How long are we meant to stay here for?" I whispered back.

"Until they capture Just in your world."

"How long will that be?"

Brad pulled the hood on his sweatshirt over his dishevelled hair and tried to act like a teenager again. "Beats me, dude."

———— · · · ————

Everybody, and I mean every single body from the school that had been brought here, gathered in a crowd. Principal Parker decided to take control, and he urged everyone to make their way *away* from the sun, to head east towards the ocean. We walked for hours, breaking here and there, but the landscape never changed. It was like we were walking in circles around a small globe of fields. After what felt like days, we found a dam and we drank. Nearby I spotted a herd of cows who stared at us in their daily boredom. Perhaps they were contained cattle, I wondered briefly, but noticed they were not tagged, and looked rather stray and unkempt. This appeared to be unclaimed land then. Barren from here to eternity, with grass so tall and yellow it looked dead, flower beds growing wildly in strange spots, and black soil in other places. After seeing the cows, Eleanore praised the lord that we were still on planet Earth, and I laughed to myself deliriously. How true was this, exactly?

At some point, as we walked through a meadow of beautiful purple flowers, JT made an unhappy sound, stopped, and checked the bottom of one of his shoes. For a moment he did nothing, but then he laughed quietly, and grabbed Hayley's sleeve. "Hey look, it's Eleanore," he said, showing her the cow patty on his sole. She did not find it amusing.

Nearing sunset, we were snapped out of our wandering daze by the strange sound of a motor running. Everybody stopped. We turned in the direction it was coming from, at first turning left, but then suddenly it sounded like it was coming from the right. Then behind us, then in front. I tilted my head to focus in, but the wind knocked the source about and soon I realised why. There was a highway not too far away, and it stretched past us for miles.

"Civilisation!" somebody cried. I think it was Mary.

"Let's wave some cars down and get the hell out of here!" Wednesday declared in exasperation.

"Out of the question," snapped Principal Parker, and he grabbed his eager daughter's arm to stop her from following as Wednesday and Friday bolted ahead. "Sugar plum, it's not safe for you."

Eleanore gave him a grim stare, and then looked down. She fumbled for a moment as she cracked her ankles.

"What else is there to do? We need water, Daddy. *I* need water! There's probably a fuel station not too far ahead."

For once, I was on her side. It was a good idea, in this particular situation, to take rides from strangers. I apparently wasn't the only one who agreed, either. A few others remained standing on the spot, up to their knees in grass. But I wasn't one of them. I searched for Annie, and when I found her I grabbed her hand and started after Wednesday and Friday, who were very far ahead now.

"What are we going to do? Hitch a ride back to Horn-Horn? It's not even here!"

"I don't know, Annie. I just need water."

A large hill was blocking the sight of the highway, but Wednesday, Friday and two others I didn't know had reached the top and stopped. When we finally caught up to them, we looked down and saw a wonderful sight. A lonesome, old service station was right at the bottom of the hill, next to the noisy highway. In the distance, across the dry and shimmering landscape, were plumes of grey smoke spread right across the setting sky. Friday shrieked with glee, and started down the hill. After walking all day, she'd perhaps expected too much from her legs, and they gave way with the steep descent. She rolled the rest of the way down, but stood up at the bottom and kept running as if nothing had happened.

Only a few of us were game to go down there. I was, of course, willing. So was Annie. Everything was the same as in our world. I was having a hard time believing it was anywhere else. Same gas pumps, same smells, same kind of cars. Same people. A few of them looked at us strangely, emerging from nowhere.

The automatic doors swung open as we walked by them, and the beep of a new customer sounded above. Air-con, glorious air-con, was only a thought in the back of our minds as we scoped the compact service station. We found Wednesday and Friday in the food aisle, grabbing hold of a few bottles of water. Wednesday was fishing money out of her friend's pants pockets when they saw us, and she walked over quickly.

"People have weird accents here..." she muttered. "It's like they don't know whether their noses are blocked or not. And there's something on the TV about terrorists..."

"Let's just pay and get out of here," I advised them.

Friday took all of the items to the man behind the bullet-proof counter. He was fat, with a curly beard and rosy cheeks. He didn't look in the least bit concerned by our dishevelled appearances. Perhaps he was distracted by the news on the small TV nearby, showing something happening with a big cloud of black smoke similar to the one we'd seen outside. He counted our items with a generous sigh, then declared that it was thirty-eight fifty for the lot. Wednesday handed him some money, and he froze for a moment before handing it back.

"Nope."

It was what we'd feared would happen. Apparently otherworldly money would not suffice. Friday looked back up the hill through the nearest window, and bit her bottom lip anxiously.

"Do you take jewellery?"

"No."

"Please, we're desperate."

"Wait," said Annie sharply.

Her eyes were looking down at the ground, moving from side-to-side, deep in thought. She finally found her own wallet in her jeans pocket and fished out a note.

"Mom gave me this strange money the other week," she said to me. "It's *green*. It says one-hundred dollars, but I don't recognise the country it's from. Some lady gave it to Brendan, and I thought that maybe… Sir, will this do?"

The man took it with barely a glance. He chucked it in the register and fished out some change as fast as lightning. It all came back in very similar green notes and coins, but the last note he held onto for a moment. He looked my sister up-and-down, taking in her ripped clothes, cuts, sooty face. He was suspicious at last.

"Were you there when it happened?" he asked in a low voice.

Annie peered deeply into his eyes, trying to understand. Then she scrunched one shoulder, and broke eye contact.

"Excuse me, where are we?" asked Wednesday.

The clerk stared blankly.

"The Atchison, Topeka and Santa Fe."

Since it was clear to us that this man was not helpful, we departed as quietly as possible, carrying the dozen or so bottles of water and snacks between us. Out on the deserted road, we stopped to take a drink. I wiped my brow and looked up at the slope ahead. Somebody from our group was watching, but the dimming sunlight behind them was blocking their face from view.

"The afterlife has money?" said Tanya, once we reached them.

"Come now, let's keep walking," said Principal Parker, and he looked off at the smoke haze. "Something is not right here…"

Hayley shouldered me violently as she walked past.

"Suddenly he's Miss Clavel!" she joked.

We continued together on our journey, through the meadows, over hills and through the dipping valleys, beyond any point of possible civilisation.

50
THOSE
IN THE DARK

By the absolute end of twilight, which dragged on for near an hour, we'd arrived at a riverbank with a tiny little cave sitting across from it. It was bereft of any wildlife, bears or the like, so mostly everybody agreed to stop and rest for the night. Many nestled together in the opening of the cave, some stayed outside. The weather here, wherever here was, seemed to be forever devoid of a real chill. We'd had a strange fog set in before sunset, but it vanished as quickly as it came. Even post-sunset was balmy. As night-time came, the stars spread across our heavens more beautifully than I'd ever seen, and so I chose to join those who slumbered outside. After a long while with my thoughts, Greg came and sat next to me. Everybody else had nodded off rather quickly. I sat up on my knees, noticing the gentle breathing of near-comatose classmates around me, most of whom had gone for a dip earlier to clean the muck off.

"They're not our stars," said Greg.

I found it odd to hear. That fact made them even more intriguing, and I couldn't pry my eyes away from them. Until Eleanore sat down on the other side of me.

"We need to talk," she said in a hush. "Shall we take a walk?"

"Only if we can make a trail with chalk."

It seemed I didn't have a choice. Before I knew it, the two of them had quite firmly grabbed me under the arms and hoisted me up. We went around the cave and into some bushes until we were deep enough in a copse that the generous remaining light from the day had become dim and unhelpful. When we stopped, I looked at the both of them and hugged myself.

"I found something," said Eleanore quietly.

I kept my eye on her as Greg moved around me; he grabbed my arm and we went on our way again, over a hill until we were presented with a giant landscape ahead of us that stretched all the way to the horizon. I felt a new wave of exhaustion. There was nothing to find out there. It was a hopelessly barren landscape without a soul to spare.

"Greg and I were..." Eleanore paused, choosing her words carefully, "...*talking* earlier, looking for berries. Then I saw that."

She pointed into the distance.

I squinted my eyes, peering closer at the darkness before me. Feeling silly, I was about to declare my failure at spotting anything when a tiny pinprick of light appeared in the immediate centre of the black yonder. Yellow and as small as a grain of sand from where we stood, it was far down in the valley below. I tried to see it better, and examined the surrounding areas with as much clarity as my failing eyes would allow. Needless to say, ten minutes later we were halfway there. Brambles and trees aside, we drifted through a tiny swamp with the last quarter moon struggling to expand its light enough for us to see clearly. Soaked and muddy, the light we'd spotted was now suddenly in clear view ahead of us, bigger than before and shockingly evident as to the source. It was a window, in a house, that looked as normal as any such structure in our world. Wooden, painted a fresh white, it was eerie to find such a cared for building in the middle of nowhere.

Upon meeting the end of the swamp, we stopped. Eleanore decided first to move forward, but Greg put a hand up to stop her. He checked behind us, sure that somebody was watching. We moved forward, slowly and as quietly as we could. The leaves under our feet crunched dreadfully, night-time seeming to amplify every move we made. All three of us made it to the house, which had no surrounding fence. I noticed a flag-pole by the front door, with a funny flag I'd never seen before lowered half-mast.

Greg was the first to peer into the window, which was the only one lit up from the inside. He didn't move a muscle. I rose up behind him, placing a hand gently on his shoulder, and stood on my tip-toes to see. It was a living room painted in a warm red, holding two sofas and an empty fireplace. Two old-fashioned twin lamps with scavo glass were lit on the wall. In the middle of the room, on a rug, sat a woman. She was wrapped in a dark blue blanket, with a box of chocolates and a bottle of whiskey by her side. Black hair scraggy and unkempt, she was on her knees, her face leaning towards the rug, and was moaning. When at last she lifted her head, I noticed she was sobbing uncontrollably.

Where are we? I asked myself again.

Then I noticed the television, a very old one in front of her. It showed a news broadcast just like the one in the service station, with a much clearer picture now of something strange going on. Did they only play the news in this world? It was a city that looked like it had been nuked, or bombed. A strange sensation crept over me. It was a tingling in my spine, a fear of the unknown. Some kind of despicable act had taken over this world, and even people in the far reaches of the woods were affected.

A ringing went off in my ears. I couldn't even grasp what it was at first, until I noticed a tiny hole in the glass of the window appear suddenly before me. The girl in the room looked up, and our eyes locked. I turned sharply, and Greg grabbed my hand. Eleanore was already far away, returning to the swamp with giant leaps. To my astonishment, a man stood at the front doorstep with a giant shot-gun in his hands, and he loaded it up and aimed it at us. We broke into a run as fast as we could, dipping left and right as we made our way feverishly towards the swamp. I was holding onto Greg's hand as another shot sounded, and I felt something whistle past my ear enough to burn. Before I knew it, Greg flung me like a rag doll into the swamp. I sputtered, awash with mud and water. Repulsed, I didn't stop, choosing to swim and dart ahead as fast as I could. After a while, the shouts and explosions from the people in that lonesome house could be heard no more, as they'd probably decided not to give chase. I finally slowed down a little. Greg was behind me, I could hear him. Making sure it wasn't an alligator, I turned and saw that not only was Greg there, but Eleanore was, too. She must have waited in the water for us after running away.

We stood up in the middle of the muddy water to wipe our faces, out of breath.

"And you thought *I* was a bad neighbour," said Eleanore.

———— • • • ————

As we made our way back up the steep ascent that led to the woods near our settlement, the mud dried and the shock set in. We returned to find the others safely where we'd left them. They were fast asleep, except for Brad who watched me bitterly from the cave entrance. Angry at me for leaving his sight, he turned and went to sleep inside, away from me. Eleanore went to sleep next to her father in the cave too, and before Greg went off to find JT, I grabbed his arm and tried to make out his face in the dark. It was the perfect time to say something to him.

"Greg. I'm sorry."

"What for?"

"For... you know. When you kissed..."

"Oh."

"It's just... with everything that's..."

"No, I get it now. Really," he said.

"Maybe another time, we could —"

"It didn't mean anything —"

"Oh," I said, puzzled.

"Wait. What?"

"Nothing. Never mind."

"Alright. Okay then. Well..."

I crossed my arms tightly, holding my breath. "Goodnight?"

"Goodnight."

He put his head down and wandered off. I hovered momentarily, swaying like a shoddy tower in strong winds, my exhausted legs stiff as wooden boards. Crap. Things were awkward again.

"Dammit Cassie, you just had to be *you*, didn't you?"

51
A
WARDROBE'S
SECRET

The next morning, as I stirred from my sleep on the ground, I was reminded of my first night in Horn-Horn when I slept uncomfortably on my bedroom floor. I cracked my legs, thinking back to the cabin in the woods, and rolled over.

Everybody was gone. I shot up like a bullet.

A series of aircraft joined my screaming. They were so loud and flew so low that I covered my ears in panic. The trees about me shook tremendously, dropping half their leaves. I watched as a good thirty of the jets swooped out of nowhere from one end of the horizon and disappeared in the other direction. Once gone, I continued searching for my friends. Confused, annoyed, my heart leapt about inside my chest. Finally, I spotted one person, somehow still asleep inside the cave.

"Brad, wake up. They're gone. Everybody's gone!"

He yawned and rubbed his eyes. "I know."

"Where did they go?"

"Home. It's safe for them now. Chelsea took them back."

"What about me?"

"I want you to stay here. Only for a little while. Chelsea and I are having difficulty contacting Wilson and the others. We think something has happened. In any case, Just has no need to bother with anyone else. He only wants you."

"Are you kidding? I won't leave my family alone with him out there. I want to go home now. Don't keep me here any more."

"No. They won't approve. It's not safe yet."

"I don't care, Brad. I *wish* to go home."

"Dammit. Hold on tight."

I did so, clutching at his trim waist. The ground left our feet and the air beat down like a hurricane. Before I knew it, gravity once again played hard to get, and I knew I was back in my own world again.

— · · · —

I opened my front door and entered the foyer with Brad. I patted down my hair after the treacherous journey back through the skies, and leaned around a few corners. Nobody was home.

"Keep in mind, it *has* been over a day since you disappeared."

"I know," I muttered dismissively, still looking, "but I didn't expect them to move on so suddenly."

We tip-toed up the stairs and checked all of the rooms. Not a single soul was here. In my room I grabbed the TV remote off the bedside table and tuned into the news channel.

Terrible explosion, the news reporter said immediately. School incinerated, all hope for faculty and students lost. I noticed that it was a recording from the night before, showing footage of families grieving in front of a decimated location. I spotted Tanya's father hugging a blonde woman, and to my sadness, Ella-May Parker clutching her twins.

They're fine, I wanted to say to them on the screen.

I quickly jumped to live TV for an update. To my relief, now it wasn't a tragic loss, but a miracle. All students returning from the grave. I spotted Tanya running to her parents, Eleanore and Principal Parker hugging Ella-May, Hayley talking generically to her own mother who looked like she'd had her head in a dog-bowl for eighteen hours... There was little talk on where the hell they'd come from, but at one point the news reporter started to interview them, and landed on Greg.

"Can you tell us what happened?" she asked him.

Greg looked right into the camera, intimidated by it.

"I don't remember," he muttered. As our eyes locked over the vastness of static space, I knew he was lying.

I collapsed onto my Legs of Luxury and moaned in relief.

"Brad, if they don't find Just soon, I'm going to wish something very horrible happen to him."

"If only you could," Brad walked to the door and peered down the hallway slowly. "He's *hoping* you'll throw a wish his way."

"Huh?"

"Ursula had the power to change age, Zag can grant wishes, van Pan had the power to turn into anything... These are all gifts, their birth-rights. Not one is the same. Therefore there are multitudes, billions upon billions. Just's birth-gift is absorbing powers. If you wished *anything* on him, he would be able to take that ability..."

"Which is to make wishes," I said slowly.

"And then we'd all be in trouble."

"That's inconvenient. Couldn't you have told me that before?"

"Seemed irrelevant."

"What's your gift?" I asked.

"I can cross into other worlds unharmed, and carry others."

"Now I know why you were with me."

Brad wasn't paying attention, and it was beginning to bother me. He wouldn't stop peering down the hallway, as if he'd heard something that was not right. I stood up and went over to him, and tried to see what he was seeing.

"What is it?"

His face dropped, and a heavy fear clutched at my stomach. He grabbed my waist to direct me over to the nearest wall, and leant us against it. Suddenly we quite literally sank *through* it, and into another world. We were at a festival, a medieval one at that, and a large woman was throwing pink petals out into the crowd around us. Amazed, it took me a moment to notice that Brad was leaning one of his ears back through the wall we'd come through. Quickly, he pulled us back into my bedroom, the silence stunning me after such noise at the festival.

Brad didn't say a word, and dragged me by the arm to my wardrobe. He opened it up and pushed me inside. I tripped over the clay head, and looked up just as he began to shut me in on my own.

"What are you doing?" I asked, trying to see through the slats.

"My job is to protect you," he whispered on the other side.

The darkness began to overwhelm me. "What's happening?"

"It isn't safe here. You have to leave."

"Where are my parents?" I demanded.

"Take five steps back from where you are. There is a trap door that will lead you to them. Trust it."

"Trap door? There's no t…"

"*Trust it.*"

"No…" I muttered, afraid.

"Five steps back. Take the clay head. When you get out…"

Heavy footsteps came thundering out of nowhere, and I listened as an angry cry of three or four men ordered Brad to put his hands up. Amidst the confusion, my throat closed and I couldn't breathe. I grabbed the clay head and hugged it, scratching at it in anxiety, and in doing so I failed to notice the four steps I took back as I tried to block the noise coming from outside. The swing of an axe, the roll of a head. The last step I took never ended. My foot continued to sink into nothingness and then I felt the strangest pressure on all sides of my body, as if I were being transported through a very thin tube. The darkness turned to red, then purple, and I could see strange flying wisps of cloud, or electricity, or fabric, flying past me.

— • • • —

If Mr. Sheppard had not been attending to the miraculous return of his only daughter that morning, he quite possibly could have borne witness to the most unusual thing to ever occur on his tenth hole green. A finger emerged first, wiggling about, and then an entire fisted hand. That was all I could fit through the ring, really, and with that I punched angrily at the wet grass that was smothering me until I burst forth with an angry moan. Muddy, soaked, shaking, I stumbled forward.

I knew that I was on a golf course. But which one? This wouldn't suffice any more. I had to know the truth. I looked down at the clay head in my spare arm, and placed my other hand on the top of its lid.

"I wish to know *exactly* what is going on!" I demanded. And I hoped, without Zag, that it would work like before.

Sure enough, it did. I let out a tremendous sneeze, and golden glitter shot out of my nostrils. For a moment my mind was blank, but then I began to discover that all the information I wished for was already in my head, as if it had been there forever. And I fell down on the short grass as a result.

Rudnick van Pan had not perished, and neither had Ursula. The two foetuses we'd seen that night were them, most certainly, but van Pan had used his power to morph, and while holding onto Ursula had disguised her as one, too. Ursula was later found in her normal form after van Pan had made his escape. Although alive, he'd beaten her to within an inch of her life, and she was now being treated on her own planet for brain damage. She'd been cleared of all charges. van Pan, the villain, was unfortunately on his way back to Danube as well, which was even worse news. Duke Wilson and his newly formed monarch were being overthrown at that very moment, although it was secretly a voluntary affair: If he didn't give van Pan the throne, van Pan would spill the beans to the world about the experimental chambers, and Wilson and many others would be in a great deal of trouble. So, Queen Wallacia was returning to the throne after nearly forty years of absence.

What van Pan wants, I thought angrily as I picked myself up and strode along, *is to kill Ursula on her own terms. Even if she has to make it look like an accident.*

It took me ten minutes until I'd managed my way to the far east side of the golf course, and I saw Ms. Berry's gigantic mansion over a hill. So I was still in Horn-Horn, which was a relief. I immediately broke into a run. My family was in that mansion. I knew this now. They were in hiding. They couldn't be tracked. Duke Wilson, upon learning of his fate and the furious mutiny right around the corner, had placed them there and put a spell on the dwelling. Knowing that nobody lived there any more, it would be the last place anybody would go looking. Most importantly of all, Zag was there. Wilson had warned him last night. If he ever ended up in the hands of van Pan, then he would most certainly use his wishes for evil. Duke Wilson could spot the type from a mile away. This was why Zag had been passed down from owner to owner, quite carefully to avoid such a fate. My having him was the most scandalous ownership in the Crux community in over eight thousand years.

I ran into the front lawn, jumping around the sprinklers and the confused gardeners, and raced up the steps onto the landing. I halted at the front door. There was a black cat sitting on the nearest swing. I wiped my wet hair from my face, puffed my cheeks, and thought for a moment. It probably wasn't the same one who'd... No, Ms. Berry had a cat. That was something I *did* know about her. Still, insanity and pride aside, I had to ask.

"Can you talk?"

It was looking at me, but it didn't say anything. It just meowed. Only, the meow had sounded an awful lot like *'yes'*. I stared for a little while longer, catching my breath, and then it declared most certainly: "I said yes, I can talk."

"Oh!"

I opened the door and went inside. The Victorian-era downstairs was grey and brown, from another time. It was also completely deserted, a situation I was becoming far too accustomed to. I could hear tiny little whispers around my ears, like buzzing mosquitos, and I glanced around in bewilderment.

The cat clawed its way through the screen door.

"No, she can't hear you."

"What?"

"Not you, Cassie," said the cat. *"You."*

He looked behind me. I turned around. Nobody was there.

"A spell has been put on the house. You need to know the magic word to see them."

"What's the magic word?"

"How do I know it's really you?"

I shrugged.

"You're the one who just called me by my name."

"You could be van Pan."

"I'm... not..." I thought for a moment. "I wish you knew."

It took him a moment to recover after I heaved some chunky golden glitter all over him. Finally, after shaking most of it off, he went to licking himself, and muttered one word to me: "Chasm."

"That's the magic word? *Chasm?*"

Mom, Dad, Brendan, Annie and Zag popped into my peripherals, and I jumped a mile in the air. They tackled me like a football quarterback, at which point Pigsworth and Tigger rushed over from another room, and I was met with five equally riveting stories melting together into white noise.

52
URSULA'S STAFF

The Danubian night sky was lit with a trillion shimmering stars. It seemed like there were more than usual, and they glowed brighter as if they knew of the excitement building.

"Welcome back, my Lord," said Pier, distantly. He was at the door to the deceased King's parlour, looking tentatively in.

A tired-looking van Pan was by the fireplace, staring deep into the glowing embers. His hair and eyebrows singed from the lightning strike, one ear bloody, completely blackened from soot. He turned to the Palace servant, but did not utter a word. Pier watched on with intrigue as the man in front of him started to undress. van Pan shimmied out of his pants, took off his battered jacket, and rattled his head so that his hair sat messy. He unpacked something pink and orange from the nearest closet and shook it out to reveal a ruffled corset.

"Well," he said, cozying into it. "As if the news that their long-lost Queen returning wasn't enough. Imagine if they knew it had been

331

me all along. Here. While you're standing there, help me into my dress."

Pier stood in his uniform: a dickie bow, a blue vest, brown pants and black, polished shoes. He moved forward and helped van Pan into an elegant and fanciful coral-coloured dress. It had beads and ribbons and laces galore.

"Forgive me for prying," he said to his new master, "but with all that is going on with Earth in the coming months… Don't a lot of people on Danube have family and friends there?"

"Probably," said van Pan, uninterested.

"Most would feel obliged to warn them of what is planned."

"Most would feel obliged to keep their mouths shut. In case you failed to notice, it's only going to hit Horn-Horn, and I doubt very many Danubians know anybody there."

"I do."

van Pan buttoned the top of the dress and arched an eyebrow. Without warning, his face and body transformed. Pier stared in bewilderment at the person before him. Somebody he hadn't seen in a very long time, and somebody who looked much older, careworn.

"Strange, I find it takes more effort these days to look like my older self," said van Pan, voice high and feminine, and he laughed. His long, white hair billowed gently across his shoulders, and his thin lips stretched to reveal tiny, yellowed teeth. "Believable?"

Pier bowed carefully. "Yes, my Lord."

"You shall call me Queen Wallacia," she said, ignoring his foolishness. "I feel better now that I'm in my old form. I've promised the Duke I won't tell the public about those experimental chambers, so the story goes that I was kidnapped long ago and have just escaped captivity, which is why I look so old. Everybody in the Kingdom will be so relieved to have a ruler that they won't ask questions. Now, you can leave. Retrieve the Princess's staff from the evidence sector. I wish to inspect its damage before I deal with other matters. Bring it to me; I will be visiting her in the health ward."

Pier backed out gently and disappeared down the long and echoey hallway. Wallacia sat there for a while, amazed and invigorated to be in her own body once again.

If only it was my resting state, she thought bitterly.

She shuddered at the notion of seeing her male face ever again, but knew that she would have to. Whenever she fell asleep, her transformation would end and she would return to the form of Rudnick van Pan.

Ignoring the crowds, some bowing before her, some gawking in awe at the sight of her terribly aged face, she glided as serenely as possible into the private hospital wing where her step-daughter lay, comatose and weak. Their battle on the cliff had almost killed them both, but she was stronger than Ursula.

"Out," she demanded of the nurse

A round woman with *Suffrolens,* she responded with a humph and closed the door behind her as she left.

Wallacia sat down by Ursula's bedside and smiled at the sleeping face which had suffered many visible traumas. She grabbed her hand and kissed it gently.

"My dear Ursula. One moment I'm determined to kill you and the next we're home and it's just like old times. And I finally got you to sleep in the end."

She turned and saw some flowers that had been placed in a vase. She reached out, grabbing them by the stems with her terribly old hands, and tore them in half with one twist.

"I don't know if you can hear me right now, but the doctors have told me that you're going to be fine. I know what you're thinking, hearing that. Why, I must be livid! In fact, I'm not in the least. I've changed my mind about you. You're the only family I've got left, and I..." Her voice caught in her throat. "With your help, we can live together in peace. You, me, Able... and Just."

She held onto her step-daughter's hand, stroking it with her thumb and forefinger, only stopping as she realised that Ursula's eyes were wide open. Wallacia wasn't sure if they were wet with tears, or out of grogginess.

"Good. You can hear me. You were never really made of the right material to rule, Ursula. Your father, he didn't know what was best for you, or his people. I'll correct everything in time. You'll see. Danube will forget him, and with me as Queen I will make sure you go back to your old, carefree life. Just as useless as you ever were."

Ursula tried to move, but Wallacia shushed her.

"You rest now," she said, stroking her wet cheek. "I'll take care of everything. Mother's here."

There was a shuffle by the door. Wallacia looked up to see the servant Pier standing with Ursula's staff in his hands, pointing it at her. She slowly stood up, noticing the large cracks in the crystal ball where the fluid inside had leaked out.

"What are you doing?" she said quietly.

Pier stood frozen, his eyes wide, lips thinned. His intentions were flowing out of him and into the staff quickly. A hot molten coloured ooze gurgled from the base and began filling up the ball, until it spilled over the sides of the cracked opening and sizzled onto the floor.

Rudnick van Pan, Queen Wallacia, whoever it was under the skin, only had a moment to spare. But then it was over. The glowing orange lava spat out in a stream and struck her in the chest. She let out an agonising yell and collapsed to her knees. Her entire body lit up as the energy boiled her from the inside. Pier pried his eyes away and they connected with Ursula's. In that moment, the true energy of the crystal ball entered Wallacia and she began to age at such a pace that by the time she stood back up and leaned forward to pry the staff away, she was nothing but a skeleton with a wafer-thin layer of skin and hair. She shrieked and clutched at its wooden roots with her burning knuckles, and as her touch affected the powers, she was thrust back by another whopping energy: her own desire to reverse the age-ing process. Only, in her hysteria the powers became too rampant, and before she knew it she was a young child again, then a baby, then...

As she realised what was next, she turned to Ursula and let out one final bone-chilling scream before her mouth and eyes closed up with skin and suffocated her moans. Then, her spine pulled her head back into her shoulders, causing her to curl up, and her body wept fluid until she was nothing but a tiny dead lump on the floor.

The crystal ball shattered. The lava cooled and fell in chunks to the floor. Pier let go of the staff, observing his work in numb curiosity.

"For the King," he said, bowing to Ursula.

She watched, paralysed in her bed, as five giant guards strode into the room and took him away.

Never to be seen again.

53

BREAKFAST
WITH WILBUR

I woke up in the middle of the night, afraid. I sat up, drenched in sweat, desperately thirsty. My throat was dry and my heart was beating rapidly. I'd had a nightmare, a strange pulling sensation as I dreamt I was drowning in lava. Shaken, I stayed curled in the unfamiliar bed made for me in Ms. Berry's mansion, and tried to make things out in the darkness. I wasn't sure if I believed in ghosts, but if they did exist, one would certainly be roaming the halls tonight. A gentle rumble of thunder flirted with my ears, and I forced my eyes closed and put my head under the covers.

Late the next morning, Mom came into my hotel room to let me know she was about to stop serving breakfast, so I'd better hurry if I wanted scrambled eggs. When I eventually got up and headed downstairs, I found my entire family gathered around the kitchen table… accompanied by a black man in a grey gardener's outfit.

"Who is this?" I asked cautiously.

Brendan tapped a spare seat next to him, insisting I join his side. "It's alright! His name is Wilbur."

Mom brought the frying pan over and served some of her world-famous scrambled eggs and bacon onto my plate.

"Wilbur is a gardener here," she explained further. "He tends to some of the housework, too, now that Ms. Berry is gone."

"He's very superstitious," said Dad, sipping his orange juice.

Zag walked in from the sitting room. His eyes were fixated on a red kazoo in his hands. My own eyes, however, practically exploded from their sockets at the sight of him. I turned to Wilbur, then back.

"Get out of here!" I yelled.

He sat down at the table with us.

"Relax, Wilbur can't see us. He hasn't said the magic word."

Zag blew on his kazoo loudly.

I noticed Wilbur indeed wasn't looking directly at anybody. In fact, he was sitting there innocently, shoulders up around his ears, staring at the table, eyes as wide as mine. Mom scraped the remainders of the eggs onto a spare plate, and chucked the hot pan and everything else into the sink with a noisy clatter.

"But he can see everything *else*, right?" I asked slowly.

My parents and siblings paused what they were doing and looked at the cutlery and newspapers in their hands. They promptly put them down, and Zag stopped blowing into his colourful toy.

"Alright, nobody move until he gets up…" said Mom. "Luckily, I have some news to tell everyone. I wanted to wait for Cassie."

"Oh?"

"Somebody rang the landline last night, so I answered it. It was that Wilson man again. I don't think he knows how to use a phone, because he kept yelling into it. Anyway, he rang to tell us he's back in charge of that place Dame Purplewink comes from."

I stared at her, engulfed by stupefaction. "Danube? Why?"

"van Pan was murdered last night, so he… *she*… isn't Queen any more," said Mom. "I guess somebody took it upon themselves to kill her. So once Dame Purplewink is better, she's going to be crowned Queen of Danube and take over."

I heaved a sigh of relief.

"We can go home then, right? We're safe?" asked Annie.

My parents exchanged concerned looks.

"They still haven't caught Just. But they've conducted a… a *spell*, I think, to keep us safe for a while," said Dad, and he turned in confusion to his wife. "I didn't know aliens could use magic…"

"What kind of spell?" asked Annie, and she slurped up a serving of scrambled eggs without moving her plate.

Wilbur's eyes shot to the source of sound.

Mom got up from the table and said: "They knew when Just was in Horn-Horn, and now they know that he's not. So what they've done is, and this is how Duke Wilson explained it to me… They've set up a sensor around the border of Horn-Horn, like a trip-wire, and if he enters again we'll know about it."

Brendan half-smiled, unsure. "I guess that's good news."

"In that case, I'm going to pack!" said Annie, standing up.

I quickly whistled at her, demanding she sit back down. There was no need for packing. With a concise wish and an even tighter cough of glitter, we disappeared in quite literally the blink of an eye.

Leaving poor Wilbur frozen solid, clueless of our swift exit.

54

HIDDEN IN THE ROSE GARDEN

The first truly chilled day since we'd moved in landed upon Horn-Horn in late September, and the landscape changed before our very eyes. Some trees shed their leaves overnight, flowers faked their deaths, and the dried grass re-emerged from the ground like a vibrant green phoenix from the ashes.

The time came, not long after, for us to return to school. It was something the town put off for a few weeks, but due to the wonders of technology we were able to submit homework via the internet, and that got things rolling. On that same cold day, being a Monday, the students of Horn-Horn High-High were starting fresh. The board of education had split the school up into five lots, and in our five lots we would attend five different schools until construction on the new school was completed. A major investigation was said to be underway, as the news reports stated the cause of the school's explosion was a very serious natural gas leak. Whether a person with an intelligent thought in his brain could swallow this tripe was not really something the government concerned themselves over — they knew what really happened, and as long as the truth didn't get out, conspiracy theorists could debate amongst themselves until the cows came home.

Annie and I were going to the same foster school. Hayley and Wednesday were the only ones from my class going to Maplethorn High School, which was luckily in the next town over. The other schools were not so close. In fact, one of the five was over an hour's drive away (these five schools being the only ones with space to accommodate). Split amongst other schools meant a lot of friends were being separated, some students feeling completely isolated. Since I didn't have friends any more, it didn't make a difference to me.

"I'll be your friend," said Annie, as we rode on a new bus.

I pressed my head against the window. "Kill me now."

Starting at a new school was not something I could have predicted doing again so soon. But there I was, sitting in a classroom with thirty or so strange teenagers. Wednesday, Hayley and I stayed together in the front row, lonely, but still not speaking to one another. The other students made fun of us, mainly because for some reason being from another school meant we were their mortal enemies.

When recess came, I rushed out of the room before our mean, hair-lipped teacher could make another subtle jab at me. I found a place to sit in a small abandoned rose garden, hunched snugly into my huge overcoat. I stared at the ground, lost in my thoughts of things normal people could not relate to.

Now that I had actually been given the gift (or curse) of time, I'd spent many hours of many days going over what had happened weeks earlier. Some nights I could barely sleep because I would lie there thinking about, well... *everything*. Ms. Berry, and Brad... Ursula most of all, and van Pan. They'd breathed extra dimensions into my life, and were these dimensions so unable to repeat that I was bound to live a disappointing life hereafter because of it? A clueless psychologist might say: yes. Because it was not real. A figment of a disturbed mind. Yet here we were weeks later, the only source of proof of those adventures sleeping every night in my wardrobe, and a feline friend for Tigger who I'd catch lapping up milk in the kitchen when he thought nobody was looking. Every time I thought of normality, the others would pop into my head, too: Greg, Eleanore, Hayley, JT, Ms. Weiss, the lot of them. Now *they* weren't the normal part of my life, either. Every single body from Horn-Horn High-

High refused to talk about their journey to the other planet. I couldn't pry a word from them. It was as if it never happened.

Any news coming out of Danube was also not for my ears. Zag and Timothy were barred, too. It had become a one-way street. They could arrive on my planet, but I wasn't allowed to even acknowledge theirs. How mighty they must think themselves. One night out of desperation, I'd made a wish to visit Ursula in her hospital wing, and that strange dull noise echoed out of the clay head and nothing came of it. I didn't even cough anything up. What frustrated me most, though — more than the silent treatment, or the Indian givers of communication — the one thing that irked me to near insanity was what a total lack of respect people from both sides had for me now. Not that I was expecting a gracious acknowledgment every time I entered a room, but I was back to being looked upon as a clueless teenager. Troublesome, stupid and disrespectful, with years to go until worldly knowledge was to enter my brain and stay there.

Goddamn it, I thought, sitting lonesome and agitated in the rose garden. *I'm not just some teenager. My name is Cassie Gellar the First. I own a Child of Crux!*

I'd gone too deep into despair again, and failed to hear the footsteps on the stone walk-way until it was too late. Wednesday and Hayley appeared in front of me, each buttoned up from the cold. Hayley sniffed one of the roses closest to her, and looked around at the strange ensemble of weeds and plants amongst us.

"It's not quite the Vineyard," she said.

I drew an infinity symbol in the ground with my finger. Between the strands of grass here and there, it was impossible to see.

"Can we sit here?" asked Wednesday.

I shrugged as a yes.

When they sat down across from me, they laughed to one another. Now they were friends. Just another inexplicable attempt to suck the universe of its natural balance.

"This place blows," said Hayley, getting serious again. She held out a juice bottle for me. "Here. JT wanted me to give this to you."

"Thanks," I said, smiling warmly.

"It's from JT, not me."

I took it and sipped away quite greedily. Finished, I placed the half-imploded bottle by my side.

Wednesday started pulling out large weed-like strands of grass.

"I can't believe I'm saying this, but I miss Horn-Horn High-High."

After a moment of reflection, Hayley sighed moodily.

"I can't believe *I'm* saying this, but… I miss *Ms. Weiss.*"

Luckily on Wednesdays from now on, the day that is, our old class would be spending the whole day together at Ms. Weiss's house to study. It was something I knew we were all looking forward to, even Eleanore.

"It's like… we're stuck," said Wednesday, and as a cold breeze went past she ducked her mouth under her collar. "This place is horrible. Everybody hates us. I don't even have any friends here, besides from you guys."

"Whoa, whoa, who said anything about being friends?" said Hayley. "When our old school re-opens we'll go back to being…"

"Enemies?" I offered.

It was an unhappy look they gave me.

"I don't even know why we were fighting…" Hayley muttered.

"I do," said Wednesday.

"Shut up."

We sat there, letting the school noises dance above, watching the birds as they flew about their business, back and forth around us in the dank and unpleasant rose garden. When the bell rang, the two of them jumped up without another word and scampered back the way they came. I stayed for a minute longer and watched a green spider making its way through the grass in front of me, camouflaged to near perfection.

55
TIMOTHY'S CONCERN

The day went along at a snail's pace. In fact, if you watched a video at half speed of a snail watching a video of a snail in half speed, that would be a more accurate description. The more time I spent with these hostile students, the more depressed I became. Wherever the other students of Horn-Horn were, I'm sure they were going through the same.

The weather turned balmy by the end of the day. We packed up our things and left the classroom in a rush. I went and sat on my own on a bench under a thriving oak tree by the front, waiting for Annie to meet me so we could hop on the bus together. I was on my phone writing my thoughts when a hideous chill smacked the top of my head and ran down my back, and into my cleavage. I hadn't a moment to collect myself as I heaved in shock. I was drenched, and whatever hit me was stinging my eyes. I managed to open them in time to see two girls walking away with empty drink bottles in their hands. They peered back at me, horrible smirks on their faces. They really didn't like us here. I found a few spare tissues in my backpack and wiped myself down as much as I could. I must've looked horrible. My hair was flat across my forehead, and now I felt all sticky. The chill of the breeze mixed with the chill of those iced drinks was something of a torture technique. A wave of emotions surfaced and I shed a few tears as discretely as I could. Everybody who walked past stared at me and I felt like I was back at square one.

It wouldn't be so bad, I thought, *if I had somebody on my side.*

"Those girls will meet the front end of a golf-cart if you say the magic word."

I looked to my left. Somebody was sat next to me and I hadn't even noticed. It was a small boy, skinny and with short jet black hair. He was wearing a grey T-shirt and khakis which looked very similar to a pair Brendan had. His words struck me as odd, so I laughed to be polite and wiped my eyes.

"No kidding," I said.

"Chasm."

I stayed silent.

"It's me. Timothy."

I doubled and faced him square on. "You're a human now?"

"This is how I really look."

"No kidding," I said again, taking him all in. "Wow. I thought you were an actual cat."

"I can transform into any animal I please," he said, and he arched his neck back to see the mean girls catching up with a mound of friends on a grassy knoll. "Things will get better, you know. They always do."

"Thanks, Reverend."

"I came with your parents. They wanted to pick you up today. From the looks of things, I'd say it was the perfect day for it."

"Sure was. Where are they?"

"In the car-park. Annie's already with them. Come on."

Glad to have somebody by my side, we started walking towards the busy car-park ahead.

"I'm not going home with you," he told me.

"Why not?"

"I think I'll fly back. The weather is lovely and I want to try becoming a bird and see what everything looks like from high up."

It sounded like a lovely idea to me.

"Why don't you wish for things to go back to normal?" he

asked, lifting his head up to bathe in the warm afternoon sun.

"I couldn't think of anything worse," I replied in all honesty.

He smiled cutely. For some reason he was amused by my answer. "You should know that a few minutes ago, a mysterious figure donated eight million dollars to Horn-Horn High-High. An old associate, I've been told, by the name of Hermione Purplewink. She's a Dame, you know. The fundamental structures of the new school will be up within the next few weeks, and classes will restart in just under a month."

My jaw set in disbelief.

"It was really Duke Wilson, of course."

"Why does *he* care about anything in Horn-Horn?"

"You must understand, Danube is a different world to yours. They have different ideas for honouring people than you do here. Zag was the King's for a long time before he gave him to Ursula, and they plan to look after him. You're his owner, Cassie, so in turn you must have a healthy environment in order for Zag to thrive. And in light of what has happened of late…"

"So what, things are going to go back to normal?"

"Vineyard and all."

A sneaky, knowing grin spread across his face.

I blinked in surprise. "How do you even…? You weren't there, you couldn't have known a thing about the Vineyard…"

I remembered the black cat that had been watching us at school the first week, just as a breeze swept past us mysteriously, giving me goosebumps.

"You *were* that cat. I *knew* it. Hang on, that was before I even *met* Ursula. Why were you following me?"

"I knew where Zag was all along," said Timothy. "While Ursula obsessed over *how* to find you, I was looking at what was right in front of us. I saw your sister in the woods that day, right before you were attacked by the moose, and I eventually put two and two together."

"Why didn't you tell Ursula?"

We stopped on the side of the road as a stream of cars drove past. He sighed. "That's a complicated question. To start, you should know that my father was a brilliant man. He was a governor on Danube in one of the lower regions near the base of the dome, but he disappeared when I was six. Then they got rid of the rest of my family and threw me into an experimental chamber. I wasn't there for very long, but I *was* there long enough to have tests done on me.

One of the side-effects of these experiments was something I never told anybody I'd developed. The ability to turn into any animal I wanted. I'm just like Ursula, like you, at least that's how I originally look. Not this form, but another... *human*-like one. But I can turn into a cat most easily, and I don't know why. However, this is a *not* a gift I was born with. The people in the experimental chambers assumed it was, as everybody has a birth-gift on Danube that is uniquely magical. What they couldn't set their minds back to, however, was my transforming into an animal *before* they started testing on me. That's because I never did. My natural, birth-given gift is the ability to read minds. That's what I've been doing my whole life."

"How did you get out of there?" I asked.

"It's not important. But as soon as Ursula and I arrived in Horn-Horn to look for Zag, I figured out what was going on in his mind, in Ursula's, in your sister's, and then in yours... Enough so that I knew what I had to do. So I kept my eye on you and made sure that Ursula wasn't to catch on, until I learned that van Pan was here. I read his mind, figured out what he was up to, and that was when I decided it was time for Ursula to find you. After that, I'm afraid it got a little bit out of control..."

"What about Just? Did you read his mind?"

"Yes, and he's afraid. He knows about the security surrounding you. He wants to kill you and Zag as much as he did before, but now that he's had time to think things over, he's not as desperate. He doesn't want to go to jail. So, he's biding his time. He'll come back one day, but he isn't planning on it any time soon."

I sighed in relief. The cold was slowly sifting back into mugginess. I looked around at the students, getting sparser and sparser in quantity as they found their own ways home. Suddenly, I spotted a giant graffiti-covered vehicle in the car park ahead.

"Of course they brought the bus..."

Before we made our way over to it, Timothy grabbed my arm to stop me. "Wait, there's one more thing that concerns me."

"What's that?"

"It's common knowledge, at least among those familiar with quantum physics, that splitting open the universe in order to get to another world can cause immense shifts in time."

I tried to keep up, and nodded effortlessly.

"It makes me wonder what kind of time disturbances your protector made when he pushed you and the entire school into that alternate world."

I thought of Brad. A burning feeling ignited in my stomach. "He said he's done that sort of thing before. It was his birth-gift."

"But Cassie, that was *big*. He had to fit your entire school population in. He even saved the birds and ants on the school-grounds."

I thought back to the planet appearing above me in the sky. I shuddered and felt dizzy. I never wanted to go through that again.

"Danube should have thought ahead. That could've... That *may have*, in fact... created some serious alterations. *Anywhere* in time."

Thinking about this as we reached the bus, I promised him I would keep my eye out for any such disturbances. Happy with my answer, he waved to my family inside the bus. Then, very suddenly, he transformed. No longer was I standing next to a small child. Instead, a tiny sparrow swirled around me merrily, booped me on the forehead, and set off into the clouds above.

I felt a terrible sense of dread as I climbed onto the bus. I was tired, I realised, of everything. My mother greeted me with a tremendous hug, and I told my family about the drinks thrown at me. I cried into Mom's sleeve, involuntarily of course, and when I turned to face the rest of them I spotted Brendan near the back, spraying his hot face with a bottle of water; Dad, wedged in the driver's seat, sweat stains under his arms; and Annie, already absorbed in one of her science books. Mom wiped some of the matted hair from my face and said gently: "It's a beautiful day. Why don't we head to the beach and get some ice-creams?"

Brendan, Annie, and even Dad jumped for joy at the idea. I sat down on my own as the engine started, and opened the window to let a breeze run through the bus.

Happiness came with the wind, and as I remembered how desperately lonely I'd felt when we first moved to Horn-Horn, something finally dawned on me. Gazing across the weathered aqua seats at my family members, I realised that I'd never *really* been on my own at all.

Not even once.

EPILOGUE
THE AMBER LANDING

Thunder echoed across the skies above Maplethorn, and rippled throughout the land. The lightning that crackled within chortled heavily and quickly, hidden from the world below by a subdued white cloud. The lightning had been pink, and it appeared and then disappeared through what was an uncharted *split* in the universe made weeks before. Through the tunnel of time it went, closing up one world and spinning into the next, and in its travels it sucked in many things. Air particles, helium, dark matter, rocks, branches, sulphur cyanide, plasma, ice, fire, and a living form were collected.

When it appeared in another time and place, it dropped all of these variants from its place in the sky. The fire, helium, ice and dark matter vaporised immediately, but the body, the rock and the branch fell surely downwards, patting gently into the soft snow below.

Broken but alive, the woman was most certainly unconscious. Missing some of an arm and a leg (for the split in time that she'd been sent through was so short in existence that they hadn't the time to get through), she rolled lazily down a slope. She'd also gained a vast array of deep slices, short in nature but prominent, all across her once smooth face. Collecting like a snowball, it wasn't until she hit a bank of rocks that everything stopped. She lay there, her glasses lost in the mysterious vastness of space. Her clothes still intact but in tatters. A hound bellowed far away, and just as some of the last streams of vibrant pink static electricity danced away from her body, a man and his Duke appeared over the snowy hillock with a canine leading the way. They were rugged up in furs and hats, with their weapons pointed at the glowing pink ball below them.

"Halt!" shouted Duke Wilson.

Prince Frederick ignored his comrade, and the two of them felt their way down the slope until they landed by the curled-up body. The Prince kicked it gently. The hound, his guide, sniffed suspiciously.

"It's a body," said Prince Frederick.

He bent down just as she began to stir. He felt her face and noticed her eyelashes flutter as he stroked past them.

"A woman, in fact. And I do believe she's still alive."

"I'll send for help," said Duke Wilson of Elmer. He turned back to the looming ice dome and used his birth-gift to let the people inside know where they were.

The woman opened her eyes and took in her surroundings as steadily as she could, though she couldn't see far, and it was night.

"Are you alright?" asked Frederick.

She nodded, and realised through her blurred vision that this handsome young man before her had no eyes.

"Yes, I'm alright," she said in a rush. "Where am I?"

"You're on the outskirts of the Palace of Danube," he replied, and he felt her face once more. "My, your bone structure suggests you are the most beautiful creature I've ever laid hands on."

The woman sat up and put her good hand to her forehead. She hadn't yet realised that some of her right arm was missing.

"Tell me. What's your name?" Frederick held her close.

She squinted as she thought. "I have no *idea*."

Help from the Kingdom was fast approaching in the dark, wintery skies above.

"I am Prince Frederick, and as long as I am here with you, you have nothing to fear. I will take care of you." He felt her face once again, taking in the sculpt and analysing it in his mind. "For now, at least, why don't we call you…"

He thought carefully.

EPILOGUE

"*…Wallacia?*"

The men and animals landed about them, bringing spells and hover-mechanisms to carry them back to the Palace safely and quickly. The mysterious woman held the blind Prince's hand in hers, and as she was lifted up to safety into one of the strange crafts above, she noticed the peculiar tingling sensation in her right arm. When she looked down, a tiny pink spark of static electricity shot out of it and disappeared into thin air.

With that, Beverly Berry closed her eyes and fell into the deepest sleep of her most unusual life.

For character insights, future storylines and more, visit:

www.tommylellan.com

OTHER BOOKS IN THIS SERIES

'Horn–Horn, Cracked'
(Book #2)

'Stars Above Horn–Horn'
(Book #3)

DID YOU LIKE THIS BOOK?

WHY NOT LEAVE A REVIEW AT GOODREADS AND AMAZON!

Did you know that reviews are an essential part of a book's success? By writing a review, you're not only helping the author, you are helping other people find 'The Horn-Horn Series'!

All books in this series are available at these leading retailers:

BARNES & NOBLE

Waterstones

goodreads

amazon

booktopia

ABOUT THE AUTHOR

Tommy Lellan was born in London and moved to Melbourne at the age of two. When not writing, he is found performing pop/rock songs and composing musical scores.

Follow Tommy Lellan @tommylellan on Social Media.

www.ingramcontent.com/pod-product-compliance
Lightning Source LLC
Chambersburg PA
CBHW020253120726
47904CB00001B/188